Praise for **James Ellroy**

"Ellroy is the author of some of the most powerful crime novels ever written."
—*The New York Times*

"Garrote-tight prose. . . . [Ellroy is] a force of nature, stringing together words into barbed-wire lariats which he then uses to choke the bejesus out of you. . . . His novels are all muscle, zero fat."
—*The Austin Chronicle*

"He's forged a style uniquely his own. Energetic and abrasive, it comes at us like a speed freak. . . . The power and pull of Ellroy's writing is unmistakable."
—*Los Angeles Times Book Review*

"Memorable, stunning, incisive. . . . It is possible, I think, to make the argument that in the past couple of decades, Mr. Ellroy has been the most influential writer in America."
—Otto Penzler, *The New York Sun*

"Nobody in this generation matches the breadth and depth of James Ellroy's way with noir."
—*The Detroit News*

"Ellroy sprays declarative sentences like machine-gun bullets, blasting to kingdom come all notions of justice, heroism, and simple decency."
—*Entertainment Weekly*

"[Ellroy] can make the night world of sleaze and street monsters come alive on the page."
—*St. Louis Globe-Democrat*

BOOKS BY JAMES ELLROY

Destination: Morgue!

The Cold Six Thousand

Crime Wave

My Dark Places

American Tabloid

Hollywood Nocturnes

White Jazz

L.A. Confidential

The Big Nowhere

The Black Dahlia

Killer on the Road

Suicide Hill

Because the Night

Blood on the Moon

Clandestine

Brown's Requiem

***James* Ellroy**

Because the Night

James Ellroy was born in Los Angeles in 1948. His L.A. Quartet novels—*The Black Dahlia*, *The Big Nowhere*, *L.A. Confidential*, and *White Jazz*—were international bestsellers. *American Tabloid* was *Time*'s Novel of the Year for 1995; his memoir *My Dark Places* was a *Time* Best Book of the Year and a *New York Times* Notable Book for 1996; his most recent novel, *The Cold Six Thousand*, was a *New York Times* Notable Book and a *Los Angeles Times* Best Book of the Year for 2001. He lives on the California coast.

Because the Night

James Ellroy

VINTAGE BOOKS A Division of Random House, Inc. New York

To Edith Eisler

FIRST VINTAGE BOOKS EDITION, OCTOBER 2005

Library of Congress Cataloging-in-Publication Data
Ellroy, James, 1948–
Because the night : a novel / by James Ellroy.
p. cm.
1. Police—California—Los Angeles—Fiction. 2. Psychiatrists—Fiction.
3. Los Angeles (Calif.)—Fiction. 4. Mystery fiction. I. Title.
PS3555.L6274 B4 2005
813'.54—dc22
2005046202

Vintage ISBN-10: 1-4000-9529-8
Vintage ISBN-13: 978-1-4000-9529-2

Book design by Georgia Küng

www.vintagebooks.com

Printed in the United States of America
10 9 8 7 6 5 4 3 2 1

I must take charge of the liquid fire,
and storm the cities of human desire

—W. H. Auden

1

THE liquor store stood at the tail end of a long stretch of neon, where the Hollywood Freeway cut across Sunset, the dividing line between bright lights and residential darkness.

The man in the yellow Toyota pulled into the bushes beside the on-ramp, twisting the wheel outward and snapping on the emergency brake in a single deft motion. He took a big-bore revolver from the glove compartment and stuck it inside a folded-up newspaper with the grip and trigger guard extended, then turned the ignition key to *accessory* and opened the car door. Breathing shallowly, he whispered, "Beyond the beyond," and walked up to the blinking fluorescent sign that spelled L-I-Q-U-O-R, the dividing line between his old life of fear and his new life of power.

When he walked through the open door, the man behind the counter noticed his expensive sports clothes and folded *Wall Street Journal* and decided he was a class Scotch buyer—Chivas or Walker Black at the least. He was about to offer assistance when the customer leaned over the counter, jabbed the newspaper at his chest and said, "Forty-one-caliber special load. Don't make me prove it. Give me the money."

The proprietor complied, keeping his eyes on the cash register to avoid memorizing the robber's features and giving him a reason to kill. He felt the man's finger on the trigger and caught the shadow of his head circling the store as he fumbled the cash into a paper bag. He was about to look up when he heard a sob behind him near the refrigerator case, followed by the sound of the robber cocking his gun. When he did look up, the *Wall Street Journal* was gone and a huge black barrel was descending, and then there was a cracking behind his ear and blood in his eyes.

The gunman leaped behind the counter and dragged the man, kicking and flailing, to the rear of the store, then crept to the cardboard beer display that stood next to the refrigerator case. He kicked the display over and saw a young woman in a navy pea coat huddled behind an old man in coveralls.

The robber weaved on his feet; nothing he had been taught had prepared him for three. His eyes shifted back and forth between the two whimpering in front of him and the counterman off to his left, searching for a neutral ground to tell him what to do. His vision crisscrossed the store, picking up geometric stacks of bottles, shelves piled with junk food, cut-outs of girls in bikinis drinking Rum Punch and Spañada. Nothing.

A scream was building in his throat when he saw the beige curtain that separated the store from the living quarters behind it. When a gust of wind ruffled the curtain he *did* scream—watching as the cotton folds assumed the shape of bars and hangman's nooses.

Now he knew.

He jerked the girl and the old man to their feet and shoved them to the curtain. When they were trembling in front of it, he dragged the counterman over and stationed him beside them. Muttering, "Green door, green door," he paced out five yards, wheeled and squeezed off three perfect head shots. The horrible beige curtain exploded into crimson.

2

DETECTIVE Sergeant Lloyd Hopkins stared across the desk at his best friend and mentor Captain Arthur Peltz, wondering when the Dutchman would end his preliminaries and get down to the reason why he had called him here. Everything from the L.A.P.D.'s touch football league to recent robbery bulletins had been discussed. Lloyd knew that since Janice and the girls had left him Dutch had to fish for conversational openers—he could never be direct when he wanted something. The rearing of families had always been their ice-breaker, but now that Lloyd was familyless, Dutch had to establish parities by roundabout means. Growing impatient and feeling ashamed of it, Lloyd looked out the window at the nightwatch revving up their black-and-whites and said, "You're troubled, Dutch. Tell me what it is and I'll help."

Dutch put down the quartz bookend he was fingering. "Jungle Jack Herzog. Ring a bell?"

Lloyd shook his head. "No."

Handing him a manila folder, Dutch said, "Officer Jacob Herzog, age thirty-four. Thirteen years on the job. An exemplary cop, balls like you wouldn't believe. Looked like a wimp, bench pressed two-fifty. Worked Metro, worked Intelligence Division plants, worked solo on Vice loan-outs to every squadroom in the city. Three citations for bravery. Known as the 'Alchemist,' because he could fake *anything*. He could be an old crippled man, a drunk marine, a fag, a low rider. You name it."

Lloyd's eyes bored in. "And?"

"And he's been missing for three weeks. You remember Marty Bergen? 'Old Yellowstreak'?"

"I know two jigs blew his partner in half with a ten-gauge and Bergen dropped his gun and ran like hell. I know he faced a trial board for cowardice under fire and got shitcanned from the Department. I know he published some short stories when he was working Hollenbeck Patrol and that he's been churning out anticop bullshit for the *Big Orange Insider* since he was fired. How does he figure in this?"

Dutch pointed to the folder. "Bergen was Herzog's best friend. Herzog spoke up for him at the trial board, made a big stink, dared the Department to fire him. The Chief himself had him yanked off the streets, assigned to a desk job downtown—clerking at Personnel Records. But Jungle Jack was too good to be put to pasture. He's been working undercover, on requests from half the vice commanders on this side of the hill. He'd been here at Hollywood for the past couple of months. Walt Perkins requested him, paid him cash out of the snitch fund to glom liquor violators. Jack was knocking them dead where Walt's guys couldn't get in the door without being recognized."

Lloyd picked up the folder and put it in his jacket pocket. "Missing Person's Rcport? Family? Friends?"

"All negative, Lloyd. Herzog was a stone loner. No family except an elderly father. His landlord hasn't seen him in over a month, he hasn't shown up here *or* at his personnel job downtown."

"Booze? Dope? A pussy hound?"

Dutch sighed. "I would say that he was what you'd call an ascetic intellectual. And the Department doesn't seem to care—Walt and I are the first ones to even note his absence. He's been a sullen hardass since Bergen was canned."

Lloyd sighed back. "You've been using the past tense to describe Herzog, Dutchman. You think he's dead?"

"Yeah. Don't you?"

Lloyd's answer was interrupted by shouting from the

downstairs muster room. There was the sound of footsteps in the hall, and seconds later a uniformed cop stuck his head in the doorway. "Liquor store on Sunset and Wilton, Skipper. Three people shot to death."

Lloyd began to tingle, his body going alternately hot and cold. "I'm going," he said.

3

THE man in the yellow Toyota turned off Topanga Canyon Road and drove north on the Pacific Coast Highway, dawdling at stoplights so that his arrival at the Doctor's beach house would coincide exactly with dusk. As always, the dimming of daylight brought relief, brought the feeling of another gauntlet run and conquered. With darkness came his reward for being the Doctor's unexpendable right arm, the one person aside from the Night Tripper who knew just how far his "lonelies" could be tapped, dredged, milked, and exploited.

Spring was a sweet enemy, he thought. There were tortuously long bouts of sunshine to contend with, transits that made nightfall that much more satisfying. This morning he had been up at dawn, running an eight-hour string of telephone credit checks on the names gleaned from the John books of the Doctor's hooker patients. A full day, with, hopefully, a fuller evening in store: his first grouping since taking three people for the mortal coil shuffle and maybe later a run to the South Bay singles bars to trawl for more rich lonelies.

The man's timing was perfect; he pulled off P.C.H. and down the access road just as the Doctor's introductory music wafted across the parking area. Six cars—six lonelies; a full house. He would have to run for the speaker room before the Night Tripper got impatient.

Inside the house, the man ignored the baroque quartet issuing over the central speakers and made for a small rectangular room lined with acoustical padding. The walls held a master recording console with six speakers—one for each upstairs bedroom, with microphone jacks for each outlet and six pairs of headphones and an enormous twelve-spooled tape deck capable of recording the activity in *all* the bedrooms with the flick of a single switch.

He went to work, first turning on the power amp, then hitting the volume on all six speakers at once. A cacophony of chanting struck his ears and he turned the sound down. The lonelies were still shouting their mantras, working themselves into the trancelike state that was a necessary precondition to the Doctor's counseling. Getting out his notebook and pen, the man settled into a leather chair facing the console, waiting for the red lights on the amplifier to flash—his signal to listen in, record, and assess from his standpoint as Dr. John Havilland's executive officer.

He had held that position for two years; two years spent prowling Los Angeles for human prey. The Doctor had taught him to control his compulsions, and in payment for that service he had become the instrument that brought about realization of Havilland's own obsession.

As the Doctor explained it, a "consciousness implosion" had replaced the "consciousness explosion" of the 1960s, resulting in large numbers of people abandoning the old American gospels of home, hearth, and country, *and* the counterculture revelations of the sixties. Three exploitable facts remained, one indigenous to the naive pre-sixties psyche, two to the jaded post: God, sex, and drugs. Given the right people, the variations on those three themes would be infinite.

His assignment was to find the right people. Havilland described his prototypical chess piece as: "White, of either gender, the offspring of big money who never fit in and never grew up; weak, scared, bored to death and without purpose, but given to a mystical bent. They should be orphaned and living on trust funds or investment capital or severely estranged from their families and living on remittances. They should accede to the concept of the 'spiritual master' without the slightest awareness that what they really want is someone to tell them what to do. They should love drugs and possess marked sexuality. They should consider themselves rebels, but their rebelliousness should always have been actualized as timid participation in mass movements. Find these people for me. It will be easier than you might think; because as you search for them, they will be searching for me."

The search took him to singles bars, consciousness workshops, the ashrams of a half dozen gurus, and lectures on everything from New Left social mobilization to macrobiotic midwifery, and resulted in six people who met Havilland's criteria straight down the line and who fell for his charisma hook, line, and sinker. Along the way he served the Doctor in other capacities, burglarizing the homes of his legitimate patients; reconnoitering for information that would lead to the recruitment of more lonelies; screening sex ads in the underground tabloids for rich older people to pimp the lonelies to; planning his training sessions and keeping his elaborately crossreferenced files.

He had moved forward with the Doctor, indispensable as his procuror of human clay. Soon Havilland would embark on his most ambitious project, with him at his side. Last night he had proved his mettle superbly.

But the headaches . . .

The light above speaker number one flashed on, causing the man to drop his pen and reach for the headphones. He had managed to adjust them and plug in the jack when he heard the Doctor cough—his signal that it was time to pay careful attention and make notes about anything that seemed special or particularly useful.

First came a profusion of amenities, followed by the two lonelies praising the bedroom's decor. The man could hear the Doctor pooh-poohing the rococo tapestries, assuring his charges that such surroundings were their birthright.

"Get to it, Doc," the man muttered.

As if in answer, the Doctor said, "So much for light conversation. We're here to break through the prosaic, not dawdle in it. How did your ménage in Santa Barbara work out? Did you learn anything about yourselves? Exorcise any demons?"

A soft male voice answered. The man recognized the voice immediately and recalled his recruitment: the gay bar in West Hollywood; the plump executive type whose wary mien was a virtual neon sign announcing "frightened first-timer seeking sexual identity." The seduction had been easy and the seducee had met all the Doctor's criteria.

"We used the coke to get things started," the soft voice said. "Our client was old and afraid of displaying his body, but the coke got his juices running. I—"

A woman's voice interrupted: "*I* got the old geezer's juices going. He wasn't even down to his skivvies when I grabbed his crotch. He wanted the *woman* to take the lead; I sensed that as soon as we walked in the door and I saw all that science fiction art on the walls—amazons with chains and whips, all that shit. He—"

The soft male voice rose to a wail. "I was savoring the lead-in! Doctor said to take it slow, the guy wasn't pre-screened. We got him from the sex ads, and Doctor said that—"

"Bullshit!" the woman barked. "You wanted to get coked yourself, and you wanted the old guy to like you because you were the one with the dope, and if we played it your way the whole assignment would have been a cocaine tea party."

The man put down his pen as the executive type started to blubber. After a short interval of silence, the Doctor whispered, "Hush, Billy. Hush. Go out and sit in the hallway. I want to talk to Jane alone."

There were the sounds of footsteps over a hardwood floor and of a door slammed in rage. The man smiled in anticipation of some vintage Havilland. When the Doctor's voice came over the speaker, he took up his pen with a glee akin to love.

"You're letting your anger run you, Jane."

"I know, Doctor," the woman said.

"Your power lies in exercising it judiciously."

"I know."

"Was the assignment fulfilling?"

"Yes. I chose the sex and made them like it."

"But it felt hollow afterwards?"

"Yes and no. It was satisfying, but Billy and the old man were so *weak*!"

"Hush, Janey. You deserve to traffic with stronger egos. I'll keep my eye on the high-line personals. We'll find you some feisty intellectuals to butt heads with."

"And a partner with balls?"

"Nooo, you'll go solo next time."

The man heard Jane weep in gratitude. Shaking his head in loathing, he listened to the Doctor deliver his coup de grâce: "He paid you the full five thousand?"

"Yes, Doctor."

"Did you do something nice for yourself with your gratuity?"

"I bought myself a sweater."

"You could have done better than that."

"I—I wanted you to have the money, Doctor. I took the sweater just as a symbol of the assignment."

"Thank you, Jane. Everything else all right? Reciting your fear mantras? Following the program?"

"Yes, Doctor."

"Good. Then leave the money with me. I'll call you at the pay phone later this week."

"Yes, Doctor."

The sounds of departure forced the man to catch up with his note-taking. As if on cue, the Doctor clapped his hands and said, "Jesus, what an ugly creature. Speaker three, Goff. Efficacy training."

Goff plugged a jack into speaker number three and hit the *record* switch. When the tape spool began to spin, he tiptoed upstairs to watch. This would be his first visual auditing since blasting his "beyond" to hell, and he had to see how far the Night Tripper was taking his recruits. Only one of them was capable of approaching his own degree of extremity, and all his instincts told him that Havilland was just about to push him to it.

Goff was wrong. Peering through a crack in the door, he saw the Professor and the Bookworm kneeling on gym mats facing the mirror that covered the entire west wall. Their hands were clasped as if in prayer and Havilland was standing over them, murmuring works of encouragment. With Billy Boy and the Bull Dagger already counseled, it meant that the Doctor was saving the foxy redhead and the real psycho for last.

Goff pressed himself into the wall and stared into the bedroom just as the two men on the mats pulled off their undershirts and began shouting their fear mantras. "*Patria infinitum patria infinitum patria infinitum patria infinitum patria infinitum.*" With each repetition of the phrase they smashed their hands into their chests, each time harder, shouting louder and louder as the blows hit home. Throughout, they retained eye to eye contact with their own mirror images, never flinching, even as blood-dotted welts rose on their torsos.

Goff checked the second hand of his watch. One minute. Two. Three. Just when he thought the chanters would have to collapse, he heard the word "*Stop*!"

Havilland knelt on the mat, facing the men. Goff watched them move their eyes from the mirror to the eyes of the Doctor, then extend their right arms and squeeze their hands into fists. Havilland reached into the pocket of his lab coat and withdrew a disposable syringe and a handful of cotton balls. First he injected the Bookworm; then he wiped the needle and injected the Professor. Both lonelies swayed on their knees but remained upright.

The Doctor got to his feet, smiled, and said, "Think pure efficacy. Robert, you have been placed in a very wealthy home on assignment. A couple, an older man and woman, are drooling for your favors. The phone rings. They both go to answer it. Where do *you* go?"

Robert stammered, "T-to the b-bathroom? To check for drugs?"

Havilland shook his head. "No. You have drugs on the brain; it's a weak point of yours. Monte, what would *you* do?"

Monte wiped sweat from his chest and twisted to stare at himself in the mirror. "*I* would wonder why the call was so important that they both had to run for the phone, especially when I was there looking so groovy. So what I would do would be to run for an extension and pick it up the very second that the old fucker did, then listen in and see if there was any salient info I could get from the call."

Havilland smiled and said, "Bravo," then slapped Monte across the face and whispered, "Bravo, but always look at *me* when you answer. If you look at yourself you get the notion that you thought independently. Do you see the fallacy in that kind of thinking?"

Monte lowered his eyes, then brought them up to meet Havilland's. "Yes, Doctor."

"Good. Robert, a hypothetical question for you. Think pure efficacy and answer candidly. My supply of legally obtained pharmaceutical drugs runs out, because of new laws passed limiting hypnotics and the like to physicians with hospital affiliations. You crave them and come to realize that they are what you like most about being in my tutelage. What do you do?"

The Bookworm pondered the question, shifting his gaze back and forth from the mirror to the Doctor. Goff grinned when he realized that Havilland had given the lonelies a Pentothal jolt.

Finally, Robert whispered, "It would never happen to you. It just couldn't."

Havilland put his hands on Robert's shoulders and gave them a gentle squeeze. "The perfect answer. Monte would have intellectualized it, but your response was pure candor and pure heart. And of course you were right. I want you to both chant your mantras now. Hold eye contact with yourself, but think of *me*."

When Havilland started for the door, Goff padded downstairs and back to the speaker room. He rewound the efficacy training tape and placed the spool in a large manila envelope, then plugged his headphones into the middle speaker just in time to hear male/female sexual grunting move into strangled sighs and girlish giggles. The giggle became a high-pitched smoker's cough, and Goff himself laughed. It *was* the tight little redhead he had picked up at the Lingerie Club, the one who had devastated him with her Kundalini yoga positions. He had been lucky to get out of her Bunker Hill Towers condo alive.

The Doctor was the first to speak. "Bravo. Bravo." His monotone sent the woman into new gales of laughter. The man she had coupled with was still trying to catch his breath. Goff imagined him lying on the bed on the verge of a coronary.

The Doctor spoke again. "Later, Helen. I want to check the victim's pulse. You may have gone too far this time."

"Beyond the beyond," Helen said. "Isn't that our motto, Doctor?"

"Touché," the Doctor said. "I'll call you Thursday."

When a full five minutes of silence followed the sound of little Helen skipping gaily out the bedroom door, Goff's gut clenched. He knew that the male lover was the real psycho and that the Night Tripper was taking him a major step closer to his brink. Thus the shattering of glass and the obscenities that came in the wake of the stillness were expected, as were the expressions of concern from the Doctor. "It's all right, Richard, it really is. Sometimes 'beyond the beyond' means hating. First you have to accept that reality, then you have to work through it. You can't hate yourself for being what you are. You are basically *good* and *powerful*, or you wouldn't be with me now. You just happen to have an exceptionally high violence threshold to overcome in order to achieve your selfhood."

Thomas Goff shifted into memories of Richard Oldfield's recruitment, beginning with the crippled whore with the three-hundred-dollar-a-day smack habit he had met at Plato's Retreat West. She had told him of the stockbroker/bodybuilder/remittance man who paid five C-notes a pop to work her over because of her resemblance to the governess who had tortured him as a child. The approach at the health club had had the thrust of a nightmare; Oldfield looked enough like Goff to be taken for his fraternal twin, and he was dead-lifting four hundred pounds. But the bodybuilder had capitulated to the Doctor's machinations like a baby going for its mother's tit.

More breaking glass. Oldfield weeping. Havilland alternately whistling a tune and murmuring, "There, there." Goff knew that the reversal was coming.

It arrived in the form of a slap in the face that filled the speaker with static. "You weakling," Dr. John Havilland hissed. "You picayune poseur. You sycophantic whoremonger. I give you the best fuck in our program, promise to take you where your chickenshit conscience would never permit you to stray, and you respond by smashing windows and bawling."

"Doctor, please," Richard Oldfield whimpered.

"Please *what,* Richard?"

"Ple—you know . . ."

"You have to say it."

"Ple-please take me as far as I can go."

The Doctor sighed. "Soon, Richard. I'm going to be collecting a great deal of information, and it should yield the name of a woman suitable for you. Think of that when you go through your fear mantras."

"Thank you, Doctor John."

"Don't thank me, Richard. Your green doors are my green doors. Go home now. I'm tired, and I'm going to dismiss the grouping early."

Goff heard the Doctor escort Oldfield to the door. The tape machine recorded a hissing silence. The Night Tripper's executive officer imagined it as being inhabited by nightmares in repose, manifested in cold manila folders spilling out data that would transform human beings into chess pieces. The Alchemist and his six offerings were just the beginning. A series of Havilland's slogans caused Goff to shudder back the headache that was burning behind a beige curtain in his mind. Last night. Three. What if the data keepers couldn't be bought? The headache throbbed through the curtain, like a hungry worm eating at his brain.

Doors slamming above him; periods of stillness, followed by the staggered departures of the lonelies. Mercedes and Audis pulling out onto P.C.H. and more silence. Suddenly Goff was terrified.

"Bad thoughts, Thomas?"

Goff swung around in his chair, knocking his shorthand pad to the floor. He looked up into the light brown eyes of Dr. John Havilland, locking his own eyes into them exactly as the Doctor had taught him. "Just thoughts, Doctor."

"Good. The papers are full of you. How does it feel?"

"It feels dark and quiet."

"Good. Does the 'psycho killer' speculation disturb you?"

"No, it amuses me because it's so far from the truth."

"You had to take out three?"

"Yes. I—I remembered your efficacy training. Some-sometime I might have to do it again."

"A cold gun? Untraceable?"

"Cold city. I stole it."

"Good. How are the headaches?"

"Not too bad. I chant if they really start to hurt."

"Good. If your vision starts to blur again, see me immediately, I'll give you an injection. Dreams?"

"Sometimes I dream about the Alchemist. He was good, wasn't he?"

"He was superb, Thomas. But he's gone. I scared him off the face of the earth."

Havilland handed Goff a slip of paper. "She's a legitimate

patient—she phoned the office for an appointment. I checked her out with some girls in the life. She's a thousand dollars a night. Check out her john book—anyone who can afford her can afford us."

Goff looked at the slip: Linda Wilhite, 9819 Wilshire Blvd, 91W. He smiled. "It's an easy building. I've hit it before."

Havilland smiled back. "Good, Thomas. Go home now and enjoy your dreams."

"How do you know I'll enjoy them?"

"I *know* your dreams. I made them."

Goff watched the Doctor about-face and walk to the latticework patio that overlooked the beach. He let the Doctor's exit line linger in his mind, then turned off the tape console and walked outside to his car. He was about to hit the ignition when he noticed a mound of wadded up plastic on top of the dashboard. He grabbed at it and screamed, because he knew that it was *beige* plastic, and that meant that *he* knew.

Goff ripped the plastic trashbag to shreds, then slammed his fists into the dashboard until the pain numbed the screaming in his mind. Turning on the headlights, he saw something white under his windshield wiper. He got out of the car and examined it. The embossed business card of John R. Havilland, M.D., Practice in Psychiatry, stared at him. He turned the card over. Neatly printed on the back were the words *I know your nightmares*.

4

AFTER thirty-six nonstop hours on the liquor store case, Lloyd Hopkins fell asleep in his cubicle at Parker Center and dreamed of annihilation. Sound waves bombarded him, predator birds attacked the willfully shut-off part of his brain where the man he had killed in the Watts riot and the man he had tried to kill last year resided. The birds tore open jagged sections of sky, letting in crystals the color of blood. When he awakened he bludgeoned the images with quiet still-lifes of Janice and the girls in San Francisco, waiting for time to heal the wounds or reinforce the division. The liquor store/charnel house memory took over from there, pushing family love back into the safety compartment with his nightmares. Lloyd was relieved.

The death scene expanded in his mind, chalked like a forensic technician's marking grid. Off to his left were an open cash register, a counter scattered with tens and twenties, broken liquor bottles all along the lower shelves. Heel marks where the proprietor had been dragged to his execution. The right hand grid revealed an overturned cardboard beer display and heel marks where the two other victims had probably crouched to hide from the killer. Bisecting the grids was the crimson wind tunnel into the store's rear room, three bodies crumpled across a once beige curtain that was torn free from the doorway by the muzzle velocity of three hollow point .41 slugs smashing through three cranial vaults. There were no discernible trajectory or spatter marks; exploded brain and bone debris had rendered the tiny stockroom a slaughterhouse.

Lloyd shook himself further awake, thinking: *Psycho-*

path. He walks into the store, pulls out a monster hand-cannon and demands the money, then sees or hears something that flips his switch. Enraged, he hops over the counter and drags the proprietor by the hair over to the doorway. The girl and the old man betray their presence. He knocks over the display cutout and makes them walk to the curtain. Then he takes them out with three bull's-eyes from a top-heavy, unvented revolver with monster recoil, leaving the money on the counter. A volcano with ice-water fuel injection.

Lloyd stood up and stretched. Feeling the last residue of sleep dissipate, he walked down the hall to the mens room and stood before the sink, alternately staring at himself in the mirror and running cold water over his face. He ignored the sound of early arriving officers laughing and primping quietly around him, aware for a split second that they were keeping their voices at a low register out of deference to his reputation and well-known hatred of loud noise. Feeling his rage start to peak, he defined his killer with self-righteous cop invective: *psychopathic scumbag. Take him out before his switch flips again*.

The first thirty-six hours of his investigation had been spent thinking and chasing computer type. After noticing a "No Parking" zone outside the liquor store and extending all the way down the block, Lloyd theorized that the killer had either walked to the location or had parked in the bushes beside the freeway on-ramp. His latter thesis had been rewarded—under fluorescent arc lights the forensic technicians had found fresh tire tracks in the soft dirt and minute yellow paint scrapings stuck to the tips of sharp branches. Four hours later the L.A.P.D.'s Scientific Investigation Division completed its tests on the paint and announced the results of the technician's plaster of paris moldings of the tire tracks: The car was a Japanese import, late model; the paint the standard brand in every Japanese automotive plant; the tires standard equipment radials—used solely by Japanese manufacturers. R & I and a computer cross-check of recent armed robbery and homicide bulletins revealed that there were no yellow Japanese imports registered to convicted and paroled armed robbers or murderers and that none had been mentioned as figuring in any robberies or homicides dating back over a year. The California Department of Motor Vehicles supplied the most frustrating information: There were 311,819 yellow Japanese automobiles, 1977 to 1984 models, registered in Los Angeles County, making a concerted check for criminal records a clerical impossibility. Even the L.A. County "Hot Sheet" yielded zilch—a total of eight yellow Toyotas, Subarus, and Hondas had been reported stolen over the past six weeks, and all eight had been recovered. The car was a dead end.

Which left the gun.

Lloyd considered the still awaited latent print workup a foregone conclusion: smudges, streaks, partials, and at best a few completes belonging to local juiceheads who patronized the store. Let the three officers he had assigned to run background checks on the victims have carte blanche there—fingerprint mania or the "kill three to get one" angle his superiors at Robbery/Homicide had told him to stress were as dead as the car. Every ounce of Lloyd's instinct told him that, just as every ounce had told him that the trinity of this case was the killer's psychosis, his cool, his *gun*.

The Ballistics Report and the Autopsy Protocol were rife with flat-out wonderment. Henry McGuire, Wallace Chamales, and Susan Wischer were killed by a .41 revolver fired from a distance of twelve to fifteen feet, all three slugs hitting them square between the eyes. The killer was a marksman, the gun an anomaly. Forty-one revolvers predated the Wild West days, going out of manufacture before the Civil War. They were too unwieldy, too heavy, and had a marked tendency toward misfiring. Forty-one ammunition was even worse: hardball or hollow point, its unpredictable reports were capable of jerking the shooter's arm seemingly out of its socket or of going off like a soggy popcorn kernel. Whoever had shot the three people at Freeway Liquor had mastered a difficult antique handgun with antique ammo and had exercised his mastery under a state of extreme duress.

Lloyd stared deeper at his own mirror image, wondering what to do now that he had already sent stolen gun queries to every police agency in California and had personally questioned every antique gun dealer in the Central Yellow Pages. Negative answers all the way down the line—no .41s in stock, let alone purchased, and it would probably be another twenty-four hours before the responses to his queries began trickling in. All the paperwork was digested; all the facts were lodged. There was nothing he could do but wait.

And waiting was antithetical to his nature. Lloyd walked back to his cubicle and stared at the walls. Snapshots of his daughters formed a spray around the fed's ten most wanted; a pincushion map of L.A. County showed that homicides were up in Hollywood, South Central, and the East Valley. On the Freeway Liquor case the obvious next step was a call to Hollywood dicks to see what their snitches had come up with. Looking for something to perk his mental juices, he picked up the file that Dutch Peltz had given him just before the start of the frantic thirty-six hours. *Herzog, Jacob Michael, 5/3/49,* was typed on the front of the manila folder and inside were Xerox copies of statistical records forms, fitness reports, commendation certificates and odd memoranda from superior officers. Thinking of Herzog as a dead man and of the folder as his epitaph, Lloyd pulled up a chair and read every word in it five times.

A singular man emerged. Jungle Jack Herzog had a 137 I.Q., barely met the L.A.P.D.'s height and weight requirements and was born in Beirut, Lebanon. He was fluent in three Middle Eastern languages and had protested the Vietnam war in college, before joining the Air National Guard. He had graduated twelfth in his academy class and received scrolls in scholarship, marksmanship, and physical training. His first four years on the job had been spent working Wilshire Patrol and Wilshire Vice, receiving Class A fitness reports, earning praise from all superior officers save one vice squad lieutenant, who shunted him back into uniform for refusing to serve in a public restroom deployment to catch persons engaged in homosexual acts. That same lieutenant had then recanted his criticism—later requesting that Herzog train his men in operating bookmaking and prostitution surveillances, heavily emphasizing the use of disguise. Herzog's "seminars" had been so successful that he gained consultant status, training plainclothes officers citywide, staying in demand while doing four and three year tours of duty at West L.A. and Venice Divisions.

Jungle Jack became known as the "Alchemist," a reference to his ability to tranform himself and render himself virtually invisible on the street. He was also spectacularly brave—twice resolving hostage situations, the first time by offering himself to the gunman who had taken over a bar he was staking out for liquor violations.

The gunman had grabbed a young prostitute and was holding a knife to her throat while his accomplice tapped the cash register and grabbed the purses and billfolds of the bar's patrons. Herzog, in the guise of a crippled drunk, taunted the knife wielder to release the girl and take him in her stead, screaming obscenities at him, inching closer as the blade drew a trickle of blood at the girl's throat. When he was two feet away, the gunman shoved the prostitute aside and grabbed Herzog, screaming when Jungle Jack's elbow crashed into his windpipe. Herzog disabled the man with a flat-handed karate chop and took off after his accomplice, catching him after a five-block foot pursuit.

The second hostage situation was resolved even more boldly. A man known to local officers as a heavy angel dust user had snatched a little girl and was holding her at gunpoint while a crowd gathered around him. Jack Herzog, in uniform, walked though the crowd and up to the man, who dropped the little girl and fired at him three times. The shots missed, and Herzog blew the man's brains out at point-blank range.

Herzog's reputation grew within the Department; requests from vice squad and plainclothes commanders multiplied. Then Sergeant Martin Bergen, Herzog's best friend, committed an act of cowardice as noteworthy as Herzog's acts of bravery. A trial board followed, and Herzog went to the wall for his friend, calling in favors in hope of saving Bergen's career, testifying as a character witness at his trial, decrying the L.A.P.D.'s hero mentality from his standpoint as one of its greatest heroes. Martin Bergen was banished from the Department in disgrace and Jungle Jack Herzog was banished to a file clerk job—a defeat as ignominious as Bergen's. Even a hero shouldn't fuck with the bosses.

Lloyd put the folder down when he realized that a shadow had fallen across the pages. He looked up to find Officer Artie Cranfield from S.I.D. staring at him.

"Hello, Lloyd. How's tricks?"

"Tricky."

"You need a shave."

"I know."

"Any leads on the liquor store job?"

"No. I'm waiting on queries. Ever hear of a cop named Jungle Jack Herzog?"

"Yeah, who hasn't? A real gunslinger."

"Ever hear of an ex-cop named Marty Bergen?"

"What is this, a guessing game? Everyone knows Old Yellowstreak and that toilet paper tabloid he writes for. Why?"

"Herzog and Bergen were best buddies. Mr. Guts and Mr. Chickenshit. You like it?"

"Not particularly. You look sardonic, Lloyd."

"Waiting makes me feel sardonic. Not sleeping makes me look sardonic."

"Are you going home to sleep?"

"No, I'm going to look for Mr. Guts."

Artie shook his head. "Before you go, say something macho about the liquor store asshole."

Lloyd smiled. "How about 'his ass is grass and I'm the fucking lawnmower'?"

"I like it! I like it!"

"I thought you would."

Lloyd drove to Jack Herzog's last known address, a twenty-unit apartment house on the valley side of the Hollywood Hills. The pink stucco building was sandwiched between two shopping malls and featured a video game arcade in the front lobby. The directory listed Herzog as living in apartment 423. Lloyd walked up four flights of stairs and checked the hallway in both directions, then jimmied the lock with a credit card and closed the door behind him, almost stumbling over the pile of unopened mail that was spread out on the floor.

He flipped a light switch and let his eyes fall on the first thing that greeted them, a trophy case filled with award scrolls and loving cups. The ink on Herzog's death certificate was the scouring powder wipe marks that covered the wood and glass surfaces. A quick check of the rest of the apartment revealed that wipe marks streaked with abrasive powder were spread over every surface capable of sustaining latent prints. It was the job of a conscientious professional.

Lloyd leafed through the envelopes on the floor. No personal letters or postcards—every piece was either a utility bill or junk mail. Letting his eyes stray over the living room walls, he saw an impersonal habitat come into focus—no artwork of any kind; no masculine disarray; furniture that had probably come with the lease. The award scrolls and loving cups had the look of hand-me-downs, and when he squinted to read the names and dates embossed on them, Lloyd saw that they were track and field awards won by Herzog's father in Lebanon during the late '40s.

The kitchen was even more spare—dishes and silverware stacked neatly by the drainboard, no food of any kind in the refrigerator or on the shelves. Only the bedroom bore signs of personality: a closet stuffed with L.A.P.D. uniforms and a huge supply of civilian clothes, outfits ranging from ragpicker overcoats to skinny-lapel pimp suits to outlaw motorcycle leathers. Beside the bed were tall shelves crammed with books. Lloyd scanned the spines. All the titles were biographies, the lives of generals, conquerors and religious iconoclasts predominating. One whole shelf was devoted to works on Richard the Lion Hearted and Martin Luther; another to books on Peter the Great. Romantic plunderers, despots, and mad visionaries. Lloyd felt a wave of love for Jungle Jack Herzog.

After checking out the bathroom, Lloyd found the phone and called Dutch Peltz at the Hollywood station. When Dutch came on the line, he said, "I'm at Herzog's pad. It's been wiped by a pro. You can scratch Herzog for real, but don't let anyone know, okay?"

"All right. Was the pad trashed?"

"No. I get the feeling the killer was just being cautious, covering his ass from all standpoints. Can you do me a few favors?"

"Name them."

"When the Vice Squad comes on, find out from Walt Perkins what bars Herzog was working. Glom any reports he may have filed. I'm going to check out Marty Bergen myself, and I'll come back here and interview Herzog's neighbors tonight. I'll call you at home around seven."

"Sounds good."

"Oh, and Dutch? Have your guys feel out their snitches on antique gun freaks, or any assholes known to use violence who've been taking up guns lately. Even if it's just street bullshit and jive, I want to know about it."

"You're fishing, Lloyd."

"I know. I'll call you at seven."

Lloyd walked through Jungle Jack Herzog's barren dwelling place. Locking the door behind him, he said, "You poor noble son-of-a-bitch, why the fuck did you have to prove yourself so hard?"

It took Lloyd half an hour to drive to the West Hollywood office of the *Big Orange Insider*. Heat, smog, and lack of sleep combined to produce a head pounding that had the pavement wobbling before his eyes. To combat it he rolled up the windows and turned the air conditioning on full, shivering as a fresh adrenaline rush overtook him. Two new cases, three dead and one presumed dead. No sleep for at least another twelve hours.

The *Big Orange Insider* occupied the first floor of a pseudo art-deco chateau on San Vicente a block south of Sunset. Lloyd walked in, bypassing the receptionist, knowing she made him for a cop and would be instantly buzzing the editorial offices to tell them the enemy was coming. He walked into a large room crammed with desks and smiled as suspicious eyes darted up from typewriters to appraise him. When the eyes turned hostile he bowed and blew the assembly a kiss. He was beginning to feel at ease when two women waved back. Then he felt a tugging at his sleeve and turned to see a tall young man pressed into him.

"Who let you back here?" the young man demanded.

"No one," Lloyd said.

"Are you a policeman?"

"I'm a defector. I've quit the cops, and I'm seeking asylum with the counterculture fourth estate. I want to peddle my memoirs. Take me to your wisest ghost writer."

"You have thirty seconds to vacate the premises."

Lloyd took a step toward the young man. The young man took two steps backwards. Seeing the fear in his eyes, Lloyd said, "Shit. Detective Sergeant Hopkins, L.A.P.D. I'm here to see Marty Bergen. Tell him it's about Jack Herzog. I'll be waiting by the reception desk."

He walked back to the reception area. The woman at the desk gave him a deadpan stare, so he busied himself by perusing the enlarged and framed editorial cartoons that adorned the four walls. The L.A.P.D. and L.A. County Sheriff's were attacked in vicious caricatures. Fat, porcine-featured policemen cloaked in American flags poked sleeping drunks with tridents; Chief Gates was dangled on a puppet's string by two men in Ku Klux Klan robes. Wolf-faced cops herded black prostitutes into a paddy wagon, while the officer at the wheel guzzled liquor, a speech balloon elaborating his thoughts: "Wow! Police work sure is exciting! I hope these bimbos are holding some cash. My car payment is overdue!"

"I'll admit it's a bit hyperbolic."

Lloyd turned to face the voice, openly sizing up the man who owned it. Martin Bergen was over six feet tall, blond, with a once strong body going to flab. His florid face was contorted into a look of mirthless mirth and his pale blue eyes were liquid but on target. His breath was equal parts whiskey and mint mouthwash.

"You should know. You had what? Thirteen or fourteen years on the job?"

"I had sixteen, Hopkins. You've got what?"

"Eighteen and a half."

"Pulling the pin at twenty?"

"No."

"I see. What's this about Jack Herzog?"

Lloyd stepped back in order to get a full-body reaction. "Herzog's been missing for over three weeks. His pad has been wiped. He was working Personnel Records downtown and on a loan-out to Hollywood Vice. No one at Parker Center or Hollywood Station has seen him. What does that tell you?"

Marty Bergen began to tremble. His red face turned pale and his hands plucked at his pants legs. He backed into the wall and slid down into a folding metal chair. The woman at the desk brought over a glass of water, then hesitated and hurried off into the ladies room when she saw Lloyd shake his head.

Lloyd sat down beside Bergen and said, "When did you see Herzog last?"

Bergen's voice was calm. "About a month ago. We still hung out. Jack didn't blame me for what I did. He knew we were different that way. He didn't judge me."

"What was his state of mind?"

"Quiet. No—he was always quiet, but lately he'd been moody, up one minute, down the next."

"What did you talk about?"

"Stuff. Shit. Books, mostly. My novel, the one I've been writing."

"Did you and Herzog discuss his assignments?"

"We never talked police work."

"I've heard Herzog described as a 'stone loner.' Is that accurate?"

"Yes."

"Can you name any of his other friends?"

"No."

"Women?"

"He had a girlfriend he saw occasionally. I don't know her name."

Lloyd leaned closer to Bergen. "What about enemies? What about men within the Department who hated him for the way he stood by you? You know the rank-and-file cop mentality as well as I do. Herzog must have engendered resentment."

"The only resentment that Jack engendered was in me. He was so much better than me at everything that I always loved him the most when I hated him the most. We were so, *so* different. When we talked last, Jack said that he was going to exonerate me. But I ran. I was guilty."

Bergen started to sob. Lloyd got up and walked to the door, looking back on the hack writer weeping underneath framed excoriations of what he had once been. Bergen was serving a life sentence with no means of atonement. Lloyd shuddered under the weight of the thought.

* * *

The return trip to the Valley eased Lloyd's fatigue. Snug in his air-conditioned cocoon, he let his mind run with images of Herzog and Bergen, intellectual cop buddies, two men who his instincts told him were as much alike as Bergen said they were different. The Freeway Liquor case receded temporarily to a back burner, and when he parked in front of Jack Herzog's building he felt his mental second wind go physical. He smiled, knowing he would have the juice for a long stretch of hunting.

Herzog's neighbors began returning home from work shortly after five. Lloyd sized the first several of them up from his car, noting that their common denominator was the weary lower middle class look indigenous to Valley residents of both genders. Prime meat for the insurance payoff ploy. He pulled a stack of phony business cards from the glove compartment and practiced his glad-hander insurance man smile, preparing for a performance that would secure him the knowledge of just how much a loner Jungle Jack Herzog was.

Three hours later, with two dozen impromptu interviews behind him, Lloyd felt Herzog move from loner to cipher. None of the people he had talked to recalled even *seeing* the resident of apartment 423, assuming that the unit was kept vacant for some reason. The obvious candor of their statements was like a kick in the teeth; the fact that several had mentioned that the landlord/manager would be out of town for another week was the finishing blow. It was a solid investigatory angle shot to hell.

Lloyd drove to a pay phone and called Dutch Peltz. Dutch answered on the first ring. "Peltz, who's this?"

"Anyone ever tell you you answer the phone like a cop?"

Dutch laughed. "Yeah, you. Got a pencil?"

"Shoot."

"Herzog was working two singles bars, the First Avenue West and Jackie D.'s, both on Highland north of the Boulevard. He was specifically looking for bartenders taking bribes to serve minors and hookers giving head in the hat-check room; we'd had a dozen complaints. He worked those joints for over six weeks, never blowing his cover, always calling narco or patrol from a pay phone when he saw something coming down. He figured in six coke busts and nine for prostitution. As a result, the A.B.C. has both joints up for suspension of their liquor licenses."

Lloyd whistled. "What about the reports he filed?"

"No reports, Lloyd. Walt Perkins' orders. The arresting officers filed. Walt didn't want Jack compromised."

"Shit. That means you can scratch revenge as a motive."

"Yeah, at least as far as his recent arrest record is concerned. What happened with Bergen?"

"Nothing. Bergen hasn't seen Herzog in over a month, says he was moody, troubled. He took the news hard. He was drunk at two in the afternoon. Poor bastard."

"We're going to have to file a Missing Persons Report, Lloyd."

"I know. Let Internal Affairs handle it, which means you and Walt Perkins are going to catch shit for not reporting it earlier and probably even heavier shit for working Herzog off the payroll."

"You might get the case if it goes to Robbery/Homicide."

"They'll never find the stiff, Dutch. This job is pro all the way. I.A.D. will go at it sub rosa, then stonewall it. Let me give it another forty-eight hours before you call them, okay?"

"Okay."

"What have you got from your snitches on the liquor store job?"

"Nothing yet. I sent out a memo to all officers on it. It's still too early for a response. What's next on Herzog?"

"Bar hopping, Dutchman. Yours truly as a swinging single."

"Have fun."

Lloyd laughed and said, "Fuck you," then hung up.

Bombarded by disco music, Lloyd competed for floor and bar space at First Avenue West. Showing his insurance agent's business card and Jack Herzog's personnel file photo to three bartenders, four cocktail waitresses and two dozen singles, he got negative responses, distinguished only by hostile looks and shakes of the head from low-rider types who made him for fuzz and annoyed brush-offs from young women who didn't like his style. Lloyd walked out the door angrily shaking *his* head as the washout continued.

Jackie D.'s, three doors down, was almost deserted. Lloyd counted heads as he took a seat at the bar. A couple doing a slow grind on the dance floor and two overaged swingers feeding coins to the jukebox. The bartender slipped a napkin in front of him and explained why: "Twofers at First Avenue West. Every Tuesday night I get killed. First Ave can afford it, I can't. I keep my prices low to do volume and I still get killed. Is there no mercy in this life?"

"None," Lloyd said.

"I just wanted a confirmation. What are you drinking?"

Lloyd put a dollar bill on the bar. "Ginger ale."

The bartender snorted, "You see what I mean? No mercy!"

Lloyd took out the snapshot of Jack Herzog. "Have you seen this man?"

The bartender scrutinized the photo, then filled Lloyd's glass and nodded. "Yeah, I seen him around here a lot."

Lloyd's skin prickled. "When?"

"A while back. A month, six weeks, maybe two months ago, right before those A.B.C. cocksuckers filed on me. You a cop?"

"That's right."

"Hollywood Vice?"

"Robbery/Homicide. Tell me about the man in the picture."

"What's to tell? He came in, he drank, he tipped well, he didn't hit on the chicks."

"Ever talk to him?"

"Not really."

"Did he ever come in with or leave with anyone?"

The bartender screwed his face into a memory search, then said, "Yeah. He had a buddy. A sandy-haired guy. Medium height, maybe early thirties."

"Did he meet him here?"

"That I can't tell you."

Lloyd walked over to the pay phone outside the men's room and called Hollywood Station, requesting Lieutenant Perkins. When he came on the line, Lloyd said, "Walt, this is Lloyd Hopkins. I've got a question."

"Hit me."

"Did Herzog work his bar assignments alone?"

There was a long moment of silence. Finally Perkins said, "I'm not really sure, Lloyd. My *guess* is sometimes yes, sometimes no. I've always given Jack carte blanche. Any arrangements he made with individual squad members would be up to him. Shall I ask around tomorrow night at roll call?"

"Yes. What about a sandy-haired man, medium height, early thirties. Herzog might have worked with him."

"That's half our squad, Lloyd."

There was another stretch of silence. Finally Lloyd said, "He's dead. I'll be in touch," and replaced the receiver. The barman looked up as he strode toward the door. "There's no mercy!" he called out.

Battered by sleeplessness and dwindling options, Lloyd drove downtown to Parker Center, hoping to find an easily intimidated nightwatch supervisor on duty at Personnel Records. When he saw the man behind the records counter dozing in his chair with a science fiction novel lying on his chest, he knew he was home.

"Excuse me, Officer!"

The records supervisor jerked awake and stared at Lloyd's badge. "Hopkins, Robbery/Homicide," Lloyd said, "Jack Herzog left some files for me in his desk. Will you show me where it is?"

The supervisor yawned, then pointed to a bank of Plexiglas enclosed cubicles. "Herzog's daywatch, so I don't know exactly where his desk is. But you go help yourself, Sergeant. The names are on the doors."

Lloyd walked into the Plexiglas maze, noting with relief that Herzog's cubicle was well out of the supervisor's sight. Finding the door unlocked, he rummaged through the desk drawers, feeling another impersonal habitat come into focus as pencils, notepads, and a series of blank office forms were revealed. One drawer; two drawers; three drawers. Herzog the cipher.

Lloyd was raising his fist to slam the desktop when he noticed the edges of several slips of paper on the floor, wedged into the juncture where the wall met the carpet. Squatting, he pulled them out, going cold when he saw file requisition slips with the officer's name, rank, date of birth, and badge number on top and the requesting officer's name and division below. Squinting, he read over the five slips. The officers' names were unknown to him, but the requesting officer's name wasn't. Captain Frederick T. Gaffaney, Internal Affairs Division, had requested all five files. Old born-again Christian Fred, who had given him grief as a Robbery/Homicide lieutenant. Squinting harder, Lloyd felt the coldness run up his spine into his brain. He knew Gaffaney's signature. These were blatant forgeries.

Lloyd got out his notebook and wrote down the names of the officers whose files had been requested. Tucker, Duane W., Lieutenant, Wilshire Division; Murrray, Daniel X., Captain, Central Division; Rolando, John L., Lieutenant, Devonshire

Division; Kaiser, Steven A., Captain, West Valley Division; Christie, Howard J., Lieutenant, Rampart Division.

He stared at the names, then on impulse ran his hand under the carpet again, coming away with a last slip of paper, going dead ice cold when he read the name printed on top: *Hopkins, Lloyd W. #1114, 2/27/42, Sergeant, Robbery/ Homicide Division.*

5

THOMAS Goff's surveillance photographs had not prepared him for the woman's beauty; nothing in Goff's oral and written reports came close to describing her aura of refinement. A thousand-dollar-a-night whore in a thousand-dollar raw silk dress. Dr. John Havilland leaned back in his chair, pretending to be tongue-tied. Give the woman the temporary upper hand, let her think her charisma had dented his professionalism. When Linda Wilhite didn't fidget under his gaze, he broke the long introductory silence. "Will you tell me something about yourself, Ms. Wilhite? The reasons why you've decided to enter therapy?"

Linda Wilhite's eyes circled the office; her hands smoothed the arms of her chair. Brilliantly varnished oak walls, a framed Edward Hopper original. No couch. The chairs she and the Doctor were sitting in were upholstered in pure cashmere. "You love nice things," she said.

Havilland smiled. "So do you. That's a very beautiful dress."

"Thank you. Why do most people come to see you?"

"Because they want to change their lives."

"Of course. Can you guess what I do for a living?"

"Yes. You're a prostitute."

"How exactly did you know that?"

"You called my service and made an appointment without asking to speak to me personally, and you wouldn't say who referred you. When a woman contacts me in that manner, I assume that she's in the Life. I've counseled a great many prostitutes, and I've published several monographs on my findings, without ever violating the anonymity of my patients. In criminal parlance I'm a 'stand-up guy.' I don't have a receptionist or a secretary, because I don't trust such people. Women in the Life trust *me* for these reasons."

Linda traced patterns on her silk and the Doctor's cashmere. "This dress cost thirteen hundred dollars. My shoes cost six hundred. I love nice things and you love nice things, and we both make a lot of money. But what I do to make money is killing me, and I have to stop."

Havilland leaned forward as the woman's words settled in on him. He brought his voice down to its lowest register and said, "Are you ready to sacrifice picayune shit like thirteen hundred dollar dresses to achieve your true power? Are you ready to dig through your past to find out why you need creature comforts at the expense of your integrity? Are you willing to break yourself down to ground zero in order to help me take you as far as you can go?"

Linda flinched at the battery of questions. "Yes," she said.

Havilland stood up, stretched and decided to go in full bore. Sitting back down, he said, "Linda, my brand of therapy is a two-way street. What you think I need to know and what I need to know may well be two different things. I would like this first session to consist of questions and answers. I'll throw out some educated guesses and assumptions about you, and you tell me how accurate I am. What I want to establish is some kind of instinctive rapport. Do you follow me?"

Her voice quavering, Linda said, "How far is as far as I can go?"

Dr. John Havilland threw back his head and laughed. "My educated guess is that you can hit the ball out of the ballpark and into the next county."

Linda smiled. "Then let's do it," she said.

Havilland got up and walked to the window, glancing down on the jetstream of cars and people twenty-six stories below him. He coughed and pressed the activator button inlaid on the window ledge, sending current to the tape recorder housed behind a section of wall panel.

Turning to face Linda Wilhite, he said, "You're thirty-one or two, large family, northern Midwest—Michigan or Wisconsin. The best and brightest of your siblings. Adored by your brothers, despised by your sisters. Your parents are new money, uneasy about it, terrified of losing their hard-earned status. You dropped out of college in your senior year and worked at odd jobs before a series of disillusionments led you slowly into the Life. How close am I?"

Linda was already shaking her head. "I'm twenty-nine, from L.A., an only child. My parents died when I was ten. I lived in a series of foster homes until I graduated from high school. I never attended college. My parents were semi-poor. I made a conscious decision to become a prostitute, just as I've made a conscious decision to quit being one. Please don't consider me typical."

Circling the office, his eyes shifting back and forth between Linda Wilhite and the Persian rug that cushioned his footfalls, Havilland said, "Is being typical a crime? No, don't answer, let me continue. You enjoy sex with certain kinds of older men among your customers, and it hurts you if they sleep with anyone else. If you find a customer attractive, then you fantasize about him and hate yourself for it afterwards. You despise hookers who consider themselves 'therapists' and the like. Your basic dilemma is a conservative nature, one grounded in the work ethic, undercut with the knowledge that what you do is shit, antithetical to every decent moral instinct you possess. You have rationalized this contradiction for years, bolstered yourself with self-help books and spiritual tracts, but now it won't wash anymore and you came to me. Touché, Ms. Wilhite?"

The Doctor's voice had risen higher and higher, little crescendos of truth that Linda knew would grow in scope and intimacy without the man's resonance ever cracking. Her hands fluttered over her lap, looking for something of and by herself to touch. When they descended on green paisley silk, she jerked them back and said, "Yes. Yes. Yes. How did you know those things?"

Dr. John Havilland sat back down and stretched his legs until his feet dangled a few inches from Linda's alligator shoes. "Linda, I'm the best there is. To be blunt, I am a work of fucking art."

Linda laughed until she felt a blush creep up from her bodice. "I've got a john who says the same thing to me. He collects Colombian art, so I know it's an informed opinion. And you know the funny thing? He calls me 'a work of fucking art,' and he never fucks me—he just takes pictures of me. Isn't that a hoot?"

Havilland laughed along, first uproariously, then sedately. When his laughter wound down, he said, "What does this man do with the photographs of you?"

"He has them blown up, then he frames them and hangs them in his bedroom," Linda said.

"How do you feel about that? Worshiped? Adored?"

"I . . . I feel worthy of my beauty."

"Did your parents recognize your beauty early on? Did they fawn over you because of it?"

"My father did."

"Did your parents take photographs of you?"

Linda flinched at the word *photographs*. She stammered, "N-no."

Havilland leaned forward and put his hand on her knee. "You've gone pale, Linda. Why?"

Flinching again, Linda said, "This is happening so fast. I wasn't going to tell you today because most of the time it seems so remote. My father was a violent man. He was a longshoreman, and he used to fight bare knuckles for money on the docks at San Pedro. He'd win or he'd lose and he'd always bet heavily on himself, so if he won he showered mother and me with gifts and if he lost he brooded and smashed things. Most of the time it was fifty-fifty, win, lose, win, lose—so that I never knew what to expect.

"Then, when I was ten, Daddy hit a losing streak. He brooded worse then ever and punched out all the windows in our house. It was winter and we were broke and the heat was shut off and cold air blew in through the broken windows. I'll never forget the day it happened. I came home from school and there were police cars in front of the house. A detective took me aside and told me what happened. Daddy had put a pillow over Mother's head and shot her in the face. Then he stuck the gun in his mouth and shot himself. I was sent to Juvenile Hall, and a couple of days later a matron told me I had to identify the bodies. She showed me photographs from the autopsy—Daddy and Mother with half their faces blown away. I cried and I cried, but I couldn't stop looking at the pictures."

"And, Linda?" Havilland whispered.

Linda said, "And I went to live with an elderly couple who treated me like a princess. I swiped the pictures the matron showed me and forced myself to laugh and gloat over them. Those pictures gave me freedom from the shitty life I had, and laughing at them was like getting revenge on my parents. I—"

Havilland raised a hand in interruption. "Let me finish. Your foster parents caught you laughing over the photographs and punished you? It was never the same with them after that?"

"Yes," Linda said.

The Doctor circled his office again, running light fingertips over the oak walls. "A few more questions, then we'll end the session. Is the type of man—of customer—that you're attracted to large and physical, possessed of intelligence and breeding but also possessed of a certain aura of violence?"

Linda's whisper was astonished. "Yes."

Havilland smiled. "World-class progress in one session. Does the day after tomorrow—Friday—suit you for our next one? Say ten-thirty?"

Linda Wilhite stood up, surprised to find her legs steady.

She smoothed the front of her dress and said, "Yes. I'll be here. Thank you."

Havilland took her arm and walked her to his outer office door. "It was my pleasure."

After Linda Wilhite was gone, the Doctor, armed with her image and facts from Goff's reconnaissance, turned off the lights and played the time-travel game.

When Linda was two and living in a San Pedro dive with her white-trash parents, he was twelve and gaining clandestine access to wealthy homes in Bronxville and Scarsdale, New York, exorcising his nocturnal heart by delivering himself to the quiet muse of other peoples' dwellings, sometimes stealing, sometimes not. . . .

When Linda was fourteen and sexually experimenting with surfer morons in Huntington Beach, he was twenty-four and graduating from Harvard Medical School at the top of his class, the legendary Doctor John the Night Tripper, the genius dope chemist/abortionist who held instructors rapt with his digressions on the theories of Kinsey, Pomeroy, and Havelock Ellis. . . .

When Linda was growing into her exquisite beauty in a series of foster homes, filled with wonder at her parents' deaths and the apostasy that their bloodletting had spawned, he—

The Time Machine screeched, shuddered, and ground to a halt. A green door opened to reveal a man in a gray uniform standing beside a salmon-pink 'fifty-six Ford Victoria ragtop. Little girls in party dresses thronged the car, and just before it exploded into flames they turned to point and laugh at him.

The Night Tripper walked to the wall and turned on the light, seeking confirmation. He found it in glass-encased tributes; framed diplomas from New York University and Harvard Med and St. Vincent and Castleford Hospitals—parchment that spelled out plainly that he was the best. The dates on them told him why the Time Machine had malfunctioned. Linda was powerful. Linda had sustained a catastrophe as he had and required that he juxtapose his story against hers from the beginning. . . .

1956. Scarsdale, New York. Johnny Havilland, age eleven, known as "Spaz," "Wimpdick," and "Shitstick." Sherry-guzzling mother with the inbred look indigenous to high-line Wasps who have never had to work for a living; big bucks father, a hunter whose shotgun volleys have decimated the varmint population of six New York counties. Johnny hates school; Johnny hates to play ball; Johnny loves to dream and listen to music on his portable radio.

Johnny's father considers him a wimp and decrees a rite to prompt his manhood: Shoot the family's senile golden retriever. Johnny refuses and is sent by his father to a "training school" run by an extremist sect of nuns. The nuns lock Johnny in a basement full of rats, with no food or water and only a shovel for protection. Two days go by. Johnny huddles in a corner and screams himself hoarse as the rats nip at his legs. On the third day he falls asleep on the floor and wakes up to find a large rat scampering off with a chunk of his lip. Johnny screams, picks up the shovel and beats every rat in the basement to death.

Johnny's father takes him home the following day, tousling his hair and calling him "Dad's little ratter." Johnny goes straight for his father's gun rack, grabs a twelve-gauge pump and strides outside to the kennel, where five Labradors and short-haired Pointers frolic behind barbed wire. Johnny blows the dogs to kingdom come and turns to face his father, who turns white and faints. Weeks go by. His father shuns him. Johnny knows that his father has given him a precious gift that is far more valuable then standard manhood. Johnny loves his father and wants to please him with his newfound strength.

1957. "Green Door" by Jim Lowe climbs the hit parade and fills Johnny with portents of dark secrets.

* * *

"Midnight, one more night without sleeping.
Watching, 'till the morning comes creeping.
Green door, what's that secret you're keeping?"

Johnny wants to know the secret so he can tell his father and make him love him.

The quest for the secret begins with a shinny up a drainpipe into a neighbor's darkened attic. Johnny finds coyotes mounted on roller-skates wheels and department store mannequins. The mannequins have been gouged in the facial and genital regions and red paint has been daubed in the holes and left to trickle off in simulation of wounds. Johnny steals a coyote's glass eye and leaves it on his father's desk. His father never mentions the gift. As other gifts from other dark houses follow, Johnny perceives that his father is terrified of him.

Johnny's housebreaking career continues; the spacious homes of Westchester County become his teacher and friend. Thoughts of earning his father's love grow mute beside the haphazard tides of passion that he assimilates in shadow-shrouded bedrooms and hallways. Green door after green door after green door bursts open. And then there was the next to the last door and the man in the uniform, and the last door opening on a pitch-black void. . . .

The darkness deepened as the Time Machine suffered its final malfunction, its chronograph needle stuck permanently on June 2, 1957. The void stretched into months. The callow Johnny Havilland who entered was only a shell compared to the self-sufficient John who emerged. . . .

Always this memory gap, the Night Tripper thought. Father was there when he entered and gone when his recollections again assumed a linear sequence. He took Goff's photographs of Linda Wilhite from his desk and fanned them like a deck of cards. Linda came briefly to life, the slash of her mouth speaking bewilderment. She wanted to know *why* he was as great as he was.

Havilland ruffled the photos again, making Linda beg for

the answer. He smiled. He would tell her, and he would not need the Time Machine to help him.

1958. Father had been gone for months; Mother, in a perpetual sherry haze, didn't seem to care. Checks came in bimonthly, drawn from the tax-exempt trust funds that Father's father had started almost half a century before. It was as if a giant puppetmaster had snatched the man into eternity, leaving his material wealth as wonder bait to ensure that Johnny could have *anything* he wanted.

Johnny wanted knowledge. He wanted knowledge because he knew it would give him sovereignty over the psychic pain that all the human race save himself was subject to. His grief over his father's disappearance had transmogrified into armor sheathed in one-way transparent glass. *He* could look out and see *all*; no one could look in and see *him*. Thus invulnerable, Johnny Havilland sought knowledge.

He found it.

In 1962 John Havilland graduated from Scarsdale High School, number one in his class, hailed by the school's principal as a "human encyclopedia." N.Y.U. and more scholastic honors followed, culminating in a Phi Beta Kappa key, Summa Cum Laude graduation and a full scholarship to Harvard Medical School.

It was at Harvard Med that John Havilland was able to combine his knowledge-lust and dominion over human feelings into dominion over other people. Like his early burglary career, it began with a shinny up a drainpipe and a vault into an open window. But where before he had come away with knicknacks to please his father, this time he came away with questions and answers that he knew would make *him* the spiritual patriarch to scores of pliant souls.

The window yielded tape recordings of confidential interviews conducted by Alfred Kinsey in 1946 and 1947. The interviewees were described in terse sentences and were then asked to describe themselves. The variance factor was astonishing—the people almost always defined themselves by some physical abnormality. The Q. and A. sessions that followed proceeded along uniform patterns, revealing mundane matters—lust, guilt and adultery—things which John Havilland's immune system had surmounted in early adolescence.

After over two hundred hours of listening to the tapes, John knew two things: One, that Kinsey was an astute interviewer, a scholar who considered factual admissions illuminating in themselves; and, two, that that knowledge was *not* enough and that Kinsey had failed because he could *not* get his interviewees to talk openly about fantasies beyond variations of fucking and sucking. He could elicit no admissions of dark grandeur, because he felt none himself. His interviewees were hicks who didn't know shit from Shinola. Kinsey operated from the Freudian/humanist ethic: Provide knowledge of behavior patterns to enable the subject a viewpoint of objectivity in which to relegate his neuroses to a scrap heap of things that don't work. Show him that his fears and most extreme fantasies are irrational and convince him to be a loving, boring, happy human being.

After over six hundred hours of listening, John knew two more things: That the most profound truth lay in the labyrinths that coiled behind a green door in the interviewee's mind the very second that Alfred Kinsey said, "Tell me about your fantasies"; and, two, that with the proper information and the correct stimuli he could get carefully chosen people to break through those doors and act out their fantasies, past moral strictures and the boundaries of conscience, taking *him* past his already absolute knowledge of mankind's unutterable stupidity into a new night realm that he as yet was incapable of imagining. Because the night was there to be plundered; and only someone above its laws could exact its bounty and survive.

Now armed with a mission, there remained only to discover and actuate the means towards its fulfillment. It was 1967. Drugs and hard rock flooded Harvard Yard, spawned by a backwash of students, townies, and traveling hippies willing to protest anything, try anything, and ingest anything in order to gain themselves, lose themselves, or achieve a "transcendental experience." Social change was in the wind, producing a "consciousness explosion" that John Havilland considered fatuous and propagated by failures, many of whom would not live to see the period dwindle out of its own emptiness, replaced by a new reactionary fervor. Giving the youth culture a life expectancy of two years at the most, he decided to become one of its ikons. People would follow him; they would have no choice.

Two abortions performed gratis in his antiseptically clean Beacon Hill apartment gained him a hushed reputation among Harvard undergrads; a record heard at a pot party provided him with a powerful sobriquet. "Doctor John the Night Tripper" was a Creole who shrieked odes to dope and sex, backed up by two saxes, drums, and an electric organ. At the party, a heavily stoned anthropology professor shoved an album cover in John Havilland's face and yelled, "That's you, man! Your name is John and you're in med school! Dig it!"

The nickname stuck, fueled by the young doctor's forays into manufacturing LSD and liquid methamphetamine. Drug concocting med students were commonplace, but a dope doc who gave the stuff away with no strings was the subject of much speculation. People started to come around to his apartment, seeking his knowledge. He told them what they wanted to hear, a hodge-podge of counterculture thought combed from all their heroes. They never knew they were being bullshitted, not even when the Night Tripper revealed that there were indeed strings.

The experiments began. Do you *really* want to find out who you are? Dr. John would ask his would-be subject. Do you *really* want to find out the depth of your potential? Do you understand that my exploring your most secret fantasies will gain for you in one weekend what psychoanalysis will never discover?

The subjects were all "pre-screened" drop-ins at the

Beacon Hill apartment. They were, male and female, all of a type: Aesthetes devoid of original thought; rich-kid spiritual seekers whose rebellious streaks cloaked long histories of overdependence on their parents. A weekend to help out Dr. John with his med school thesis? Sure.

The weekends would begin with high quality marijuana and jokingly phrased sex questionnaires. More weed and oral questions followed, the Doctor regaling the subjects with made-up sexual anecdotes of his own. When the subjects were plied almost to sleep with weed and music, Dr. John would give them a skin pop of sodium Pentothal and tell them horror stories and gauge their responses. If they responded with glee, he would go straight for the fantasy jugular, interweaving his horror stories with the subject's own, creating tapestries ranging from family slaughter to wholesale sexual conquest. When the subject fell asleep, the Night Tripper would fall asleep at his side, savoring the feel of clothed bodies almost touching in the fellowship of nightmares.

Increasingly smaller doses of sodium Pentothal accompanied by visual aids took up the rest of the weekend, bringing the subject to the fantasy/reality juncture point where they had some cognizance of what they had revealed. Anti-war activists guffawed over photographs of napalm barbecued babies, felt momentary remorse, then laughed it off in the joy of new-found freedom. The Doctor described beloved parents in postures of debasement with barnyard creatures; the subjects supplied gory and humorous embellishments. Psyches broke through green doors, retreated into normalcy and left their weekend revelations to simmer benignly, waiting for the right time or the right catalyst, or waiting for nothing.

After four months of weekends, Dr. John discontinued his experiments. They had become boringly repetitive, and he had reached the point where he could unfailingly predict the responses of his subjects. He had quantum leaps to take in his mission, but he knew those leaps were years away.

Upon graduation from medical school in 1969, Havilland

was assigned to the Intern Program at St. Vincent's Hospital in the Bronx, New York, where he spent twelve-hour shifts tending to the needs of welfare families. It was boring medicine, and he grew more restive by the day, sending out resumés to every hospital in the metropolitan New York area known to have a lackluster psychiatric staff. A three-year residency was required of all physicians training in psychiatry, and he wanted to be sure that he would be able to dominate his instructors—even at entry level.

Sixteen applications sent out; sixteen acceptances. Three months of detective work. Conclusion: Castleford Hospital, one hour north of New York City. Low pay, alcoholics in key administrative posts, a psychiatric staff of four aged doctors and a pillhead R.N. Heavy Medicaid contracts with the New York State Parole Board, which meant plenty of court-referred criminal types. He would play the game with all the finesse he was capable of and they would give him carte blanche. On March 4, 1971, Dr. John Havilland moved into his new quarters outside the main administration building at Castleford Hospital in Nyack, New York, knowing that something was about to happen. He was right. After six months of counseling dreary low-lifes, he met Thomas Goff.

At their first counseling session Goff had been hyperkinetic and witty, even under the stress of a migraine headache. "My goal in life used to be to do *nothing* exceedingly well; my downfall was the fact that I liked to do it in stolen cars. . . . I'll do anything to keep from going back to prison, from skindiving for Roto-rooter to servicing Jewish spinsters in Miami Beach. What do you recommend, Doc? Grow gills or get circumcised? Jesus fucking Christ, these daylight headaches are killing me!"

Havilland had felt instincts clicking into place, telling him to act now. Obeying those instincts, he gave Goff a large intravenous shot of Demerol. While Goff was off on a painless dope cloud he asked him questions and found out that Goff liked to hurt people and that he never talked about it because they put you in jail for that. He had hurt lots of people, but the Trashbag Man had been his cellie at Attica and the headaches had started about then, and wasn't that wild psychedelic ceiling *beige*? *Give me back my headaches!*

Havilland had put him completely out, reading his file while he was unconscious. Thomas Lewis Goff, D.O.B. 6/19/49/; light brown and blue, 5ft. 10in., 155. High school dropout, 161 I.Q., car thief, burglar, pimp. Suspect in three aggravated assault cases, cases dismissed when the women victims refused to testify. Convicted of first degree auto theft with two priors, sentenced to five years in state prison, sent to Attica on 11/4/69, considered a model prisoner. Paroled after the recent riots, when psychiatrists at the prison judged that he would go psychotic if he remained incarcerated. Psychosomatic headaches and terror of daylight chief symptoms, dating from the time of the riot, when he was shut in a secluded cell block with one Paul Mandarano, a convicted murderer known as the "Trashbag" killer. Mandarano had committed suicide by hanging himself from the cell bars, and Goff had remained in the cell with his body until the riot was quelled. No presense of neurological damage; judged an excellent parole risk.

Fate embraced Dr. John Havilland. When Thomas Goff regained consciousness, he said, "It's going to be all right, Thomas. Please trust me."

The Night Tripper stalked Goff's nightmares, then blunted them with drugs and fantasies until Goff wasn't sure that Attica and the Trashbag Man had really happened. Under sodium Pentothal and age regression hypnosis, the Doctor took him back to the trauma flux point, learning that Paul Mandarano had hung himself with a beige plastic trashbag and that a blower fan stationed outside the cell block had blown the loose ends of the bag continually over the bars, acting in concert with safety arc lights, turning the cell where Goff had huddled with a rotting body into an alternately brightly lit and pitch-black horror show. Classic symbolism: Light magnified the terror; darkness diminished it. After seven months of therapy sessions in a cool, dim room, Thomas Goff's fear of daylight abated to the point where it became tolerable. "I'll always hate oysters, Doc; but somtimes I'll have to watch other people eat them. Daylight is pretty unavoidable, but as Nietzsche said, 'What does not destroy me makes me stronger.' Right, Doc?"

The Night Tripper felt tremors of love at Goff's words. It was right for Goff to love him, but the reverse was not tolerable. "Yes, Thomas, Nietzche was right. You'll find that out even more as we continue our journey together."

That journey was interrupted for over ten years.

Thomas Goff disappeared, gone into mists that would always be at best a witches brew of fantasy and reality. The Doctor grieved for the loss of his would-be right hand and concentrated on practicing the craft of psychiatry, specializing in counseling criminals and prostitutes at Castleford and then in private practice in Los Angeles, seeking and storing knowledge, writing and publishing monographs and establishing a reputation of maverick brilliance that grew and grew as his designs for conquest seethed within him. And then one day Thomas Goff was at his door, whimpering that the headaches were back and would the Doctor please help him?

Fate snapped its fingers. "Yes," Dr. John Havilland said.

Neuro scans, electro-encephalograms, blood tests, and extensive therapy followed, each physical and mental probe another step toward the starting gate of the Night Tripper's mission. Thomas Goff's last ten years had been extraordinary. Havilland described them in his journal:

> Since my previous analysis of the subject, he has gone on to assume classic criminal behavior patterns, exemplifying the paranoic/sociopathic textbook personality, but with one notable exception: His criminal behavior is pathologically derived, but not pathologically executed. Goff shows great adaptability in subjugating his violent urges to circumspection in the choosing of his victims,

and he always stops short of inflicting great bodily harm or murder. He has committed nighttime burglaries all over the East Coast for a decade and has never been caught; he has performed an estimated two hundred assaults on women, experiencing simultaneous sexual release *without reverting to the mayhem that characterized his assault career prior to our 1971 counselings.* Since Goff is, in the truest sense a psychopath, this restraint (and his pride in it, that he attributes to my earlier counseling!) is beyond extraordinary—it is almost unbelievable. It is evident that he credits me with saving his life (i.e., alleviating his terror of daylight and blunting his memory of the suicide he witnessed at Attica); and that, implicitly, he credits me with "teaching" him the restraint that has armed him with a virtual criminal carte blanche. In fact, Goff (a 161 I.Q.!), says that *I have taught him to think.* It is evident that this brilliant criminal is seeking a father-son bonding with me, and that his "headaches" are a psychosomatic device to bring the two of us together to achieve the purposes he senses I have planned. His attraction to me is *not* either overtly or covertly homosexual; Goff simply equates me, on the sensory/stimuli level, with peace, tranquillity and the fulfillment of dreams.

Three weeks into the new counseling, with Goff's recurring headaches quelled with hallucinogen-laced codeine, the Night Tripper went in full tilt and gained complete capitulation.

"Do you know that I love you, Thomas?"

"Yes."

"Do you know that I am here to take you as far as you can go?"

"Yes."

"Will you help me to help other people? To bring them out the way I've brought you out?"

"You know I will."

"Will you help me gain knowledge?"

"Name it, point the finger, I'll do it."

"Would you kill for me?"

"Yes."

That night the Doctor outlined Goff's role in his mission. Recruit lonely men and women, journeymen spiritual seekers, spineless "new agers" with no family and plenty of money. The counterculture consciousness circuit and singles night-spots should be rife with them. Goff was to judge their susceptibility, draw them out, and bring them to him, utilizing the greatest discretion and caution, employing no physical violence. He was also to perform burglary-reconnaissance forays, entering the homes of the Doctor's hooker patients, checking their john books for the names of wealthy customers—the objective being men with weak wills and monogamous relationships with their whores. "Be slow and cautious, Thomas," Havilland said. "This is a lifetime process."

That process yielded three lonelies in the first year. Havilland was satisfied with the progress he was making with their psyches, but frustrated by the lack of pure knowledge he was reaping. Eight more months passed; another three lonelies were recruited. The Doctor refined his techniques and filled up hundreds of pages on what he had learned. Yet still he hungered for pure data; molding clay that he could hold in his hands, savor and then mix into the human tapestry he was creating. The frustration had him slamming his desk in rage, beseeching time warps in his past for the answer to unanswerable questions. Then two events coincided and provided an answer.

Despite medication, Thomas Goff's headaches grew worse. Havilland ran a new series of tests and found his psychosomatic diagnosis rebuked. Goff had leptomeningitis, a chronic brain inflammation. It was the cause of his headaches and had probably been a contributing factor to his violent behavior throughout the years. For the first time in his professional life, the Doctor found himself in a crisis. Leptomeningitis could be cured by surgery and a wide assortment of drugs. His executive officer could be restored to health, and it would be business as usual. Leptomeningitis was also known to induce homicidal rages in normally peaceful men and women, yet, somehow, Thomas Goff, a violent sociopathic criminal, had sustained the disease for over a decade without letting it push him across the line into mindless slaughter. Without treatment, Goff would soon go insane and die of a massive cerebral hemorrhage. *But if, through a careful application of antibiotics and painkillers, Goff's disease could be de-escalated and escalated to suit his whims, he would possess his very own terminal man, and it would provide him with the opportunity to observe an absolutely emotionless human machine run gauntlets of stress unparalleled in psychiatric history. And if need be, Goff could be put to use as the ultimate killing machine.*

The Night Tripper decided to sacrifice his executive officer/protégé/son to the god of knowledge.

Then the Alchemist appeared.

Goff's leptomeningitis was three weeks into a "remission" when he told the Doctor of the vice cop he had met, the disguise artist reader of hero biographies who he could tell was just dying to bend to someone. Havilland had at first been wary—the man was, after all, a police officer—but then after seven counseling sessions devoted to bringing the Alchemist through his obvious green door, the cop supplied the last piece of the Night Tripper's long-sought puzzle: cruel, merciless data. Levers of manipulation that would allow him to bend hundreds of people like twigs. The six folders that he offered in acquiesence to the Doctor's charisma were the first key. Four data keepers and two police legends. The Alchemist had tried very hard to please him, and in his gratitude the Doctor had brought him through his green door much too fast, and he had run from the self-discoveries that were unfolding before him.

Now the Alchemist was gone. Only his legacy of potential knowledge remained.

Back in the present, the Night Tripper let his mind play over the files in his wall safe. Cops. Men used to violence as a way of life. Goff would have to be his go-between, but he was approaching his terminus—the lepto would become uncontrollable within a few months. His training mission was unsettling, a violation of his efficacy counseling. He should have searched the liquor store for possible witnesses, then retreated until the proprietor was alone. One killing was perfection; three was dangerous.

Havilland walked to his window and looked out, watching the microcosmic progression of the people below him, scuttling like laboratory animals in an observation maze. He wondered if they would ever know that at odd moments he loved them.

6

SEVENTY-TWO hours into the liquor store case; over two thousand man hours spent probing every possible scientific angle. Yield: Zero. Extensive background checks on the three victims: Zero multiplied by the silence of the random factor—decent people at the wrong place at the wrong time, loved ones importuning God for the reason why, the unearthing of dull facts leading nowhere. The fingerprint report was a pastiche of swirls, streaks, and smudges; the heel marks and fabric elements found at the death scene were all attributed to the victims. The snitch reports that filtered back to Hollywood Division officers had the air of hyperbole and were inimical to Lloyd's concept of the killer as being very smart and very cool and not at all interested in reaping renown for his handiwork. If the queries on stolen .41 revolvers came back negative, the only remaining option would be to initiate nationwide gun queries and have a team of computer jockeys and astute paperwork detectives run through the over three-hundred thousand automobile registration records for yellow Japanese imports, crosschecking them with criminal records and records of known criminal affiliates, looking for combustion points. If no two facts struck sparks and if the gun queries washed out, the case would be shunted into the bureaucratic backlog.

Lloyd recoiled at the knowledge that time was running out. Seated at Dutch Peltz's desk, savoring the feel of a silent Hollywood Station drifting toward dusk, he read over Xeroxes of the Field Interrogation Reports he had requisitioned citywide. On the night of April 23, eleven yellow Japanese cars had been stopped for traffic violations and/or "suspicious behavior." Four of the people cited and detained had been women, five had been ghetto black men, two with no criminal record, three with misdemeanor records for possession of drugs and nonpayment of child support. The two remaining white men were a lawyer stopped and ultimately arrested for drunk driving and a teenager popped for driving under the influence of a narcotic substance, which the arresting officer surmised to be airplane glue. No sparks.

Lloyd yelled, "Shit!" and stormed through his makeshift command post looking for a pen and paper. Finding a yellow legal pad and a stack of pencils atop Dutch's bookcase, he wrote:

> Dutchman—time running out. There's a shitload of hotel stick-ups downtown, so I'll probably get yanked to a robbery assignment soon. The 4/23 F.I.s and the snitch feedback are goose-egg. Will you do the following for me?
>
> 1. Have another team of uniformed officers house to house (6-8 block radius) the area surrounding Freeway Liquor. Have them ask about:
>
> A. Yellow Jap cars recently seen in area. (Lic. #)
>
> B. Recent loiterers.
>
> C. Recent conversations with the three deceased. All 3 victs. were locals. Did *they* mention anything suspicious?
>
> D. *Have officers check previous canvass report filed by patrolmen who house-to-housed the night of the killings. Have them check residences of people who were not home that night.*
>
> E. Tell the men that Robbery/Homicide has allocated unlimited overtime on this case—they'll get the $ in their next check.
>
> 2. Glom all H.W. Div. F.I.'s for past 6 mos. mentioning yellow Jap. autos. Set aside all incoming F.I.s featuring same, and collate all incoming rob. & homicide bulletins mentioning same.
>
> 3. Re: Herzog. I've got a weird feeling about this—

even beyond the fact J.H. stole my file. I want some kind of handle on it before we call I.A.D. Have you run your grapevines on the 6 officers? Are the files still missing? I'm going to sleep at J.H.'s pad for the next several nights—(886–3317) see what happens—also, if the Rob./Hom. brass can't find me, they can't reassign me—L.H.

There was a knock at the door, followed by the sound of coughing. Lloyd put his memo under Dutch's quartz bookend and called out, "Enter!"

Lieutenant Walt Perkins walked in and shut the door behind him. When he shuffled his feet nervously, Lloyd said, "Looking for me or the Dutchman, Walt?"

"You," Perkins said.

Lloyd pointed to a chair. Perkins ignored it. "I checked with the squad," he said. "Herzog always worked alone. A lot of the men wanted to work with him because of his rep, but Jack always nixed it. He used to joke that ninety-five percent of all vice cops were alcoholics. He . . ." Perkins faltered as Lloyd came alive with tension. The sandy-haired man was not a cop.

Perkins shuffled his feet again, drawing figure eights on the floor. "Lloyd, I don't want I.A.D. nosing around the squad."

"Why?" Lloyd asked. "The worst you'll get is a reprimand. Vice commanders have been working Herzog off the payroll for years. It's common knowledge."

"It's not that."

"Then what is it?"

Perkins ceased his figure eights and forced himself to stare at Lloyd. "It's you. I know the whole story of what happened with you last year. I got it straight from a deputy chief. I admire you for what you did, that's not it. It's just that I know the promotion board has a standing order not to ever promote you or Dutch, and I—"

Lloyd's peripheral vision throbbed with black. Swallowing to keep his voice down, he said, "And you want me to sit on this? A brother officer murdered?"

Shaking his head and lowering his eyes, Perkins whispered, "No. I paid off a clerk at Personnel Records. He's going to carry Herzog present for another week or so, then report him missing. There'll be an investigation."

Lloyd kicked out at a metal wastebasket, sending a mound of wadded paper onto Perkins's pantslegs. The lieutenant flinched back into the door and brought his eyes up. "The born-agains in I.A.D. have a hard-on for you, Hopkins. Gaffaney especially. You're a great cop, but you don't give a fuck about other cops and the people close to you get hurt. Look at what you've done to Dutch Peltz. Can you blame me for wanting to cover my ass?"

Lloyd released the hands he had coiled into fists. "It's all a trade-off. You're an administrator, I'm a hunter. You're a well liked superior officer, which means that the guys you command are shaking down hookers for head jobs and ripping off dope dealers for their shit and slopping up free booze all over Hollywood. I'm not so well liked, and I get strange, scary ideas sometimes. But I'm willing to pay the price and you aren't. So don't judge me. And get out of the way if you don't want to get hurt, because I'm seeing this thing through."

Lloyd pretended to fiddle with the papers on Dutch's desk. The second he averted his eyes, Perkins slipped out the door.

An hour later, when the last remnants of twilight dissolved into night, Lloyd drove to Jackie D.'s bar. The barman he had talked to two nights before was on duty and the place was still empty. The barman had the same weary look and automatically put down a napkin as Lloyd took a seat at the bar, shaking his head and saying, "No mercy. The ginger ale drinkers always return. There is no mercy."

"What's the complaint this time?" Lloyd asked.

"Wet T-shirt contest next door. First I gotta compete with

free booze, now I gotta compete with free tits. I heard the guy who owns that puspocket is gonna throw in female mud wrestling, maybe female bush shaving, maybe female dick measuring, make a bundle and go into something stable like pushing heroin. No mercy!"

"Isn't his liquor license up for suspension, too?"

"Yeah, but he's young and he's got the chutzpah to think big and diversify. You know, a forty-story swingers' condo shaped like a dick, with an underground garage shaped like a snatch. You drive in and an electric beam shoots you an orgasm. No mercy!"

"There is mercy. I'm here to prove it."

The barman poured Lloyd a ginger ale. "Cops do not give mercy, they give grief."

Lloyd drew a paper bag from his jacket pocket. "You remember the man I was asking you about the other night? You said you saw him here with another man, sandy haired, early thirties?"

"Yeah, I remember."

"Good. We're going to create a little picture of that guy. You're going to be the artist. Come over on this side of the bar."

Lloyd spread out his wares on the bartop. "This is called an Identikit. Little composite facial features that we put together from a witness' description. We start with the forehead and work down. We've got over thirty nose types and so forth. See how the slots fit together?"

The barman fingered cardboard eyebrows, chins, and mouths and said, "Yeah. I just put these pieces together until it looks like the guy, right?"

"Right. Then I put the finishing touches in with a pencil. You got it?"

"Do I look dumb?"

"You look like Rembrandt."

"Who's he?"

"A bartender who drew pictures on the side."

It took the barman half an hour of sifting, comparing, rejecting, and appraising to come up with a composite. Lloyd looked at the portrait and said, "Not bad. A good-looking guy with a mean streak. You agree with that?"

"Yeah," the barman said. "Now that you mention it, he did look kinda mean."

"Okay. Now show me what these composite pieces have missed."

Lloyd took out a pencil and poised it over the Identikit picture. The barman studied his portrait from several different angles, then grabbed the pencil and went to work himself, shading the cheeks, broadening the nose, adding a thin line of malevolence to the lips. Finishing with a flourish, he said, "There! That is the cocksucker in the flesh!"

Holding the cardboard up to the light, Lloyd saw a vividly lean countenance come into focus, the thin mouth rendering the handsomeness ice cold. He smiled and felt the barman tugging at his sleeve. "Where's this fucking mercy you were telling me about?"

Lloyd stuck the portrait in his pocket. "Call the A.B.C. tomorrow at ten o'clock. They'll tell you the complaints against you have been removed and that you're no longer facing a license suspension."

"You've got that kinda clout?"

"Yeah."

"Mercy! Mercy prevails!"

Driving over the Cahuenga Pass to Jack Herzog's apartment, Lloyd thought: Only the hunt prevails. Trace all evidential links backward and forward in time and you will find that you are in the exact place that you were in four or eight or sixteen years ago, chasing ghouls too twisted to be called human and too sad to be called anything else, finding or not finding them, holding surveillance on patterns of hatred and fear, imparting morally ambiguous justice, running headlong into epiphanies that were as ever-changing as your need to know them was immutable. That the hunt was always conducted on the same landscape was the safest mark of permanence. Los Angeles County was thousands of miles of blacktop, neon, and scrub-brush-dotted hillside, arteries twisting in and around and back on themselves, creating human migrations that would unfailingly erupt in blood, stain the topography and leave it both changed and the same.

Lloyd looked out the window, knowing by off-ramp signs exactly where he was. He strained his eyes to see Ray Becker's Tropics, a bar he had worked as a vice officer fifteen years before. It wasn't there. The whole block had been razed. The Tropics was now a coin laundry, and the Texaco Station on the corner was a Korean church. A thought crossed his mind. If the city became unrecognizable, and the blood eruptions became the only sign of permanence, would he go insane?

The entrance foyer of Herzog's building was crowded with teenagers playing Pac-man. Lloyd walked past them to the elevator and took it up to the fourth floor. The corridor was again deserted, with a wide assortment of music and TV noise blasting behind closed doors. He walked to the door of 423 and listened. Hearing nothing, he picked the lock and moved inside.

Flipping the wall switch, he saw the same sterile apartment illuminated, the only addition since his previous entry a fresh stack of junk mail and final notices from Bell Telephone and L.A. County Water and Power. Knowing the bedroom and the kitchen would be the same, Lloyd sat down on the couch to be still and think.

His mind was doing tic-tac-toe, .41 revolvers and Herzog's file requisition slips as x's and o's, when the phone rang. Lloyd picked up the receiver and slurred into the mouthpiece, "Hello?"

"Dutch, Lloyd."

"Shit."

"Expecting someone else?"

"Not really. I'd forgotten I left the number."

"Anything new on Herzog?"

"A good composite I.D. on a man Herzog was seen with. That's it."

"I've got some feedback on those file slips. Got a pencil?"

Lloyd dug a pen and spiral notebook out of his pocket. "Shoot."

"Okay," Dutch said. "First off, all the files are still missing. Second, they were *not* requisitioned from anywhere within the Department. Third, all the six officers are in good standing in the Depart—"

Lloyd cut in. "What about common denominators? I'm the only one of the six below lieutenant. Have you—"

"I was getting to that. Okay, six files. One, there's you, regarded as the best homicide dick in the L.A.P.D. Two, there's Johnny Rolando. You've heard of him—he's been a technical advisor on half a dozen TV shows. Both of you fall into what you might call the legendary-cop category. Now the other four—Tucker, Murray, Christie, and Kaiser—are just hardworking uniformed brass with over twenty years on the job. What—"

Lloyd interrupted: "That's *all* you've got?"

Dutch sighed. "Just listen, okay? The other four have one thing in common: Moonlight gigs as head of security for industrial firms. You know the kind of deal—plants that hire lots of cheap labor, lots of dopers and ex-cons on the payroll, lots of pilfering, lots of chemicals lying around that can be used to manufacture dope, so you have to keep the lid on—let the employees only rip you off so much, that kind of thing."

Lloyd's mental wheels turned. "How did you grapevine this info, Dutch?"

"Through a friend on the feds. He said the four firms—Avonoco Fiberglass, Junior Miss Cosmetics, Jahelka Auto King, and Surferdawn Plastics are what you'd call semi-sleazy. Shitkicker security guards who couldn't make the cops, files with lots of juicy dirt on their employees, to use as levers in case they go batshit from sniffing too much paint thinner. *Heavy* files on the workers at Avonoco—they've got a class-two security rating. They make fasteners for the space program at Andrews Air Force Base and they pay the minimum wage to everyone below management level. You like it?"

"I don't know. What's the theory behind it? Hire legit cops as figureheads, keep the shitkickers in line, have them act as go-betweens if a wayward employee gets busted?"

Dutch yawned. "Basically, yeah, I'd say that's it."

"Any *hard* dirt on the officers themselves?"

"Not really. Johnny Rolando screws TV stars; Christie, the Avonoco Fiberglass security man, has a history of compulsive gambling and psychiatric care; you like to give superior officers shit and never go home to sleep. Just a random sampling of L.A.'s finest."

Lloyd didn't know whether to laugh or take offense at the remark. Suddenly regret coiled around him and forced the words out. "I'll apologize to Perkins."

Dutch said, "Good. You owe him. I'll move on your liquor store memo and I'll give you another forty-eight on Herzog. After that *I'm* reporting him missing. Herzog's father is old, Lloyd. We owe it to him to give him the word."

"Yeah. What's Perkins afraid of, Dutch?"

"None of the stuff you hit him with. He runs one of the cleanest Vice Squads in the city."

"What, then?"

"You. A forty-two-year-old hardcharger cop with nothing to lose is a scary fucking thing. Sometimes you even scare me."

Lloyd's regret settled like a stone at the center of his heart. "Good night, Dutch."

"Good night, kid."

Lloyd replaced the receiver, immediately thinking of new angles on the case. His mental x's and o's were settling around blackmail, but his eyes kept straying back to the phone. Call

Janice and the girls in San Francisco? Tell them that the house was sealed off almost exactly the way they had left it, that he only used the den and the kitchen, preserving the rest of the rooms as a testament to what they had once had and could have again? His phone conversations with Janice had at last progressed beyond civility. Was this the time to push for the fullest possible restoration of the family's past?

The job provided the answer. No. The officers who took over the formal investigation of Herzog's disappearance would check his phone bill and discover the long distance call. Janice's snotty off-and-on live-in lover would probably not accept a collect call. Fucked again by the verities of being a cop.

Stretching out on the couch, Lloyd dug in for a long stint of mental machinations. He was at it for half an hour, playing variations on blackmail themes, when there was a rapping on the door, followed by a woman's softly spoken words, "Jack? Jack, are you there?"

Lloyd walked to the door and opened it. A tall blond woman was framed by the hall light. Her eyes were blurry and her blouse and designer jeans were rumpled. She looked up at him and asked, "Are you Marty Bergen? Is Jack here?"

Lloyd pointed the woman inside, scrutinizing her openly. Early thirties, a soft/strong face informed with intelligence. A lean body clenched against stress and bringing it off with grace. *Play her soft.*

When she was standing by the couch, he said, "My name is Hopkins. I'm a police officer. Jack Herzog has been missing from both his work assignments for close to a month. I'm looking for him."

The woman took a reflexive step backward, bumping the couch with her heels and then sitting down. Her hands flew to her face, then grasped her thighs. Lloyd watched her fingers turn white. Sitting down beside her, he asked, "What's your name?"

The woman released her hands, then rubbed her eyes and stared at him. "Meg Barnes."

Taking her steady voice as a signal to press the interrogation, Lloyd said, "I've got a lot of personal questions."

"Then ask them," Meg Barnes answered.

Lloyd smiled. "When did you see Herzog last?"

"About a month ago."

"What was the basis of your relationship?"

"Friends, occasionally lovers. The sexual part came and went. Neither of us pushed it. The last time I saw Jack he told me he wanted to be alone for a while. I told him I'd come by in a month or so."

"Which you did tonight?"

"Yes."

"Did Herzog contact you at any time during the month?"

"No."

"Was the sexual part of your relationship on immediately before you saw Herzog last?"

Meg flinched and said, "No, it wasn't. But what does this have to do with Jack's disappearing?"

"Herzog is an exceptional man, Miss Barnes. Everything I've discovered about him has pointed that out. I'm just trying to get a handle on his state of mind around the time he disappeared."

"I can tell you about that," she said. "Jack was either exhilarated or depressed, like he was on a roller-coaster ride. Most of his conversation had to do with vindicating Marty Bergen. He said he was going to fuck the L.A.P.D. high brass for what they did to him."

"Why did you think I was Bergen?" Lloyd asked.

"Because Bergen and I are the only friends Jack has in the world, and you're big, the way Jack described Bergen."

Lloyd spent a silent minute mustering his thoughts. Finally he asked, "Did Herzog say specifically how he was going to vindicate Bergen or fuck the high brass?"

"No, never."

"Can you give me some specific instances of his exhilarated or depressed behavior?"

Meg Barnes pondered the question, then said, "Jack was either very quiet or he'd laugh at absolutely everything, whether it was funny or not. He used to laugh hysterically about someone or something called Doctor John the Night Tripper. The last time I saw him he said he was really scared and that it felt good."

Lloyd took out his Identikit portrait. "Have you ever seen this man?"

She shook her head. "No."

"Do the names Howard Christie, John Rolando, Duane Tucker, Daniel Murray, or Steven Kaiser mean anything to you?"

"No."

"Avonoco Fiberglass, Jahelka Auto King, Surferdawn Plastics, Junior Miss Cosmetics?"

"No. What are they?"

"Never mind. What about my name—Lloyd Hopkins?"

"No! Why are you asking me these things?"

Lloyd didn't answer. He got up from the couch and tossed the upholstered pillow he was leaning against on the floor, then carried the coffee table over to the wall. When he turned around, Meg Barnes was staring at him. "Jack's dead," she said.

"Yes."

"Murdered?"

"Yes."

"Are you going to get the person who did it?"

Lloyd shuddered back a chill. "Yes."

Meg pointed to the floor. "Are you sleeping here?" Acceptance had taken the controlled edge off her voice. Lloyd's voice sound numb to his own ears. "Yes."

"Your wife kick you out?"

"Something like that."

"You could come home with me."

"I can't."

"I don't make that offer all the time."

"I know."

She got up and walked to the door. Lloyd saw her strides as a race between her legs and her tears. When she touched the door handle, he asked, "What kind of man was Herzog?"

Meg Barnes' words and tears finished in a dead heat. "A kind man afraid of being vulnerable. A tender man afraid of his tenderness, disguising it with a badge and a gun. A gentle man."

The door slammed shut as tears rendered words unnecessary. Lloyd turned off the lights and stared out the window at the neon-bracketed darkness.

"TELL me about your dreams."

Linda Wilhite measured the Doctor's words, wondering whether he meant waking or sleeping. Deciding the latter, she plucked at the hem of her faded Levi skirt and said, "I rarely dream."

Havilland inched his chair closer to Linda and formed his fingers into a steeple. "People who rarely dream usually have active fantasy lives. Is that true in your case?" When Linda's eyelids twitched at the question, he thrust the steeple up to within a foot of her face. "Please answer, Linda."

Linda slapped at the steeple, only to find the Doctor's hands in his lap. "Don't push so hard," she said.

"Be specific," Havilland said. "Think exactly what you want to say."

Linda breathed the words out slowly. "We're barely into the session and you start taking command. I had some things I wanted to discuss, things that I've had on my mind lately, and you barge right in with questions. I don't like aggressive behavior."

The Doctor collapsed the steeple and clasped his hands. "Yet you're attracted to aggressive men."

"Yes, but what does that have to do with it?"

Havilland slumped forward in his chair. "Touché, Linda. But let me state my case before I apologize. You're paying me a hundred and fifteen dollars an hour, which you can afford because you earn a great deal of money doing something you despise. I see this therapy as an exercise in pure pragmatism: Find out why you're a hooker, then terminate the therapy. Once you stop hooking you won't need me or be able to afford me, and we'll go our separate ways. I feel for your dilemma, Linda, so please forgive my haste."

Linda felt a little piece of her heart melt at the brilliant man's apology. "I'm sorry I barked," she said. "I know you're on my side and I know your methods work. So . . . in answer to your question, yes, I do have an active fantasy life."

"Will you elaborate?" Havilland asked.

"About six years ago I posed for a series of clothed and semi-nude photographs that ultimately became this arty-farty coffee table book. There was this awful team of gay photographers and technicians, and they posed me in front of air conditioners to blow my hair and give me goose bumps and beside a heater to make me sweat buckets, and they turned me and threw me around like a rag doll, and it was worse than fucking a three hundred pound drunk."

"And?" Havilland whispered.

"And I used to fantasize murdering those fags and having someone film it, then renting a big movie theatre and filling it with girls in the Life. They'd applaud the movie and applaud me like I was Fellini."

The Doctor laughed. "That wasn't so hard, was it?"

"No."

"Is that a recurring fantasy?"

"Well . . . no . . ."

"But variations of it recur?"

Linda smiled and said, "You should have been a cop, Doctor. People would tell you whatever you wanted to know. Okay, there's this sort of upbeat version of the movie fantasy. You don't have to be a genius to see that it derives from my parents' deaths. I'm behind a camera. A man beats a woman to death, then shoots himself. I film it, and it's real and it isn't real. What I mean is, *of course* what happens is real, only the people aren't *permanently* dead. That's how I justify the fantasy. What I think I—"

The Doctor cut in: "Interpret the fantasy."

"Let me finish!" Linda blurted out. Lowering her voice, she said, "I was going to say that somehow it all leads to love. These real or imaginary or whatever people die so that I can figure out what my fucked-up childhood meant. Then I meet this big, rough-hewn man. A lonely, no-bullshit type of man. He's had the same kind of life as me and I show him the film and we fall in love. End of fantasy. Isn't it syrupy and awful?"

Looking straight at the Doctor, Linda saw that his features had softened and that his eyes were an almost translucent light brown. When he didn't answer, she got up and walked over to the framed diplomas on the wall. On impulse, she asked, "Where's your family, Doctor?"

"I don't really have a family," Havilland said. "My father disappeared when I was an adolescent and my mother is in a sanitarium in New York."

Turning to face him, Linda said, "I'm sorry."

"Don't be sorry, just tell me what you're feeling right now."

Linda laughed. "I feel like I want a cigarette. I quit eight months ago, one of my little control trips, and now I'm dying for one."

Havilland laughed in return. "Tell me more about the man you fall in love with."

Linda walked around the office, running her fingertips along the oak walls. "Basically, all I know is that he wears a size forty-four sweater. I know that because I had a john once who had the perfect body and he wore that size—for some reason I looked at the label while he was getting dressed. When I first started having these fantasies I used to picture the john's face—then I made myself forget his face, because it interfered with my fantasy. Once I even drove downtown to Brooks Brothers and spent two hundred dollars on a size forty-four navy blue cashmere sweater."

Linda sat down and drummed the arms of her chair. "Do you think that's a sad story, Doctor?"

Havilland's voice was very soft. "I think I'm going to enjoy taking you beyond your beyond."

"What's that?"

"Just a catch phrase of mine dealing with patients' potentialities. We'll talk more about that later. Before we conclude, please give me a quick response to a hypothetical situation. Among my patients is a young man who wants to kill. Wouldn't it be terrible if he met a young woman who wanted to die and if someone were there with a camera to record it?"

Linda slammed the arms of her chair. The floor reverberated with her words: "Yes! But why does that idea titillate me so?"

Havilland got up and pointed to the clock. "No souls saved after fifty minutes. Monday at the same time?"

Linda took his hand on the way to the door. "I'll be here," she said, her voice receding to a whisper.

Havilland drove home to his condominium/sanctuary in Beverly Hills and went straight to his inner sanctum, the only one of the six rooms not walled from floor to ceiling with metal shelves spilling psychology texts.

The Night Tripper thought of his three dwellings as a wheel of knowledge exploration, with himself as the hub. His Century City office was the induction spoke; his condo the fount of study and contemplation; the Malibu beach house the spoke of dispatch, where he sent his lonelies beyond their beyonds.

But the central point of his work was here behind a door he had personally stripped of varnish and painted an incongruous bright green. It was the control room of the Time Machine.

A swivel chair and a desk holding a telephone were centered in the room, affording a swivel view of four information-covered walls.

One wall held a huge map of Los Angeles County. Red pins signified the addresses of his lonelies, blue pins denoted the pay phones where he contacted them—a safety buffer he had devised. Green pins indicated homes where the lonelies had been placed on assignment, and plastic stick figures marked Thomas Goff, ever mobile in his quest to find more red pins.

Two walls comprised a depth gauge, to probe the Night Tripper's childhood void. Serving as markings on the gauge were WCBS top-forty surveys from Spring 1957, attached to the walls with red and blue pins, and a shelf containing roller-skate wheels that were once the feet of dead animals, lockets of soft brown hair stolen from inside a family Bible, and a swatch of carpet stained with blood.

Clues.

The remaining wall was covered with typed quotations from inhabitants of the void, taped on in approximate chronological order:

> *December, 1957:* Mother—"Your father was a monster, and I'm glad he's gone. The administrators of the trust fund have been instructed to tell us nothing, and I'm glad. I don't want to know." (Current disposition: Residing in a Yonkers, N.Y., sanitarium with severe alcoholic senility.)

> *March, 1958:* Frank Baxter (father's lawyer)—"Just think the best, Johnny. Think that your dad loves you very much, which is why he's sending you and your mother all that nice money." (Disposition: Committed suicide, August, 1960)

> *Spring, 1958:* (Imagined? Recalled from previous summer?) Police detectives questioning mother as to father's whereabouts—obsequious; deferential to wealth. (Disposition: Complete disregard of all my inquiries to Scarsdale P.D. and Westchester County P.D. 1961-1968) *Dreamt*?

June, 1958: Nurse & doctor at Scarsdale Jr. High (overheard)—"I think the boy has a touch of motor aphasia"; "Bah! Doctor, that boy has got a tremendous mind! He just wants to learn what he wants to learn"; "I'll believe the X ray before I believe your analysis, Miss Watkins." (Disposition: doctor dead, nurse moved away, address unknown. Note: X rays and other tests taken at Harvard indicate no aphasiac lesions.)

Walls of clues. Hubs within the hub of himself and all the spokes of his wheels.

Havilland swiveled in his chair, pushing off with his feet, spinning himself faster and faster, until the room was a blur and the four walls and their clues metamorphosed into rapid-fire images of Linda Wilhite and her home movie fantasies. He shut his eyes and Richard Oldfield was standing nude in front of a movie camera, with other lonelies laboring over arc lights and sound equipment. The chair was close to toppling off its casters when the phone rang and froze the moment. Deep breathing to bail out of his reverie, the Night Tripper let the chair come to a halt. When he was certain his voice would be calm, he picked up the phone and said, "Is this good news, Thomas?"

Goff's voice was both self-satisfied and hoarse with tension. "Bingo. Junior Miss Cosmetics. I never even had to contact the cop. I played one of his stooges like an accordion. Murray won't know anything about it."

"Have you got them?"

"Tonight," Goff said. "It's only costing us a grand and some pharmaceutical coke."

"Where? I want to know the exact time and place."

"Why? You told me this was my baby."

"Tell me, Thomas." Hearing the hoarseness in his own voice, Havilland coated his words with sugar. "You've done brilliantly, and it *is* your baby. I just want to be able to picture your triumph."

Goff went silent. The Doctor pictured a proud child afraid

to express his gratitude at being wooed with cheap praise. Finally the child bowed to the father. "At ten-thirty tonight. The end of Nichols Canyon Road, in the little park with the picnic benches."

Havilland smiled. Throw the child a crumb. "Beyond brilliant. Perfection. I'll meet you at your apartment at eleven. We'll celebrate the occasion by planning our next grouping. I need your feedback."

"Yes, Doctor." Goff's voice was one step above groveling. Havilland hung up the phone and replayed the conversation, realizing that Linda Wilhite had remained a half step back in his mind the whole time, waiting.

At nine-thirty Havilland drove to Nichols Canyon and parked behind a stand of sycamore trees adjacent to the picnic area. He was shielded from view by mounds of scrub-covered rock which still allowed him visual access to Goff's meeting spot. The lights that were kept on all night to thwart off gay assignations would frame the picture, and unless Goff and the security stooge spoke in a whisper their voices would carry up to his hiding place. It *was* perfection.

At ten past ten, Goff's yellow Toyota pulled up. Havilland watched his executive officer get out and stretch his legs, then withdraw a large revolver from his waistband and go into a gunfighter's pirouette, swiveling in all directions, blowing away imaginary adversaries. The overhead lights illuminated a throbbing network of veins in his forehead, the storm warning of a lepto attack. Havilland could almost feel Goff's speeded-up heartbeat and respiration. When the sound of another car approaching hit his ears and Goff stuck his gun back and covered the butt with his windbreaker, Havilland felt his body go cold with sweat.

A battered primer-gray Chevy appeared, doing a little fishtail as the driver applied the brakes. A fat black man in a skin-tight uniform of pale blue shirt, khaki pants, and Sam Browne belt got out, making a big show of slamming the door and chugging from a pint of whiskey. Havilland shuddered as he recalled one of Goff's favorite death fantasies: "Drawing down on niggers."

The black man sauntered up to Goff and offered him the bottle. Goff declined with a shake of the head and said, "You brought them?" Havilland squinted and saw that Goff's fingers were trembling and involuntarily plucking at his waistband.

The black man knocked back a long drink and giggled. "If you got the money, I've got the honey. If you got the dope, I got the . . . shit, I can't rhyme that one. You look nervous, homeboy. You been tootin' a little too much of your own product?"

Goff took a step backward. His whole left side was alive with tremors. Havilland could see his left leg buckle as though straining to kick out at a right angle. The black man raised his hands in a supplicating gesture, fear in his eyes as he saw Goff's face contort spastically. "Man, you reelin' with the feelin'. I get you the stuff and you pay me off, and we do this all real slow, all right?"

Goff found his voice. Willing it even made his tremors subside. "Rock steady, Leroy. You want it slow, you got it slow."

"My name ain't Leroy," the black man said. "You dig?"

"I dig you, Amos. Now cut the shit and bring me the stuff. *You* dig?" Goff's thumbs were hooked in his belt loops. His hands twitched in the direction of the gun. Havilland saw the black man bristle, then smile. "For a K note and two grams of righteous blow you can call me anything short of Sambo." He walked to his car and reached into the backseat, coming away with two large cardboard suitcases. Returning to Goff and putting them down at his feet, he said, "Fresh off the Xerox machine. Nobody but me knows about it. Come up green, homeboy."

Goff stuck a shaking hand into his windbreaker and pulled out a plastic baggie, then tossed it in the dirt beside the black man's car. "Ride, Leroy. Buy yourself a Cadillac and get your hair processed on me."

The black man picked up the baggie and balled it in his fist, then killed the pint and threw it at Goff's Toyota. When it hit the trunk and shattered, Goff grabbed at his waistband, then stifled a shriek and jerked his gun hand to his mouth and bit it. Havilland stifled his own outcry and watched the black man raise his hands and back up slowly toward his car, murmuring, "I'll be rockin' steady, rockin' steady real slow. *Reeeal* slow." His back touched the driver's side door and he squirmed in behind the wheel, rolled up the window and gunned the car in reverse. When the dust from his exit cleared, Havilland could see Thomas Goff weeping, aiming his handcannon at the moon.

An hour after Goff's sobbing departure, the Doctor drove to his underling's apartment in the Los Feliz district, the moon catching the edge of his vision, constantly drawing his eyes from the road. Parking outside Goff's building, he checked the contents of his black leather "Truth Kit": sodium Pentothal ampules, ten c.c. bottles of liquid morphine and an assortment of disposable syringes. He would quash Goff's pain and gauge the degree of his slippage.

Goff opened the door on the first knock. He was stripped to the waist, his torso oozing sweat. Havilland stepped inside and felt the chill of an air-conditioner on full blast. He looked at Goff. His extremities were tensed as if to contain earthquakes and his eyes were a feverish yellow. Doing a quick hypothetical run-through based on observation and carefully studied case histories, he gave his pawn a month to live.

When the door closed on his diagnosis, the Doctor took Goff by the arm and led him to the couch. The two cardboard suitcases rested by the coffee table, unopened. Goff smiled through his tremors and pointed to them. "We're on our way, Doctor John."

Havilland smiled in return and opened his leather bag. He

withdrew a fresh syringe and a morphine bottle, poking the needle through the porous rubber top, extracting just enough dope for an enticing mainline. Goff wet his lips and said, "It's the worst it's ever been. I've been doing some more reading on migraines. They get worse in a person's thirties. I think I'm really scared."

The Doctor took a bead on a large pulsating vein behind Goff's left ear. He formed a tourniquet with the flat of his hand, placing it just above Goff's collarbone. Whispering, "Easy, Thomas, easy," he inserted the needle square into the vein and depressed the stopper. A sharp jet of blood squirted out as the morphine entered. Goff's features unclenched in relief and Havilland smiled and amended his death sentence: A small dose still brought comfort. Sixty days.

Goff's limbs went languorous and the veins in his forehead receded to their normal dimensions. Havilland studied his patient and devised a spur of the moment contingency plan: If the pain began again within the next half hour, give Goff thirty days of maintenance doses, risk him on one more security-file run, then take him out of L.A. to terminate, and go solo on the remaining runs. If the pain remains abated, give him sixty days of tether for two more runs. Play the truth game with him to explain the tension with the jigaboo. The problem was *covered*.

Goff closed his eyes and drifted off into a dope/exhaustion cloudbank. Havilland got up and walked around the living room, purposely averting his eyes from the suitcases. The low ceiling was painted black and the walls were painted a military brown. Goff's therapy-controlled brightness phobia had driven him to turn a cheery dwelling place into a neuroses decompression chamber. Every time he visited the apartment, the Doctor looked for splotches of color, indicators that he had at long last instigated a total failure of memory, thereby giving Goff some peace of mind to go with his total acquiescence. But everything that could be purchased or rendered dark remained that way, room carpeting to cabinet hardware.

The Doctor surveyed the decompression chamber from a possible farewell standpoint. Various shades of darkness hit his senses, producing a pleasant vertigo that resurrected a childhood memory of a ferris wheel at a Bronx amusement park. The wheel was about to grab him when a burst of non-sequitur pink threw a wrench into its gears.

Snapping back to the present, Havilland saw that it was a pink slip of paper on the end table near the bedroom door, partially covered by a black ceramic ashtray. He picked it up and felt the room reel. It was an L.A.P.D. release slip, issued to Thomas Goff upon the presentation of sixty-five dollars bail money. The charge was 673.1—Failure to appear in traffic court. The Doctor read the heavily abbreviated type at the bottom and crumpled the paper in his hand. His executive officer had been arrested for non-payment of jaywalking citations.

The ferris wheel stopped at the top of its circuit, then plummeted to earth, dropping him into a land of treason. He looked over at Goff, who stirred in his stupor, kneading his shoulders into the couch.

The Doctor felt a wave of rage and loathing hit him like a one-two punch in the solar plexus. To combat it he breathed in-out, in-out until the counterproductive emotions leveled off into professional calm. When he was certain he could maintain his decorum he arrayed the tools of his truth kit on the coffee table, filling one syringe with morphine and another with sodium Pentothal. As Goff's stirrings became more violent, he reached over and pinched his nostrils shut and counted slowly to ten. At nine Goff jerked fully awake and screamed. Havilland took his hand from his nostrils and clamped it over his mouth, pinning his head to the wall. Whispering, "Easy, Thomas, easy," he took the morphine syringe and skin-popped Goff in his left arm and left pectoral muscle. Seeing that Goff's relief was instantaneous, he released his hand and said, "You didn't tell me that you were arrested last month."

Goff shook his head until his body shook with it all the way down to his toes. "I haven't been in the slam since Attica, you know that, Doc."

It was the hoarse rasp of a terrified man speaking the perfect truth. Havilland smiled and whispered, "Your left forearm, Thomas." When Goff obeyed, he jammed a 30 c.c. jolt of sodium Pentothal into the largest vein at the crook of his elbow. Goff gasped and began to giggle. Havilland withdrew the needle and leaned back on the couch. "Tell me about the Junior Miss file transaction," he said.

Goff giggled and fixed his glazed eyes on the far wall. "I scoped out the security bimbos from the bar across from the parking lot," he slurred. "All white trash and niggers. The niggers looked too shifty, so I settled on this Okie type. I asked some of the regulars about him, casual like. They said he was a coke fiend, but controlled, and a closed-mouthed type. He sounded like prime meat, so I brought him out slowly and closed the deal yesterday. I met him a couple of hours ago. Those two suitcases are the files."

Havilland felt his mind buzz, like someone had stuck a live wire into his brain. Goff was so far gone that he was now immune even to massive doses of hypnotic drugs. Time was running out for his executive officer—he had two weeks to live. At best.

Thomas Goff continued to squeal with laughter, his hands dancing over his body. Havilland examined the pink release slip. No vehicle license plate mentioned. Goff had obviously been stopped for questioning while on foot, a routine warrant check turning up his old jaywalking tickets. He waved the slip in front of Goff's eyes. Goff ignored the flash of brightness and laughed even harder.

Havilland got to his feet and swung a roundhouse open hand at Goff's face. Goff screeched, "No please," as the blow made contact, then wrapped his head in his hands and curled into a fetal ball on the couch. The Doctor squatted beside him and put a hand on his shoulder. "You need a rest, Thomas," he said. "The migraines are sapping your strength. We're going to take a little vacation together. I'm going to confer with some specialists about your headaches, then treat you myself. I want you to stay home and rest, then call me in forty-eight hours. All right?"

Goff twisted to look at the Doctor. He wiped a trickle of blood from his nose and whimpered, "Yes, but what about the next grouping? We were going to plan it, remember?"

"We'll have to postpone it. The important thing now is to deal with your migraines."

Thomas Goff's eyes clouded with tears. The Doctor extracted a bottle of tetracyline-morphine mixture from his bag and prepped a syringe. "Antibiotics," he said. "In case your migraines have gone viral." Goff nodded as Havilland found a vein in his wrist and inserted the needle. His tears spilled over at the act of mercy, and by the time the doctor withdrew the syringe he was asleep.

Dr. John Havilland picked up the two suitcases, surprised to find that he wasn't thinking of the merciless information inside. As he turned off the light and shut the door behind him, he was thinking of a black vinyl Vietnam body bag he had won as a joke prize at a med school beer bust and of dogs exploding into red behind a barbed wire fence.

8

LLOYD awoke in his den, already calculating hours before he was fully conscious. Thirty-six since Dutch's ultimatum and no new leads—report Herzog missing. Well over a hundred hours since the liquor store slaughter—all leads deadended. Start cross-checking the three hundred thousand yellow Jap cars and begin hauling in known armed robbers, leaning on them hard, squeezing all known and suspected pressure points in hope of securing information. Shit work all the way down the line.

Lloyd stretched and rolled off the convertible bed in one motion, then walked into the kitchen and opened the refrigerator, letting the cold air bring him to full consciousness. When goose bumps formed beneath his T-shirt and boxer shorts he shivered and dug out a half consumed container of cottage cheese, eating with the spoon that was still stuck inside. Almost gagging on the sticky blandness, he looked round the three small rooms he had allotted himself in his family's absence: den to sleep, think and study in; kitchen for the preparing of such gourmet fare as cottage cheese and cold chili from the can; the downstairs bathroom for hygiene. When he started doing calculations as to the number of hours since Janice and the girls had left, his mental calculator quit in midtransaction. If you start running tabs you'll go crazy and do something crazy to get them back. Let it be. If you stalk them, they'll know you haven't changed. It's a penance waiting game.

Finishing his breakfast, Lloyd showered hot and cold, then dressed in a day old button-down shirt and his only clean suit, an unseasonable summer pinstripe. Murmuring "Now or never," he sat down at his desk, dug out a spiral notebook and wrote:

> 4/28/84
> To: Chief of Detectives
> From: Det. Sergeant Lloyd Hopkins, Rob/Hom. Div.
>
> Sir:
>
> Four days ago I was contacted by my friend, Captain Arthur Peltz, the commander of Hollywood Division. He told me that Officer Jacob Herzog, a Personnel Records clerk at Parker Center who was working on a sub-rosa loan-out to Hollywood Vice, had been missing for nearly a month. Captain Peltz asked me to investigate, and in doing so I discovered that Herzog's (intact) apartment had been professionally wiped of fingerprints. I questioned Herzog's best friend, former L.A.P.D. Sergeant Martin Bergen, who told me that *he* hadn't seen Herzog in over a month and that Herzog had been "moody" at the time of their last meeting. An interview with Herzog's girlfriend confirms his month long absence and "moody" behavior. My opinion is that Herzog is the victim of a well-planned homicide and that his disappearance should be immediately and fully investigated. I realize that I should have reported this earlier, but my sole purpose in *not* reporting was to first establish evidence (however circumstantial) of wrongdoing. Captain Peltz ordered me to report to you immediately, but I violated that order.
>
> Respectfully, Lloyd Hopkins, #1114

Lloyd read over his words, strangely satisfied at having taken the bulk of the risk in incurring high brass wrath. He ripped the page out of the notebook and put it in his inside jacket pocket, then clipped on his .38 and handcuffs and made for the front door. He had his hand on the doorknob when the phone rang.

He let it ring ten times before answering—only Penny pursued a phone call that persistently.

"Speak, it's your dime."

Penny's giggle came over the wire. "No, it's *not*, Daddy! It's my dollar-forty."

Lloyd laughed. "Excuse me. I forgot inflation. What's the scoop, Penguin?"

"The same old same old. What about you? Are you getting any?"

Lloyd feigned shock. "Penny Hopkins, I'm surprised at you!"

"No, you're not. You told me I was jaded in my crib. You didn't answer my question, Daddy."

"Very well, in answer to your question, I am *not* getting any."

Penny's giggle went up an octave. "Good. Mom read me that first letter of yours, you know. We were talking about it the other night. She said it was excessive, that *you* were excessive, and even when you were admitting to be being a sleazy womanizer your admissions were excessive. But I could tell she was impressed."

"I'm glad. Is Roger still staying with you?"

"Yes. Mom sleeps with Roger, but she talks about you. One of these nights I'm going to get her stoned and get her to admit you're her main love. I'll report her words to you verbatim."

Lloyd felt a little piece of his heart work itself loose and drift up to San Francisco. "I want all of you back, Penguin."

"I know. I want to come back, and so does Anne. That's two votes for you. Mom and Caroline want to stay in Frisco. Dead heat."

"Annie and Caroline are okay?"

"Anne is big into vegetarianism and Eastern thought and Caroline is in love with this punk rock fool next door. He's a high school dropout. Gross."

Lloyd laughed. "Par for the teen age course. Let me hit you with something. Doctor John the Night Tripper. Ring any bells?"

"Ancient ones, Daddy. The 'sixties. He was this wild rock and roller. Caroline has one of his records—'Bad Boogaloo.'"

"That's it?"

"Yeah. Why?"

"A case I'm on. Dutch is on it, too. It's probably nothing."

Penny's voice went low and shrewd. "Daddy, when are you going to tell me about what happened right after the breakup? I'm no dummy, I know you were shot. Uncle Dutch practically admitted it to Mom.

Lloyd sighed as their conversation came to its usual conclusion. "Give it another couple of years, babe. When you're a world-weary fifteen I'll spill my guts. Right now all it means is that I owe a lot of people."

"Owe what, Daddy?"

"I don't know, babe. That's the tricky part."

"Will you tell me when you figure it out?"

"You'll be the first to know. I love you, Penny."

"I love you, too."

"I've got to go."

"So do I. Love love love."

"Likewise."

"Bye."

"Bye."

With "Owe what, Daddy?" trailing in his mind, Lloyd drove downtown to Parker Center. His memo to the Chief of Detectives rested like a hot coal in his jacket pocket. Deciding to check his incoming basket before dropping it with the Chief's secretary, he took the elevator to the sixth floor and strode down the hall to his cubicle, seeing the note affixed to his door immediately: "Hopkins—call Det. Dentinger, B.H.P.D., re: gun query."

Lloyd grabbed his phone and dialed the seven familiar digits of the Beverly Hills Police Department, saying, "Detective Dentinger," when the switchboard operator came on the line. There was the sound of the call being transferred, then a man's perfunctory voice: "Dentinger. Talk."

Lloyd was brusque. "Detective Sergeant Hopkins, L.A.P.D. What have you got on my gun query?"

Dentinger muttered "shit" to himself, then said into the mouthpiece, "We got a burglary from two weeks ago. Unsolved, no prints. A forty-one-caliber revolver was listed on the report of missing items. The reason you didn't get a quicker response on this is because the burglary dicks who originally investigated think that the report was padded, you know, for insurance purposes. A bunch of shit was reported stolen, but the burglar's access was this little basement window. He couldn't have hauled all the shit out—it wouldn't have fit. I've been assigned to investigate the deal, see if we should file on this joker for submitting a false crime report. I'll give you the sp—"

Lloyd cut in. "Do you think there *was* a burglary?"

Dentinger sighed. "I'll give you my scenario. Yes, there was a burglary. Small items were stolen, like the jewelry on the report, the gun, and probably some shit the victim didn't report, like cocaine—I've got him figured for a stone snowbird, really whacked out. You know the clincher? The guy owns two of these antique guns, mounted in presentation cases, with original ammo from the Civil War, but he only reports *one* stolen. I don't doubt that the fucker *was* stolen, but any intelligent insurance padder would stash the other gun and report it stolen too, am I right?"

Lloyd said, "Right. Give me the information on the victim."

"Okay," Dentinger said. "Morris Epstein, age forty-four, eight-one-six-seven Elevado. He calls himself a literary agent, but he's got that Hollywood big bucks fly-by-night-look. You know, live high on credit and bullshit, never know where your next buck is coming from. Personally, I think these—"

Lloyd didn't wait for Dentinger to finish his spiel. He hung up the phone and ran for the elevator.

* * *

8167 Elevado was a salmon pink Spanish-style house in the Beverly Hills residential district. Lloyd sat in his car at the curb and saw Dentinger's "big bucks fly-by-night" label confirmed: The lawn needed mowing, the hedges needed trimming, and the chocolate brown Mercedes in the driveway needed a bath.

He walked up and knocked on the door. Moments later a small middle-aged man with finely sculpted salt-and-pepper hair threw the door open. When he saw Lloyd, he reached for the zipper at the front of his jumpsuit and zipped up his chest. "You're not from Roll Your Own Productions, are you?" he asked.

Lloyd flashed his badge and I.D. card. "I'm from the L.A.P.D. Are you Morris Epstein?"

The man shuffled back into his entrance foyer. Lloyd followed him. "Isn't this out of your jurisdiction?" the man said.

Lloyd closed the door behind them. "I'll make it easy on you, Epstein. I have reason to believe that the forty-one revolver you reported stolen might have been used in a triple homicide. I want to borrow your other forty-one for comparison tests. Cooperate, and I'll tell the Beverly Hills cops that your insurance report was exaggerated, not padded. You dig?"

Morris Epstein went livid. Spittle formed at the corners of his mouth. He flung an angry arm in the direction of the door and hissed, "Leave this house before I have you sued for police harassment. I have friends in the A.C.L.U. They'll fix your wagon for real, flatfoot."

Lloyd pushed past Epstein's arm into an art-deco living room festooned with framed movie posters and outsized gilt-edged mirrors. A glass coffee table held a single-edged razor blade and traces of white powder. There was a large cabinet against the wall by the fireplace. Lloyd opened and shut drawers until he found the glassine bag filled with powder. He turned to see Epstein standing beside him with the telephone in his hand. When he held the bag in front of Epstein's eyes, the little man said, "You can't bluff me. This is illegal search and seizure. I'm personal friends with Jerry Brown. I've got clout. One phone call and you are adios, motherfucker."

Lloyd grabbed the telephone from Epstein's hand, jerked the cord out of the wall and tossed it on the coffee table. The table shattered, sending glass shards exploding up to the ceiling. Epstein backed into the wall and whispered, "Now look, pal, we can bargain this out. We can—"

Lloyd said, "We're past the bargaining stage. Bring me the gun. Do it now."

Epstein unzipped the top of his jumpsuit and kneaded his chest. "I still say this is illegal search and seizure."

"This is a legal search and seizure coincident to the course of a felony investigation. Bring me the gun—in its case. Don't touch the gun itself."

Morris Epstein capitulated with an angry upward tug of his zipper. When he left the room, Lloyd gave it a quick toss, searching the remaining drawers, wondering whether or not he should go to the Beverly Hills Station and check out the burglary report. Dentinger had said that no prints were found, but maybe there were F. I.'s on yellow Jap imports or other indicators to jog his brain.

He went through the last drawer, then turned his attention to the mantel above the fireplace. He could hear Epstein's returning footsteps as his eyes caught a cut-glass bowl filled with match books. He grabbed a handful. They were all from First Avenue West—one of the two bars that Jungle Jack Herzog was working.

"Here's your gun, shamus."

Lloyd turned around and saw Epstein holding a highly varnished rosewood box. He walked to him and took the box from his hands. Opening the lid, he saw a large blue steel revolver with mother-of-pearl grips mounted on red velvet. Arranged in a circle around it were copper-jacketed soft-nosed bullets. Taking a pen from his pocket, he inserted it into the barrel and raised the gun upward. Clearly etched on the barrel's underside were the numbers 9471.

"Satisfied?" Epstein said.

Lloyd lowered the barrel and closed the lid of the box. "I'm satisfied. Where did you get the guns?"

"I bought them cheap from the producer of this Civil War mini-series I packaged last year."

"Do you know the serial number of the other gun?"

"No, but I know the two guns had consecutive numbers. Listen, do the Beverly Hills fuzz really think I padded that burglary report?"

"Yes, but I'll slip them the word about how you cooperated. I saw some matches here from First Avenue West. Do you go there a lot?"

"Yeah. Why?"

Lloyd took a photograph of Jack Herzog from his billfold. "Ever see this man?"

Epstein shook his head. "No."

Withdrawing a photocopy of his Identikit portrait of the man seen with Herzog, Lloyd said, "What about him?"

Epstein looked at the picture, then flinched. "Man, this is fucking weird. I did some blow with this guy outside Bruno's Serendipity one night. This is a great fucking likeness."

Lloyd felt two divergent evidential lines intersect in an incredible revelation. "Did this man tell you his name?" he asked.

"No, we just did the blow and split company. But it was funny. He was a weird, persistent kind of guy. He kept asking me these questions about my family and if I was into meeting this really incredibly smart dude he knew. What's the matter, shamus? You look pale."

Lloyd gripped the gun box so hard that he could hear his finger tendons cracking. "Did you tell him your name?"

"No, but I gave him my card."

"Did you tell him about your guns?"

Epstein swallowed. "Yeah."

"When did you talk to the man?"

"Maybe two, three months ago."

"Have you seen him since?"

"No, I haven't been back to Bruno's. It sucks."

"Did you see the man get into a car?"

"Yeah, a little yellow job."

"Make and model?"

"It was foreign. That's all I know. Listen, what's this all about? You come in here and hassle me, break my coffee table—" Epstein stopped when he saw Lloyd run for the door. He called out, "Hey, shamus, come back and shmooze sometime! I could package a bad-ass fuzz like you into a series!"

Running roof lights and siren, Lloyd made it back to Parker Center in a record twenty-five minutes. Cradling the gun box in the crook of his arm, he ran the three flights of stairs up to the offices of the Scientific Identification Division, then pushed through a series of doors until he was face to face with Officer Artie Cranfield, who put down his copy of *Penthouse* and said, "Man, do you look jazzed."

Lloyd caught his breath and said "I *am* jazzed, *and* I need some favors. This box contains a gun. Can you dust it for latents real quick? After you do that, we need a ballistics comparison."

"This is a suspected murder weapon?"

"No, but it's a consecutive serial number to the gun I think is the liquor store murder weapon. Since the ammo in this box and the murder ammo is antique, probably from the same casting, I'm hoping that the rifling marks will be so similar that we can assume th—"

"We can't make those kind of assumptions," Artie interjected. "That kind of theorizing won't hold up in court."

Lloyd handed Artie the gun box. "Artie, I'll lay you twenty to one that this one gets settled on the street. Now will you please dust this baby for me?"

Artie took a pencil from his desk and propped open the lid of the box, then stuck another pencil in the barrel of the revolver, the end affixed to the upper hinge of the box, forming a wedge that held the gun steady. When the box and gun were secure, he took out a small brush and a vial of fingerprint powder and spread it over every blue steel, mother of pearl, and rosewood surface. Finishing, he shook his head and said, "Smooth glove prints on the grip, streak prints on the barrel. I dusted the box for kicks. Smudged latents that are probably you, glove prints that indicate that the box was carefully opened. You're dealing with a pro, Lloyd."

Lloyd shook his head. "I really didn't think we'd find anything good. He stole the companion gun, but I figured he might have touched this one, too."

"He did, with surgical rubber gloves." Artie started to laugh.

Lloyd said, "Fuck you. Let's take this monster down to the tank and see how it kicks."

Artie led Lloyd through the Crime Lab to a small room where water and tufted-cotton-layered ballistics tanks were sunk into the floor. Lloyd slipped three slugs into the .41's chamber and fired into the top layer of water. There was the sound of muffled ricocheting, then Artie squatted and opened up a vent on the tank's side. Withdrawing the "catcher" layer of cotton, he pulled out the three expended rounds and said, "Perfect. I've got a comparison microscope in my office. We'll sign for the liquor store shells and run them."

Lloyd signed a crime lab chit for the three rounds taken from the bodies of the liquor store victims and brought them, in a vinyl evidence bag, to Artie's office. Artie placed them on the left plate of a large, double-eyepieced microscope, then placed the three ballistics tank rounds on the right plate and studied both sets, individually and collectively, for over half an hour. Finally he got up, rubbed his eyes and voiced his findings: "Discounting the fact that the set of rounds fired at the liquor store were flattened by their contact with human skulls, while the tank rounds were intact, and the fact that the impact of the liquor store rounds altered the rifling marks, I would say that the basic land and groove patterns are as identical as slugs fired from two different guns can be. Nail the bastard, Lloyd. Give him the big one where it hurts the most."

Bruno's Serendipity was a singles bar/backgammon club on Rodeo Drive, in the heart of Beverly Hills' boutique strip. The club's interior was dark and plush, with a long sequin-studded black leather bar dominating one half of the floor space, and lounge chairs and lighted backgammon boards the other. A sequined velvet curtain divided the two areas, with a raised platform just inside the doorway that was visible from both sides of the room. Lloyd smiled as he approached the bar. It was a perfect logistical setup.

The bartender was a skinny youth with a punk haircut. Lloyd sat down at the bar and took out his billfold, removing a ten dollar bill and his Identikit portrait and letting the bartender see his badge all in one motion. When the youth said, "Yes, sir, what can I get you?" Lloyd tucked the ten into his vest pocket and handed him the photocopy.

"L.A.P.D. Have you seen this man here before? Take it over to the light and look at it carefully."

The bartender complied, switching on a lamp by the cash register. He studied the picture, then shook his head and said, "Sure. Lots of times. Kind of an intense dude. I think he swings both ways, I mean I've seen him in these really intense conversations with both men and women. What did he do?"

Lloyd gave the youth a stern look. "He molests little boys. When was the last time you saw him?"

"Jesus. Last week sometime. This guy's a chicken hawk?"

"That's right. What time does he usually show up?"

The bartender pointed in the direction of the backgammon tables. "You see how dead it is? Nobody shows up here much before eight. We only open up this early because we usually get some businessmen boozehounds in the late afternoon."

Lloyd said, "I noticed that you don't have a parking lot. Have you got any kind of valet parking setup?"

The youth shook his head. "We don't need one. Plenty of street parking after the boutiques close." He pointed to the platform inside the doorway. "You'll be able to see him real good, though. After dark, every time the door opens disco music goes on and colored lights flash down from the ceiling, white, then blue and red, you know, to let people know who's arriving. You'll be able to see him real good."

Lloyd put a dollar bill on the counter, then walked to a stool at the far end of the bar. "Ginger ale with lime. And bring me some peanuts or something. I forgot to eat lunch."

For six hours Lloyd drank ginger ale and plumbed logic for something to explain his two cases converging into a single narrative line. Nothing but a sense of his own fitness for the unraveling emerged from his ruminations, which were accompanied by a disco light show at the club's front door. From six o'clock on, every person who entered was centered in a flashing light show that was stereo-synced to upbeat arrangements of tunes from *Saturday Night Fever.* Most of the people were young and stylishly dressed and did a brief dance step before heading for the bar or backgammon tables. Lloyd scrutinized every male face as the first white light hit it; no one even vaguely resembled his suspect. Gradually the male and female faces merged into an androgynous swirl that made his eyes ache, combining with the noise of subtle and blatant mating overtures to tilt all his senses out of focus.

At eleven o'clock, Lloyd went to the men's room and soaked his head in a sink filled with cold water. Revived, he dried himself with paper towels and walked back into the club proper. He was about to take his seat at the bar when the Identikit portrait walked past him in the flesh.

Lloyd's skin prickled and he had to ball his gun hand to

kill a reflex reach for his .38. The men's eyes locked for a split second, Lloyd averting his first, thinking: *Take him outside at his car.* Then he heard a hoarse gasp behind him, followed by a clicking of metal on metal.

Both men turned at the same instant. Lloyd saw the Identikit man raise his monster handgun and sight it straight at him. He ducked to his knees as the muzzle burst with red and the report of the shot slammed his ears. Bottles exploded behind the bar as the shot went wide; screams filled the room. Lloyd rolled on the floor toward the sequined divider curtain, drawing his .38 and attempting to aim from a backward roll as odd parts of frantic bodies blocked a shot at his target. Two more thunderous explosions; the bar mirror shattering; the screaming reaching toward a crescendo. Lloyd rolled free of the curtain, crashing into a backgammon table. He got to his feet as another shot hit the curtain housing and sent the curtain crashing to the floor. People were huddling under tables, pressing together in a tangle of arms and legs. Muzzle smoke covered the bar area, but through it Lloyd could see his adversary arcing his pistol, looking for *his* target.

Lloyd extended his gun arm, his left hand holding his wrist steady. He fired twice, too high, and saw the Identikit man turn and run back in the direction of the restrooms. Stumbling over an obstacle course of trembling bodies, Lloyd pursued, flattening himself to the wall outside the men's room, nudging the door inward with his foot. He heard strained breathing inside and pushed the door open, firing blindly at chest level, jerking himself backwards just as a return shot blew the door in half.

Lloyd slid to the floor, counting expended rounds: five for psycho, three for himself. Charge him and kill him. He fumbled three shells from his belt into the chamber of his snub nose, then fired into the bathroom in hope of getting a return shot in panic. When none came, he pushed through the half-destroyed door, catching a blurry glimpse of a pair of legs pulling themselves up and out of a narrow window above the toilet.

Stripping off his jacket, Lloyd leaped up and tried to squeeze out the window. His shoulders jammed and splintered the woodwork, but even by squirming and contracting every inch of his body he wouldn't fit. Jumping down, he ran back through the club proper, now a wasteland of shattered glass, upended furniture, and shelter-seeking mounds of people. He was only a few feet from the entrance promenade when the door burst open and three patrolmen with pump shotguns came up in front of him and aimed their weapons at his head. Seeing the fear in their eyes and sensing their fingers worrying the triggers, Lloyd let his .38 drop to the floor. "L.A.P.D.," he said softly. "My badge and I.D. are in my jacket pocket."

The middle cop poked Lloyd in the chest with the muzzle of his shotgun. "You ain't got a jacket, asshole. Turn around and put your hands on the wall above your head, then spread your legs. Do it real slow."

Lloyd obeyed in the slowest of slow motion. He felt rough hands give him a thorough frisking. In the distance he could hear the wail of sirens drawing nearer. When his hands were pinned behind his back and cuffed, he said, "My jacket is in the bathroom. I was here on a homicide stakeout. You've got to issue an A.P.B. and a vehicle detain order. It's a yellow Japan—"

A heavy object crashed into the small of his back. Lloyd twisted around and saw the middle cop holding his shotgun, butt extended. The other two cops hung a few feet back, looking bewildered. One of them whispered, "He's got a cross draw holster. I'll check the bathroom."

The middle cop silenced him. "Shitcan it. We'll take him in. You check these people, look for anyone wounded, take statements. The meat wagon will be here in a second, so you help the paramedics. Jensen and I will take asshole in."

Lloyd squinted and read the leader cop's nameplate—Burnside. Straining to keep his voice steady, he said, "Burnside, you are letting a mass murderer and probable cop killer walk. Just go into the bathroom and get my jacket."

Burnside spun Lloyd around and shoved him out the door and into a patrol car at curbside. Lloyd looked out the window and saw other Beverly Hills' black-and whites and paramedic vans pull up directly on the sidwalk. As the patrol car accelerated, he looked in vain for a yellow Japanese import and felt his whole body smolder like dry ice.

The ride to the Beverly Hills Station took two minutes. Burnside and Jensen hustled Lloyd up the back stairs and led him down a dingy hallway to a wire mesh holding tank. Shoving him inside, still cuffed, Burnside said to his partner, "This bust feels like fat city. Any legit L.A.P.D. dick would have taken one of our guys with him on a stakeout. Let's go get the skipper."

When the two cops locked the cage door and ran off down the hallway, Lloyd leaned back against the wire wall and listened to the laughing and shouting coming from the drunk tank at the far end of the corridor. Letting his mind go blank, he gradually assimilated a mental replay of the events at Bruno's Serendipity. One thought dominated: Somehow the Identikit man had instantly seized upon him as his enemy. True, his size and outdated business suit would alert any streetwise fool; but the I.K. man had glimpsed him for only a brief moment in a crowded, artificially lighted environment. Lloyd held the thought, testing it for leaks, finding none. *Something was way off the usual criminal ken.*

"You fucked up, Sergeant."

Lloyd shifted his gaze to see who had spoken. It was a Beverly Hills captain, in uniform. He was holding his suit coat and .38 and shaking his head slowly.

"Let me out and give me my jacket and gun," Lloyd said.

The captain shook his head a last time, then slid a key into the cage door and swung it open. He took a handcuff key from his pocket and unlocked Lloyd's cuffs. Lloyd rubbed his wrists and took his coat and gun out of the captain's hands, realizing that the man was at least a half dozen years his junior. "Yeah, I fucked up," he said.

"Nice to hear the legendary Lloyd Hopkins admit to fallability," the captain said. "Why didn't you notify the head of our detective squad of your stakeout? He would have given you a backup officer."

"It happened too fast. I was going to wait for the suspect outside by his car. I would have called for one of your units to assist me, but he made me for a cop and freaked out."

"What are you, six-four? Two-twenty five? It doesn't take a genius to figure out what you do for a living."

"Yeah? Your own officers couldn't figure it out too well."

The captain flushed. "Officer Burnside will apologize to you."

Lloyd said, "Goody. In the meantime a stone psychopathic killer drives out of Beverly Hills a free man. An A.P.B. and a vehicle detain order might have gotten him."

"Don't try my patience, Hopkins. Just be grateful that no one at Bruno's was hurt. If you had been responsible for the injury or death of a constituent of mine, I would have crucified you. As it stands, I'll let your own Department deal with you."

Lloyd's vision pulsed with red. He shut his eyes to keep the throbbing localized and said, "Do you want to hear the whole story?"

"No. I want a complete report, in triplicate. Go upstairs and find a desk and write it now. I've informed your superiors at Robbery/Homicide. You are to report to the Chief of Detectives tomorrow morning at ten. Good night, Sergeant."

Fuming, Lloyd watched the captain walk away. He gave himself ten minutes to cool down, then took an elevator to the third floor vehicle registration office. A night clerk gave him a yellow legal pad and a pen, and over the next two hours he block printed three reports detailing the events at Bruno's and summarizing his investigations into the liquor store homicides and the disappearance of Officer Jack Herzog, copying over his unsubmitted memo to the Chief of Detectives verbatim in hopes that it would be construed as an effort at "team play." When he finished, he left the pages with the night desk officer and headed for the parking lot. He was almost out the door when an intercom voice jerked him back in. "Urgent call for Sergeant Hopkins. Paging Sergeant Hopkins."

Lloyd walked to the night desk and picked up the phone. "Yes?"

"It's Dutch, Lloyd. What happened?"

"Lots of shit. Who told you?"

"Thad Braverton. You're supposed to see him tomorrow."

"I know. Is he pissed?"

"Depends on what you have to say. What *happened*?"

Lloyd laughed through his anger and fatigue. "You won't *believe* what happened. The same guy did the liquor store job and killed Jack Herzog. I'm sure of it. He fired on me with his liquor store piece. We did our best to destroy a Beverly Hills singles bar. It was wild."

Dutch shouted, "*What!*"

"Tomorrow, partner. I'll call you after I talk to Braverton."

Dutch's voice was soft. "Jesus fucking Christ."

Lloyd's was softer. "Yeah, on a popsicle stick. You got any good news for me? I could use some."

Dutch said, "Two items. One, I checked around on that weird name you asked about. Doctor John the Night Tripper. He was a rock bimbo from years ago, and it's also the nickname of a psychiatrist who does lots of counseling of hookers and court-referred criminal types. He's very well respected. His real name if John Havilland and his office is in Century City. Two, you're in good shape with I.A.D. I called Fred Gaffaney this morning and reported Herzog missing. I took the grief, which consisted of Gaffaney screaming 'fuck' a few times."

Lloyd memorized the first item and laughed at the second. "Good work, partner. I'll talk to you tomorrow."

Dutch laughed back. "Stay alive, kid."

Lloyd hung up and walked out into the parking lot, threading his way through a maze of erratically parked black-and-whites and unmarked cruisers. When he got to the sidewalk he saw Officer Burnside striding toward him. Burnside snickered as he passed, and Lloyd halted and tapped him on the shoulder. "You got something to say to me?"

Burnside turned and said, "Yeah. Ain't you a little old to be hotdogging outside your jurisdiction?"

Lloyd smiled and drove a short right hand into Burnside's midsection. Burnside gasped and doubled over. Lloyd propped up his chin with his left hand, then swung a full force right at the bridge of his nose, feeling it crack beneath his fist. Burnside flew back onto the pavement, moaning and drawing himself into a ball to escape more blows. Lloyd walked to his car feeling old and numb and tired of his profession.

9

THE Night Tripper was on his fourth reading of the Junior Miss Cosmetics files when the phone in his private study rang, twenty-four hours before Goff's next scheduled call. Picturing his terminal man straining against a bacterial fever, he picked up the receiver and whispered, "You're early, Thomas. What is it?"

Goff's reply came out in series of gasps. "Cop! Big man from the cop files! I tried to wax him like the liquor store scum, but he—" The gasps became a horrified wailing.

Havilland envisioned Goff hyperventilating and frothing and burning up the phone booth with his fever and bewildered rage. Passing sentence in his mind, he said aloud, "Go home, Thomas. Can you understand that? Go home and wait for me. Draw in three breaths and tell me you'll go home. Will you do that for me?"

The three breaths drew out the semblance of a human voice. "Yes . . . yes . . . please hurry."

The Doctor replaced the receiver and held his hands in front of his eyes. They were perfectly steady. He walked into the bathroom and stared at himself in the mirror. His light brown eyes were unwavering in their knowledge that although Goff had fallen, he was invulnerable. He reached below the sink and picked up the death kit he had prepared the previous night, then went back to his study and stuffed it inside the old leather briefcase he had saved since med school. Squatting down, he pulled up a section of loose carpeting and opened his floor safe, extracting a single manila folder, thinking for a split second that the man in the photo attached to the first page looked exactly like his father.

Thus armed for mercy, he left his apartment and walked out to the street to look for a cab. One cruised by a few minutes later. "Michael's Restaurant on Los Feliz and Hillhurst," Havilland told the driver. "And please hurry." The driver sped through the late evening traffic, never looking back at his passenger. Pulling up in front of the restaurant, he said, "Fast enough for you?"

The Doctor smiled and handed him a twenty. "Keep the change," he said.

When the cab drove away, Havilland walked the four blocks to Goff's apartment, noting with relief that all the lights in the adjoining units were off. He rapped softly on the door, hearing otherworldly moans respond to his knock. The inside chain was withdrawn, and Goff was framed in the doorway, beseeching him with terrified eyes and hands pressed together in prayer. The doctor stared at the hands as they trembled a few inches in front of him. The fingers were bloody stubs, as if Goff's animal panic had driven him to try to dig a way out of his life. Looking at the inside of the door, he saw gouge marks and trickles of blood.

Havilland put gentle hands on Goff's shoulders and pushed him back into the living room, seeing his cordite-stinking handgun on the coffee table. Shutting and bolting the door, he pointed Goff to the couch, then rummaged in his briefcase for his instruments of accusation and mercy. Laying the manila folder face down on the floor and filling a syringe from a lab vial of strychnine, he whispered, "Two questions before I sedate you, Thomas. One, did the police see your car?"

Goff shook his head and tried to form 'no' with his lips. The Doctor looked into his eyes. *Probable truth*.

Whispering, "Good, good," he clasped his left hand over Goff's mouth and pressed his head to the wall with all his strength. Goff's eyes bulged but remained locked into the eyes of his master. Havilland took the manila folder from the floor and slipped off the front page photograph. Holding it up for Goff to see, he said, "Is this the policeman?"

Goff's eyes widened, the pupils dilated. A scream rose in his throat and he twisted his head and bit at the Doctor's hand. Havilland pushed forward with all his weight, flailing with his free arm for the syringe, finding it just as Goff's teeth grazed his palm. Throwing himself across Goff's squirming torso, he stabbed the needle into his neck, missing his target vein, pulling it free as the point struck muscle tissue. Aiming again, he saw his father and the cop in the photo fuse into one persona just as the ferris wheel at the Bronx amusement park began its descent. The spike struck home; his thumb worked the plunger; the poison entered. Goff's back arched as his feet twisted and pushed off the wall in a huge full-body seizure. Both master and minion were thrown to the floor. Goff writhed, foam at his mouth. Havilland got to his knees, seeing his father and the cop separate into individual entities, replaced by a little girl in a fifties-style party dress laughing at him. He shook his head to destroy the vision, then heard Goff's vertebrae popping as he attempted to turn himself inside-out. Getting to his feet, he saw a door opening on blackness and headstones behind a barbed wire fence. Then he held his hands in front of his face and saw that they were steady. He looked down on the floor and saw Thomas Goff, dead, frozen in a final configuration of anguish.

"Father," the Night Tripper whispered. "Father. Father."

Now only the disposal remained.

The Doctor dug through his briefcase, removing the black vinyl body bag and laying it out lengthwise on the floor, zipped open. He tossed Goff's handgun into the bottom, then stuffed in Goff himself and zipped the bag up.

Goff's car keys were on the coffee table. Havilland pocketed them, then squatted down and hoisted the pain-free Goff onto his right shoulder. Picking up his briefcase and flicking off the ceiling light, he shut the door and walked outside to the street.

Goff's Toyota was parked four buildings down. Havilland unlocked the trunk and wedged the dead man inside, securing the body bag by placing a spare tire and bumper jack across Goff's midsection. Satisfied with the concealment, the Doctor slammed the trunk shut and drove him to his final resting place.

Thomas Goff's grave was the basement maintainence area of a storage garage in the East Los Angeles industrial district. It was owned by one of the Doctor's former criminal counselees, currently doing ten to life for a third armed robbery conviction. Havilland paid the taxes and sent the man's wife a quarterly check; the gloomy old red-brick fortress would be his for at least another eight years.

It took the Night Tripper ten minutes to secure the gravesite, rummaging through the ring of keys his counselee had given him, opening up a series of double padlocked doors, driving through an obstacle course of mildewed cartons and rotting lumber until he was in the pitch black bowels of the building. Wiping the car free of his fingerprints and retracing his steps in the dark, he felt a sense of satisfaction and completion hit him harder with each padlock he snapped shut: Thomas Goff had spent his adult life seeking the absence of light and the Doctor had promised to help; now he would have layer upon layer of darkness to cradle his eternity.

When the street door lock was fastened behind him, the Night Tripper walked toward downtown L.A. and shifted his thoughts to the future. With Goff dead, he was flying solo; all the file runs were his. It was time to put off his current lonelies with talk of forthcoming "ultimate" assignments and concentrate on the acquisition of data and his possible combat with the policeman who so resembled his father. Crossing the Third Street bridge, the lights of the downtown business monoliths hovering in front of him, Havilland thought of chess moves: Richard Oldfield, clinically insane yet superbly cautious, who resembled the late Thomas Goff like a twin brother. *Pawn to queen*. Linda Wilhite, the hooker who fantasized snuff films and who desired a life of blissful domesticity with a big, rough-hewn man. *Queen to king*.

And finally the highly tarnished "king" himself: Detective Sergeant Lloyd Hopkins, the outsized L.A. cop with the off-the-charts I.Q., the man of whom the Alchemist had said: "I glommed his file because he is simply the best there is. If he weren't such an up-front womanizer and so outlaw in his methods, he'd be Chief of Detectives. He's got close to complete autonomy within the Department, because the high brass knows he's the best and because they think he's slightly off his nut. He was the one who closed the 'Hollywood Slaughterer' case last year. No one really knows what happened, but the rumor is that Hopkins simply went out and killed the bastard."

Havilland replayed the words in his mind, juxtaposing them with the superlative arrest record and erratic homelife detailed in the folder. *Checkmate*. Staring deeper into the lights before him, he thought of unlocking the door to his childhood void with symbolic patricide.

10

"BEFORE we start, I want you to read this morning's *Big Orange Insider*."

Lloyd shifted in his chair and lowered his eyes, wondering if Thad Braverton bought his look of phony contrition. Their handshake had been a good start, but Braverton's eyes were pinpoints of barely controlled rage, belying the authoritative calm of his voice.

"Martin Bergen's byline?" Lloyd asked.

The Chief of Detectives shook his head. "No. Surprisingly, it was written by some other cop-hating hack. Just read it, Hopkins. The comments of one Officer Burnside are particularly interesting."

Lloyd stood up and took the folded tabloid from the Chief, handing him his neatly typed report on the liquor store-Herzog case in return. Sitting back down, he read the *Insider*'s hyperbolized account of the shootout at Bruno's Serendipity. The three-column piece was written as an indictment of "Gunslinger Justice" and heavily emphasized the "Innocent young singles whose lives were placed in jeopardy by a trigger-happy L.A.P.D. detective." The concluding paragraph featured the observations of Beverly Hills Officer Carl D. Burnside, twenty-four, "whose nose was in a splint from a recent jogging accident."

> "Sergeant Hopkins attempted to arrest his suspect in a room filled with innocent people, even though he knew the guy was armed and dangerous. He should have had a Beverly Hills officer go with him. His callous disregard for the safety of Beverly Hills citizens is disgusting. Hot-

dog cops like Hopkins give sensitive, safety-conscious policemen like me a bad name."

Lloyd stifled a burst of laughter by wadding up the tabloid and watching the Chief of Detectives read his report. He had labored over it at home for five hours, detailing his two cases from their beginnings, charting their convergence step by step, underlining his certainty of Martin Bergen's innocence in Jack Herzog's presumed death, Herzog's theft of the six L.A.P.D. Personnel files and how the Identikit man *had to have seen those files*—it was the only way he could have identified him as a policeman in a crowded, smoky room.

The last page was the clincher, the evidence documentation that Lloyd hoped would bowl Thad Braverton over and save him the ignominy of departmental censure. At dawn he had driven back to Bruno's Serendipity and had bribed the two workmen cleaning up the previous night's damage into letting him make a check for expended .41 rounds. By charting approximate trajectories and scanning the walls with a flashlight he had been able to recover two flattened slugs. Artie Cranfield and his comparison miscroscope had done the rest of the work, delivering the irrefutable ballistics confirmation: *The three liquor store rounds and the two rounds extracted from the walls at Bruno's Serendipity had been fired by the same gun.*

Thad Braverton finished reading the report and fixed Lloyd with a deadpan stare. "Muted bravo's, Hopkins. I was going to suspend you, but in the light of this I'll let you slide with a reprimand: Do not ever go into another department's jurisdiction without greasing the skids with their watch commander. Do you understand me?"

Lloyd screwed his face into a semblance of sheepishness. "Yes, Chief."

Braverton laughed. "Don't try to act contrite, you look like a high school kid who just got laid. You're the official Robbery/Homicide supervisor on the liquor store job, right?"

"Right."

"Good. Stay on that full time. I'm turning over the Herzog case to I.A.D. They'll go at it covertly, which is essential; if Herzog was engaged in any criminal activity I don't want it getting back to the media. They're also better equipped to check out the file angle discreetly—those security firms are big bucks, and I don't want you stepping on their toes. *Comprende*?"

Lloyd flushed. "Yes."

"Good. I'll set up some sort of liaison so that you and I.A.D. can compare notes. What's your next move?"

"I want a full-scale effort to identify this asshole. The Identikit portrait is an exceptional likeness, and I want every cop in the county to have a look at it. Here's what I'm thinking: A closed briefing here at the Center this afternoon. Representatives of every L.A.P.D. and Sheriff's division to attend. No media shitheads. I'll get up about ten thousand copies of the I.K. portrait and tell the men to distribute them at their roll calls. I'll brief the men on my experience with the suspect and offer my observations on his psych makeup and M.O. Every cop in L.A. County will be looking for him. Once we get a positive I.D., we can issue an A.P.B. and take it from there."

Thad Braverton slammed his desk with both palms and said, "You've got it. I'll have my secretary start phoning the various divisions immediately. How's two-thirty sound? That will allow time for the men to go back to their stations and put out the copies before nightwatch. You can take care of getting them in the meantime."

Lloyd got to his feet and said, "Thanks. You could have given me lot of grief, but you didn't." He started to walk for the door, then turned around and added, "Why?"

Braverton said, "You really want to know?"

"Yes."

The Chief of Detectives sighed. "Then I'll tell you. Only four men know *exactly* what happened with you last year. You and Dutch Peltz, obviously, and the big chief and myself. I'm sure you know that rumors have circulated and that some cops admire you for what you did while other cops think you should be in Camarillo for it. I love you for what you did. I'm a hard ass with most people, but I'll take a lot of shit from the people I love."

Lloyd ducked out the door at the Chief's last words. He didn't want him to see that he was a half step away from tears.

Four hours later, Lloyd stood behind the lectern at the front of Parker Center's main briefing room, staring out at what he estimated to be two hundred uniformed and plainclothes police personnel. Every man and woman present had been issued a manila folder upon entering the room. Each folder contained fifty copies of the Identikit portrait of the man designated and M.O.-typed as:

> Multiple homicide suspect, W.M., 30-35, lt. brn, eye color unknown, 5′9″-5′11″, 150-160. Drives late model yellow Japanese import; armed with .41 antique handgun. Known to frequent singles bars and use cocaine. *This man is the perpetrator of the April 23 Hollywood liquor store killings. Consider him armed and extremely dangerous."*

When the last late-arriving officers took their seats, Lloyd held up a copy of the *Los Angeles Times* and spoke into the microphone. "Good afternoon. Please give me your complete attention. On page two of today's *Times* there is an accurate report of my encounter last night with the man whose portrait you are now holding. The only reason I am alive today is because this man uses a single-action revolver. I heard him cock the hammer before he fired at me and was able to avoid his first shot. Had he been using a more practical double-action weapon, I would be dead."

Lloyd let his eyes circuit the audience. Feeling them securely in his hand, he continued, "After exchanging fire with me, the man escaped. All the *hard* facts regarding him are on your Identikit pictures. The portrait, by the way, is a superb likeness—it was put together by an intelligent witness and was immediately confirmed by two others. *That is our man*. What I would like to add are my observations of this killer."

He paused and watched the assembled officers study their folders and take out pens and notepads. When there was a gradual shifting of eyes to the lectern, he said, "Last week this man killed three people with clean head shots worthy of a practiced marksman. Last night he fired at me from a distance of ten feet and missed. His four subsequent rounds were wild, fired in panic. I believe that this man is psychotic and will kill until he himself is killed or captured. There must be a concerted effort to identify him. I want these portraits distributed to *every* officer in L.A. County and every trustworthy snitch. He uses coke and frequents singles bars, so every vice and narco officer should utilize *their* snitches and question *their* bar sources. Witnesses have said that he has mentioned 'an incredibly smart dude' he knows, so our suspect may have a partner. I want men *strongly* resembling this suspect to be *carefully* detained for questioning, at *gunpoint*. All suspects detained should be brought to the Central Division Jail. I'll be there from five o'clock on, with a legal officer and a stack of false arrest waivers. Some innocent men are going to be rousted, but that's unavoidable. Direct all queries from police and non-police sources to me, Sergeant Lloyd Hopkins, at Central Division, extension five-one-nine."

Lloyd let the officers catch up on their note taking, knowing that up to now their rapt attention had been on a purely professional level. Clearing his throat and tapping the microphone, he went straight for their purely personal jugulars. "I've given you ample reasons why the apprehension of this suspect is the number one police priority in Southern California, but I'll go a notch better: This man is the prime suspect in the disappearance and probable murder of a Los Angeles police officer. Let's nail the motherfucker. Good day."

* * *

It took Lloyd two hours to establish a command post at the Central Division jail's booking facility. Anticipating a deluge of phone calls, he had first appropriated three unused telephones from the Robbery/Homicide clerical supply office, plugging them into empty phone jacks adjacent to the jail's attorney room, securing an immediate hookup to the existing extension number by intimidating a series of Bell Telephone supervisors. Central Division switchboard operators were instructed to screen incoming calls and give all police *and* civilian calls regarding the Identikit picture first priority in the event of tied-up lines. Any *live* suspects brought in were to be placed in a soundproof interrogation room walled with one-way glass. Once Lloyd's negative identification certified their innocence, they were to be gently coerced into signing false arrest waivers by Central Division's ad hoc "Legal Officer," a patrolman who had graduated law school, but had failed the California Bar exam four times. The detainee would then be driven back to his point of "arrest" and released.

Lloyd settled in for a long tour of duty, setting out notepads and sharpened pencils for jotting information and a large thermos of coffee for fuel when his brain wound down. Every angle had been covered. The two officers working under him on the liquor store case had been yanked from their current duties and told to compile a list of all singles bars in the L.A.P.D.'s jurisdiction. Once this was accomplished, they were to phone vice squad commanders citywide and have them deploy surveillance teams. Watch commanders had been instructed to highlight the Identikit man at evening roll call and to order all units to approach all suspects with their pump riot guns. If the I.K. man was on the street, there was a good chance of taking him.

But not alive, Lloyd thought. Ruffling through the false arrest forms on his desk, he knew that his killer would not give up without a fight and that on this night the odds of innocent blood being spilled were at their optimum. A panicky, overeager cop might fire on a half-drunk and belligerent businessman who resembled the I.K. suspect; an overly cautious officer might approach a yellow Jap import with a placating smile and get that smile blown off his face by a .41 hollow point. The detain/identify/release approach was desperation—any experienced homicide dick would know it implicitly.

At six o'clock the first call came in. Lloyd guessed the source immediately: Nightwatch units had been on the street for an hour, and scores of patrolman had been putting out the word to their snitches. He was right. A self-described "righteous dope dealer" was the caller. The man told Lloyd how he was certain the liquor store killer was a "nigger with a dye job" who "wasted" the three people as part of a "black power conspiracy." He then went on to offer *his* definition of black power: "Four coons pushing a Cadillac into a gas station for fifty cents worth of gas." Lloyd told the man that his definition would have been amusing in 1968 and hung up.

More calls followed.

Lloyd juggled the three phone lines, sifting through the ramblings of drunks, dopers, and jilted lovers, writing down every piece of information that issued from a reasonably coherent voice. The offerings were of the third- and fourth-hand variety—someone who knew someone who said that someone saw or knew or *felt* this or that. It was in all probability a labyrinth of *mis*information, but it had to be written down.

At ten, after four hours on the phones, Lloyd had filled up one entire legal pad, all with non-police input. He was beginning to despair of ever again dealing with a fellow professional when a pair of callow-looking Newton Street Division patrolmen brought in the night's first "hard" suspect, a rail-thin, six-foot-six blond youth in his early twenties. The officers acted as though they had death by the tail, each of them clasping a white-knuckled hand around the suspect's biceps.

Lloyd took one look at the terrified trio, said, "Take off

the cuffs," and handed the youth a false arrest waiver. He signed it as Lloyd told the officers to take their "killer" wherever he wanted and to buy him a bottle of booze on the way. The three young men departed. "Try to stay alive!" Lloyd called after them.

Within the next two hours, three reasonable suspect facsimiles were brought in, two by Hollywood Division patrol teams, one by Sheriff's detectives working out of the San Dimas Substation. Each time Lloyd shook his head, said, "Cut him loose" and force-fed the suspect a hard look, a waiver and a pen. Each time they signed willingly. Lloyd imagined them envisioning every "innocent man falsely imprisoned" movie ever made as they hurriedly scrawled their names.

Midnight came and went. The calls dwindled. Lloyd switched from coffee to chewing gum when his stomach started to rumble. Thinking that the twelve o'clock change of watch would allow him a hiatus from the phones, he settled back in his chair and let the normal jail noises cut through his caffeine fatigue and lull him into a half sleep. Full sleep was approaching when a voice jerked him awake. "Sergeant Hopkins?"

Lloyd swiveled his chair. An L.A.P.D. motorcycle officer was standing in front of him, holding an R&I computer printout. "I'm Confrey, Rampart Motor," the officer said. "I just came on duty and saw your I.D. kit want. I popped a guy who looks exactly like it last month. Jaywalking warrants. I remembered him because he had this weirdness about him. I got his R. and I. sheet and his D.M.V. record. There's a mug shot from my warrant bust."

Lloyd took the sheet and slipped off the mug-shot strip. The Identikit man jumped out at him, every plane and angle of his face coming into focus, like a paint-by-numbers portrait finally completed.

"Is it him?" Confrey whispered.

Lloyd said, "Yes," and stared at the full-face and profile

shots of the man who had almost killed him, trembling as he read the cold facts that described a monster:

> Thomas Lewis Goff, W.M., D.O.B. 6/19/49, brn., blu. 5'10", 155. Pres. Add.—3193 Melbourne #6, L.A. Crim. Rec. (N.Y. State): 3 agg. asslt. arrst.—(Diss.); 1 conv.-1st Deg. Auto Theft-11/4/69-sent. 3-5 yrs. Paroled 10/71. (Calif. State): Failure to app.—3/19/84-Bail $65—paid. Calif. dr. lic. # 01734; Vehic.—1980 Toyota Sed. (yellow) lic. # JLE 035; no mov. viol.

Lloyd put the printout down and said, "Who's the morning watch boss at Rampart?"

Confrey stammered, "Lu-Lieutenant Praeger."

"Good. Call him up and tell him we've got the big one on Melbourne and Hillhurst. Hold him for me; I'll be right back."

While Confrey made the call, Lloyd ran down the hall to the Central Division armory and grabbed an Ithaca pump and box of shells from the duty officer. When he returned to the jail area, Confrey handed him the phone and whispered, "Talk slow, the loot is an edgy type."

Lloyd took a deep breath and spoke into the mouthpiece. "Lieutenant, this is Hopkins, Robbery/Homicide. Can you set something up for me?"

"Yes," a taut voice answered. "Tell me what you need."

"I need a half dozen unmarked units to check the area around Melbourne and Hillhurst for a yellow nineteen-eighty Toyota, license JLE oh-three-five. No approach—sit on it. I need the thirty-one hundred block of Melbourne sealed at both ends in exactly forty minutes. I want five experienced squadroom dicks to meet me at Melbourne and Hillhurst in exactly forty minutes. Tell them to wear vests and to bring shotguns. Have them bring a vest for me. I want *no* black-and-whites inside the area. Can you implement this now?"

Lloyd didn't wait for an answer. He handed the phone back to Confrey and ran for his car.

* * *

By zigzagging through traffic and running red lights, Lloyd made it to Melbourne and Hillhurst in twenty minutes. No other unmarked cruisers were yet on the scene, but he could feel the too perfect silence that preceded impending explosions all around him. He knew that the silence would soon be broken by approaching headlights, two-way radio crackle and the hum of powerful engines held at idle. Last name introductions and his orders would follow, leaving nothing but the explosion itself.

Parking under a streetlamp at the edge of the intersection, Lloyd turned on his emergency flashers as a signal to the other officers and jacked shells into his shotgun, pumping one into the chamber and setting the choke on full. Grabbing his flashlight, he walked down Melbourne, staying close to the trees that bordered the sidewalk, grateful that there were no late night strollers or dog walkers out. The street was a solid mass of two-story apartment buildings, identical in their sideways exposures and second story landings. Three-one-nine-three was in the middle of the block, a dark gray stucco with wrought-iron railings and recessed door without screens. Lloyd flashed his light on the bank of mailboxes at the front of the building. T. Goff—Apt. 6, true to the R. & I. printout. He counted mail slots, then stepped back and counted the doorways themselves, playing his beam over them to illuminate the numerals embossed at eye level. Ten units; five up, five down. Apartment six was the first unit on the second story. Lloyd shivered when he saw muted light glowing behind drawn curtains.

He walked back to Hillhurst, scanning parked cars en route. No yellow Toyotas were stationed at curbside. When he got to the intersection, he found it blocked off by sawhorse detour signs affixed with blinking red lights. Radio static broke the silence, followed by hoarse whispers. Lloyd squinted and saw three unmarked Matadors parked crossways behind the barricade. He blinked his flashlight at the closest one, getting a double blink in return. Then there was the opening of car doors and five men wearing bullet-proof vests and holding shotguns were standing in front of him.

"Hopkins", Lloyd said, getting "Henderson," "Martinez," "Penzler," "Monroe," and "Olander" in return. A vest was handed to him. He slipped into it and said, "Vehicle?"

Five negative head shakes answered him at once. One of the officers added, "No yellow Toyotas in an eight block radius."

Lloyd shrugged. "No matter. The target building is halfway down the block. Second story, light on. Henderson and I are going in the door. Martinez and Penzler, you stand point downstairs, Monroe and Olander, you hold a bead on the back window." Feeling a huge grin take over his face, he bowed and whispered, "Now, gentlemen."

The men formed a wedge and ran down Melbourne to 3193. When they were on the sidewalk in front of the building, Lloyd pointed to the first upstairs back window, the only one on the second story burning a light. Monroe and Olander nodded and hung back as Martinez and Penzler automatically took up their positions at the bottom of the stairs. Lloyd nudged Henderson with his gun butt and gestured upwards, whispering, "Opposite sides of the door. One kick."

With Lloyd at the lead, they tiptoed up the stairs and fanned out to cover both sides of the door to apartment 6. Henderson put his ear to the doorjamb and formed "nothing" with his lips and tongue. Lloyd nodded and stepped back and raised his shotgun. Henderson took up an identical position beside him. Both men raised their right feet simultaneously and kicked out at the same instant. The door burst inward, ripped loose at both sides, dangling from one remaining hinge. Lloyd and Henderson pressed into the wall at the sound of the implosion, listening for reflex movement within the apartment. Hearing nothing but the creaking of the door, they stepped inside.

Lloyd would never forget what he saw. While Henderson

ran ahead to check the other rooms, he stood in the doorway, unable to take his eyes from the nightmare hieroglyphics that surrounded him on all sides.

The living room walls were painted dark brown; the ceiling was painted black. Taped across the walls were photographs of nude men, obviously clipped from gay porno books. The bodies were composites formed of mismatching torsos, heads, and genital areas, the figures linked by magazine photos of antique handguns. Each collage had a slogan above it, block printed in contrasting yellow paint: "Chaos Redux," "Death's Kingdom," "Charnel Kong," and "Blitzkrieg." Lloyd studied the printing. Two of the slogans were in an unmistakable left-hander's slant; the other two in a straight up right-handed motion. Squinting at the wall area around the cutouts, he saw that they were bracketed by abrasive powder wipe marks. He ran his fingers over the walls in random circles. A film of white powder stuck to them. Like Jack Herzog's apartment, this place had been professionally secured against latent print identification.

Henderson came up behind Lloyd, startling him. "Jesus, Sarge, you ever see anything like it?"

Lloyd said "Yes," very softly.

"Where?"

Lloyd shook his head. "No. Don't ask me again. What are the other rooms like?"

"Like a normal pad, except for the colors of the wall and ceiling paint. All the surfaces have been wiped, though. Ajax or some shit like that. This motherfucker is whacked out, but smart."

Lloyd walked to the door and looked out. Martinez and Penzler were still stationed downstairs and there was as yet no general awakening of the other tenants. He turned and said to Henderson, "Go round up the other men, then wake up the citizens." He handed him the mug-shot strip of Thomas Goff and added, "Show this to every person and ask them when they saw the bastard last. Bring anyone who's seen him in the past twenty-four hours to me."

Henderson nodded and went downstairs. Lloyd counted to ten to clear his mind of any preconceived notions of what he should look for and let his eyes take a quick inventory of the living room, thinking: darkness beyond the aesthetic limits of the most avant garde interior decorator. Black naugahyde sofa; charcoal gray deep-pile rug; black plasticene high-tech coffee table. The curtains were a thick olive drab velour, capable of shutting out the brightest sunlight, and the one floor lamp was sheathed in black plastic. The overall effect was one of containment. Although the living room was spacious for a small apartment, the absence of color gave it a stiflingly claustrophobic weight. Lloyd felt like he was enclosed in the palm of an angry fist. In reflex against the feeling he slipped off his bullet-proof vest, surprised to find that he was drenched in sweat.

The kitchen and bathroom were extensions of the darkness motif; every wall, appliance and fixture had been brushstroked with a thick coat of black enamel paint. Lloyd scrutinized potential print-sustaining surfaces. Every square inch had been wiped.

He walked into the bedroom. It was the disarrayed heart of the angry fist; a small black rectangle almost completely eclipsed at floor level by a large box spring and mattress covered by a purple velour bedspread. Lloyd stripped the bedspread off. The dark blue patterned sheets were crumpled and rank with sweat. Male clothing, varied in color, was strewn across them. Squatting to examine it, he saw that the pants and shirts were stylish and expensive and conformed in size to Thomas Goff's dimensions. An overturned cardboard box lay next to the front of the bed. Upending it, Lloyd sifted through a top layer of male toiletries and a second layer of paperback science fiction novels, coming to a tightly wedged stack of battered record albums on the bottom.

He thumbed through them, reading the titles on the

jackets. Dozens of albums by the Beatles, Rolling Stones, and Jefferson Airplane, all bearing the block printed warning: "Beware! Property of Tom Goff! Hands off! Beware!" Lloyd held two albums up and examined the printing. It was right-hand formed and identical to the printing on the living room walls. Smiling at the confirmation, he read through the remaining records, knowing that the common denominator of Goff's musical taste was the 1960s, going cold when he saw a garish album entitled, "Doctor John the Night Tripper—Bayou Dreams."

Lloyd studied the jacket. A frizzy-haired white man wearing red satin bell bottoms was honking a saxaphone at a snarling alligator. The song titles listed on the back were the typical 'sixties dope, sex, and rebellion pap, almost nostalgic in their naïveté. Putting the album down, he wondered if it were a Herzog-Goff link beyond general aesthetic strangeness—a link that could be plumbed for evidence.

There was a rapping on the wall behind him. Lloyd stood up and turned around, seeing Henderson and a small man in a terrycloth bathrobe. The man was casting unbelieving eyes over the black walls, mashing shaky hands together inside the pockets of his robe. "This guy's the manager, Sarge. Said he saw our buddy this afternoon."

Lloyd smiled at the man. "My name's Hopkins. What's yours?"

"Fred Pellegrino. Who's going to pay for my busted door and this crazy paint job?"

"Your insurance company," Lloyd said. "When did you see Thomas Goff last?"

Fred Pellegrino pulled rosary beads from his pocket and fondled them. "Around five o'clock. He was carrying a suitcase. He smiled at me and hotfooted it out to the street. 'See you soon,' he said."

"You didn't ask him where he was going?"

"Fuck no. He's paid up three months in advance."

"Was he alone?"

"Yeah."

"How long has he lived here?"

"About a year and a half or so."

"Good tenant?"

"The best. No noise, no complaints, always paid his rent on time."

"Did he pay by check?"

"No, always cash."

"Job?"

"He said he was self-employed."

"What about his friends?"

"*What* friends? I never seen him with *nobody*. What if my insurance company don't pay for this batshit paint job?"

Lloyd ignored Pellegrino and motioned Henderson over to the far side of the room. "What did the other tenants have to say?" he asked.

"The same spiel as Pops," Henderson said. "Nice, quiet, solitary fellow who never said much besides 'good morning' or 'good night.'"

"And no one else has seen him today?"

"No one else has seen the scumbag in the past week. This is depressing. I wanted to eighty-six the cop-killer motherfucker. Didn't you?"

Lloyd gave a noncommittal shrug and took Goff's R. & I. printout from his pocket. He handed it to Henderson and said, "Go back to Rampart and give this to Praeger. A.P.B., All Police Network. Tell him to add 'armed and extremely dangerous' and 'has left-handed male partner,' and to call the New York State Police and have them wire me all their existing info on Goff. Tell Pellegrino that I'm spending the night here as a safety precaution and shoo him back to his pad."

"You're gonna crash here?" Henderson was slack-jawed with disbelief.

Lloyd stared at him. "That's right, so move it."

Henderson walked away shaking his head, taking a pliant

Fred Pellegrino by the arm and leading him out of the apartment. When they were gone, Lloyd walked to the landing and looked down on the knot of people milling in the driveway. Bullet-proof vested cops with shotguns were assuring pajama-clad civilians that everything was going to be all right. After a few minutes the scene dispersed, the citizens walking back to their dwellings, the cops to their unmarked Matadors. When Henderson pointed a finger at his head and twirled it, then pointed upstairs, Lloyd dragged the sofa over to the devastated front door and barricaded himself in to think.

Two divergent cases had merged into one and had now yielded one *known* perpetrator and one accomplice, an *unknown* quantity whose only *known* crime thus far was defacing rented property. With an A.P.B. in effect and I.A.D. covering the personnel file angle, his job was to deduce Thomas Goff's behavior and go where less intelligent cops wouldn't think to look.

Lloyd let his eyes circuit the living room, knowing that it would merge with another horror chamber the very second he closed them, knowing that it was essential to juxtapose the imagery and see what emerged.

He did it, shuddering against the memory of Teddy Verplanck's bay-windowed apartment, deciding that *it* was worse because he had known the extent of the Hollywood Slaughterer's carnage and that he was driving to be destroyed. Thomas Goff's home bespoke a more subtle drive—the drive of a seasoned street criminal who had very probably not been arrested for anything since 1969, a man with a partner who might well be a restraining influence; a man who spread his insanity all over his walls and walked away saying 'see you soon' a few hours ahead of a massive police dragnet.

Lloyd walked through the apartment again, letting little observations snap into place and work in concert with his instincts: the photos of nude men and guns spoke "homosexual," but somehow that seemed wrong. There was no telephone, which confirmed Goff as a basic loner. The lack of dishes, cooking utensils, and food were typical of ex-convicts, men who were used to being served and who often developed a craving for cafeteria food. The incredible darkness of the rooms was sheer insanity. All indicators pointing to the enormous question of *motive*.

Lloyd had almost completed his run-through of the apartment when he noticed a built-in wall cupboard in the hall between the living room and bedroom. It had been painted over like the rest of the wall, but cracks in the paint by the wooden opener knob indicated that it had been put to use. He swung the cupboard door open and recoiled when he saw what was affixed to the back.

There was a magazine cutout of a blue uniformed policeman with his hands upraised as if to placate an attacker. Surrounding the cop were outsized porno book penises studded with large metal staples. A circle of handgun cutouts framed the scene, and square in the middle of the cop's chest was a glued-on white paper facsimile of an L.A.P.D. badge, complete with a drawing of City Hall, the words, "Police Officer" and the number 917.

Lloyd slammed the cupboard with his fist. Jack Herzog's badge number burned in front of his eyes. He tore the door off by the hinges and hurled it into the living room. Just then Penny's "Owe what, Daddy?" hit him like a piledriver, and he knew that getting Thomas Goff would be the close-out on all his debts of grief.

11

THE Night Tripper stared at the stunning female beauty that now adorned the walls of his outer office. Thomas Goff's surveillance photographs of Linda Wilhite were blown up and framed behind glass, woman bait that would lure his policeman/adversary into a trap that would be sprung by his own sexual impluses. The Doctor walked into his private office and thought of how he had planned over a decade in advance, creating a series of buffers that would prevent anyone from knowing that he and Thomas Goff had ever met. He had destroyed Goff's file at Castleford Hospital; he had even stolen his prison file while visiting Attica on a psychiatric seminar, returning it three weeks later, altered to show a straight, no-parole release. He had never been seen with Goff, and they had always communicated via pay phones. The only possible connection was several times removed—through his lonelies, all of whom Goff had recruited. If the manhunt for his former executive officer received pervasive media play, one of them might snap to a newspaper or TV photograph accompanied by scare rhetoric.

Yet even that avenue of discovery was probably closed, Havilland thought, picking up the morning editions of the *L.A. Times* and *L.A. Examiner*. There was no further mention of the shoot-out at Bruno's Serendipity and no mention of the late night raid on Goff's apartment. If Hopkins had initiated some sort of media stonewall to keep a lid of secrecy on his investigation, then his complicity in his own destruction would reach epic proportions.

The Night Tripper trembled as he recalled the past thirty-six hours, and his acts of courage. After disposing of Goff's body, he had walked through downtown L.A., thinking of the probable course of events that had led Hopkins to at least identify Goff at the level of physical description. One thing emerged as a reasonable certainty: It was the Alchemist's disappearance and presumed death, *not* the liquor store killings, that had led the policeman to Goff. Goff and Herzog had spent a good deal of time together at bars, and some perceptive witness had probably provided Hopkins with the description that took him to Bruno's Serendipity. Thus, hours later, after he had smeared Goff's walls with homosexual bait, he had left the albums that Goff had stashed at Castleford in 'seventy-one and added the touch that would arouse Hopkins' cop rectitude. Pique his rage with the faggot image of the Alchemist; pique his brain with the wipe marks, diverse script styles, and Goff's old copy of "Bayou Dreams."

The most thrilling act of courage had been in implementing Richard Oldfield, dressing him in a bulky sweater that downplayed his musculature and a tweed cap that was very much in Thomas Goff's style, yet shielded his upper face and non-Goff haircut. He had pumped him up for hours, promising him his very own handpicked victim as his "ultimate assignment," then had watched from a parked rental car across the street as Oldfield went through his impersonation perfectly, fooling Goff's landlord dead to rights, with Hopkins and his dragnet only hours away.

Havilland unlocked his desk drawer and dug out the Junior Miss Cosmetics file he had been studying, hoping that fresh work and thoughts of the future would quiet the sense of excitement that made him want to *live* in the hours just past.

It didn't help. He kept recalling the flashlights approaching and how he knew that he was now *inside* the police cordon; how he had hunkered down in the car seat and had heard the officers repeat Goff's license number over and over, one of them whispering that "Crazy Lloyd" was "leading the raid," his partner replying with something about "Crazy

Lloyd going after that Hollywood psycho with a thirty-ought-six and a forty-four mag." When the raid itself transpired a half hour later, he could see Hopkins across the street, holding a shotgun, much taller than any of the men he led, looking exactly like his father. It had taken monumental self-control to drive away from the scene without confronting the policeman face to face.

With an effort, the Night Tripper returned to the cosmetics file, reading notations on the life and sleazy times of the woman whom he was certain would become his next pawn.

Sherry Shroeder was a thirty-one-year-old former assembly line worker at Junior Miss Cosmetics, recently fired for stealing chemicals used in the manufacture of angel dust. It had been her fourth and final pilfering "arrest" within the company, resulting in her dismissal under threats of criminal prosecution. Daniel Murray, the L.A.P.D. captain who moonlighted as the Junior Miss security chief, had made her sign a confession and had told her that it would not be submitted to the police if she signed a waiver stating that she would not apply for unemployment benefits or workmen's compensation. Her three previous "arrests" had been resolved through Daniel Murray's coercion. Sherry Shroeder was a frequent co-star of low budget pornographic films. Murray had obtained a print of one of her features and had threatened to show it to her parents should she fail to return the chemicals she had stolen. Sherry agreed, eager to retain her four-dollar-an-hour job and spare her parents the grief of viewing her performance. There was no photograph attached to the folder, but her vital statistics of five-seven, 120, blond hair, and blue eyes were enticing enough. There was a final notation in the file, stating that since her dismissal Sherry Shroeder had been seen almost daily in the bars across the street from Junior Miss, drinking with her former fellow employees and "turning tricks" in the back of her van on paydays.

Havilland wrote down Sherry Shroeder's address and phone number and put it in his pocket. Relieved that his next move was ready to be implemented, he let his thoughts return to Lloyd Hopkins, making a spur of the moment decision that felt uncommonly sound: If the policeman didn't come his way within forty-eight hours, he would initiate the confrontation himself.

12

AFTER a twenty-four hour stint of Robbery/Homicide conferences and paper chasing at Parker Center, Lloyd drove to Century City to grasp at the wildest of straws, getting honest with himself en route: His investigation was stymied. Every cop in Southern California was shaking the trees for Thomas Goff, and he, the supervising officer and legendary "big brain," did not yet have a psychological mock-up to work from. If he could use the legendary criminal shrink's nickname as his entree, he could probably interest him in the Goff case and get him to offer his observations. It was slim, but at least it was movement.

The twenty-four hours at the Center had yielded nothing but negative feedback. The New York State Police had reacted promptly to his inquiry on Thomas Goff, issuing the L.A.P.D. a teletype that ran to six pages. Lloyd learned that Goff was a sadist who picked women up in bars, seduced and then beat them; that he liked to steal late model convertibles, that he had "no known associates" and was given a no-parole release from Attica, most likely a bureaucratic stratagem to encourage his departure from New York State.

The day's major frustration had been at a late afternoon conference in Thad Braverton's office, where the Chief of Detectives had read a strongly worded memo from the *Big* Chief stating that there was to be a total media blackout on the Goff case, for reasons of "public safety." Lloyd had laughed aloud, then had sat fuming as Braverton and his old nemesis Captain Fred Gaffaney of I.A.D. gave him the fish-eye. He knew that "public safety" translated to "public relations," and that the media kibosh was undertaken out of apprehension regarding Jack Herzog's possible criminal activities and his relationship with the disgraced cop Marty Bergen. The icing on that cake was the industrial firm and the brass hats who were moonlighting for them. It would not do to step on their toes. A media blitz might flush Goff out, but the Department was covering its ass.

Lloyd parked in a subterranean facility on Olympic and Century Park East, then took an elevator up to ground level and found the shrink's building, a glass and steel skyscraper fronted by an astroturf courtyard. The directory in the foyer placed "John Havilland, M.D.," in suite 2604. Lloyd took a glass-encased elevator to the twenty-sixth floor and walked down a long hallway to an oak door embossed with the psychiatrist's name. He pushed the door open, expecting to be confronted by the saccharine smile of a medical receptionist. Instead, he was transfixed by photographic images of the most beautiful woman he had ever seen.

She was obviously tall and slender, with classic facial lines offset by little flaws that made her that much more striking, that much less the trite physical ideal. Her nose was a shade too pointed; her chin bore a middle cleft that gave her whole face an air of resoluteness. Dark hair cascaded at the edge of soft cheekbones and formed a compliment with large eyes whose focus was intense, but somehow indecipherable. Walking up to the wall to examine the photographs at close range, Lloyd saw that they were candid shots, and that much more stunning for the fact. Closing his eyes, he tried to picture the woman nude. When new images wouldn't coalesce, he knew why: her beauty rendered all attempts at fantasy stillborn. This woman demanded to be seen naked in reality or not at all.

"She's exquisite, isn't she?"

The words didn't dent Lloyd's reverie. He opened his eyes and saw and heard and felt nothing but the feminine power captured in front of him. When he felt a tap on his shoulder, he turned around and saw a slight man in a navy blazer and gray flannel slacks staring up at him, hand outstretched, light brown eyes amused by his reaction to the photographs. "I'm John Havilland," the man said. "What can I do for you?"

Lloyd snapped back into a professional posture, taking the man's hand and grasping it firmly. "Detective Sergeant Hopkins, Los Angeles Police Department. Could I have a few minutes of your time?"

Dr. John Havilland smiled and said, "Sure. We'll go into my office." He pointed toward an oak door and added, "I've got over half an hour until my next session. You're blushing, Sergeant, but I don't blame you."

Lloyd said, "Who is she?"

"A counselee of mine," Havilland said. "Sometimes I think she's the most beautiful woman I've ever seen."

"I was thinking the same thing. What does she think about being your pinup girl?"

Havilland's cheeks reddened; Lloyd saw that the man was smitten beyond the bounds of professionalism. "Forget I asked, Doctor. I'll keep it to business from here on in."

The Doctor lowered his eyes and led Lloyd into an oak paneled inner office, pointing him to a chair, taking an identical seat a few feet away. Raising his eyes, he said, "Is this personal or an official police inquiry?"

Lloyd stared openly at the psychiatrist. When Havilland didn't flinch, he realized that he was in the company of an equal. "It's both, Doctor. The starting point is your nickname. I—"

Havilland was already shaking his head. "It's a second-hand nickname," he said. "Doctor John the Night Tripper was a 'sixties rock and roller. I was given the monicker in med school, because my name was John and I did a certain amount of night tripping. I've also counseled a great many criminals, court referred and otherwise. These people have perpetuated the nickname. Frankly, I like it."

Lloyd smiled and said, "It does have a certain ring." He dug two snapshots out of his jacket pocket and handed them to Havilland. "Have you ever counseled either of these men?"

The Doctor looked at the photos and handed them back. "No, I haven't. Who are they?"

Lloyd ignored the question and said, "If you had treated them, would you have told me?"

Havilland formed his fingers into a steeple and placed the point on his chin. "I would have given you a 'yes' or 'no' answer, then asked, 'Why do you want to know?' "

"Good direct answer," Lloyd said. "I'll reciprocate. The light-haired man recently walked into a liquor store and blew three people to shit. The dark-haired man is an L.A. policeman, missing and presumed dead. Before he disappeared he was hysterical and obsessed with your nickname. I'm certain that the light-haired man killed him. Old light-hair is a world class psycho. Two days ago we shot it out in a Beverly Hills singles bar. You probably read about it in the papers. He escaped. I want to cancel his ticket. Atascadero or the morgue, preferably the latter."

Lloyd leaned back and loosened his necktie, chagrined that he had raised his voice and probably blown his professional parity with the psychiatrist. He felt a headache coming on and shut his eyes to forestall it. When he opened his eyes, Dr. John Havilland was beaming from ear to ear and shaking his head in delight. "I love macho, Sergeant. It's one of my weak points as a headshrinker. Since we've established a certain base of candor, can I ask a few candid questions?"

Lloyd grinned. "Shoot, Doc."

"All right. One, did you honestly think that I knew these two men?"

Lloyd shook his head. "No."

"Then is it safe to assume that you came to exploit my renowned knowledge of criminal behavior?"

Lloyd's grin widened. "Yes."

The Doctor grinned back. "Good. I'll be glad to offer my

observations, but will you phrase your case or questions or whatever nonhypothetically? Give me the literal information as succinctly as possible, then let me ask questions?"

Lloyd said, "You've got it," then walked to the window and looked down on the street twenty-six stories below him. With his back to the doctor, he spoke for ten uninterrupted minutes, recounting a streamlined version of the Herzog/Goff investigation, excluding mention of the security files and Herzog's relationship with Marty Bergen, but describing the Melbourne Avenue horror show in detail.

When he concluded, the Doctor whispered, "God, what a story. Why hasn't there been mention of this man Goff on TV? Wouldn't that help flush him out?"

Turning to face Havilland, Lloyd said, "The high brass have ordered a total media blackout. Public safety, public relations, take your pick—I don't want to go into it. Also, my options are dwindling. I haven't got the slightest handle on Goff's partner. The A.P.B. is hit or miss. I'll be staking out some bars myself, but that's needle in a haystack stuff. If I don't get any leads soon, I'll have to fly to New York and interview people who knew Goff there, which, frankly, seems futile. Run with the ball, Doc. What I'm interested in are your assumptions on Goff's relationship with his partner and the condition of his apartment. What do you think?"

Havilland got up and paced the room. Lloyd sat down and watched him circuit the office. Finally the Doctor stopped and said, "I buy your appraisal of Goff's basic psychoses and the left-handed man as a restraining influence, but only to a degree. Also, I don't think that the men are homosexual lovers, despite the symbolism of the wall cutouts. I think you're dealing with subliminally exposited false clues; the nude men and the slogans especially. The slogans are reminiscent of the 'sixties—maybe Goff and his friend were inspired by the sloganeering of the Manson family. I think that the left-behind record albums point to the subliminality of the subterfuge, because every single record was some kind of 'sixties musical archetype. The apartment was cleaned out thoroughly, yet these albums were left behind. That strikes me as odd. Now one thing is obvious—Goff's cover was blown after his gunplay with you; he knew he had to run, that he would be positively identified very soon. *So his friend wiped the walls to eliminate his own fingerprints*, probably after Goff had vacated—but he didn't remove the cutouts because they pointed only to *Goff's* psychoses. He didn't *see* the cupboard cutout that bore the missing officer's badge number, because it was an inside surface that he himself had never touched, and because he didn't know that Goff had created it. The other wall clues could be construed as ambiguous, but not the cupboard cutout. It pointed to the murder of a Los Angeles policeman. Had Goff's friend known of it, he would have destroyed it. What do *you* think, Sergeant?"

Riveted by the brilliantly informed hypothesis, Lloyd said, "It floats on all levels. I was thinking along similar lines, but you took it two steps further. Can you wrap the whole package up for me?"

The Doctor sat down facing Lloyd, drawing his chair up so that their knees were almost touching. He said, "I think that the basic motivational clues, subliminal and overt, are the nude men, which represent not homosexual tendencies, but a desire to destroy male power. I think that Goff's friend is highly disturbed while Goff himself is psychotic. I think both men are highly intelligent, highly motivated pathological cop haters."

Lloyd let the words sink in, retaining eye contact with the Doctor. The thesis was sound, but what was the next investigative step?

Finally Havilland lowered his eyes and spoke. "I'd like to help you, Sergeant. I have lots of informed criminal sources. My own mini-grapevine, so to speak."

"I'd appreciate it," Lloyd said, taking a business card from his jacket pocket. "This has my office and home numbers on it. You can call me regardless of the time." He handed

Havilland the card. Havilland pocketed it and said, "Could I have that picture of Goff? I'd like to show it to some of my counselees."

Lloyd nodded. "Don't mention that Goff is a homicide suspect," he said as he placed the snapshot in the Doctor's hand. "Try to sound casual. If your patients think this is a big deal, they might try to exploit the situation for money or favors."

"Of course," Havilland said. "It's the only professional way to do it. By the same token, let me state this flat out: I cannot and will not jeopardize the anonymity of my sources, under any circumstances."

"I wouldn't expect you to."

"Good. What will you do next?"

"Hit the bricks, chew on your thesis, go over the existing paperwork forty or fifty times until something bites me."

Havilland laughed. "I hope the bite won't be fatal. You know, it's funny. All of a sudden you look very grave, and just like my father. Bad thoughts?"

Lloyd laughed until his sides ached and tears ran down his cheeks. Havilland chuckled along, forming a series of steeples with his fingers. Regaining his breath, Lloyd said, "God, that feels good. I was laughing at how ironic your question was. For a solid week I've had nothing but homicide on my brain, but when you said 'bad thoughts' I was thinking of that incredible woman on your walls."

Laughing wildly himself, the Doctor blurted out, "Linda Wilhite has that effect on a man. She can tur—" He caught himself in mid-sentence, stopped and said, "She can move men to the point of wanting to speak her name out loud. Forget what I said, Hopkins. My counselees' anonymity is sacred. It was unprofessional of me."

Lloyd got to his feet, thinking that the poor bastard was in love, beyond rhyme or reason, with a woman who probably caused traffic jams when she walked down the street to buy a newspaper. He smiled and stuck out his hand. When Havilland took it, he said, "I do unprofessional things all the time, Doc. Guys with our kind of juice should fuck up once in a while out of *noblesse oblige*. Thanks for your help."

Dr. John Havilland smiled. Lloyd walked out of his office, willing his eyes rigid, away from the photographs of Linda Wilhite.

13

THE Night Tripper began to hyperventilate the very second that Lloyd Hopkins walked out his door. The suppressed tension that had fueled his performance, *his brilliant performance*, started to seep out through his pores, causing him to shiver uncontrollably and grab at his desk to fight his vertigo. He held the desktop until his knuckles turned white and cramps ran up his arms to his shoulders. Concentrating on his own physiology to bring his control back to normal, he calculated his heartbeat at one twenty-five and his blood pressure as stratospheric. This professional detachment in the face of extreme fear/elation calmed and soothed him. Within seconds he could feel his vital signs recede to something approaching normalcy. "Father. Father. Father," Dr. John Havilland whispered.

When his physical and mental calm united, the Doctor replayed his performance and assessed the policeman, astonished to find that he was not the right-wing plunderer he had expected, but rather a likable fellow with a sense of humor that was offset by the violence he held in check just below the surface of his intellect. Lloyd Hopkins was a bad man to fuck with. So was he. He had taken their first round easily, running on instinct. Round two would have to be meticulously planned.

Checking his desk calendar, the Doctor saw that he had no patients for the rest of the day and that Linda Wilhite's next session was still two days off. Thoughts of Linda spawned a long series of mental chess moves. Hopkins would be leaving for New York, unless he discovered evidence to keep him in

Los Angeles. It would not do to have "Crazy Lloyd" talk to the administrators at Attica. Round two would have to be initiated today, but how?

Just then it hit him. At their first session Linda had spoken of a "client" who collected Colombian art and who took nude photos of her and hung them in his bedroom. *Another pawn.*

Havilland opened the wall safe hidden behind his Edward Hopper original and took out Thomas Goff's verbatim transcription of Linda's john book/journal. He sifted through pages of sexual facts, figures, and ruminations before he found mention of the man.

> 8/28/83; Stanley Rudolph, 11741 Montana (at Bundy) 829-6907. Referred by P.N.
>
> A truly ambivalant man. He lives in a condo full of Colombian art (aesthetic!) that he claims he buys dirt cheap from doper rip-off bimbos (macho obnoxiousness!). The statues were atavistic, *virile*, wonderful. Stanley talks them up so much prior to business that I know he wants something other than straight fucking—especially when he starts calling me a work of fucking art. Lead in to (of course!) a photography session! (Reading between the lines—Stan baby is impotent, digs nudie shots juxtaposed against his phallic statues). Stan takes his shots (no beavers—actually tasteful)—(Stan the Aesthete)—then tells me stories about all the women who beg for his donkey dick (Stan the macho buffoon). I lounge around nude trying to keep from cracking up. $500.00.
>
> 9/10/83—Ambivalent Stan has become a regular at $500.00 per. I am now framed on his walls in naked splendor. Weird. I wish my breasts were bigger.

Havilland replaced the transcript in his safe and thought of another faceless pawn living a sleazy life in the Valley industrial district, then locked up his office and went looking for her.

* * *

Junior Miss Cosmetics was situated at the northeast edge of the San Fernando Valley, a squat green stucco building enclosed by rusted cyclone fencing. Outside the wire perimeter was a huge dirt lot filled with carelessly parked cars, and across the street stood an entire city block of cocktail lounges, all of them flashing neon signs at three o'clock in the afternoon. Parking underneath a sign advertising "Nude Workingman's Lunch," Dr. John Havilland felt like he had just entered hell.

The Doctor locked his car and counted neon blinking doorways all the way up the block, ending with a total of nine. He walked into the first door, wincing against a blast of country western music, squinting until he could make out a bandstand and an overweight redhead doing a listless nude boogie. There was a horseshoe-shaped bar off to his left. Steeling himself for his role, Havilland took a twenty dollar bill from his money clip and walked over.

The bartender looked up as he approached. "You drinking or you want the lunch?" he asked.

Havilland placed the twenty flat on the bar and willed his voice to suit the environment. "I'm looking for Sherry Shroeder. A buddy of mine says she hangs out here."

"Sherry's eighty-six," the bartender said. "She gets coked or juiced and gets rowdy. You looking to pour some pork?"

The Doctor gawked, then said, "What?"

The bartender spoke slowly, as if to an idiot child. "You know, push the bush? Slake the snake? Drain the train? Siphon the python?"

Havilland swallowed and took another twenty from his pocket. "Yes. All those things. Where can I find her? Please tell me."

Snatching up the two bills, the bartender leaned over and spoke into the Doctor's ear. "Go down the street to the Loafer Gopher. Sherry should show up there sooner or later. Sit at the bar, and sooner or later she'll come up and try to sit on your face. And, buddy? Keep your roll to yourself. They got some righteous shitkickers down there."

The Loafer Gopher was dark and featured punk rock. Havilland sat at the bar and sipped scotch and soda while Cindy and the Sinners sang their repertoire of "Prison of Your Love," "Nine Inches of Your Love," and "Gimme Your Love" over and over. He arrayed a stack of one dollar bills in front of him and tried to avoid eye contact with the topless barmaid, who considered eye to eye meetings a signal to refresh drinks. Playing Mozart in his mind to kill the hideous music and conversation surrounding him, the Doctor waited.

The waiting extended into hours. Havilland sat at the bar, buying a drink ever twenty minutes, nursing the top, then, unseen, dumping the rest on the floor. When mental Mozart began to pall, he fantasized Sherry Shroeder as everything from a Nordic ice maiden to a platinum-coiffed slattern, using her security file statistics as his physical spark point. He was nearing the limits of both his patience and imagination when coy fingers caressed his neck and a coy female voice asked, "Care to buy a lady a drink?"

Havilland swiveled his stool to face the come-on. The woman who had delivered it looked like a burned-out beach bunny. Her face was seamed from too much sun and chemical ingestion, with deep furrows around the mouth and eyes that bespoke many desperate attempts to be fetching and an equal number of rejections. Her blond hair was set in a lopsided frizzy style that added to her look of anxiousness. But her features were pretty, and her designer jean and tanktop-clad body was lean and womanly. If this was his actress, Richard Oldfield would love her.

"I'm Sherry," the woman said.

Havilland signaled the barmaid and smiled at his pawn. "I'm Lloyd."

She giggled as the barmaid placed a tall drink in front of her and grabbed two of the Doctor's one dollar bills as payment. She took a long sip and said, "That's a good name.

It goes with your blazer. You don't really dress for the Gopher, but that's okay, 'cause there's so many bars on this strip that you can't go home and change every time you hop one, can you? I mean, is that the truth?"

"That's the truth," Havilland said. "I dress conservatively because the bigwigs at the studio demand it. I'm just like you. I can't go home and change every time I go out on a talent search."

Sherry's eyes widened. She gulped the rest of her drink and stammered, "Ar-ar-are you an agent?"

"I'm an independent movie producer," Havilland said, snapping his fingers at the barmaid and pointing to Sherry's empty glass. "I sell art movies to a combine of millionaires, who screen the films in their special screening rooms. As a matter of fact, I'm here looking for actresses."

Sherry downed her fresh drink in three fast swallows. Havilland watched her eyes expand and bodice flush. "I'm an actress," she said in a rush of breath. "I've done extra work and I've done loops and other stuff. Do you think you—"

Havilland silenced her with a finger to her lips, then looked around the bar. No one seemed interested in their business. "Let's go outside and talk," he said. "This place is too loud."

Sherry led him across the street to the Junior Miss parking lot and her battered VW van. "I used to work there," she said as she unlocked the passenger door. "They fired me because I was overqualified. They found out I had a bigger I.Q. than the president of the company, so they let me go."

Havilland sat down in the passenger seat and made a mental note not to touch anything inside the vehicle. Sherry walked around the front of the van and squeezed in behind the wheel. When she looked at him importuningly, the Doctor said, "Sherry, I'll be frank. I produce high-budget adult films. Normally I would not advise a serious young actress like yourself to appear in such a movie, but in this case I would—because only a private audience of Hollywood bigshots will be viewing it. Now let me ask you, have you had experience in adult films?"

Sherry's answer came out in a gin-fueled torrent of words. "Yeah, and this is perfect because before I did loops and the camera guy said my mom and dad would never know. We shot in the boys' gym at Pacoima Junior High, 'cause the camera guy knew the janitor and he had the key, and we had to shoot late at night 'cause then nobody would be around. Ritchie Valens went to Pacoima Junior High, but he got killed with Buddy Holly on February 3, 1959. I was just a little girl then, but I remember."

The final memory numbed the Doctor. He took out his billfold and said, "We'll be shooting in two days or so, at a big house in the Hollywood Hills. Two performers—you and a very handsome young man. Your pay is a thousand dollars. Would you like an advance now?"

Sherry Shroeder threw her arms around Havilland and buried her head in his neck. When he felt her tongue in his ear, he grabbed her shoulders and pushed her away. "Please, Sherry, I'm married."

Sherry gave a mock pout. "Married men are the best. Can I have a C-note now?"

Havilland took three hundreds from his billfold. He handed them to Sherry and whispered, "Please keep quiet about this. If word gets out, other actresses will be bothering me for parts, and I think I want to stick with you exclusively. All right?"

"All right."

Havilland smiled. "I need your phone number."

Sherry reached in the glove compartment, then flicked on the dashboard light and handed the Doctor a red metallic flaked business card bearing the words, "Sherry—Let's Party! Incall and outcall, 632-0140." Havilland put the card in his pocket and nudged the passenger door open with his shoulder. He smiled and said, "I'll be in touch."

Sherry said, "Party hearty, Lloyd baby," and gunned her

engine. The Doctor watched the VW van peel rubber into the night.

The Night Tripper drove to a pay phone and called Richard Oldfield at his home, speaking a single sentence and hanging up before Oldfield could reply. Satisfied with the force of his words, he drove to the Hollywood Hills and his third stellar performance of the day.

Oldfield had left the front door unlocked. The Night Tripper walked through it to find his pawn kneeling on the living room floor in his efficacy training posture, head thrust out and eyes closed, hands clasped behind his back. He was stripped to the waist, and his pectoral muscles were twitching from a recent workout.

Havilland walked up and flung a whiplike backhand at Oldfield's face, gashing his cheek with his Harvard signet ring. Oldfield leaned into the blow and remained mute. Havilland reared back and swung again, catching his pawn on the bridge of the nose, ripping flesh and severing a vein below his left eye. When Oldfield betrayed no pain, the Doctor unleashed a whirlwind of open palms and backhands, until his pawn's face contorted and a single tear escaped from each eye and merged with the blood from his lashings.

"Are you ready to hurt and twist and loathe and gouge the woman who ruined you as a child?" the Night Tripper hissed. "Are you ready to go as far as you can go? Are you ready to enter a realm of pure power and relegate the rest of the world to the shit heap that it really is?"

"Yes," Richard Oldfield sobbed.

The Doctor took a silk handkerchief from his blazer pocket and swabbed his counselee's face. "Then you shall have all of it. Now listen and don't ask questions. The time is two days from now, the place is here. Don't go out of the house until I tell you, because a policeman is looking for someone who looks exactly like you. Do you understand all these things?"

"Yes," Oldfield said.

Havilland walked to the phone and dialed seven digits he had memorized early that afternoon. When a weary voice answered, "Yes?", he said, "Sergeant, this is John Havilland. Listen, I've got a line on your suspect. It's rather vague, but I think I credit the information."

"Jesus fucking Christ," Lloyd Hopkins said. "Where did you get it?"

"No," Havilland said, "I can't tell you that. I can tell you this—the man is right-handed, and in my professional opinion he knows nothing about any homicides, or about Goff's whereabouts."

Lloyd said, "I've got my notebook, Doc. Talk slowly."

"All right. This man says he met Goff last year at a singles bar. They pulled a burglary together, he forgets the location, and stole some art objects. Goff had a customer for the stuff. My man says his name was either Rudolph Stanley or Stanley Rudolph. He had a condo in Brentwood, somewhere near Bundy and Montana."

"That's it?"

"Yes. My counselee is a basically decent, very disturbed young man, Sergeant. Please don't press me for his identity. I won't yield on that."

"Don't sweat it, Doc. But if I get Goff on your info, be prepared for the best dinner of your life."

"I look forward to it." Havilland waited for a reply, but the policeman had already hung up.

Putting down the phone, he saw that Richard Oldfield had not budged from his supplicant position. He looked at the blood on his hands. Twist the cop. Gouge him. Maim him. Make him pay for the childhood darkness and infuse the void with light.

14

AT dawn, Lloyd was stationed in his car at the southeast corner of Bundy and Montana, armed with skin-tight rubber gloves and a selection of burglar's picks. After receiving Havilland's phone call, he had made a battery of his own calls, to the L.A.P.D.'s R. & I., the All Police Computer Network, the feds, and the California Department of Motor Vehicles Night Information line. The results were only halfway satisfying: A man named Stanley Rudolph lived at 11741 Montana, # 1015, but he possessed no criminal record and had never been cited for anything more serious than running a red light. A solid citizen type who in all probability would scream for his attorney when confronted with the fact that he was a receiver of stolen goods. There was only the tried-and-true and highly illegal daylight recon run. Rudolph's D.M.V. application had yielded the facts that he was unmarried, worked as a broker at the downtown stock exchange, and was the owner of a light blue 1982 Cadillac Seville bearing the personalized license plate "Big Stan," which was now parked directly across the street. Lloyd fidgeted and looked at his watch. 6:08. The exchange would be opening at seven. "Big Stan" would have to leave soon or be late for work.

Sipping coffee directly from the thermos, he thought of his other, nonprofessional telephone inquiries. Against his better judgment, he had called R. & I. and the D.M.V. to learn what he could about Linda Wilhite. The information gleaned was lackluster: Date of birth, physical stats, address, and phone number and the facts that she was "self-employed," drove a Mercedes and had no criminal record. But the act of pursuit was thrilling, fueled by fantasies of what it would be like to need and be needed by a woman that beautiful. Thoughts of Linda Wilhite had competed with thoughts of his investigation for control of his mind, and it was only Haviland's astonishing phone call that bludgeoned them to second place.

At 6:35, a portly man wearing a three-piece business suit trotted up to the Cadillac, holding a sweet roll in one hand and a briefcase in the other. He got in the car and gunned it southbound on Bundy. Lloyd waited for three minutes, then walked over to 11741 Montana and took the elevator up to the tenth floor.

1015 was at the end of a long carpeted corridor. Lloyd looked in both directions, then rang the bell. When thirty seconds went by without an answer, he studied the twin locks on the door and jammed his breaker pick into the top mechanism, feeling a very slight click as a bolt loosened. He leaned his shoulder into the door, accentuating the give of the top lock. With his free hand he stuck a needle-thin skeleton pick into the bottom keyhole and twisted it side to side. Seconds later the bottom lock slid open and the door snapped inward.

Lloyd stepped inside and closed the door behind him. When his eyes became adjusted to the darkness, he found himself in a treasure trove of primitive art. There were shelves filled with Colombian fertility statues and African wood carvings covering the tops of empty bookcases. Windowsills and ottomans held Mayan pottery, and the walls were festooned with framed oil paintings of Peruvian Indians and shrines in the Andes. The living room carpeting and furniture were bargain basement quality, but the artwork looked to be worth a small fortune.

Lloyd slipped on his rubber gloves and reconnoitered the rest of the condo, coming to one nonincriminating conclusion: Except for the artwork and the late model Cadillac, "Big Stan" lived on the cheap. His clothing was off the rack and his refrigerator was stuffed with TV dinners. He shined his own shoes and owned nothing electronic or mechanical except the built-in appliances that came with the pad and an inexpensive 35mm camera. Stanley Rudolph was a man obsessed.

Lloyd took a generic brand cola from the refrigerator and sat down on a threadbare sofa to consider his options, realizing that it would be impossible to secure latent prints from any art objects that Goff or Havilland's anonymous source might have touched. Stanley Rudolph had probably fondled the statues and pottery repeatedly, and the shrink had said that his source was both right-handed and innocent of knowledge of Goff's whereabouts and homicides in general. Havilland was a pro; his assessments could be trusted.

This left three approaches: Lean hard on "Big Stan" himself; toss the pad for levers of intimidation, and find his address book and run the names through R. & I. Since "Big Stan" was unavailable, only the last two approaches were practical. Lloyd killed his soft drink and went to work.

It took him three hours to comb every inch of the condo and confirm his conclusion that Stanley Rudolph was a lonely man who lived solely to collect art. His clothes were poorly laundered, his bathroom was a mess and the bedroom walls were blanketed with dust, except for rectangular patches where paintings had obviously recently hung. The sadness/obsessiveness combo made Lloyd want to send up a mercy plea for the entire fucked-up human race.

This left the address book, resting beside the telephone on the living room floor. Lloyd leafed through it, noting that it contained only names and phone numbers. Turning to the G's, he saw that there was no mention of Thomas Goff and that Stanley Rudolph's scrawl was unmistakably right-handed. Sighing, he thumbed back to the A's and got out his notepad and pen and began copying down every name and phone number in the book.

When he got to "Laurel Benson," Lloyd felt a little tremor drift up his spine. Laurel Benson was a high-priced call girl he had rousted while working West L.A. Vice over ten years before. Thinking that it was merely a coincidence and that it was nice to know that "Big Stan" got laid occasionally, he continued his transcribing until he hit "Polly Marks" and put down his pen and laughed out loud. Thus far, the only two women listed in the book were hookers. No wonder Rudolph had to shine his own shoes and drink generic soda pop—he had *two* expensive habits.

The N through V section contained the names of over fifty men and only four women, two of them hookers that Lloyd had heard about from vice squad buddies. Writers cramp was coming on when he turned to the final page and saw "Linda Wilhite—275-7815." This time the little tremor became a 9.6 earthquake. Lloyd replaced the address book and left the obsessive little condo before he had time to think of his next destination and what it all meant.

Parked outside Linda Wilhite's plush high rise on Wilshire and Beverly Glen, Lloyd ran through literal and instinctive chronologies in an attempt to logically explain the remarkable coincidence that has just fallen into his lap. Dr. John Havilland was in love with Linda Wilhite, who was probably a very expensive prostitute, one who had tricked with Stanley Rudolph, who had bought stolen goods from Thomas Goff and the Doctor's anonymous source. Havilland did not know Goff or Rudolph, but did know Wilhite and the source. The coincidence factor was strong, but did *not* reek of malfeasance. Unanswered questions: Did Linda Wilhite know Goff or the source; or, the wild card—was the shrink, who had the air of a man in love, protecting Linda Wilhite, *the real source,* by giving him correct information from a bogus "informant," this way protecting both his professional ethics and the woman he loved? Was the Doctor playing a roundabout game, *wanting* to aid in a homicide investigation, yet not wanting to relinquish confidential information? Lloyd felt anger overtake his initial sex flush. If Linda Wilhite knew *anything* about Thomas Goff or his left-handed friend, he would shake it out of her.

He ran into the high rise and bolted three flights of service stairs. When he raised his hand to knock on the door of Linda Wilhite's apartment, he saw that *he* was shaking.

A security peephole slid open. "Yes?" a woman's voice said.

Lloyd put his badge up in front of the hole. "L.A.P.D.," he said. "Could I speak to you for a moment, Miss Wilhite?"

"What's this about?"

Lloyd felt his shaking go internal. "It's about Stanley Rudolph. Will you open up, please?"

There was the sound of locks being unlatched, and then *she* was there, wearing an ankle-length paisley caftan. Lloyd tried to stare past her into the apartment, but Linda Wilhite held the center of his vision and rendered the background dull black.

"What *about* Stanley Rudolph?" she asked.

Lloyd walked into the apartment uninvited, taking a quick inventory of the entrance hall and living room. It was still hazy background stuff, but he knew that everything was tasteful and expensive.

"Don't be shy, make yourself right at home," Linda Wilhite said, coming up behind Lloyd and pointing him toward a floral-patterned easy chair. "I'll have the butler bring you a mint julep."

Lloyd laughed. "Nice pad, Linda. Out of the low-rent district."

Linda feigned a return laugh. "Don't be formal, call me suspect."

Lloyd stuck his hand in his jacket pocket and pulled out snapshots of Thomas Goff and Jungle Jack Herzog. He handed them to Linda and said, "Okay, suspect, have you seen either of these men before?"

Linda looked the photos over and returned them to Lloyd. There was not the slightest flicker of recognition in her eyes or her hands-on-hips pose. "No. What's this about Stan Rudolph? Are you with Vice?"

Lloyd sat down in the easy chair and stretched his legs. "That's right. What's the basis of your relationship with Rudolph?"

Linda's eyes went cold. Her voice followed. "I think you know. Will you state your purpose, ask your questions, and get out?"

Lloyd shook his head. "What do *you* know?"

"That you're no fucking Vice cop!" Linda shouted. "You got a snappy comback for that one?"

Lloyd's voice was his softest; the voice he saved for his daughters. "Yeah. You're no hooker."

Linda sat down across from him. "Everything in this apartment calls you a liar."

"I've been called worse than that," Lloyd said.

"Such as?"

"Some of the choicer shots have included 'urban barracuda,' 'male chauvinist porker,' 'fascist cocksucker,' 'wasp running dog,' and 'pussy hound scumbag.' I appreciate articulate invective. 'Motherfucker' and 'pig' get to be boring."

Linda Wilhite laughed and poked a finger at Lloyd's wedding ring. "You're married. What does your wife call you?"

"Long distance."

"What?"

"We're separated."

"Serious splitsville?"

"I'm not sure. It's been a year and she's got a lover, but I intend to outlast the bastard."

Linda stretched out her legs, matching Lloyd's pose, but in the opposite direction. "Do you always discuss intimate family matters with total strangers?"

Lloyd laughed and stilled an urge to reach over and touch her knee. "Sometimes. It's good therapy."

"I'm in therapy," Linda said.

"Why?" Lloyd asked.

"That's your first dumb question," Linda said. "Everyone has problems, and people who have money and want to get rid of them go to shrinks. *Comprende*?"

Lloyd shook his head. "Most troubled people are swamped by petty neuroses, stuff that they haven't got the slightest handle on. Offhand, I'd say that you're not that kind of person. Offhand, I'd say that some sort of catalyst led you to the couch."

"My shrink doesn't have a couch. He's too hip."

"That's a strange thing to call a psychiatrist."

"All right. Hip translates to brilliant, concerned, dedicated, and brutally honest."

"Are you in love with him?"

"No. He's not my type. Look, this conversation is getting a little weird and a bit far afield. You *are* a cop, aren't you? That wasn't a dime-store badge you showed me, or anything like that, was it?"

Lloyd saw a large stack of newspapers lying on top of a coffee table an arm's length away. He pointed to them and said, "If you've got Tuesday's *Times*, look at the second page. 'Shootout at Beverly Hills Nightclub.' "

Linda went to the table and leafed through the papers, then read the article standing up. When she turned around to face Lloyd, he had his badge and I.D. card extended. Linda took the leatherette holder and examined it, then smiled from ear to ear. "So you're Sergeant Lloyd Hopkins and one of those pictures is the unidentified homicide suspect you shot it out with. Very impressive. But what do Stan Rudolph and I have to do with it?"

Lloyd mulled the question over as Linda sat back down without relinquishing the I.D. holder. Deciding on an abridged version of the truth, he said, "An informant told me that Thomas Goff, my previously 'unidentified homicide suspect,' sold Stanley Rudolph some art objects, aided by a still unidentified partner. I came across Rudolph's address book and noticed the names of several call girls I'd busted years ago. I also noticed your name, and concluded that since the only other women in the book were in the Life, you had to be also. I needed an outside lever to pry some information out of Rudolph, and since the other women probably still hate me for busting them, I decided on you."

Linda handed the I.D. holder back. "Are you that fucking brash?"

Lloyd smiled. "Yes," he said.

"Why don't you just question Stan baby yourself?"

"Because he'd probably want an attorney present. Because any admission of knowing Goff is an implicit admission of receiving stolen goods, accessory to first degree burglary and criminal conspiracy. What kind of man is Rudolph?"

"A pathetic little nerd who gets his rocks off taking nude pictures. A loud-mouthed buffoon. What specifically did this guy Goff do?"

"He's murdered at least three people."

Linda went pale. "Jesus. And you want me to pry information about him out of Stan baby?"

"Yes. And about his partner, who I'm certain is left-handed. Does Rudolph ever talk about his art collection and how he accquired it?"

Linda tapped Lloyd's arm and said, "Yes. His art collection is his favorite topic of conversation. It's all tied in to his sex M.O. He's told me a dozen times that he buys his stuff from rip-off guys. That's as specific as he gets. He used to have nude photographs of me on his bedroom walls, but he took them down because he was expecting some more Colombian statues. I haven't tricked with him in six weeks or so, so maybe he and Goff got together recently."

Lloyd thought of the rectangular patches on Rudolph's bedroom wall, imagining the nude Linda he could have seen had he pulled his B & E a few months before. "Linda, do you think you—"

Linda Wilhite silenced him with a breathtaking coconspirator's smile. "Yes. I'll call Stan baby and set up a date, hopefully for tonight. Call me around one A.M., and don't worry, I'll be very cool."

Lloyd's conspiratorial smile felt like a blush. "Thank you."

"My pleasure. You were right, you know. I did enter therapy for a reason."

"What was it?"

"I want to quit the Life."

"Then I was right on two counts."

"What do you mean?"

"I told you you were no hooker."

Lloyd got up and walked out of the apartment, letting his exit line linger.

With the Stanley Rudolph angle covered, Lloyd remembered an investigatory approach so rudimentary that he knew its very simplicity was the reason he had forgotten to explore it. Cursing himself for his oversight, he drove to a pay phone and called Dutch Peltz at the Hollywood Station, asking him to go across the street to the Hollywood Municipal Court and secure a subpoena for Jack Herzog's bank records. Dutch agreed to the errand, on the proviso that Lloyd fill him in at length on the case when he came by the station to pick up the paperwork. Lloyd agreed in return and drove to Herzog's apartment house in the Valley, thinking of Linda Wilhite all the way.

At Herzog's building, Lloyd went straight to the manager's apartment, flashed his badge, and asked him what bank the missing officer's rent checks were drawn on. Without hesitation, the frail old man said, "Security-Pacific, Encino branch," then launched into a spiel on how other officers had been by the previous day and had sealed the nice Mr. Herzog's nice apartment.

After thanking the manager, Lloyd drove back over the Cahuenga Pass to the Hollywood Station. He found Dutch

Peltz in his office, muttering, "Yes, yes," into the telephone. Dutch looked up, drew a finger across his throat and whispered, "I.A.D." Lloyd took a chair across from him and put his feet up on the desk. Dutch muttered, "Yes, Fred, I'll tell him," and hung up. He turned to Lloyd and said, "Good news and bad news. Which would you prefer first?"

"Take your pick," Lloyd said.

Dutch smiled and poked Lloyd's crossed ankles with a pencil. "The good news is that Judge Bitowf issued your subpoena with no questions asked. Wasn't that nice of him?"

Lloyd took in Dutch's grin and raised his feet as if to kick his precious quartz bookend off the desk. "Tell me what Fred Gaffaney had to say. Omit nothing."

"More good news and bad news," Dutch said. "The good news is that *I* am your official liaison to I.A.D. on all matters pertaining to the Goff-Herzog case. The bad news is that Gaffaney just reiterated in the strongest possible language that you are to go nowhere near the officers working the moonlight gigs or go near the firms themselves. Gaffaney is preparing an approach strategy, and he and his top men will be conducting interviews within a few days. *I* will be given Xeroxes of their reports, *you* can get copies from me. Gaffaney also stated that if you violate these orders, you will be suspended immediately and given a trial board. You like it?"

Lloyd reached over and patted the bookend. "No, I don't like it. But you do."

Dutch flashed a shark grin. "I like anything that keeps you reasonably restrained and thereby a continued member of the Los Angeles Police Department. I would hate to see you get shitcanned and go on welfare. You'd be drinking T-bird and sleeping in the weeds within six months."

Lloyd stood up and grabbed the subpoena off Dutch's desk. He laid the notebook containing the names from Stanley Rudolph's address book in its place and said, "I know why you're acting so sardonic, Dutchman. You had a martini with your lunch. You have one drink a year, and your low tolerance gets you plowed. I'm a detective. You can't fool me."

Dutch laughed. "Fuck you. What's with this notebook and where do you think you're going? You were going to fill me in on the case, remember?"

Lloyd took a playful jab at the bookend. "Fuck you twice. I don't confide in alcoholics. Have one of your minions run those names through R. & I., will you?"

"I'll think about it. Hey Lloydy, how come you took my bad news so easy? I expected you to throw something."

Lloyd tried to imitate Dutch's shark grin, but knew immediately that it came out a blush. "I think I'm in love," he said.

Lloyd drove back to the Valley, highballing it northbound on the Ventura Freeway in order to hit the Encino branch of the Security-Pacific Bank before closing time, making it with two minutes to spare. He showed his I.D. and the subpoena to the manager, a middle-aged Japanese man who led him to the privacy of a safe deposit box examination room, returning five minutes later with a computer printout and a thick transaction file. Bowing, the manager closed the door, leaving Lloyd in impeccable silence.

That silence soon became inhabited by dates and figures that detailed an atypical cop life. Jack Herzog's savings and checking accounts went back five years. Lloyd started at the beginning of the transaction file and waded through paychecks deposited twice monthly, rent checks drawn monthly and savings stipends deposited every third L.A. City pay period. Jack Herzog was a frugal man. There were no large withdrawals indicating spending sprees; no checks for amounts exceeding his monthly rent payment of $350.00, and out of every third paycheck he deposited $300.00 in a 7½% growth savings account. When Herzog opened his dual accounts in 1979, his total balance was less than six hundred dollars. At the transaction file's last entry date four months before, he was worth $17,913.49.

Noting that the last entry was on 1/4/84, Lloyd turned to the computer sheet, hoping it contained facts updating Herzog's two accounts to the present.

It did. The same deposit/check withdrawal motif continued, this time detailed in hard-to-read computer type. Lloyd was about to shake his head at the sadness of close to nineteen grand belonging to a dead man when the final transaction came into focus, grabbing him by the throat.

On March 20, around the time of his disappearance, Jack Herzog closed out both his accounts and purchased an interbranch bank draft for his total balance of $18,641.07. There was a photocopy of the draft clipped to the computer sheet. It stated that the above amount was to be transferred to the West Hollywood branch of Security-Pacific, to the savings account of Martin D. Bergen. Lloyd let the facts sink in, then walked slowly out of the examination room and through the bank proper, bowing to the bank manager and running as soon as he hit the sidewalk.

By speeding through the Hollywood Hills, Lloyd was able to reach the *Big Orange Insider* office in just under half an hour. The same receptionist gave him the same startled look as he pushed through the connecting door to the editorial department, and seconds later the young man he had tangled with on his previous visit attempted to block his progress by standing in his path with his legs dug in like a linebacker. "I told you before you can't come back here," he said.

Lloyd took a bead on his head, then caught himself. "Marty Bergen," he said. "Official police business. Go get him."

The young man wrapped his arms around his chest. "Marty is on vacation. Leave now."

Lloyd took the bank subpoena from his pocket and rolled it up, then tickled the underside of the young man's chin with the end. When he jerked backward, Lloyd said, "This is a court order to search Bergen's desk. If you don't comply with it, I'll get an order to search the entire premises. Do you dig me, Daddy-o?"

Turning beet red, then pale, the youth flung an arm toward the back of the room. "The last desk against the wall. And let me see that court order."

Lloyd handed the subpoena over and weaved through a crammed maze of desks, ignoring the stares of the people sitting at them. Bergen's desk was covered with a pile of papers. Lloyd leafed through them, pushing the stack aside with he saw that every page contained notes scrawled in an indecipherable shorthand. He was about to go through the drawers when a woman's voice interrupted him. "Officer, is Marty all right?"

Lloyd turned around. A tall black woman wearing an ink-stained printer's smock was standing beside the desk, holding a long roll of tabloid galley paper. "Is Marty *all right*?" she repeated.

"No," Lloyd said. "I don't think so. Why do you ask? You sound concerned."

The woman fretted the roll in her hands. "He's been gone since the last time you were here," she said. "He hasn't been at his apartment and nobody from the *Orange* has seen him. And right before he took off he grabbed all his columns for the following week, except one. I'm the head typesetter, and I needed to set those issues. Marty really screwed the *Orange*, and that's not like him."

"Has he taken off like this before?"

The women shook her head. "No! I mean sometimes he rents a motel room and goes on a toot, but he always leaves copies of his column for the time he expects to be gone. This time was *weird* because he took *back* his columns, and *they* were really *weird* to begin with."

Lloyd motioned the woman to sit down. "Tell me about

those columns," he said. "Try to remember everything you can."

"They were *just weird*," the woman said slowly. "One was called 'Moonlight Malfeasance.' It was about these bigshot L.A. cops who had these figurehead jobs bossing around all these low-life rent-a-cops. *Weird*. The other columns were off-shoots on that one, about the L.A.P.D. manipulating the media, because they got all the inside dirt from the moonlight cops. *Weird*. I mean the *Orange*'s meat is it's anti-fuzz policy, but this stuff was *weird*, even for Marty Bergen, who was a lovable dude, but *weird* himself."

Lloyd felt fragments of his case burst into a strange new light: *Marty Bergen had seen the missing L.A.P.D. Personnel files*. Swallowing to hold his voice steady, he said, "You told me that Bergen let you keep one of the columns. Have you still got it?"

The woman nodded and rolled out her galley sheet on the desk. "Marty gave real specific instructions on how to set it," she said. "He said it had to have a heavy black border and that it had to run on May the third, because that was the birthday of this buddy of his. *Weird*." She located the section and jabbed it with her finger. "There. Read it for yourself."

The black-bordered piece was entitled "Night Train to the Big Nowhere." Lloyd read it over three times, feeling his case move from its strange new light into a stranger darkness.

> When a cop jumps on the Night Train to the big nowhere, he doesn't care about its exact destination, because any terminus is preferable to living inside his own head, with its awful knowledge of how the solar age will never penetrate the Big Iceberg.
>
> When my friend jumped on the Night Train to the Big Nowhere, he probably foresaw only relief from his locked-in knowledge of the big nightmare, and the vice grip of the new nightmare that spelled out his role to play in the shroud dance that owns us all.

That you didn't purchase your ticket with your gun spoke volumes. Like me, you were a blue-suit sham. You did not use that tool of your trade in your nihilist last hurrah, reaffirming your masquerade. Instead you strangled on a pink cloud of chemical silence, giving yourself time to think of all the puzzles you had solved, and of the cruelty of your final jigsaw revelations. At the end you confronted, and *knew*. It was your most conscious act of courage in a life vulgarized by fearful displays of bravery. I love you for it, and offer you this twenty-one gun verse valedictory:

Resurrect the dead on this day,
open the doors where
they dare not to stray;
Cancel all tickets to the horror shroud dance,
Burn down the night in the rage of a trance.

Lloyd handed the sheet back to the bewildered typesetter. "Print it," he said. "Redeem your piece of shit newspaper."

The woman said, "It ain't *The New York Times*, but it's a regular gig."

Lloyd nodded, but didn't reply. When he walked out of the office the strident young man was scrutinizing the bank subpoena with a magnifying glass.

Knowing that he couldn't bear to recon Marty Bergen's apartment, Lloyd drove home and called the West Hollywood Sheriff's, briefly explaining the case and relegating the job to them, omitting his knowledge of the bank draft, telling them to make a check of local motels and to detain Bergen if they found him.

New questions burned in the morass that the Herzog-Goff case had become. Was Jungle Jack Herzog a suicide? If so, where was his body, who had disposed of it, and who had wiped his apartment free of fingerprints? Marty Bergen's "weird" columns indicated that he had seen the files Herzog had stolen. Where were the files, what was the literal gist of the suicide column, where was Bergen, and what was the extent of his involvement in the case?

When nothing came together for him, Lloyd knew that he was overamped, undernourished, and coming unconnected, and that the only antidote was an evening of rest. After a dinner of cold sliced ham and a pint of cottage cheese, he sat down on his porch to watch the twilight dwindle into darkness, warming to the idea of not thinking.

But he thought.

He thought of the terraced hills of the old neighborhood, and of sleepless 'fifties' nights spent listening to the howling of dogs imprisoned in the animal shelter two blocks away. The shelter had given his section of Silverlake the nickname of "Dogtown," and for the years of 'fifty-five and 'fifty-six, when he had been a peewee member of the Dogtown Flats gang, it had supplied *him* with the sobriquets of "Dogman" and "Savior." The constant howling, plaintive as it was, had been mysterious and romantic dream fuel. But sometimes the dogs chewed and clawed their way to freedom, only to get obliterated by late-night hot-rodders playing chicken on the blind curve blacktop outside his bedroom window. Even though the corpses were removed by the time he left for school in the morning, with the pavement hosed down by old Mr. Hernandez next door, Lloyd could feel and smell and almost taste the blood. And after awhile, his nights were spent not listening, but cringing in anticipation of coming impacts.

Lack of sleep drew Lloyd gaunt that fall of 'fifty-six, and he knew that he had to act to reclaim the wonder he had always felt after dark. Because the night was there to provide comfort and the nourishing of brave dreams, and only someone willing to fight for its sanctity deserved to claim it as his citadel.

Lloyd began his assault against death, first blocking off "Dead Dog Curve" at both ends with homemade sawhorse detour signs to prevent access to chicken players. The strategem worked for two nights, until a glue-sniffing member of the First Street Flats crashed his 'fifty-one Chevy through the barricade, sideswiping a series of parked cars as he lost control, finally coming to a halt by rear-ending an L.A.P.D. black-and-white. Out on bail the next day, the driver went looking for the *puto* who had put up the sawhorse, smiling when Dogtown buddies told him it was a crazy fourteen-year-old kid called Dogman and Savior, a loco who was planning to flop in a sleeping bag by Dead Dog Curve to make sure that nobody played chicken on his turf.

That night fourteen-year-old Lloyd Hopkins, six foot one and a hundred and eighty pounds, began the series of *mano a mano* choose-off's that rendered the nicknames Dogman and Savior passé and earned him a new title: "Conquistador." The fights continued for ten nights straight, costing him a twice broken nose and a total of a hundred stitches, but ending chicken on Griffith Park and St. Elmo forever. When his nose was set for the second time and his swollen hands returned to their normal size, Lloyd quit the Dogtown Flats. He knew he was going to become a policeman, and it would not do to have a gang affiliation on his record.

The ringing of a telephone jerked him back to the present. He walked into the kitchen and picked it up. "Yes?"

"Hopkins, this is Linda."

"What?"

"Are you spaced out or something? Linda Wilhite."

Lloyd laughed. "Yeah, I am spaced out. How's tricks?"

"Not funny, Hopkins, but I'll let you slide because you're spaced. Listen, I *did* just trick with Stanley, and I very subtly pried some not too encouraging info out of him."

"Such as?"

"Such as you were misinformed somehow. Stan baby has never heard of Goff. I described the picture you showed me to him, and he doesn't know anyone resembling it. Ditto any left-handed man. Stan said he buys his stuff from a black guy who works solo. He *did* buy some stuff from a white guy, once, last year, but the guy charged too much. Sorry I couldn't be of more help."

"You were a lot of help. How did you get my phone number?"

Linda laughed. "You *are* spaced. From the phone book. Listen, will you let me know how this turns out?"

"Yes. And thanks, Linda."

"My pleasure. And by the way, if you feel like calling, you don't have to have a reason, though I'm sure you'll think one up."

"Are you telling me I'm devious?"

"No, just lonely and a bit guilt-ridden."

"And you?"

"Lonely and a bit curious. Bye, Hopkins."

"Good-bye, Linda."

15

AFTER a handshake and brief salutations, Linda Wilhite took her seat across from the Doctor and began to talk. When Havilland heard vague self-analysis fill the air, he clicked off his conscious listening power and shifted into an automatic overdrive that allowed him to juxtapose Linda's beauty against the single most important aspect of his life: *thinking one step ahead of Lloyd Hopkins*.

Since they were both geniuses, this kept the Night Tripper's mental engine pushed to its maximum horsepower, searching for loopholes and overlooked flaws in the logical progression of this game. With his physical concentration zeroed in on Linda, he thought of the game's one possible trouble spot: Jungle Jack Herzog.

Their relationship had been based on mutual respect—Herzog's genuine, the Doctor's feigned. The Alchemist was a classic psychiatric prototype—the seeker after truth who retreats into a cocoon of rationalization when confronted with harrowing *self*-truths. Thus the Doctor had played into his pathetic fantasy of using the stolen files to create an "L.A.P.D. credibility gap" that would by implication exonerate his friend Marty Bergen, while at the same time plumbing the basis of his attraction to a man whose cowardly actions he despised. The truth had finally become too strong, and Herzog had run to some unknown terminus of macho-driven shame. Goff had wiped his apartment shortly after he disappeared, and the odds against his leaving records or contacting Bergen or L.A.P.D. colleagues were astronomical—his shameful new self-knowledge would preclude it. Yet Hopkins had tied in Herzog to the late Thomas Goff, although he had *not* mentioned the missing files. *That* was potentially damaging, although Herzog had had no knowledge of his *hard* criminal activity. The most important part of the game was now to convince Hopkins that he was shielding someone close to Goff; that he was strangling on the horns of an ethical dilemma. He would play the role of every wimpy liberal man of conscience that policemen hated, and "Crazy Lloyd" would buy it—hook, line, and sinker.

The Night Tripper mentally decelerated, catching bits of psychobabble sloganeering as Linda's monologue wound down. Knowing that she would expect him to respond, he made brief mental notes to contact and placate his lonelies with excuses for his absence, then smiled and said, "I let you go on like that without interjecting questions because such thinking is living in the problem, not the solution. You've got to be able to exposit *facts*, gauge them for their basic truths and nuances, solicit my feedback, accept it or reject it, then move on the next *fact*. You've obviously read every lunatic and well-intentioned self-help book ever written, and it's mired you down with a great deal of *useless* food for thought. *Give me facts*."

Linda flushed, clenched her jaw and slammed the arms of her chair. "Facts," she said. "You want facts, then I'll give you facts. Fact: I'm lonely. Fact: I'm horny. Fact: I just met a very interesting man. Fact: I can tell that he's turned on to me. Fact: He's mooning for his estranged wife and will probably not hit on yours truly, as much as he'd like to. Fact: I'm pissed off about it."

Havilland smiled. The litany sounded like his fish swallowing a huge chunk of bait. "Tell me about the man. Facts, physical and otherwise, then your conclusions."

Linda smoothed the hem of her skirt and smiled back. "All right. He's about forty and very large, with intense gray eyes and dark brown hair, sort of unkempt. Ruddy complexion. His clothes are out of style. He's funny and arrogant and sarcastic. He's very smart, but there's nothing contrived or academic about it. He just *has* it. He's a *natural*."

At Linda's last words the Doctor felt his fish gobble the bait, then inexplicably start to chew through the line. When he spoke, his voice sounded disembodied, as if it had been filtered through an echo chamber. "He *has* it? He's a *natural*? Those aren't facts, Linda. Be more specific."

"Don't get angry," Linda said. "You wanted conclusions."

Havilland leaned back in his chair, feeling his own line snap with the realization that he had displayed anger. "I'm sorry I raised my voice," he said. "Sometimes nonspecific information makes me angry."

"Don't apologize, Doctor. You know human emotions better than I do."

"Yes. More facts then, please."

Linda stared at her clenched hands, then counted facts on her fingers. "He's a cop, he's proud to a fault, he's lonely. He—oh shit, he just has *it*."

Havilland felt barbed-wire hooks gouge his jugular, Linda's beauty the hook wielder. Her voice supplied a verbal gouging that honed the hooks to razor sharpness. "I just don't feel factual about this man, Doctor. It's weird meeting him so soon after entering therapy, and nothing will probably come of it, but my only facts are my *intuitions*. Doctor, are you all right?"

Havilland stared through Linda to a mental chessboard he had constructed to resurrect his professional cool. Kings, queens, and knights toppled; and in the wake of their fall he was able dredge up a smile and a calm voice. "I'm sorry, Linda. One of my little bouts of vertigo. I'm also sorry for impugning your intuitions. One thing struck me when you were describing this fellow, and that's that he sounds very much like your size forty-four sweater fantasy man. Has that occurred to you?"

Linda covered her mouth and laughed. "Maybe the Rolling Stones were wrong."

"What do you mean?"

"You're obviously not a rock fan," Linda said. "I was referring to an old Stones tune called 'You Can't Always Get What You Want.' Although they could be *right*, because if Lloyd-poo doesn't want to be had, then I'm sure that he will *not* be had. That's part of his charm."

Havilland made a steeple and brought it up to his face, framing Linda inside the triangle. "How has he affected your fantasy life?"

Linda gave the Doctor a rueful smile. "You don't miss much. Yes, this man is the basic forty-four sweater prototype; yes, he possesses that certain aura of violence I mentioned earlier; yes, I have cast him as the man who watches my gory home movies with me. I also like the fact that he's a cop. And you know why? Because he doesn't judge me for being a prostitute. Cops and hookers work the same street, so to speak."

Collapsing the steeple into his lap, the Doctor said, "For the record, Linda, you've made a great deal of progress in only three sessions. So much so that I'm considering a rather avant garde visual aid session a week or so down the line. Would you be up for that?"

"Sure. You're the doctor."

"Yes," Havilland said, "I am. And doctors have certain results that they must achieve. Mine involve confronting my counselee's most hideous secrets and fears, taking them through their green doors and beyond their beyonds. You know that your confrontations are going to be particularly painful, don't you, Linda?"

Linda stood up and adjusted the pleats in her skirt, then slung her handbag over her shoulder. "No pain, no gain. I'm tough, Doctor. I can handle all the truth you can hit me with. Friday at ten-thirty?"

Havilland got to his feet and took Linda's hand. "Yes. One thing before you go. What were your parents wearing at the time of their deaths?"

Linda held the doctor's hand while she pondered the question. Finally she said, "My father was wearing khaki pants, a plaid lumberjack shirt and a Dodger baseball cap. I remember the pictures the policemen showed me. The detectives were amazed that he could blow his brains out and still keep the cap on his head. My mother was doing part-time practical nursing then, and she was wearing a white nurse's uniform. Why?"

Havilland lowered her hand. "Symbolic therapy. Thank you for digging up such an unpleasant memory."

"No pain, no gain," Linda said as she waved good-bye.

Alone in his office with the scent of Linda's perfume, the Night Tripper wondered why validation of his most audacious move should cause such a bizarre reaction. He played back the session in his mind and got nothing but a static hiss that sounded like an air-raid siren about to screech its doom warning. Reflexively, he grabbed his desk phone and dialed one of his pawn's numbers, getting a recorded message: "Hi, lover, this is Sherry! I'm out right now, but if you want to party or just rap, talk to the machine. Bye!"

He put down the receiver, knowing immediately that he had made a mistake. Sherry Shroeder lived in the Valley. He had made a toll call that would appear on his phone bill. Havilland took a deep breath and closed his eyes, searching for a train of thought to provide a counteraction to the blunder. It arrived in the form of *facts*: the remaining Junior Miss Cosmetics files were boring. They were boring because they detailed unimaginative sleaze. Thus a higher class line of confidential dirt should be procured. The Avonoco Fiberglass Company had a class two security rating. The Alchemist had said, "If you cut a fart they've got a file on you. They hire lots of parolees and work furlough inmates as part of an L.A. County kickback scam." The L.A.P.D. file on their security chief had described him as a compulsive gambler with a history of psychiatric counseling. Choice meat for Thomas Goff. *Choicer* meat for a trained pshychiatrist.

The Night Tripper locked up his office and took the elevator down to the bank of payphones in the lobby. He was leafing through the Yellow Pages when the reason for his erratic behavior stunned him with its implications of cheap emotion: *he was jealous of Linda Wilhite's attraction to Lloyd Hopkins*.

16

LLOYD spent the morning at the West Hollywood Sheriff's Substation, reading over the report filed by the team of detectives who had searched Marty Bergen's apartment.

The report ran a total of eight pages, and contained both the officers' observations regarding the apartment's condition and a six page inventory of items found on the premises. There was no mention of the personnel files or any other official police document, and nothing that pointed to Jack Herzog or his murder/suicide/disappearance. What emerged was a clipped word portrait of an alcoholic ex-cop reaching the end of his tether.

On the ambiguous pretext of a "routine check," the detectives had learned from Bergen's landlady that she had not seen her tenant in over a week, and that in her opinion he was "holed up swacko in some motel on the Strip." The state of Bergen's apartment confirmed this appraisal. Empty scotch bottles were strewn across the floor, and there were no clothes or toilet articles to be found. All four rooms reeked of booze and waste, and a portable typewriter lay smashed to pieces on the kitchen floor.

The officers had followed the landlady's advice and had checked every motel and cocktail bar on the length of the Sunset Strip, showing Bergen's *Big Orange Insider* byline photo to every desk clerk and bartender they encountered. Many recognized Bergen as a frequent heavy binger, but none had seen him in over two weeks. Deciding to sit on the information before assigning L.A.P.D. detectives to search for the ex-cop/writer, Lloyd drove to West L.A. and his last remaining uncharted link to the whole twisted mess, wondering if his motives were entirely professional.

Linda Wilhite opened her door on the second knock, catching Lloyd in the act of straightening his necktie. Pointing him inside, she looked at her watch and said, "Noon. Fourteen hours after my call, and you're here in person. Got a good reason?"

Lloyd sat down on a floral patterned sofa. "I came to cop a plea," he said. "I haven't been entirely honest with you, and I—"

Linda silenced him by leaning over and adjusting the knot in his tie. "And you want something. Right?"

"Right."

"So tell me," Linda said, sitting down beside him.

Lloyd gave her an unrepentent stare. "Dr. John Havilland put me on to you, unconsciously. I saw those pictures of you in his outer office. Then he—"

Linda grabbed his arm. "What!"

"The framed photographs of you. Don't you know about that?"

Linda shook her head angrily, then sadly. "That poor, wonderful man. I told him about this arty-farty picture book I posed for, and he went out and bought it. How sad. I figured he was some sort of ascetic asexual, then this morning I told him about a man I'm attracted to, and he freaked out. I've never seen anyone so jealous."

"He blurted your name when I commented on the pictures," Lloyd said. "And he obviously takes them down before he sees you. Havilland counsels lots of criminal types. In the course of my investigation I blundered onto his name and decided to exploit his expertise in matters of the criminal psyche. As I suspected, he had his own underworld grapevine. He queried his source and came up with a man who, along with Thomas Goff, sold Stanley Rudolph some art objects. I snuck into Rudolph's pad and found your name in his phonebook. Even though Rudolph himself doesn't know Goff, this anonymous man *does*. The whole Rudolph connection was a weird bunch of information and *mis*information, which doesn't alter the fact that Havilland's source *knows Goff*."

Lloyd paused when he saw that Linda's face had become a mask of rage. Lowering his voice, he continued. "Havilland is legally protected by a shitload of statutes regarding professional privilege. He does not have to reveal the name of his source, and all my instincts tell me that no amount of coercion would move him to divulge the name of Goff's cohort."

Lloyd put his hand on Linda's shoulder. She cringed at his touch, then batted his hand away and hissed, "There are people who can't be coerced, Hopkins, and the doctor is one of them. He can't be coerced because unlike you, he has principles. There are also people who can't be manipulated, and even though I'm a whore, I'm one of them. Do you honestly think that I'd manipulate information out of a man who wants to help me and give it to a man who at best wants to fuck me? You want an addition to your epithet list, Sergeant? How about 'uncaring manipulative sleazebag'?"

Seeing red, Lloyd walked out of the apartment and down to the street and his unmarked cruiser. Ten minutes later he was sitting in Dr. John Havilland's outer office, staring at the photographs of Linda Wilhite and asking his seldom sought God not to let him do anything stupid.

The Doctor appeared just as the red throbbing behind Lloyd's eyes began to subside. He was ushering an elderly woman wearing a "Save the Whales" T-shirt out of his private office, cooing into her ear as she checked the contents of her purse. When he saw Lloyd, he said, "One moment, Sergeant," issued a final good-bye to his patient, then turned and laughed. "That very rich woman thinks that she can communicate telepathically with whales. What can I do for you? Have you made any progress in your investigation?"

Lloyd shook his head and spoke with a deliberate slowness. "No. Your source was somewhat inaccurate in his information. I questioned Stanley Rudolph. He has no knowledge, guilty or otherwise, of Thomas Goff. His primary source of stolen goods is a black man who works by himself. Rudolph bought goods from a *solo* white man only once, sometime last year. You said that your source met Goff at a singles bar. Did he tell you the name of it?"

Havilland sighed and sat down in an armchair across from Lloyd. "No, he didn't. To be frank, Sergeant, the young man has a drug problem, an addiction that sometimes involves blackouts. His memory isn't always completely trustworthy."

"Yet you believe that he knows Goff?"

"Yes."

"And you credit his statement that he has no knowledge of Goff's whereabouts and no knowledge regarding the liquor store homicides?"

Havilland hesitated, then said, "Yes."

Keeping his voice deliberately slow, Lloyd said, "No, you don't. You're shielding someone who knows something hot about Goff, and you're scared. You want to tell me what you know, but you don't want to compromise your ethics and jeopardize your patient's well being. I understand these things. But understand *me*, Doctor. You're my only shot. We're dealing with mass murder here, not petty neuroses. You have to tell me his name, and I think you know it."

"No," Havilland said. "That's absolute."

"Will you reconsider over a period of twenty-four hours? I'll have an attorney present when I question the man, and he won't know that you informed on him. I'll concoct a story that would satisfy a genius."

Havilland lowered his eyes. "God damn it, I said no!"

Lloyd felt his slow-motion strategy burst. He jammed his hands into his front pockets, closing them around open handcuff ratchets and a metal studded sap. Staring straight at the doctor, he squeezed the concealed weaponry so hard that the pain forced his words out in a wince. "You fuck with me and I'll hit you with an I.R.S. audit and more writs, petitions, subpoenas, and court orders than you thought existed. I'll initiate motions requesting the case files of every court-referred patient who ever crossed your door. I'll hire shyster lawyers out of my own pocket and keep them on retainer just to dream up ways to hassle you. I'll have bad-ass nigger vice cops keep your office under surveillance and scare the shit out of the rich neurotics you feed from. Twenty-four hours. You've got my number."

A red tide propelled Lloyd out of the office. When he took his hands from his pockets, he saw that they were bleeding.

Hook, line, and sinker.

Havilland walked into his private office and removed an array of bait from his wall safe. Ten thousand dollars in a brown paper bag and a newly typed psychiatric report accompanied by a snapshot. He placed the report in his top desk drawer, then looked at his watch. One-thirty. He had six hours until his next move. Leaning back in his chair, the Night Tripper closed his eyes and tried to will a dreamless sleep.

He succeeded and failed.

Sleep came, interspersed with semi-conscious moments that he knew to be his memory. As each image passed through him he felt like a surgical bonesaw was slicing his body in two, leaving him the choice of going with his symbolic past or of drifting into the cloud cover of anesthesia. Off to his left was sleep; off to his right was a blood-spattered corkboard equipped with arm and legholes, a rigor-mortised ankle encircled by a steel manacle, and the Bronx ferris wheel spinning off its axis. Full consciousness was a pinpoint of light between his eyes, an escape hatch that could trigger *full sleep* if concentrated upon in tandem with recitation of his mantra, *patria sanctorum*. Three roads inward: to wakefulness, to oblivion, to his childhood void. Feeling fearless, the Night Tripper succumbed to memory and let his right side disengage.

A huge magnifying glass descended on the void, serving up details: "McEvoy-D Block," etched on the manacle; gouged and cauterized arteries marking the ankle; father whispering in his ear as the ferris wheel reached its apex, suspending them above blocks of Puerto Rican tenements. Straining to read the lips of the people traversing below him, he caught long snatches of conversation and shock waves of laughter. Then his two sides fused.

Havilland awoke, refreshed, at six-forty-five. His yawn became a smile when the new void embellishments passed the credibility test by returning to his conscious mind. His smile widened when he realized that his one-on-one with Lloyd Hopkins was the catalyst that had supplied the fresh details. Thus fortified by sleep and memory, he picked up his bag of money, locked the office, and drove to Malibu and the acquisition of data.

The rendezvous point was a long stretch of parking blacktop overlooking the beach. Havilland left his car in the service area of a closed gas station on the land side of the Pacific Coast Highway and took the tunnel underpass across to the bank of lighted pay phones adjoining the spot where he was to meet the Avonoco Fiberglass security chief. He checked his watch and walked to the railing: 8:12 P.M., the last remnants of an amber sun turning the ocean pink. Savoring the moment, he watched the ball of fire meld into a pervasive light blue. When the blue died into a dark rush of waves, he walked to the phone booth nearest the railing and dialed the number of his actress pawn.

"Hello?"

Havilland grimaced; Sherry's salutation was slurred into three stoned syllables.

"Hello? Who's this? Is that you, Otto, you horny hound?"

Havilland's grimace relaxed. Though loaded, his pawn was lucid. "This is Lloyd, Sherry. How are you?"

"Hi, Lloyd!"

"Hi. Do you remember our deal?"

"Of course, baby. I got ripped off to the max on 'Steep Throat' and 'Nuclear Nookie.' I'm not letting this one get away."

Havilland turned around and stretched, catching a glimpse of a man hunched over the phone in the last booth at the end. Even though the caller was a good ten yards away, he turned back and lowered his voice to a whisper. "Good. We're shooting tomorrow night. Your co-star will pick you up. That's a little idea of mine. You know, let the stars get acquainted so that they can perform more realistically. He'll bring an outfit for you to wear. Is that your current address on your business card?"

"Yeah, that's my crib. And I'll get the rest of my money then?"

"Yes. Your co-star's name is Richard. He'll pick you up at nine. I'll see you on the set."

Sherry laughed. "Nine p.m. Tell Richard to be there or be square. Bye, Lloyd."

"Good-bye, Sherry."

Havilland hung up and stared through the Plexiglas booth enclosures, noting with relief that the caller was gone. He checked his watch again, then walked to the railing and over to the approximate middle of the parking strip. 8:24. Hopefully, Lieutenant Howard Christie would be punctual.

At precisely eight-thirty, slow footsteps echoed on the blacktop. The Doctor squinted and saw a man materialize out of the shadows and walk straight toward him. When he was ten feet away, a sudden burst of moonlight illuminated his features. It was the man in the phone booth. Shunting that knowledge aside, the Doctor walked forward with his hand extended, watching an archetypal cop come into focus.

He was a big crew-cutted man going to fat. He had a blunt face and cold eyes that measured the Doctor up, down, and sideways without revealing a hint of his appraisal. When they were face to face, he took the extended hand and said, "Doctor Havilland, I presume?"

The words rendered the Doctor mute and faint. He tried to jerk his hand free. It was futile; the force that grasped it was crushing it into numbness.

The force spoke: "Did you think you were dealing with amateurs? I've been a cop for twenty-two years, fourteen of them on the take. I know the ropes. I saw you park your car half an hour ago, and ran you through the D.M.V. The White Pages told me the rest. A psychiatrist. Very fucking unimpressive. Do you know how many shrinks I've gamed to get out of trouble in the Department? Did you think I'd let you pull this clandestine rendezvous horseshit anonymously? Did you think I believed that snow job you gave me on the phone? A book about secret information abuse? Really, Doctor, you insult my intelligence."

With a final squeeze, Howard Christie released the Doctor's hand, then put an arm around his shoulders and led him to the railing. Havilland concentrated on his mantra. He sat on the railing and forced an appropriately frightened laugh. When Christie laughed in return, he felt his newfound courage click in.

Christie took a deep breath of ocean air. "Don't look so scared, Doc. One thing my first shrink taught me: In all relationships, power bondings are established in the first five minutes. I had to establish the fact that *I* am the power broker, because *I* have what *you* want, and since we are dealing with class two security clearance stuff, this scam is felonious. Capice?"

"Yes," Havilland said. "I understand. But where are the files?" He ran his right foot nervously over the blacktop in wider and wider circles. A big rock caught his toe. He nudged it toward him and added, "Does anyone else know my name or that I contacted you?"

Christie shook his head. "I told you I knew the ropes. No one at Avonoco knows, and I just found out your name from a D.M.V. clerk who's already forgotten it. But listen: Where did you get *my* name?"

Lowering his head, Havilland saw a holstered revolver clipped to Christie's belt, half covered by his open sports jacket. "I—I—met an L.A.P.D. officer at a bar. He—he told me you had a gambling problem."

Christie slammed the railing with both palms. "Loud-mouthed motherfuckers. For your info, Doc, cops are just like crooks, you can't trust any of them. What was his name?"

"I—I—don't remember. Honestly."

"No problem. People who go to bars forget things fast, which is why they go to bars. I'm glad I'm not a drunk. Two addictions would be too fucking much. Let's cut the shit and get down to business. First off, don't tell me why you want the files—I don't want to know. Second, we're talking about a long process of photocopying them and moving them out a few at a time. If you want quick gratification, tough shit—discuss it with *your* shrink. Third, your offer of ten thou doesn't cut it. I owe a lot of money to some *very* bad dudes to owe money to. I want thirty K, no less. *Capice*?"

Havilland faked a coughing attack, leaning over with his head between his knees. When he felt Christie slap his back, he pretended to retch and braced his hands on the pavement, palming the rock, then shoving it into his right jacket pocket as he resumed a sitting position. Wiping his eyes, he inched closed to his adversary, seeing the gun butt fully exposed, Christie's badge attached to his belt next to it.

Christie slapped his back a last time. "Breathe deep, Doc. That good sea air will put hair on your chest. What do you think of my terms?"

Havilland took a deep breath and stuck his hand in his pocket, closing it around the rock. He calculated potential arcs and slid over to where his left shoulder and Christie's right shoulder were brushing. "Yes, it's a deal. You're holding all the aces."

Christie laughed. "No gambling metaphors, I'm trying to quit." He reached his arms up as if to embrace the sky, then brought them down in a huge yawn. "I'm tired," he said.

"Let's wrap this up for tonight. Here's what I'm thinking: Six payments of five K apiece, the files to be very cautiously siphoned out at my discretion. You'll have to trust me on that. I'm the dominant ego in this relationship, but I'll be benevolent about it. Look at it as a father-son type of gig. *Capice*?"

Dr. John Havilland gasped at the worst insult ever hurled at him. He recalled a quote from Christie's L.A.P.D. file: *Long history of overdependence upon supportive figures*. Thinking, *So be it,* the Doctor said, "What do you think *I* am, an amateur? Don't you think I know that compulsive gamblers have a need to counterbalance their self-destruction by asserting themselves in business relationships, an unconscious ploy to overrule their awful dependency on their closest loved ones, the ones who rule them and own them and give them the tit they suck on?"

Christie stood up and stammered, "W-w-why you little fuck," just as Havilland smashed the rock into his face. The cop teetered on the railing, grabbing it with one hand, wiping blood from his eyes with the other. Havilland reached for his waistband and pulled the gun free, then closed his eyes and aimed at where he thought Christie's face should be. He pulled the trigger twice, screaming along with the explosions, then opened his eyes and saw that Christie's face was not a face, but a charred blood basin oozing brain and skull fragments. He fired four more times, eyes open and not screaming, ripping Christie's badge from his belt just as his last shot sheared off his head and sent him pitching over the railing to the rocks thirty feet below. Drenched in blood and inundated by horror and memory, the Night Tripper ran.

17

AT ten o'clock, after nine straight hours of prowling singles bars and simple drinking bars for Thomas Goff and Marty Bergen, Lloyd gave up, surrendering himself to the idea of a trip to New York to prowl Goff's old haunts. The Department would pay for his ticket and per diem, and before he left he would consult an attorney on legal loopholes to exert against Dr. John Havilland. Defeat loomed like a stark black banner. Lloyd succumbed to the knowledge that there was no place to go but backward in time.

The old neighborhood greeted him with banners that mocked his cop exigencies. Parking at Sunset and Vendome, he sprinted up the cracked concrete steps to the highest point in Silverlake, hoping to find a reprise of old themes that would affirm the forty-two-year-old warrior persona he had paid so dearly to assume.

But the timeless L.A. haze blanketed, then shut down his would-be reverie. He could not see his parents' house a scant half mile away; whole vistas of landmarks were covered by a witch's brew of evaporating low clouds, industrial fumes and neon. Lloyd's affirmation became a rhapsody of high prices paid for dubious conquests.

In the 1965 Watts riot he had killed a fellow National Guardsman who had fired into a storefront church filled with innocent blacks partaking of coffee and prayer. No one had ever made him for the killing, and two months later he entered the Los Angeles Police Academy.

His career as a policeman was sustained brilliance, his concurrent role as husband and father a series of blundering attempts to instill his family with benign equivalents of his knowledge. When the force of his will elicited anger and hurt, he ran back to the job, and when the job swirled him into vortexes of boredom and terror and loathing, he found women who wanted to touch briefly what he was, offer their innocence as barter, and then get out before his hard line fervor destroyed their hard-earned and fatuous sense of life's amenities.

And then, last year, Teddy Verplanck merged into his path, turning his universe into chaos. When that symbiosis was completed, death and rebirth occurred simultaneously, and as his wounds healed, Lloyd became a hybrid warrior formed of his past and its validity and of accredited blood testimony as to where it would ultimately take him.

And his hard line fervor cracked and solidified, leaving him to tread air in the middle of a fissure.

Before he could consciously recall his vow of abstinence, Lloyd drove to Whilshire and Beverly Glen and the only destination that gave the softer part of his fissure credibility. Finding the door open, he walked into the entrance hall and cleared his throat to announce his presence. His answer was the shuffle of feet and an unexpected giggle.

"You're early," Linda called out.

Trying to track the voice, Lloyd said, "It's Hopkins, Linda."

Linda stepped out of a closet next to the dining room, dressed in a silk robe. "I know it is."

Lloyd walked forward to meet her. "Am I that predictable?"

Nodding her head both "yes" and "no," Linda said, "I don't know. Just don't apologize for this afternoon. I was as out of line as you. No pretexts this time?"

"No."

"Want to talk before or after?"

"After."

Linda smiled and tilted her head toward the bedroom, then let Lloyd step ahead of her and walk in. When his back was turned, she slipped off her robe and let it fall to the floor. Lloyd swiveled to face the soft sound, seeing Linda nude, framed in the doorway, backlighted by the glow of a hall lamp. Keeping the frame at arm's length, he undressed, wincing when his gunbelt hit the carpet. Linda giggled at the impact, then laughed outright when he leaned over and fumbled off his shoes and socks and snagged his zipper and nearly fell out of his pants. Whispering something that sounded like "beyond the beyond," she slid past him and lay down on the bed. Lloyd saw her take up a beckoning position, a single shaft of light fluttering across her abdomen. Using the light as a beacon, he came to her.

She talked while he held her and felt her and tasted her; little sighs about love and green doors. When his kisses became more persistent and then trailed down to her breasts, those sighs became the gasped word "Yes." Lost in the word's repetition, he let his lips move lower, until "yes" crescendoed into "Now, please, now!"

Lloyd obeyed, joining their two halves in a single abrupt motion, then pulling back to a sustaining movement as Linda coiled herself around him and pushed upward. He moved slowly; she with the unrestrained fervor of a graceful animal exploding with gracelessness, forming a point-counterpoint give and take that battered awareness of technique to death. Then he began to move with her fury, and the cop/whore entity pushed itself into a wordless, gasping trance.

Linda succumbed to reality first, twisting her head from the crook of Lloyd's collarbone. She traced his back with her palms and kissed his neck softly, until he pulled his head from the pillow and looked down on her, revealing a blank, tear-mottled face. All she could think of to say was, "Hopkins."

Lloyd rolled over and took her hand. When he remained silent, Linda said, "It's after. We were going to talk, remember?"

Twisting sideways to face her, Lloyd said, "What do you want to talk about?"

"Anything except what just happened. It was perfect; let's not mess with it."

Lloyd positioned himself so that his eyes and Linda's were only inches apart. "No earth-shaking postcoital revelations?"

Nodding her head so that their noses rubbed, Linda said, "Yes. I'm quitting the Life. I've got seventy grand tucked away, which should set me up in some kind of business enterprise. I'm quitting the shrink, too. If I quit hooking on my own I won't need him, and therapy is too expensive for a fledgling businesswoman."

"He'll be very sorry to see you go."

"I know. He's a very brilliant shrink, but I shouldn't associate with men who are obsessed with me. Having pictures of me on the wall is just too sad. Even though he takes them down for my visits, I still feel manipulated. Do you remember the pictures? Exactly how I was posed?"

"You weren't posed. They were candid type shots."

Linda's face clouded. "Really? That's strange. *All* the pictures in the book were posed."

Lloyd shrugged, then felt an overlooked connection hit him. "*Never* underestimate your power, even over hardnoses like Havilland. Listen, did you ever mention Stanley Rudolph to him?"

Linda said, "Yes, but not by name. All I mentioned was that he liked to take nude pictures of me. Why? I don't want to talk about *your* case or *my* clients."

"Neither do I. What do you want to talk about?"

"Tell me why you broke up with your wife."

"It's not a pretty story."

"It never is."

Lloyd turned over on his back, wanting to distance himself from Linda. He tried to find the appropriate words to begin his story, then realized that unless he looked her straight in the eye, his prelude would be self-serving lies. Twisting back around and locking into eye contact, he said, "It happened last year. I had been neglecting my family and cheating on my wife with various women for years before that, but last year was when it all exploded.

"I was working Robbery/Homicide, pretty much on the cases I pleased, when I got an anonymous phone call that led me to a murder victim. A young woman. I headed the investigation and dug up information that pointed to a mass murderer who was so fucking smart that no police agency in L.A. County connected any of his killings. At the time I went to my superiors with my information, he had killed at least sixteen women."

Linda raised a hand to her face and bit the knuckles. Lloyd said, "My superiors wouldn't authorize an investigation; it was too potentially embarassing to too many police departments. So I went after him myself. Janice left me about that time, taking the girls with her. There was just me and the killer. I found out who he was—a man named Teddy Verplanck. He made the media very big as the Hollywood Slaughterer. You probably heard about him. I went out to get him, but a woman I was seeing got in the way. He killed her. I went out to kill Verplanck. We shot each other up, and another officer, my best friend, killed him. That part of it never hit the media. Janice and the girls don't know exactly what happened, but they do know that I was shot, and that the whole episode almost cost me my career. Now I've got some nightmares to live with and a lot of innocent blood to atone for."

Linda astonished Lloyd by smiling. "I was expecting some tawdry little tale of other men and other women, not a gothic epic."

Baffled by the reaction, Lloyd said, "You almost sound titillated by it."

Linda kissed his lips softly. "My father shot my mother and then blew his brains out. I was ten. I'm no neophyte. Sometimes my thoughts are very dark. Let's go to sleep on a happy note, though. I want us to be together."

Lloyd got up and closed the bedroom door, shutting out all traces of light. "So do I," he said.

* * *

The morning began with a muffled cadence counting issuing from the living room. Lloyd put it off as Linda gyrating to a TV exercise program and went back to sleep, only to be awakened again minutes later by a firm bite on his neck. He opened his eyes and saw Linda squatting beside the bed in a black leotard. She was sweating and holding one hand behind her back. He leaned forward to kiss her, only to have her dart out of the way of his lips. "What size sweater do you wear?" she asked.

Lloyd sat up and rubbed his eyes. "No kiss? No offer of breakfast? No 'when will I see you again?'"

"Later. Answer my question."

"Size forty-six. Why?"

Linda muttered "shit," and handed Lloyd a Brooks Brothers box tied with a pink ribbon. He opened it and saw a carefully folded navy blue pullover sweater. Stroking its downy front, he whistled and said, "Cashmere. Did you buy this for me?"

Linda shook her head. "I'll tell you the story some day. It's a size too small, but please wear it."

Standing up, Lloyd grabbed Linda and consummated their morning kiss. "Thank you. I'll lose weight so it'll fit better."

"I wouldn't put it past you. What's the matter, Hopkins? You're scowling."

Lloyd broke the embrace. "Delayed reaction to joy. My already complicated life has just gotten much more complicated. I'm glad."

"It's mutual. What happens next?"

"I'm going to New York in a day or so. Thomas Goff comes from there. I'm going to cruise his old haunts and talk to people who knew him. It's my only remaining out. When I get back I'll call you."

"You'd better. Why don't you shower while I make some

coffee and toast? I've got my yoga class in an hour, but at least we can have breakfast together."

Lloyd showered, alternating hot and cold jets of water over his body, lost in the sound of the spray and the hum of music coming from the kitchen. After drying off and dressing, he walked into the kitchen and found Linda fiddling with the radio dial. "I hate to be a downer," she said, "but I just heard some bad news. An L.A. policeman was murdered in Malibu. I didn't get all the details, but—"

Lloyd grabbed the radio and flipped the tuner to an all-news station, catching static and the conclusion of a weather report. He sat down and looked at Linda, then put a finger to her lips and said, "They'll repeat the story. Cop killings are hot news."

The weatherman said, "Back to you, Bob," and a stern-voiced announcer took over: "More details on that Malibu killing. L.A. County Sheriff's detectives have just announced that the dead man found on the beach near Pacific Coast Highway and Temescal Canyon Road is a twenty-two-year L.A.P.D. veteran named Howard Christie, a lieutenant assigned to the Rampart Division. Christie's decapitated body was found early this morning by local surfers, who called the Malibu Sheriff's Substation to inform them of the grisly find. Captain Michael Seidman of the Malibu Station told reporters: 'This is a homicide, but as yet we do not know the cause of death and have no suspects. We have, however, determined that Lieutenant Christie was killed in the parking lot immediately above the spot on the beach where his body was found. We are now appealing to anyone who was in the vicinity of Pacific Coast Highway and Temescal Canyon Road last night or early this morning, people who might have seen or heard something suspicious. Please come forward. We need your assistance.' Further details on this story as it breaks. And now—"

Linda turned off the radio and stared at Lloyd. "Tell me, Hopkins."

"It's Goff," Lloyd said, with a death's-head grin. "I'm not going to New York. If you don't hear from me in forty-eight hours, send up a flare." He grabbed his sweater and ran out the door. Linda shuddered, imagining her new lover's departure as a race into hell.

Pacific Coast Highway and Temescal Canyon Road was a pandemonium of police vehicles with cherry lights flashing, TV minicam crews, mobs of reporters, and a large crowd of rubbernecks that spilled over from the parking blacktop, forcing southbound P.C.H. traffic into the middle lane.

Lloyd pulled up to the dirt shoulder on the land side of the highway and killed his siren, then pinned his badge to his jacket front and dodged cars over to a diagonal stretch of pavement sealed with a length of rope hung with "Official Crime Scene" warnings. The area behind the cordon was filled with plainclothes officers and technicians with evidence kits, and a long bank of pay phones was crowded with uniformed sheriff's deputies calling in information. At the rear of the scene a half dozen plainclothesmen squatted beside the wooden railing overlooking the cliffs and the ocean, spreading fingerprint powder on a cracked piece of timber.

"I'm surprised it took you this long."

Recognizing the voice, Lloyd pivoted and saw Captain Fred Gaffaney push his way through a knot of patrol deputies and plant himself in his path. The two men stared at each other until Gaffaney fingered his cross-and-flag tie bar and said, "This is one sensitive piece of work, and I forbid you to interfere. It's in the Sheriff's jurisdiction, with I.A.D. handling any connections to collateral cases."

Lloyd snorted, "Collateral cases? Captain, this is Thomas Goff all the way down the line!"

Gaffaney grabbed Lloyd's arm. Lloyd buckled, but let himself be led over to the shadow of an empty pay phone.

"Internal Affairs is moving on the other officers whose

files were stolen," the Captain said. "They're going to be interrogated and perhaps taken into protective custody, along with their families. Except for you. Let's put the past aside, Sergeant. Tell me what you've got so far, and if possible, I'll help you move on it."

Lloyd drummed his fingers on the side of the phone booth. "Marty Bergen has at the very least *seen* the stolen files. He's missing, but some columns that he left for advance publication indicate conclusively that Herzog passed the files to him. I think we should issue an A.P.B. on Bergen, and get a court order to seize everything at the *Big Orange Insider*."

Gaffaney whistled. "The media will crucify us for it."

"Fuck the media. I've also got a hearsay line on Goff, through a hotshot psychiatrist who has a patient who knows him. But the cocksucker is hiding behind professional privilege and won't kick loose with the name of his source."

"Have you considered talking to Nathan Steiner?"

Lloyd nodded. "Yeah. I'm going to run by his office today. What have *you* got? The radio report said Christie was decapitated, which sounds like possible forty-one stuff."

Gaffaney's hands played over his tie bar. "I've got an excellent reconstruction from a team of very savvy sheriff's dicks. The M.E.'s verdict won't be in for hours, but this is the way they see it:

"One—yes, it's a gunshot homicide. Christie was shot over by that broken piece of railing, and was blown down to the beach by the impact. I saw the body. It landed on some rocks up from the tide, so it stayed dry. I saw powder burns on his shirtfront, so the shots were obviously fired point-blank. Two—Christie *was* decapitated, but the biggest piece of his head the technicians have been able to find so far is a skull fragment about the size of a half dollar. You know why? He was almost certainly killed with his own gun. It wasn't found on his body or anywhere around here. His badge was stolen, too. I talked to one of the top dogs at Rampart, and he told me that Christie packed a three-fifty-seven Python on and off duty, and that he kept it loaded with teflon-tipped dum-dum's." Gaffaney reached into his pants pocket and handed Lloyd a copper-jacketed slug. "Feel the weight of that monster, Hopkins. I took it off of Christie's gunbelt while the medics weren't looking. The expended rounds and Christie's head are probably halfway to Catalina by now."

Lloyd gouged the slug's teflon head with his fingernail. "Shit. Those Sheriff's dicks are probably right; this is a much heavier load than a forty-one. What else? Anything from Avonoco? Christie's vehicle? Other vehicles? Witnesses? Blood tracks on the pavement?"

The Captain put a restraining hand on Lloyd's chest. "Slow down, you're making me nervous. There's nothing on any of that yet, except a trail of blood leading from the railing across the parking lot and through the underpass to the other side of P.C.H. The trail got fainter as it went along, which indicates that the killer himself wasn't wounded, he was just soaked with Christie's blood. The techs are doing their comparison tests now; we'll know for sure soon. What's *your* next move?"

"Pump Nate Steiner for some legal advice. Hassle the shrink. You?"

Captain Fred Gaffaney grinned. "Interrogate the other security chiefs, go over their records, rattle skeletons. The feds are at Avonoco now. Christie's security rating makes him a quasi-federal employee, so this is a collateral F.B.I. beef. Stay in touch, Hopkins. If you want transcripts of the I.A.D. interrogations, call Dutch Peltz."

Lloyd walked back to his car, oblivious to the ghouls lining P.C.H., drinking beer and standing on their tiptoes to get a glimpse of the drama. He had his hand on the door when the young man from the *Big Orange Insider* drove by and flipped him the finger.

Nathan Steiner was a Beverly Hills attorney who specialized in defending drug dealers. His forte was "obstructionist" tactics—filing writs and court orders, suits and countersuits, and motions requesting information on prospective jurors, potential witnesses, and courtroom functionaries; all strategies aimed at securing dismissals on the grounds of prejudiced testimony or "courtroom bias." These strategies often worked, but more often "Nate the Great" won his cases by outlasting judges and prosecutors and by harassing them into foolish blunders with his paperwork onslaughts. It was well known that many judges granted his minor petitioning requests automatically, in the hope that it would keep his clients *out* of their courtrooms and thus save them the pain of a protracted Steiner performance; it was *not* well known that "Nate the Great" felt deep guilt over the scores of dope vultures cut loose from jail as the result of his machinations and that despite his loud advocacy of civil liberties, he atoned for that guilt by advising L.A.P.D. officers on ways to circumvent laws regarding probable cause and search and seizure.

Thus, when Lloyd barged through his office door unannounced, he was ready to listen. Taking a seat uninvited, Lloyd outlined a hypothetical case involving a doctor's legal right not to divulge professionally secured information, stressing that *all* of the doctor's records would have to be seized, because at this point the name of the patient was unkown.

Concluding his case, Lloyd sat back and waited for an answer. When Steiner grunted and said, "Give me three or four days to look at some statutes and think about it," Lloyd got to his feet and smiled. Steiner asked him what the smile meant.

"It means that I'm an obstructionist, too," Lloyd said.

After stopping at a taco stand and wolfing a burrito plate, Lloyd drove home and changed clothes, outfitting himself in soiled khaki pants and shirt, work boots, and a baseball cap advertising Miller High Life. Satisfied with his workingman's garb and one-day stubble, he rummaged through his garage and came up with a set of burglar's tools he had scavenged from a Central Division evidence locker ten years before: battery-powered hand drill with cadmium steel bits; assorted hook-edged chisels, and a skinny-head crowbar and mallet. Packing them inside a tool kit, he drove to Century City and the commission of a Class B felony.

The reconnoitering took three hours.

Parking on a residential side street a half mile from Century City proper, Lloyd walked to Olympic and Century Park East and found a uniformed custodian sweeping the astroturf lawn in front of his target building. He explained to the man that he was here to help with a private wiring job for a firm situated on the skyscraper's twenty-sixth floor. Only one thing worried him. He needed an electrical hook-up with wall sockets big enough to accommodate his industrial-sized tools. Also, it would be nice to have a sink in which to scrape off rusted parts. The location didn't matter; he had plenty of cord. Was there a custodian's storeroom or something like that on the twenty-sixth floor?

The man had nodded with a befuddled look in his eyes, making Lloyd grateful for the fact that he seemed stupid. Finally he gave a last nod and said that yes, every floor had a custodial room, in the identical spot—the northest edge of the building. Would the custodian on that floor let him use it for his job? Lloyd asked.

The man's eyes clouded again. He was silent for several moments, then replied that the best thing to do was wait until the custodians went home at four, then ask the guard in the lobby for the key to the storeroom. That way, everything would be cool. Lloyd thanked the man and walked into he building.

He checked the northeast corners of the third, fifth, and eighth floors, finding identical doors marked "Maintenance." The doors themselves looked solid, but there was lots of wedge space at the lock. If no witnesses were around, it would be easy.

With two hours to kill before the custodial crew left work, Lloyd took service stairs down to ground level, then walked to a medical supply store on Pico and Beverly Drive and purchased a pair of surgical rubber gloves. Walking back slowly to Century City, all thoughts of the Goff/Herzog/Bergen/Christie labyrinth left his mind, replaced by an awareness of one of his earliest insights: crime was a thrill.

Stationed in the shade of a plastic tree on the astroturf lawn in front of his target, Lloyd saw a dozen men wearing maintenance uniforms exit the building at exactly 4:02. He waited for ten minutes, and when no others appeared, grabbed his toolbox and walked in, straight past the guard and over to the serivce stairs next to the elevators, donning his gloves the second he hit the privacy of the empty stairwell. Breathing deeply, he treaded slowly up twenty-six stories and pushed through a connecting doorway, finding himself directly across from Suite 2614.

The hallway was empty and silent. Lloyd got his bearings and assumed a casual gait as he walked past Dr. John Havilland's door. When he got to the maintenance room, he scanned the hallway one time, then took the crowbar from his tool kit and wedged it into the juncture of door and jamb. He leaned forward with all his weight, and the door snapped open.

The storeroom was six feet deep and packed with brooms, mops and industrial chemicals. Lloyd stepped inside and flicked on the light switch, then closed the door and loaded his hand drill with a two-inch bit. Squatting, he pressed the start switch and jammed the bit into the door two feet above floor level. Pushing the drill forward and rotating it clockwise simultaneously, he bored a hole that was inconspicuously small yet provided a solid amount of air. Hitting the kill switch, he sat down and tried to get comfortable. Seven o'clock was the earliest safe break-in time; until then, all he could do was wait.

Swallowed up by darkness, Lloyd listened to the sounds of departing office workers, checking their departures against the luminous dial of his wristwatch. There was a deluge at five, others at five-thirty and six. After that it was uninterrupted silence.

At seven, Lloyd got up and stretched, then opened the storeroom door halfway, reaccustoming his eyes to light. When all his senses readjusted, he picked up his tool kit and walked down the hall to Suite 2604.

The lock was a single unit steel wraparound, with the key slot inset in the doorknob. Lloyd tried his burglar's picks first, starting with the shortest and working up, getting inside the keyhole but jamming short of the activator button. This left the options of drilling or jimmying. Lloyd gauged the odds of individual suites in a security building having individual alarms and decided that the odds were in his favor. He got out his skinny-head crowbar and pried the door open.

Darkness and silence greeted him.

Lloyd shut the door quietly, brushing slivers of cracked wood off the doorjamb and onto the outer office carpet. He fumbled for the wall switch, found it, and lit up the waiting room. Linda Wilhite beamed down from the walls. Lloyd blew her a kiss, then tried the door to Havilland's private office. It was unlocked. He flicked off the waiting room light and took a penlight from his pocket, letting its tiny beam serve as his directional finder. Whispering, "Let's go real slow, let's be real cool," he walked inside.

Playing his light over the walls, Lloyd caught flashes of highly varnished oak, framed diplomas, and the Edward Hopper painting he had seen on his initial visit. Arcing his light at waist level, he circuited the entire room, picking up bookcases filled with leather-bound medical texts, straight-backed chairs facing each other, and Havilland's ornate oak desk. *No filing cabinets.*

Thinking, *safe,* Lloyd felt along with walls, stopping to read the diplomas before reaching behind them. Harvard Medical School; St. Vincent's and Castleford Hospitals. East Coast money all the way, but nothing except wood paneling in back of them.

Lloyd slid back the Hopper painting and hit pay dirt, then slammed the wall when he saw that the safe was an Armbruster "Ultimate," triple lead-lined and impregnable. It was the shrink's desk or nothing.

Lloyd moved to the desk, holding the penlight with his teeth and getting out his burglar's picks. He grabbed the top drawer to hold it steady for the insertion, then nearly fell backward when it slid open in his hand.

The drawer was stuffed with pens, blank paper, and paper clips and a bottom layer of manila folders. Lloyd pulled them out and scanned the index tabs stuck to their upper right hand corners. Typed last names, first names, and middle initials. *Patients.*

There were five folders, all of them filled with loose pages. Seeing that the first three bore women's names, Lloyd put them aside and read through the fourth, learning that William A. Waterston III had difficulty relating to women because of his relationship with his domineering grandmother, and that he and Havilland had been exploring the problem twice a week for six years, at the rate of one hundred and ten dollars per hour. Lloyd scrutinized the photograph that accompanied the psychiatric rundown. Waterston did not sound or look like the type of man who would know Thomas Goff; he looked like an aristocratic nerd who needed to get laid.

Lloyd checked the index tab on the last file, seeing that a string of aliases forced the typist to move from the tab onto the front of the folder: Oldfield, Richard; a.k.a. Richard Brown; a.k.a. Richard Green; a.k.a. Richard Goff.

The last alias went through Lloyd like a convulsion. He opened the folder. A color snapshot was attached to the first page; a head and shoulders shot of a man who resembled Thomas Goff to a degree that fell just short of twinhood. Lloyd read through the entire fourteen pages of the file, shuddering when the facts of the resemblance were made clear.

Richard Oldfield was Thomas Goff's illegitimate half-brother, the result of a union between Goff's mother and a wealthy upstate New York textile manufacturer. He had entered therapy with Dr. John Havilland four years before, his love/hate relationship with his half-brother his "salient neurosis." Thomas Goff was a brilliant criminal; Richard Oldfield a stockbroker-remittance man living largely on stipends shamed and coerced out of his father by Goff's alcoholic mother, who had raised the two boys together. After wading through long paragraphs of psychiatric ruminations, Lloyd felt the blood theme emerge: Richard Oldfield's desire to emulate Thomas Goff had driven him to undertake a sporadic criminal career, burglarizing homes known to contain art objects, acting on information from stock exchange acquaintances. *Hence the Stanley Rudolph connection*, obscured by Havilland's cowardly manipulations: he wanted to surrender *the Goff connection* to police scrutiny, without divulging the name of his patient. Richard Oldfield's occasional usage of his half brother's name was what Havilland termed "cross-purpose identification—the desire to assume a person's identity and act out both loved and hated aspects of their personalities, thereby restoring order to their own psyches, resolving the love-hatred ambivalance into an acceptable norm."

Reading the file a second time, paying close attention to the most recently dated additions, Lloyd learned that Oldfield's surrender to the Goff psyche was becoming more pronounced, assuming "pathological dimensions." Goff hated women and prowled bars looking for ones to abuse; Oldfield paid prostitutes to let him beat them. Goff hated policemen and spoke often of his desire to kill them; Oldfield now aped his half brother's broadsides. The last file entry was dated 2/27/84, slightly over two months earlier, and stated that "Richard Oldfield was assuming the proportions of the classic paranoid/schizophrenic criminal type."

Lloyd put the folder down, wondering if Oldfield had discontinued therapy in February or if Havilland had more data on him elsewhere. He rummaged through the other drawers until he found a metal Rolodex file. Oldfield's address and phone number were right there under the O's—4109 Windemere, Hollywood, 90036; 464-7892.

Lloyd sat still for a full minute, fuming at the fact that his illegal entry would destroy the possibility of ever hanging an accessory rap on Havilland. Then he thought of Richard Oldfield and went calm beneath his rage. Putting the files back in their proper place, and sorting the ramifications of the B & E, he picked up the tool kit and made for the door, thinking: Don't let Havilland know that his secrets have been plundered; don't give him reason to warn Oldfield, who might warn Goff. *Cover your tracks.*

Lloyd looked at the splintered doorjamb and calculated more odds, then got out his crowbar and padded over to the door of the adjoining suite. Thinking, *just do it,* he pried the door open.

Only the sound of cracking wood assailed him. He hit the next door and the door after that, then heard the blare of an alarm cut through the echoes of his destruction.

The noise grew, then leveled off to a piercing drone. Lloyd grabbed his tool kit and ran toward the maintenance storeroom, checking the elevator bank as he passed it. The flashing numbers on top said that armed help was on the sixth floor and ascending rapidly.

Lloyd opened the storeroom door, then let it close halfway. He paced off three yards to the service stairs across the hallway and closed the door behind him, leaving himself just enough of a crack to peer through. Seconds later he heard the elevator door open, followed by the sounds of running footsteps and strained breathing drawing nearer. When he saw a single uniformed guard draw his gun and step cautiously inside the storeroom, he nudged his door open and hurled himself across the hallway, pushing the storeroom door shut. There was a panicked "What the fuck!" from the guard trapped inside, and then six shots tore through the door and ricocheted down the hallway.

Lloyd stepped inside the service stairs, picked up his toolbox and hurtled down twenty-six stories to ground level. Chest heaving and soaked with sweat, he pushed the connecting door into the lobby open. No one. He walked out the door and across the astroturf lawn to Century Park East, restraining himself by assuming a nothing-to-hide gait. He was safely inside his unmarked cruiser when he heard the wail of sirens converge on the scene of his crime. With shaking hands, he drove to the Hollywood Hills.

Windemere Drive was a residential side street in the shadow of the Hollywood Bowl. One-story tudor cottages dominated the 4100 block, and the sidewalk was free of tree and shrub overhang. It was a good surveillance spot.

Lloyd parked at the corner and circled the block on foot. No yellow Toyota. Coming back around, he flashed his penlight at the numbers stenciled on the curb. 4109 was two doors down from where he had left his car, on the opposite side of the street. He checked his watch. At 8:42 the stucco and wood tudor house was pitch dark.

He walked back to his unmarked Matador and grabbed the Ithaca pump stashed under the driver's seat. After jacking a shell into the chamber, he walked over to 4109 and rang the doorbell.

No answer and no light coming from inside. Lloyd pressed his face to the front picture window. Heavy curtains blocked his vision. Hugging close to the walls, he padded across the porch and around the driveway to the back yard. No car; thick drapes covering all the windows. The opposite side of the house was shielded from foot access by an overgrown hedge connected to the house next door. Lloyd craned his neck to get a quick look, glimpsing more darkened windows. Sounds from brightly lit neighboring dwellings underlined 4109's lack of habitation. He walked back to his car to wait.

Slouching low in the driver's seat, Lloyd waited, keeping a sustained eyeball fix on 4109. It was almost an hour later that a white Mercedes pulled to the curb in front of the house. A man too tall to be Thomas Goff and a woman in a white nurse's uniform got out and moved into a side-by-side lovers' drape. The woman squealed as the man nuzzled her neck. Together they walked up the steps and into the house. A light glowed behind the heavy curtains as the door was shut.

Lloyd stared at the curtains and thought of the woman. If she was a prostitute, Oldfield would probably pay her to stand his abuse. But that didn't click; her uniform and affectionate manner spelled girlfriend or pick-up. Keeping his impatience at bay by concentrating on the need not to risk the woman's safety, Lloyd settled in to wait out the night.

18

LAUGHING voices and a burst of light cut across the Night Tripper's field of vision, casting a rainbow haze over his infrared image of Lloyd Hopkins slouching in the front seat of his car. He put down the magnification lens he was holding to his eye and smiled. "Hello, Sherry. Hello, Richard," he said.

Sherry giggled. "Hi, Lloyd." Her uniform was a size too small and looked like it would split down the middle should she attempt anything more strenuous than walking in a straight line. She sniffed back a wad of mucous and giggled again. Havilland smiled. Coked to the gills.

He sized up his leading man.

Oldfield stood with his back up against the bolted door, in a posture that reminded the Doctor of a staunch medieval warrior trying to keep demons at bay, never guessing that they resided inside him. Last night Havilland had called him to his Malibu grouping retreat and had primed him for his performance by whispering death poems in his ear while he scrubbed Howard Christie's blood from the seats of his Volvo. The recitation had had a calming effect on them both; and now Richard Oldfield was a quiet nuclear warhead.

Sherry laughed and undid the top button of her uniform blouse. Oldfield walked to the middle of the living room and said, "Ready when you are, C.B."

Sherry giggled at the remark; Havilland could hear traces of stage fright. He walked to Oldfield and threw an arm around his shoulder. "Hold on just a minute, will you, Sherry? I want to talk to your co-star alone."

Sherry nodded and kicked off her shoes. The Doctor led

Oldfield back to the bedroom and swept an arm toward its new furnishings. "Isn't it wonderful, Richard? One of your co-counselees helped me set it up while you were asleep out at the retreat."

Oldfield darted his eyes over white velvet curtains shuttering the windows; his mattress removed from the bedstead and centered on the middle of the floor, covered with light blue silk sheets; a movie camera on a tripod with its gaze zeroing downward. He dry swallowed and whispered, "Please take me as far as I can go."

Havilland embraced him, letting his lips touch his ear. "Yes. You helped *me* last night, Richard. I was afraid. You took me through that fear, just as I have taken you through your fears. Just one reminder. When she abuses you, think of all the abuse that governess made you take as a child. Keep your fuel intake at optimum, right up until the moment. Now wait here."

The Doctor walked back into the living room. Sherry Shroeder was sitting on the couch, her uniform top completely unbuttoned. "I didn't know whether or not to strip," she said.

Sitting down beside her, Havilland said, "Not yet. Button up your outfit while I give you directions." He put a hand on her knee as she fumbled at her top. "What we are filming is a variation on the corny old nurse routine. You know, nurses are supposed to be very experienced, because they know so much about bodies."

Sherry laughed. Havilland noticed that her nervousness had subsided. Squeezing her knee gently, he said, "This variation is the nurse spanking the boy, who of course is Richard—really a man—and then getting so aroused that she has to seduce him. What I want you to do is pull down Richard's pants and spank him *hard,* very *hard,* then do the most seductive striptease you are capable of. After that I'll give both of you more specific instructions. Do you understand?"

Sherry waggled her eyebrows. "I used to play tennis

when I was a little girl. I've got a great backhand." She laughed and covered her mouth. "Richard's got a really sharp bod. Where's the camera guy?"

"Well . . ." Havilland said, "to be frank, I can't afford one, so I'm filling in. You and Richard came too high, so to cut costs, I'm standing in behind the camera myself. I—"

Sherry poked a teasing finger in the Doctor's ribs. "Come on, Lloyd. As Gary Gilmore said, 'Let's do it.'"

They walked into the bedroom. Oldfield was sprawled on his back across the mattress, fully clothed. Havilland got behind the camera, adjusting the tripod and swiveling the lens until the mattress was captured in a wide-angle shot. Clearing his throat, he said, "Since this is a silent movie, please feel free to talk—but *quietly*. I don't want to upset the neighbors." He turned the camera on and listened to the whir of film. "Sherry, you know what to do. Richard, follow Sherry's lead, but position your face on the *near* side of the mattress, so I can get some close shots. Okay, action!"

Sherry sat down on the edge of the mattress, facing the camera. She extended her legs in front of her, resting her heels on the floor. Patting her lap, she said, "Come on, you bad boy."

Oldfield obeyed, getting to his feet and loosening his belt, then lying down across Sherry's legs, positioning his buttocks just above her knees. "Bad, bad boy," she said as she pulled down his pants and undershorts. "Bad, bad boy."

Havilland zoomed in for a close-up reaction shot just as Sherry's first slap hit naked flesh. Oldfield grimaced. "Harder, Sherry," the Doctor said.

Sherry redoubled her efforts, grunting "Bad, bad boy," each time her palm made contact. Oldfield's lens-framed eyes contracted with the blows. Havilland hissed, "Harder, Sherry, harder. Remember your tennis stroke."

"Bad bad bad bad boy!" Sherry brought her hand down full force. Oldfield's eyes glazed over and dry spittle formed at the corners of his mouth. Havilland took his eye from the camera and saw that raised red dots were forming on his buttocks. "Bad bad bad bad bad boy!"

"Cut!"

The Doctor's own shout startled him. "Cut," he repeated softly. "That's a print. Richard, go wait in the hall. Sherry, step off the mattress and do your striptease."

The actors obeyed, Oldfield drawing himself to his feet and cinching his pants without meeting Sherry's eyes; Sherry kneading her flushed right hand. When Richard was outside the bedroom, Havilland said, "Be your sexiest," and swung the camera up. "Now," he said.

Sherry Shroeder began to undress, plucking at the buttons on her uniform. She took off her blouse and dropped it on the floor, then snagged the zipper at the back of her skirt. Jerking it loose, she muttered, "Shit," then caught herself and pouted at the camera, stepping out of the skirt and twirling it on a finger above her head. Letting it drop, she unhooked her bra and pulled down her stockings and panties. Nude, she did a pelvis grinding dancestep that caused her breasts to shake in opposite directions. Covered with goosebumps, she silently mouthed song lyrics and tried to pout at the same time. Zooming in for a close-up, the Doctor thought that he could detect the words to "Green Door."

"Cut!"

Again the Doctor's own voice jolted him. "Lie down, Sherry," he said. "Richard, you can come in now."

Oldfield reentered the bedroom, naked, holding his hands over his genitals. Havilland pointed to the bed, then shut off the camera and checked the expended film cylinder. Film to burn. He framed a long shot of the mattress and the two performers on it, then locked in the tripod and said, "I'm a little shy, so I'll let you pros do what comes naturally. I'll come back and check on you in a few minutes."

Sherry laughed and Oldfield flinched. Havilland flipped the automatic forward switch and walked out to the dining room. Poking his infrared lens through a crack in the curtains, he saw his *best* actor perform.

Lloyd Hopkins, stuffed fat with bait, was still sitting inside his car, still staring daggers at the house. The allusions to illegal searches in his personnel file had been accurate—he was not above committing crime to solve crimes. He was a hypocritical snake, *and* a cowardly one—undoubtedly afraid of approaching his suspect for fear of jeopardizing the fair damsel in the bedroom. Havilland watched him yawn, scratch, and stretch without ever taking his eyes from the tudor cottage. Each tiny move was like a laser beam piercing the childhood void.

Checking his watch, the Doctor saw that ten minutes had passed. He walked to the bedroom. Sherry and Richard were lying on opposite sides of the mattress. He turned the camera off and stared at his performers. Sherry was positioned on one elbow, an arm across her breasts. Richard lay rock still, eyes closed, twitching.

"We did it soft," Sherry said. "I think we faked it pretty good. Richard couldn't, you know, but I think it still looked okay. If you want we can try again and shoot some hard shots."

Havilland walked to the bedroom closet and ran his hand over a ledge at the back, coming away with a thick roll of adhesive bandage. "No, that does it, except for some clothed shots I want to get. You can get dressed now."

"*Really*?"

"Really. I'll give you the rest of your money in a minute."

Richard's eyes twitched open at the phrase. He got to his feet and stretched, then pulled on his pants and shirt and took the tape from the Doctor's hand. "Thank you for helping me go beyond my beyond," he said.

Havilland looked into his eyes and saw frozen rage. He focused the camera at Sherry and hit the on switch. Sherry finished buttoning her blouse and said, "Lloyd, can we make this quick? There's a party in the Valley at eleven-thirty, and since this was quicker than I thought, I'd like to make it."

Havilland nodded assent and telescoped the lens so that Sherry's face was held in an extreme close-up. "Now, Richard," he said.

The viewfinder went black as Richard Oldfield hurled himself beyond his beyond. A high-pitched shriek died into a struggle for breath; crashing bodies caused a blank wall to sway before the camera's eye. The Night Tripper tried to refocus, then gave up. Richard pinned Sherry to the floor with his knees, one hand holding her head, the other swirling tape up from her mouth to her nose. When both passages were shut air tight, he stood up and watched her face turn red, then blue and her arms and legs flail. Soon her entire body became a collective gasp; her torso pushing off the floor in an adrenaline-fueled death throe.

Oldfield fell to his knees and pummeled the flailing body, throwing right-left combinations at the groin and ribcage until all resistance ended in a last shudder of asphyxiation. Now weeping, he stood up on wobbly legs and saw the Doctor with the camera strapped to his shoulder, bending down, pulling the bandage off of Sherry Shroeder's face.

"Now, Richard. Now, Richard. Now, Richard."

The Night Tripper was holding out a silencer-fitted revolver. Richard took it in his hand, then looked down, seeing the dead woman's face covered with a transparent plastic pillow.

"Now, Richard. Now, Richard. Now, Richard."

The camera zoomed in and whirred; Oldfield pressed the barrel to the pillow and pulled the trigger. There was a dull plop, then the hiss of escaping air, then a spread of crimson as the deflated plastic filled with blood.

"Yes, Richard. Yes, Richard. Yes, Richard."

The Night Tripper steadied the camera, pushing the eyepiece out of his way. He took the gun from Richard's hand and flipped the cylinder open, letting the spent round fall to the floor. The Bronx ferris wheel became a whirling corkboard. He took two fresh rounds from his pocket and placed them in adjoining chambers, then flicked the cylinder shut and spun it.

Richard Oldfield stood slack-jawed, swaying to self-contained music. The Night Tripper took a Dodger baseball cap and Howard Christie's badge from his jacket, placing the cap on Richard's head, pinning the badge to his left breast pocket. He placed the camera back on the tripod, then filmed close-ups of the badge, the cap and Richard's face. Thinking of Linda Wilhite and toppling chess pieces, he picked the gun up off the floor and placed it in Richard's right hand. Getting back behind the camera, he said, "Do you feel complete now, Richard?"

"Yes," Richard said.

"Articulate how you feel."

"I feel as if I've conquered my past, that I've broken through all my green doors with the promise of peace as my reward."

"Will you go one step further for me? It will help a beautiful woman to resolve her nightmares."

"Yes. Name it."

"Stick the gun in your mouth and pull the trigger twice."

Richard obeyed without question. The hammer clicked on empty chambers. The Night Tripper captured his finest moment on film, then ran to the dining room curtains and looked out with his blood-colored lens. Lloyd Hopkins was asleep, his head cradled into the half-open car window.

19

LLOYD awoke at dawn, startled out of a dreamless sleep by a sharp cramp in his leg. Rubbing his calf, he looked out of the car window and saw the tudor cottage and the white Mercedes parked in the same spot as the night before. Oldfield's shackup was still in progress. He had time to go home and call for reinforcements to aid him in a continued surveillance and possible approach.

Lloyd swung his Matador around and pulled up behind the Mercedes. He wrote down the license number, then called R. & I. on his two way radio and read it off, requesting a complete readout on both vehicle and owner. After three minutes of static crackle, the operator came back on the air with her information. FHM 363—No wants; no warrants. Registered to Richard Brian Oldfield, 4109 Windemere, L.A. 90036. No wants; no warrants; no criminal record. Discouraged and exhausted despite his hours of sleep, Lloyd drove home, thinking of a shave, a shower, and lots of coffee.

A three-day accumulation of newspapers greeted him on his front porch. The previous day's *L.A. Times* bore a banner headline: "Policeman Murdered in Malibu." A sidebar added, "Execution Style Death for L.A.P.D. Lieutenant." Lloyd kicked the papers aside and unlocked the door, seeing the stapled together notebook pages on the floor immediately. Picking them up, he read:

> Memo to: Lloyd
> From: Dutch.
> *Read now.*
>
> L.—Where have you been? Shacking? I thought you turned over a new leaf. I'm your liaison, and we were

supposed to be in daily contact, remember? This info is straight from Gaffaney. I'll save the good stuff for last.

*A.P.B. issued on Marty Bergen—no response as yet.

*Seizure order for *Big Orange Insider* granted, yield—zilch. Punk kid editor had contents of M.B.'s desk destroyed after your last visit. Is threatening "police brutality" suit.

*Intensive questioning of P.C.H./Temescal Cyn. area residents—zilch.

*Phone-in info. on Christie—so far crank bullshit. (No eyewitnesses have come forth.)

*Blood on pavement—conclusively Christie's.

*Additional skull fragment and flattened slug found on beach (.357 teflon tipped). This, + coroners report—"Death caused by massive neurological destruction inflicted by gunshots fired at point-blank range," indicate that Christie was killed with his own gun.

*Sacramento D.M.V. night info. operator (she saw account of Christie's death in papers) called in, said that Christie called at 8:30 or so on the night of the murder, requesting D.M.V. make on car license. She gave info., but cannot remember the name of the person she gave him, or the lic. #, or the make of the car. Interesting, because the M.E. fixed the time of H.C.'s death at around the time of the call.

*On afternoon of his death, Christie was seen around classified file section at Avonoco. He told secretary he was meeting a "heavy hitter" at the beach that night. When secretary asked why, he clammed up. She said he seemed agitated and elated.

*Re: I.A.D. interviews—Rolando, clean. Kaiser, Tucker, Murray, in protective custody, appear to be clean.

****! Important—while I.A.D. officers were checking out offices of Junior Miss Cosmetics, security guard freaked out and tried to run. He was apprehended and taken into custody (Pos. of marijuana.) Gaffaney is convinced he has guilty knowledge. This man (Hubert Douglas, M.N., age 39) yelped for you (said you were "cool"

when you busted him for G.T.A. years ago). *Will talk only to you.* Come to P.C. *immediately.* (Gaffaney's orders) before Douglas makes bail or wangles a writ.
***Call me—D.P.

Lloyd didn't bother to shave or shower or change clothes. Still wearing his B & E outfit, he drove straight to a liquor store. As he recalled, Hubert Douglas was a bonded sourmash fiend. A pint of Jack Daniel's seemed like the ticket to soothe his soul and loosen his tongue. After purchasing the bottle, he raced downtown to Parker Center.

Hubert Douglas was being held in an interrogation cubicle adjoining Fred Gaffaney's office. Lloyd looked through the one-way glass and saw him sitting across a table from the captain, dressed in security guard's uniform replete with gold epaulets and a Sam Browne belt. A loudspeaker about the window crackled with his story of Come-San-Chin, the Chinese cocksucker. Gaffaney listened with his head bowed, fingering his cross-and-flag tie bar.

Lloyd walked in the door just as Douglas delivered his punch line and doubled over with laughter, slapping the table and exclaiming, "Dig it! Dig it!" Seeing Lloyd, he said, "Hopkins, my man!" and got up and extended his hand. Lloyd took it and said, "Hello, Hubert. My colleagues treating you okay?"

Douglas nodded toward Gaffaney, who looked up and glared at Lloyd. "This joker keeps asking me questions. I keep tellin' him I'll talk to you, and he keeps tellin' me you out of touch, the heavy implication bein' that you out pourin' the pork somewhere. I know my rights. I been in custody almost twenty-four hours. You gots to arraign me within twenty-four hours or cut me loose."

Lloyd looked at Gaffaney, then back at Douglas. "Wrong, Hubert. This is Saturday. We can legally hold you until Monday morning. Have a seat. I'll be back to talk to you after I have a few words with the captain."

Gaffaney got up and followed Lloyd outside. Measuring him with disdainful eyes, he said, "You need a shave and your clothes are filthy. Where have you been?"

"Out pulling burglaries," Lloyd said. "What's with Hubert?"

Gaffaney pushed the cubicle door shut. "I was at Junior Miss Cosmetics, along with an aide. We were talking to Dan Murray in his office. We had just gotten word that Christie was checking out the classified file section at Avonoco several hours before he was shot. Since my instincts regarding Murray's behavior told me he was clean, I mentioned it. Douglas was washing windows in the next room. My aide thought he looked hinky and cop-wise, so he kept an eye on him. He bolted when the conversation turned to files. My aide caught him with a big bag of weed in his pocket. He *knows* something, Hopkins. Get it out of him."

Lloyd let his mental wheels spin. "Captain, have you thrown the name Thomas Goff at that D.M.V. operator who called in about Christie?"

"Yes. I talked to her myself. She said that Goff was *not* the name she dug up for Christie. I also gave her the license number and a description of Goff's vehicle. Negative on that too. What do you—"

Lloyd hushed the captain with a hand on his shoulder. "Has Douglas seen the mug shots of Goff?"

"No."

"Then get me a copy of them now, and run me a complete all-police computer check on this name—Richard Brian Oldfield, white male, about thirty. Four-one-oh-nine Windermere, Hollywood. White Mercedes, FHM-three-six-three. He's clean on wants and warrants, but I need all the details I can get."

Gaffaney nodded, then said, "What are you fishing for?"

"I'll tell you after I've spoken to Douglas. Will you get me those mug shots now?"

The Captain walked into his office, flushing from his neck

all the way up to his crewcut. Returning to Lloyd and handing him the mug-shot strip, he hissed, "Don't make Douglas any promises of leniency."

Lloyd gave his superior officer a guileless smile. "No, sir." When Gaffaney walked back to his office, he entered the cubicle and flipped off the loudspeaker. "Let's make a deal," he said to Hubert Douglas, placing the pint of Jack Daniel's on the table between them. "Tell me what I want to know, and you walk. Fuck me around, and I hotfoot it up to Narco Division and glom a pound of reefer to add to the bag the I.A.D. bulls took off you, making it a felony possession bust. What'll it be?"

Douglas grabbed the bottle and downed half of it in one gulp. "Do I look stupid, Hopkins?"

"No, you look intelligent and handsome and full of *savoir-faire*. Let's accomplish this with a minumum of bullshit and jive. The I.A.D. bulls think that you have some guilty knowledge regarding the classified files at Junior Miss. Let's take it from there."

Douglas coughed and breathed bourbon in Lloyd's face. "But what if that there guilty knowledge involves coppin' to some illegal shit I pulled?"

"You still walk."

"No shit, Dick Tracy?"

"If I'm lyin', I'm flyin'. Talk, Hubert."

Douglas knocked back a drink and wiped his lips. " 'Bout three weeks ago I was drinkin' in a juke joint down the street from Junior Miss. This paddy dude starts a conversation with me, asks me if I like workin' security at Junior Miss, what my duties was, how tight I was in with the security boss, that kind of rebop. He buys me drinks up the ying yang, gets me righteously lubed, then splits. I ain't no dummy, I knows this dude and I ain't seen the last of each other."

Douglas paused and grabbed the bottle. Lloyd snatched it out of his hand before he could bring it to his lips. Placing the mugshot strip on the table, he said, "Is this the man?"

Douglas stared at the photos and grinned from ear to ear. "Righteous. That's the dude. What kind of shit did he pull?"

"Never mind. Finish your story."

Casting sad eyes at the pint, Douglas said, "I was right. The dude shows up the very next day, and offers to get me coked. We toot some righteous pharmaceutical blow in the john, then he starts talkin' about this righteous smart fuckin' buddy of his, how the guy was fuckin' obsessed with fuckin' *data*, you know, obsessed with knowin' the fuckin' skinny on other peoples lives. You dig?"

"I dig," Lloyd said. "Did he tell you the man's name? Did he describe him? Did he say that the man was his half-brother?"

Douglas shook his head. "The fucker didn't even tell me his own fuckin' name, let alone the name of his fuckin' buddy. But dig, that day he makes his pitch: one K and two grams of pharmacy blow for Xerox copies of all the classified files. I tell him it's gonna take time, I gotta make them copies a couple at a time, on the sly. So I does it, without Murray or anyone else at Junior Miss knowin' about it. The dude calls me at the bar to set the tr—"

Lloyd interrupted: "Did he give you an address or a phone number where he could be reached?"

"Fuck, no! He kept callin' himself a 'justified paranoid' and said that he covered his tracks when he took a fuckin' piss, just to stay in fuckin' practice. He wouldn't even call me at my fuckin' crib; it had to be the fuckin' bar. Anyways, we sets up the trade-off, last week sometime, Tuesday or Wednesday night, and man, it was righteously fuckin' strange. Kick loose with that jug, will you, homeboy? I'm thirsty."

Lloyd slid the bottle across the table. "Tell me about the trade-off. Take it slow and be very specific."

Douglas guzzled half of the remaining whiskey. "Righteous. Anyway, I been observin' the dude, and to my mind he seems like he ain't wound together too tight. You know, this seems to be a dude that you might wanta call seriously nervous and itchy. We sets up the meet for Nichols Canyon Park, at night. The dude shows up in his little yellow car, lookin' sweaty, shaky and bug-eyed, lookin' like a righteous fuckin' rabid dog lookin' to die, but lookin' to get in a few righteous fuckin' bites before he goes. He kept grabbin' at himself like he was packin' a roscoe and he kept baitin' me with all this racist shit. Hopkins, this fucker looked like righteous fuckin' *death*. I gave him the files and he gave me the K and the blow and I got the fuck out fast. I don't know what the fucker done, but I wouldn't worry too much about catchin' him, because no fuckin' human bein' can look like that and fuckin' survive. I been to Nam, Hopkins. Righteous fuckin' Khe Sahn. I seen lots of death. This fucker looked worse than the terminal yellow jaundice battle fatigue walkin' dead over there. He was righteous fuckin' death on a popsicle stick."

Lloyd let the barrage of words settle in on him, knowing that they confirmed Thomas Goff's Melbourne Avenue horror show, and *possibly* the killing of Howard Christie; but that they somehow contradicted the revelation of Richard Oldfield and his sibling rivalry with Goff. He said, "Kill the jug, Hubert, you've earned it," and walked out into the hallway. A secretary passed him and said, "Captain Gaffaney went to lunch, Sergeant. He left your query reply with the duty officer."

Lloyd thanked the woman and nonchalantly walked into Gaffaney's office. A plastic bag of marijuana tagged with an official evidence sticker was lying on his desk. He pulled off the sticker and put it in his pocket, then opened the window and hurled the bag out into the middle of Los Angeles Street, where it came to rest in the bed of a passing Dodge pickup.

"Support your local police," Lloyd called out. When only traffic noise answered him, he walked by the interrogation cubicle and gave Hubert Douglas the thumbs up sign. Douglas grinned through the open doorway and raised his empty pint in farewell.

Lloyd took the elevator down to the first floor and walked to the front information desk. The duty officer did a double-take on his outfit and handed him a slip of paper. He leaned against the desk and read: Subject D.O.B. 6/30/53, L.A. Calif. driv. lic. # 1679143, issued 7/69, no moving violations; no wants, warrants or record in Cont. U.S. *squeaky clean*-F.G.

Lloyd felt nameless little clicks assail him. He put his mind through a twenty-four hour instant replay until he hit the source of his confusion: Thomas Goff was born and raised and sent to prison in New York State. Havilland's psychiatric report on his half-brother Richard Oldfield stated that their mother raised the two boys together, presumably in New York. Yet this computer run-through fixed Oldfield's place of birth as Los Angeles. Also, Oldfield was issued a California driver's license in 1969, shortly after his sixteenth birthday, which at least *hinted* at long-term California residency.

Lloyd grabbed the desk phone and dialed Dutch's office number at the Hollywood Station.

"Captain Peltz speaking."

"It's me, Dutch. You busy?"

"Where the hell have you been? Did you get my memo?"

"Yeah, I got it. Listen, I need your help. Two-man stakeout on a pad near the Hollywood Bowl. It's got to be very cool, no unmarked units, nothing that smacks of heat. I don't want to approach this guy just yet; I only want him pinned."

"*This guy*? Who the hell is *this guy*?"

"I'll tell you about him when I see you. Can you meet me at my place in an hour? I want to change clothes and grab my civilian wheels."

Dutch sighed. "I've got a meeting in half an hour. Make it two hours."

Lloyd sighed back. "Deal."

Driving home, his little clicks worked themselves into the tapestry of the case, assuming the shape of a man who might or might not be Richard Oldfield; a man adept at manipulating *violent men* in order to achieve his purpose, which now emerged as the accruing of potential blackmail knowledge. Fact: Jack Herzog had stolen six L.A.P.D. Personnel files for his *personal* aim of "vindicating" Marty Bergen, and had told his girlfriend that he was "really scared" in the days before his disappearance/murder/suicide. Bergen considered his best friend's attempt at vindication ridiculous and had destroyed the columns the files had inspired. Yet, Thomas Goff and/or his still unknown "hotshot," "really smart" accomplice/partner, had used the L.A.P.D. information to cunningly circumvent Captain Dan Murray, wresting confidential file copies from his stooge Hubert Douglas, *killing* Lieutenant Howard Christie, probably for his refusal to deliver the files or on the basis of his demands for exorbitant amounts of money. This evidential and theoretical narrative line was cohesive and arrow straight.

But it contradicted most of his instincts regarding Thomas Goff. Goff was obsessed with his .41 revolver. He had used it on the three liquor store victims, a crime *still lacking a motive*; he had fired it at Lloyd himself, its single-action clumsiness giving him away. *Yet* . . . Howard Christie was killed with his own gun. Goff, assuming he was the killer, had eschewed a violent pattern in a time of stress, grabbing a weapon from a seasoned police officer, then shooting him with it. *It didn't wash*. The Christie job had the earmarks of a killing perpetrated by a novice, someone who had lulled the cop/security chief into considering him harmless—not the fever- or dope-driven Goff.

This left four potential suspects—Herzog, Havilland, Bergen, and Oldfield. The first three were ridiculous prospects: Herzog was a ninty-nine percent sure dead man; Havilland a love- and conscience-struck coincidental link with no motives; Bergen a pathetic, guilt-ridden drunk. Only Oldfield remained, and even he was shot full of logical holes.

His blood relationship with Goff was, of course, the key tie-in. Still, hearsay evidence indicated that Goff was dominated by his unknown partner, while Havilland's psychological workup portrayed Oldfield as being subservient to Goff. And the fact that he strongly resembled Goff and still walked around the streets pointed to his innocence. If he were Goff's accomplice, he would know that every cop in Southern California was looking for his mirror image. He would not go out and cruise for comely nurses to bring back to his pad.

Lloyd hit the Harbor Freeway southbound, feeling his clicks work into truth. He was dealing with two killers, two men whose drives had spawned an apocalypse.

20

THE chess game progressed. The lonelies had been tapped for data purchasing capital, and tonight, with his cop/adversary dead, he would inject himself with sodium Pentothal and images of his past hours and make the void explode. The homecoming was in sight.

The Night Tripper stood on his balcony and stared at the ocean, then closed his eyes and let the sound of waves crashing accompany a rush of fresh images: Hopkins departing Windemere Drive at dawn; the industrial-sized trashbag containing Sherry Shroeder thumping against Richard Oldfield's shoulder as he carried it to his car; the sated look on Richard's face as they lowered her to her grave in the shadow of the Hollywood sign. Satisfying moments, but not as fulfilling as watching his lonely Billy develop and then edit his movie into a co-mingling of Linda Wilhite's childhood trauma and adult fantasy. Billy had at first warmed to the challenge of a rush job, then had become frightened when Sherry Shroeder died in his developing room. It had taken a brilliantly adlibbed therapy session to see him through completion of the assignment.

Opening his eyes, Havilland recalled the day's *minor* testimonials to his will: The manager of his office building had called his condo with the news that he had been burglarized and that workmen were now repairing the damage to his front office door; his answering service had an urgent "call me" message from Linda Wilhite. Those telephone tidings had been such obvious capitulations to his power that he had succumbed to their symbolism and had used the beach phone to call the lonelies with an "assessment" request—ten thousand dollars per person. They had all answered "Yes" with doglike servility.

Let the capitulations continue.

The Night Tripper walked over to the kitchen wall phone and punched Linda Wilhite's number. When he heard her "Hello?", he said, "John Havilland, Linda. My service said that you needed to speak to me."

Linda's voice took on force. "Doctor, I realize that this is short notice, but I want to let you know that I'm quitting therapy. You've opened me up to lots of things, but I want to fly solo from here on in."

Havilland breathed the words in. When he breathed his own words out, they sounded appropriately choked with sentiment. "I'm very sad to hear that, Linda. We were making such progress. Are you sure you want to do this?"

"I'm positive, Doctor."

"I see. Would you agree to one more session? A special session with visual aids? It's my standard procedure for final sessions, and it's essential to my form of therapy."

'Doctor, my days are very tied up. There's lots of—"

"Would tonight be all right? My office at seven? It's imperative we conclude this therapy on the right foot, and the session will be free."

Sighing, Linda said, "All right, but I'll pay."

Havilland said, "Good-bye," and hung up, then punched another seven digits and bègan hyperventilating.

"Yes?" Hopkins's voice was expectant.

"Sergeant, this is John Havilland. Strange things have been happening. My office was broken into, and besides that, my source just contacted me. I—I—I—"

"Calm down, Doctor. Just take it slow."

"I—I was going to say that I still can't give you his name, but Goff contacted *him*, because he heard that he was in need of a gun and some money Goff owed him. The money and the gun are in a locker box at the Greyhound Bus Depot downtown. Fr-frankly, Sergeant, my source is afraid of a setup. He's considering returning to therapy, so I was able to get this information out of him. He-he has a strange relationship with Goff. . . . It's fr-fraternal almost."

"Did he give you the number of the box?"

"Yes. Four-one-six. The key is supposed to be with the man at the candy counter directly across from the row of lockers. Goff gave it to him yesterday, my man told me."

"You did the right thing, Doctor. I'll take care of it."

Dr. John Havilland replaced the receiver, thinking of Richard Oldfield stationed in the bar across from Box 416, armed with Lloyd Hopkins' personnel file photo and an Uzi submachine gun.

21

LLOYD was leadfooting it northbound on the Harbor Freeway when he realized that he had forgotten to leave Dutch a note explaining his absence. He slammed the dashboard with his palm and began shouting obscenities, then heard his cursing drowned out by the wail of sirens. Looking in his rearview mirror he saw three black-and-whites roar past with cherry lights flashing, heading for the downtown exits. Wondering why, he flipped on his two-way radio. When a squelch filtered voice barked "All units, all units, code three to the bus depot, Sixth and Los Angeles, shot fired," he shuddered back a wave of nausea and joined the fray.

Sixth and Los Angeles Streets was a solid wall of double-parked patrol cars. Lloyd parked on the sidewalk outside the bus terminal's south entrance and ran in past a bewildered-looking group of patrolmen carrying shotguns. They were jabbering among themselves, and one tall young officer kept repeating "Psycho. Fucking psycho," as he fondled the slide of his Ithaca pump. Pushing through a knot of unkempt civilians milling around in front of the ticket counters, Lloyd saw a uniformed sergeant writing in a spiral notebook. He tapped him on the shoulder and said, "Hopkins, Robbery/Homicide. What have we got?"

The sergeant grinned. "We got a machinegun nut case. A wino was checking the doors of the lockers across the walkway from the gin mill by the Sixth Street entrance when this psycho runs out of the bar and starts shooting. The wino wasn't hit, but the lockers were torn up and an old bag lady got grazed by a ricochet. The meat wagon took her to Central

Receiving. The juicehounds inside the bar said it sounded like a tommy gun—rat-tat-tat-tat-tat-tat-tat-tat. My partner is at the gin mill now, taking statements from the wino and potential witnesses. Rat-tat-tat-tat-tat-tat-tat-tat."

Lloyd felt little clicks resound to the beat of the sergeant's sound effects. "Is there a candy counter directly across from the shooting scene?"

"Yessir."

"What about the suspect?"

"Probably long gone. The wino said he tucked the burpgun under his coat and ran out to Sixth. Easy to get lost out there."

Lloyd nodded and ran to the hallway by the Sixth Street entrance. Gray metal lockers with coin slots and tiny key holes covered one entire wall, the opposite wall inset with narrow cubicles where vendors dispensed souvenirs, candy and porno magazines. Checking the lockers close up, he saw that numbers 408 through 430 were riddled with bullet dents, and as he had suspected, the bar the gunman had run out of was directly across from 416.

Crossing to the bar, Lloyd eyeballed the man at the candy counter, catching a cop-wise look on his face. Doing a quick pivot, he walked over and stuck out his hand. "Police officer. I believe someone left a key for me."

The candy man went pale and stammered, "I—I—didn't think there'd be no gunplay, Officer. The guy just asked me if I wanted to make twenty scoots for holding on to the key, then whipping it on the guy who asked for it. I didn't want no part of no shooting."

The fury of his mental clicking made Lloyd whisper. "Are you telling me that the man who gave you the key is the man who fired off the machinegun?"

"Th-that's right. This don't make me no kind of accessory after the fact, does it?"

Lloyd took out a well-thumbed mugshot of Thomas Goff. "Is this the man?"

The candy man shook his head affirmatively and then negatively. "Yes and no. This guy looks enough like him to be his brother, but the gun guy had a skinnier face and a longer nose. It's a real close resemblance, but I gotta say no."

Taking the key from the vendor's shaking hands, Lloyd said with a shaking voice, "Describe the wino the gunman fired at."

"That's easy, officer. He was a big husky guy, ruddy complexion, dark hair. He looked kinda like you."

The final click went off like a flashing neon sign that spelled, "Fool. Patsy. Dupe. Sucker bait." *It was Havilland.* The setup was for *him*, not Oldfield; it was perpetrated by *Oldfield,* not Goff. Whatever the unrevealed intricacies of the case, Havilland had set him up from the beginning, acting on knowledge of his methods gathered from his L.A.P.D. file. The shrink had set up the psychiatric report on Oldfield as a calculated move based on old Hollywood Division fitness reports that had mentioned his penchant for "search methods of dubious legality." He had been strung out from before their first meeting; the Night Tripper albums and the Linda Wilhite office photos ploys, with Linda and Stanley Rudolph and Goff and Oldfield and Herzog and how many others dangling on their own puppet strings as the Doctor's willing or unwitting accomplices? The simple brilliance of it was overpowering. He had pinioned himself to a steel wall with self-constructed steel spikes.

Before the spikes could draw more blood, Lloyd walked to Box 416 and inserted the key. The door jammed briefly, then came open. Inside was a .357 Colt Python and a roll of twenty dollar bills held together with a rubber band. He picked the gun up. The cylinder was empty, but the barrel exuded a faint odor of paraffin and the underside of the vent housing bore a plastic sticker reading Christie–L.A.P.D.

The spikes dug in again, wielded from within and without. Lloyd slammed the locker door shut and drove to Parker Center.

* * *

He found the sixth floor I.A.D. offices packed with detectives and civilian personnel. A uniformed officer passed him in the hallway and threw words of explanation: "My partner and I just brought in Marty Bergen, grabbed him in MacArthur Park, feeding the ducks. He waived his rights. Some Internal Affairs bulls are getting ready to pump him."

Lloyd ran to the attorney room at the end of the hall. A knot of plainclothes officers were staring through the one-way glass. Squeezing in beside them, he saw Marty Bergen, Fred Gaffaney, a stenographer, and an unidentified woman who had the air of a deputy public defender sitting around a table covered with pencils and yellow legal pads. The woman was whispering in Bergen's ear, while the stenographer poised fingers over his machine. Gaffaney worried his tie bar and drummed the tabletop.

Noticing wires running along the ceiling wainscoting, Lloyd nudged the officer nearest him and said, "Is there a backup transcription going down?"

The officer nodded. "Tape hookup to the skipper's office. He's got another steno at his desk."

"Headphones?"

"Speaker."

Lloyd took out his notepad and wrote, John Havilland, M.D., office 1710 Century Park East—*All phone #'s from business & residence calls for past 12 mos.*, then walked down the hall and rapped on the glass door of Fred Gaffaney's outer office. When his secretary opened it and gave him a harried look, he handed her the notepad. "The captain wants me to listen in on the interview. Could you do me a favor and call Ma Bell and get this information?"

The woman frowned. "The captain told me not to leave the office. Some marijuana that constituted evidence was stolen earlier. He had to release a suspect, and he was very angry about it."

Lloyd smiled. "That's a rough break, but this request is direct from Thad Braverton. I'll hold down the fort."

The woman's frown deepened. "All right. But please keep all unauthorized people out." She closed her hand around the notepad and walked off in the direction of the elevator bank. Lloyd locked the door from the inside and moved to the captain's private office. A grandmotherly stenographer was sitting at the desk, pecking at her machine while Gaffaney's sternly enunciated words issued from a wall speaker above her head.

" . . . and legal counsel is present. Before we begin this interview, Mr. Bergen, do you have anything you wish to say?"

Lloyd pulled up a chair and smiled at the stenographer, who put a finger to her lips and pointed to the speaker just as a burst of electronically amplified laughter hit the room, followed by Marty Bergen's voice. "Yeah. I wish to go on the record as saying that your tie clasp sucks. If the L.A.P.D. were a just bureaucracy, you would be indicted on five counts of aesthetic bankruptcy, possession of fascist regalia, and general low class. Proceed with your interview, Captain."

Gaffaney cleared his throat. "Thank you for that unsolicited comment, Mr. Bergen. Proceeding, I will state some specific facts. You may formally object if you consider my facts erroneous. One, you are Martin D. Bergen, age forty-four. You were dismissed from the Los Angeles Police Department after sixteen years of service. While on the Department, you became friends with Officer Jacob M. Herzog, currently missing. Are these facts correct?"

"Yes," Bergen said.

"Good. Again proceeding, six days ago you were questioned by an L.A.P.D. detective as to the current whereabouts of Officer Herzog. You told the officer that you had not seen Herzog in approximately a month, and that on the occasions of your last meetings Herzog had been 'moody.' Is that correct?"

"Yes."

"Again proceeding, do you wish to alter your statement to that officer in any way?"

Bergen's voice was a cold whisper. "Yes, I do. Jack Herzog is dead. He killed himself with an overdose of barbiturates. I discovered his body at his apartment along with a suicide note. I buried him in a rock quarry up near San Berdoo."

Lloyd heard Bergen's attorney gasp and begin jabbering words of caution at her client. Bergen shouted, "No goddamn it, I want to tell it!" There was a crescendo of voices, with Gaffaney's finally predominating: "Do you remember where you buried the body?"

"Yes," Bergen said. "I'll take you there, if you like."

The speaker went silent, then slowly came to life with the sound of animated whispers. Finally Gaffaney said, "Not wanting to put words in your mouth, Mr. Bergen, would you say that the previous statement you made to the police regarding Officer Herzog was misleading or incorrect?"

"What I told Hopkins was pure bullshit," Bergen said. "When I talked to him Jack was already three weeks in his grave. You see, I thought I could walk from all this. Then it started eating at me. I went on a drunk to sort it out. If those cops hadn't found me I would have come forward before too long. This has got to be heavy shit that Jack was involved in, or you wouldn't have put out an A.P.B. on me. I figure that you've got me for two misdemeanors—some jive charge for disposing of Jack's body and receiving stolen documents. So just ask your questions or let me make my statement, so I can get charged and make bail. Okay, Fred baby?"

There was another long silence, this one broken by Fred Gaffaney. "Talk, Bergen. I'll interject questions if I find them necessary."

Breath noise filled the speaker. Lloyd's body clenched in anticipation. Just when he thought he would snap from tension, Bergen said, "Jack was always stretched very thin, because he didn't have the outlets that other cops have. He didn't booze or carouse or chase pussy; he just read and brooded and competed with himself, wanting to be like these warrior mystics he worshipped. He got on mental kicks and ran wild with them. For about six months prior to his death he was obsessed with this notion of exonerating me by creating this L.A.P.D. credibility gap—showing the Department in a bad light so that the shame of my dismissal would be diminished by comparison. He talked it up and talked it up and talked it up, because he was a hero, and since he loved me he had to turn me from a coward into a hero to make our friendship real.

"About this time he met some guy in a bar. The guy introduced him to another guy, a guy that Jack called a 'file-happy genius.' This guy was some kind of guru who charged big bucks to all these sad guru-worshipper types, helping them with their problems and so forth. He convinced Jack to steal some personnel files that would suit their individual purposes—Jack's 'credibility gap' and the guru's loony hunger for confidential information. Jack showed me the files. Four of them were brass working outside security gigs where more personnel files were involved, one was Johnny Rolando, the TV guy, and the other was, you know, Lloyd Hopkins. Jack figured that the information in these files would comprise a sleazy picture of the L.A.P.D. *and* satisfy the guru's needs."

"Do you still have the files?" Gaffaney asked.

"No," Bergen said. "I read them and gave them back to Jack. I tried to put the information to use in a series of columns, as a memorial tribute to him, but finally I decided that it was just a tribute to his disturbance and gave up on the idea."

"Tell me more about this so-called guru and his friend."

"All right. First off, I don't know either of their names, but I do know that the guru was counseling Jack, helping to bring him through some things that were disturbing him. The guru used ambiguous phrases like 'beyond the beyond' and 'behind the green door,' which is an old song title. Both those phrases were included in Jack's suicide note."

Lloyd grabbed the telephone and dialed a number that he knew was a ninety-nine percent sure bet to confirm Havilland's complicity all the way down the line.

"Hello?"

Turning his back on the stenographer, he whispered, "It's me, Linda."

"Hopkins baby!"

"Listen, I can't talk, but the other night you whispered 'beyond the beyond' and something about green doors. Where did you get those phrases?"

"From Dr. Havilland. Why? You sound really spaced, Hopkins. What's all this about?"

"I'll tell you later."

"When?"

"I'll come by in a couple of hours. Stay home and wait for me. Okay?"

Linda's voice went grave. "Yes. It's him, isn't it?"

Lloyd said "Yes," and hung up, catching Bergen in mid-sentence. ". . . so from the froth around Jack's mouth I knew he'd o.d.'d on barbiturates. He used to say that if he ever took the Night Train, he'd never do it with his gun."

Gaffaney sighed. "Sergeant Hopkins searched Herzog's apartment and said that the surface had been wiped free of prints by scouring powder. When you discovered the body, did you notice any wipe marks?"

"No. None."

"Do you recall the exact words of Herzog's suicide note, in addition to those phrases you mentioned? Did Herzog elaborate on his reasons for killing himself?"

"This is where we part company, Fred baby," Bergen said. "I'll tell you anything you want to know, except that. And you haven't got the juice to get it out of me."

The sound of palms slamming a table top rattled the speaker. "On that note we'll break for a few hours. We've prepared a detention cage for you, Mr. Bergen. Your attorney can keep you company if she wishes to. We'll pick up where we left off later. Sergeant, show Mr. Bergen to his interim housing."

The speaker went dead. Lloyd got up and walked to the outer office window, catching a glimpse of a plainclothes officer hustling Marty Bergen and his attorney to the stairs leading to the fifth floor detention cages. Bergen's post-confession posture signified pure exhaustion: stooped shoulders; glazed eyes; shuffling walk. Lloyd saluted his back as he rounded the corner out of sight, then turned to see Gaffaney's secretary tapping on the door, holding up a sheaf of papers for him.

"I got your information, Sergeant."

Lloyd opened the door and took the woman's pages. "Let me explain this readout," she said. "The supervisor got me the business and residence calls up to two days ago; that's as far up-to-date as their computer is fed. When you go through it you'll notice that only a few of the numbers have names or addresses after them. That's because virtually all of this person's calls were made to pay phones. Isn't that strange? The locations of the pay phones are listed next to the number. Is this what you wanted?"

Lloyd felt another soft click. "This is excellent. Will you do me one other favor? Call the *top* managing supervisor at Bell and have her try to get me the numbers called from both phones in the past two days. Have her call me at Robbery/Homicide with the information. Tell her it's crucial to an important murder investigation. Will you do that for me?"

"Yes, Sergeant. Are you going to talk with the captain? I know that he's interested in what you're doing."

Lloyd shook his head. "No. If he needs me, I'll be in my office. I'm not going to bother him with this phone business until I have something conclusive. He has enough to worry about."

Gaffaney's secretary lowered her eyes. "Yes. He works much too hard."

Lloyd jogged up to his office, wondering if the born-again witch hunter cheated on his wife. Closing the door, he read over the list of phone numbers dialed from Havilland's office and Beverly Hills apartment, feeling his clicks collide with Hubert Douglas' snatch of Thomas Goff dialogue: "He kept callin' himself a 'justified paranoid' and said that he covered his tracks when he took a fuckin' piss, just to stay in fuckin' practice."

The pay phone calling translated to *Havilland's* "justified paranoia." The majority of the calls were made to phone booths situated within a quarter mile radius of the homes of Jack Herzog, Thomas Goff, and Richard Oldfield. The calls to Herzog began last November, which coincided with Marty Bergen's statement that Herzog met "the guru" six months ago; they ended in late March, around the time of Herzog's suicide. The Goff calls ran from the beginning of the readout until the day after the liquor store slaughter; the Oldfield communications all the way through until the readout terminated forty-eight hours before.

Turning his attention to the other pay phone locations, Lloyd got out his Thomas Brothers L.A. County street map binder, hoping that his theory meshed with Bergen's statement about the "guru" charging "big bucks" to "these sad guru-worshipper types." Phone readout to map index to map; five locations, five confirmations. Click. Click. Click. Click. Click. All five pay phones were located in shopping centers in expensive residential neighborhoods—Laurel Canyon, Sherman Oaks, Palos Verdes Estates, San Marino, and the Bunker Hill Towers complex. Conclusion: Not counting other potential "worshipper types" living *inside* his non-toll-call area of Century City and Beverly Hills, Dr. John Havilland had at least five people, perhaps innocent, perhaps violently disturbed, that he was "counseling." Unanswered question: Citing Havilland's "justified paranoia" structure, it was obvious that he wanted to be heavily buffered against *any* kind of scrutiny. *Then were did he meet with his patients?*

Lloyd recalled the diplomas on Havilland's office wall: Harvard Medical School; two hospitals from the metropolitan New York area. Click. Click. Click. Thomas Goff was New York born and bred. Could his association with the Doctor date back to his days as a psychiatric resident? All the clues lay in the past, cloaked in medical secrecy. Lloyd imagined himself as a guru-worshipper type about to write a book, armed with nothing but good intentions and a telephone. Five minutes later that telephone became a time machine hurtling toward Dr. John Havilland's past.

The book ploy worked. Years before he became dedicated to secrecy, John Havilland had possessed an autobiographical bent, one that was captured for posterity in the form of a Harvard Medical School entrance essay that his faculty advisor called "the very model of both excellence in English skills and the exposition of sound motives for becoming a psychiatrist."

From the gushing advisor's recollections of Havilland and his essay, Lloyd learned that the guru shrink was born in Scarsdale, New York in 1945, and that when he was twelve his father disappeared, never to be seen again, leaving young John and his mother lavishly well provided for. After weeks of speculating on his father's absence, John sustained a head injury that left him with fragmented memories and fantasies of the man who had sired him, a patchwork quilt of truth and illusion that his alcoholic mother could not illuminate in any way. Recurring memory symbols of good and evil—loving rides on a Bronx ferris wheel and the persistent questioning of police detectives—tore at John and filled him with the desire to know *himself* by unselfishly helping others to know *themselves*. In 1957, at age twelve, John Havilland set out to become the greatest psychiatrist who ever lived.

Lloyd let the advisor gush on, learning that while at Harvard Med Havilland studied symbolic dream therapy and wrote award-winning papers on psychological manipulation and brainwashing techniques; that during his Castleford

Hospital residency he counseled court-referred criminals with astounding results—few of the criminals ever repeated their crimes. After concluding with the words, "and the rest of Dr. Havilland's work was performed in Los Angeles; good luck with your book," the advisor waited for a reply. Lloyd muttered, "Thank you," and hung up.

Calls to Castleford and St. Vincent's Hospitals proved fruitless; they would not divulge information on Havilland and would not state whether Thomas Goff had ever been treated there. The only remaining telephone destination was a twelve-year-old boy's "memory symbol" of evil.

Lloyd called the Scarsdale, New York, Police Department and talked to a series of desk officers and clerk typists, learning that the department's records predating 1961 had been destroyed in a fire. He was about to give up when a retired officer visiting the station came on the line.

The man told Lloyd that some time back in the fifties a filthy rich Scarsdale man named Havilland had been the prime suspect in the murder of a Sing Sing Prison guard named Duane McEvoy, who was himself a suspect in the sex murders of several young Westchester County women. Havilland was also suspected of torching a whole block of deserted houses in an impoverished section of Ossining, including a ramshackle mansion that the then Scarsdale police chief had described as a "torture factory." Havilland had disappeared around the time that McEvoy's knife hacked body was found floating in the Hudson River. So far as the retired officer knew, he was never brought to justice or seen again.

After hanging up, Lloyd felt his clicking form a tight web of certainty. John Havilland had seized upon him as an adversary, casually remarking on his resemblance to his father at their initial meeting. An obsession with paternal power had led him to acquire a coterie of weak-willed "offspring"—Goff and Oldfield among them—that he was molding into carriers of his own plague and dispatching on missions of horror. Thomas Goff had probably collided with the Doctor at

Castleford Hospital, some time shortly after his parole from Attica. Havilland's "counseling" had steered him away from the criminal tendencies that had ruled his life to that time, accounting for his post-Attica one hundred percent clean record. He had probably been Havilland's recruiter of "guru-worshipper types"—his bar prowling M.O. and the testimony of Morris Epstein and Hubert Douglas pointed to it.

Lloyd's clickings departed the realm of certainty and jumped into the realm of pure supposition with a wild leap that nonetheless felt *right*: Thomas Goff was dead, murdered by Havilland after he freaked out at the liquor store with his .41. Havilland had done the interior decorating at Goff's apartment; leaving the "Doctor John the Night Tripper" album as bait. The man that Goff's landlord had seen the afternoon before the police raid was *Oldfield—impersonating Goff*. Havilland himself had killed Howard Christie.

Fool. Dupe. Patsy. Chump. Sucker bait. The reprisals jarred Lloyd's mind. He got up and started down the hall to Thad Braverton's office, then stopped when the door embossed with "Chief of Detectives" loomed in his path as a barrier rather than a beacon. *All of his evidence was circumstantial, suppositional, and theoretical*. He had no evidential basis on which to arrest Dr. John Havilland.

Shifting physical and mental gears, Lloyd walked down to the fifth floor detention area, finding Marty Bergen alone in the first cage, staring out through the wire mesh.

"Hello, Marty."

"Hello, Hopkins. Come to gloat?"

"No. Just to say thanks for your statement. It was a help to me."

"Great. I'm sure you'll make a smashing collar and carve another notch on your legend."

Lloyd peered in at Bergen. The crisscrossed wire cast shadows across his face. "Have you got any idea how big this thing is?"

"Yeah. I just heard most of the story. Too bad I can't report it."

"Who told you?"

"A source. I'd be a shitty reporter if I didn't have sources. Got any leads on the guru guy?"

Lloyd nodded. "Yes. I think it's almost over. Why didn't you tell me what you knew when I talked to you before?"

Bergen laughed. "Because I didn't like your style. I did what I had to do by coming forward, Hopkins, so I'm clean. Don't ask me to kiss your ass."

Lloyd gripped the wire a few inches from Bergen's face. "Then kiss this, motherfucker: if you'd talked to me before, Howard Christie would be alive today. Add that one to your guilt list."

Bergen flinched. Lloyd walked away, letting his words hang like poisonous fallout.

Driving west toward Hollywood, Lloyd asked himself his remaining unanswered questions, supplying instinctive answers that felt as sound as the rest of his hypothesis. Did John Havilland know that Jungle Jack Herzog was dead? No. Most likely he assumed that the shame of Herzog's "beyond" would prevent him from clueing in the world at large or the police in specific to the man who had "brought him through" it. The wipe marks in Herzog's apartment? Probably Havilland; probably the day after the liquor store murders, when he realized that Goff was irrevocably flipped out. Goff had recruited Herzog, so it was likely that he might have visited Jungle Jack's pad and left prints. Havilland would want that potential link to him destroyed. Yet the Doctor had left himself vulnerable at the level of Herzog.

Lloyd forced himself to say the word out loud. Homosexual. It was there in Herzog's hero worship; in his awful need to court danger as a policeman; in his lack of sexual interest in his girlfriend immediately before his death. Bergen would not elaborate on the suicide note because that piece of paper said it explicitly, illuminating Havilland's tragic flaw by implication:

he wanted Jack Herzog to roam the world as a testimonial to the power of a man who brought a macho cop out of the closet.

Hatred gripped Lloyd in a vice that squeezed him so hard he could feel his brains threaten to shoot out the top of his head. His foot jammed the gas pedal to the floor in reflex rage, and Highland Avenue blurred before his eyes. Then a line from Marty Bergen's memorial column forced him to hit the brake and decelerate. "Resurrect the dead on this day." He smiled. Jungle Jack Herzog was going to return from "beyond the beyond" and frame the man who sent him to his death.

Lloyd passed the Hollywood Bowl and turned onto Windemere Drive, cursing when he saw that Oldfield's Mercedes was not in front of his house and that a profusion of front lawn barbecues would prevent him from a quick B&E. After parking, he walked over and peered in the front window, finding it still covered with heavy curtains. Swearing again, he gave the front lawn a cursory eyeballing, stopping when he saw a patch of white on the otherwise green expanse.

He walked over. The patch was a piece of adhesive bandage, with a streak of what looked like congealed blood on the sticky side. Another soft click, this one followed with a soft question mark. Lloyd picked the bandage up and headed south toward the purchasing of material for his frame.

Parked outside the Brass Rail gun shop on La Brea, he took Howard Christie's .357 Magnum from the glove compartment and checked the grips. They were checkered walnut with screw fasteners at the top and bottom; interchangeable, but too ridged to sustain fingerprints. Cursing a blue streak, Lloyd took the gun into the shop and flashed his badge at the proprietor, telling him that he wanted a large handgun with interchangeable smooth wooden grips that would also fit his magnum. The proprietor got out a small screwdriver and arrayed a selection of revolvers on the counter. Ten minutes later Lloyd was three hundred and five dollars poorer and the owner of a Ruger .44 magnum with big fat cherrywood grips, the proprietor having waived the three day waiting period on the basis of a certified police affiliation. Thus armed, Lloyd crossed his fingers and drove to a pay phone, hoping that his luck was still holding.

It was. The Robbery/Homicide switchboard operator had an urgent message for him—call Katherine Daniel—Bell Telephone, 623-1102, extension 129. Lloyd dialed the number and seconds later was listening to a husky-voiced woman digress on how her respect for her late policeman father had fueled her to "kick ass" and get him the information he needed.

". . . and so I went down to the computer room and checked the current feed-in on your two numbers. No calls were made either yesterday or today from either the business or residence phones. That got my dander up, so I decided to do some checking on this guy Havilland. I started by checking the computer files on his phone bills, going back a year and a half. He paid by check on both bills—with the exception of last December, when a man named William Nagler paid both bills. I then checked this Nagler guy out. He paid his *own* bill every month, plus the bill for a number in Malibu. He *lives* in Laurel Canyon, because his checks have his address on them, and *his* number has a Laurel Canyon prefix. But—"

Lloyd interrupted: "Take it slow from here on in, I'm writing this down."

Katherine Daniel drew in a breath and said, "All right. I was saying this guy Nagler paid the bill for this number in Malibu—four-five-two, six-one-five-one. The address is unlisted—as long as Nagler pays the bill on the phone there, Ma Bell doesn't care if it's in Timbuctu. Anyway, I ran a random sampling of the six-one-five-one toll calls over the past year, and got a lot of the same pay phone numbers the other supervisor gave you on your earlier query. I also ran the computer feed-in from yesterday and today and got some toll calls, all in this area code. Do you want them?"

"Yes," Lloyd said. "Slow and easy. Have you got names and addresses on them?"

"Do you think I'd do a half-assed job, Officer?"

Lloyd's forced laugh sounded hysterical to his ears. "No. Go ahead."

"Okay. Six-two three, eight-nine-one-one, Helen Heilbrunner, Bunker Hill Towers, unit eight-forty-three; three-one-seven, four-zero-four-zero, Robert Rice, one-zero-six-seven-seven Via Esperanza, Palos Verdes Estates; five-zero-two, two-two-one-one, Monte Morton, one-twelve LaGrange Place, Sherman Oaks; four-eight-one, one-two-zero-two, Jane O'Mara, nine-nine-zero-nine Leveque Circle, San Marino; two-seven-five, seven-eight-one-five, Linda Whilhite, nine-eight-one-nine Wilshire, West L.A.; four-seven-zero, eight-nine-five-three, Lloyd W. Hopkins, three-two-nine-zero Kelton, L.A. Hey, is that last guy related to you?"

Lloyd had his laugh perfected. "No. Hopkins is a common name. Have you got Nagler's phone number and address?"

"Sure. Four-nine-eight-zero Woodbridge Hollow, Laurel Canyon. Four-six-three, zero-six-seven-zero. Is that it?"

"Yes. Farewell, sweet Katherine!"

Husky chuckles came over the line.

Sweating, his legs weak from tension, Lloyd called Dutch's private line at the Hollywood Station, connecting with a desk sergeant who said that Captain Peltz was out for the afternoon, but would be calling in hourly for his messages. Speaking very slowly, Lloyd explained what he wanted: Dutch was to dispatch trustworthy squadroom dicks to the following addresses and have them lay intimidating "routine questioning" spiels on the people who answered the door, using "beyond the beyond" and "behind the green door" as buzzwords. Holding back William Nagler's name and address, he read off the others, having the officer repeat the message. Satisfied, Lloyd said that *he* would be calling back hourly to clarify the urgency of the matter with Dutch and hung up.

Now the risky part. Now the conscious decision to jeopardize an innocent woman's life for the sake of a murder indictment, an action that was an indictment of his own willingness to deny everything that had happened with Teddy Verplanck. Driving to Linda's apartment, Lloyd prayed that she would do or say something to prove the jeopardy move right or wrong, saving them both indictments on charges of cowardice or heedless will.

Linda opened the door with a drink in one hand. Lloyd looked at her posture and the light in her eyes, seeing indignation moving into anger, a prostitute who got fucked once too often. When he moved to embrace her, she stepped out of his way. "No. Tell me first. Then don't touch me, or I'll lose what I'm feeling."

Lloyd walked into the living room and sat down on the sofa, outright scared that Linda's rectitude said all systems go. He pulled out the .44 magnum and laid it on the coffee table. Linda took a chair and stared at the gun without flinching. "*Tell me,* Hopkins."

With his eyes tuned in to every nuance of Linda's reaction, Lloyd told the entire story of the Havilland case, ending with his theory of how the Doctor had played off the two of them, counting on at least a one-way attraction developing. Linda's face had remained impassive during the recounting, and it was only when he finished that Lloyd could tell that her gut feeling was awe.

"Jesus," she said. "We're dealing with the Moby Dick of psychopaths. Do you really think he has the hots for me, or is that just part of his scam?"

"Good question," Lloyd said. "I think initially it was part of the scam, because he wanted to portray himself as a fellow lover of women. Afterwards, though, I think he was genuinely jealous of your attraction to me, if only because he has me slotted in the role of adversary. Make sense? You know the bastard better than I do."

Linda considered the question, then said, "Yes. My first impression of Havilland was that he was essentially asexual. What next, Hopkins? And why is that gun on my table?"

Lloyd flinched inwardly. Linda was allaying his doubts with perfect responses and the right questions. A light went on in his mind, easing the constricted feeling in his chest. Only if she made the perfect statement voluntarily would he sanction the jeopardy gambit. "I have no hard evidence. I can't arrest Havilland and make it stick. He called you today, right?"

"Yes. How did you know that?"

"That telephone read-out I mentioned. What did he want?"

"I called to tell him I was quitting therapy. His service forwarded the call to him. He almost begged me to come for one more session. I agreed."

"When?"

"Tonight at seven."

Lloyd checked his watch. 6:05. "One question before we get to the gun. The other night you told me about your parents' deaths and said that sometimes you have very dark thoughts. Does Havilland know about that? Has he emphasized your parents' deaths in the course of his counseling?"

Linda said, "Yes. He's obsessed with it, along with some violent fantasies I have. Why?"

Lloyd choked back a wave of fear. "I need Havilland's fingerprints on the grips of that gun. Once I have them, I'll switch the grips to Howard Christie's gun, get Havilland's prints from the D.M.V. and arrest him for Murder One and make it stick while I dig up corroborative evidence. I want you to take the gun to your session tonight. Keep it in your purse and don't touch the grips. Tell Havilland that your fantasies are becoming more violent and that you bought a gun. Hand it to him nervously, holding it by the cylinder housing and barrel. If my reading of him is correct, he'll grab it by the grips, showing you the proper handling procedure, then give it back. Hold it nervously by the barrel and trigger guard and put it back in your purse. After the session, go home and wait for my call. Havilland has no idea that I'm on to him, so you'll be in no danger."

Linda's smile reminded Lloyd of Penny and how she was her most beautiful in moments of rebellion. "You don't believe that, Hopkins. You're shaking. I'll do it on one condition. I want the gun loaded. If Havilland freaks out, I want to be able to defend myself."

A green light flashed in response to Linda's perfect voluntary statement. Lloyd took six .44 shells from his jacket pocket and put them on the coffee table. The moment froze, and he felt himself treading air. Linda put a hand on his arm. "I think I've been waiting a long time for this," she said.

22

THE Time Machine sped backward, fueled by a high octane sodium Pentothal mainline. Calendar pages ruffled in the wind. Bombardments of imagery from recent gauntlets pushed the pages closer and closer, until the black-on-white type smothered him, then turned him outside in.

Saturday, June 2, 1957. Johnny Havilland has heard from the J.D.'s at school that an auto graveyard on the edge of Ossining niggertown is a chrome treasure trove. The old jig who looks after the place sells nifty hood ornaments for the price of a pint of jungle juice, and if you hop the fence you can swipe something sharp and get away before he catches you. Jimmy Vandervort got a bulldog from a Mack truck for thirty-nine cents; Fritz Buckley got a gunsight hood hanger off a 'forty-eight Buick for free, flashing a moon on the spook when he demanded the scratch for some T-bird. Johnny imagines all manner of chrome gadgetry that he could kipe and give to his father to jazz up his 'fifty-six Ford Vicky ragtop. He takes a series of buses up to Ossining, and within an hour he is walking the streets of a negro shanty town in the shadow of Sing Sing Prison.

The streets remind him of photographs he has seen of Hiroshima after Uncle Sam slipped the Japs the A-bomb: Rubble heaps on the front lawns of abandoned houses; gutters filled with empty wine bottles and sewage overflow; emaciated dogs looking for someone or something to bite. Even the Negroes reinforce the A-bomb motif: they look gaunt and suspicious, like mutant creatures fried by atomic fallout. Johnny shivers as he recalls the spate of horror movies he has seen against his mother's wishes. Somehow this is scarier, and because it is scarier he will become that much more of a man by stealing here.

Johnny is about to ask one of the Negroes for directions to the auto graveyard when he spots a familiar flash of color down the block. He walks over and sees his father's Vicky parked outside an old wood-framed house patched over with tarpaper. Painted obscenities and swastikas cover all sides of the house. Johnny climbs in through a broken window, as if drawn by a magnetic force.

Once inside, standing in darkness on rotting wood planks, Johnny's magnet takes on the form of his father's laughter, issuing from the top of a staircase off to his left. He walks over, hearing his father's baritone glee meld with the high-pitched squealing of another man. The whir and click of gears joins with the voices as Johnny treads up the stairs, holding tightly to the banister.

When he reaches the second story landing, Johnny sees a door and squints in the darkness to see if it is green. The laughter and the gear noise grow louder, then the door blows open a crack. Johnny tiptoes over and peers inside.

A stench assails him as his eyes hone in on the backs of his father and a man in a gray uniform standing in front of a whirling circular object. The smell is of blood and body waste and sweat. A green blanket marked off like a crap table lies on the floor, covered with coins and folding money. The walls and ceiling are dotted with bright red, and rivulets of pale red drip toward the floor. Johnny squints and sees that his father is holding a chisel. He moves the chisel towards the whirling object, and a spritz of red liquid cuts the air. The man in the gray uniform laughs and exclaims, "Shit, that's a ten pointer!" He steps back and sticks his hand in his pocket, then drops a wad of cash on the blanket. The whirling circular object comes to a halt and into view.

A nude woman is attached to a plywood reinforced corkboard mounted on a foundation of bricks. A gear train composed of motorcycle chains and lawnmower belts stands behind it. The woman is manacled at the ankles and pinioned at the top with spikes through her wrists. Slash wounds oozing blood cover her chest and extremities, and a black rubber handball is stuck in her mouth, held there by crisscrossed strips of friction tape.

Johnny bites his hand to keep from screaming, feeling his fingers crack beneath his teeth. He squints at the first naked woman he has ever seen and notes her swollen belly and knows that she is pregnant.

His father grabs a handle at the top of the corkboard and leans his whole body into a downward pull. The woman spins end over end, and the man in the uniform squeals, "How about ten bucks on a roulette abortion?"

Johnny watches the chisel descend, clamping his eyes open with self-mauled fingers, knowing he has to see, knowing what *must* be happening, but seeing instead his daddy sitting beside him in the whirling ferris wheel at Playland in the Bronx, whispering that everything would always be all right and that he could go on *all* the rides and eat all the cotton candy he wanted and that Mommy would quit drinking and they would be a real family. Then the uniform man was saying "It's a boy!" and he hears the sound of his own scream, and the uniform man was on top of him with his chisel, and then father was stabbing the uniform man with a knife and stabbing *him* with a needle, whispering, "Easy, Johnny, easy, beauty, easy, babe."

The Time Machine pushed through days of sedative haze filled with the sound of mother weeping and Baxter the lawyer telling her that the money would always be there, and stern-looking men in cheap summer suits asking her where father was, and did he know a man named Duane McEvoy? Mother's scream: "No, you cannot talk to the boy—he knows nothing!" Then Baxter the lawyer takes him to a horror triple feature in White Plains and tells him father is gone forever, but he will be his pal. Midway through *The Curse of Frankenstein* images of the whirling circular object hit him. It all starts to come back, and thoughts of the ferris wheel die, slaughtered by a Cinemascope and Technicolor replay of the Caesarean birth.

"It's a boy!"

Johnny runs out of the theatre and hitchhikes to Ossining niggertown. The same A-bomb Negroes and hungry dogs maneuver on the periphery of the area, but the block itself has burned to the ground.

But it happened here.

No, it was a nightmare.

But it *did* happen here.

I don't know.

Weeks pass. The newspapers attribute the Ossining fire to "heedless Negro children playing with matches" and express gratitude that no one was hurt. Johnny grieves for his lost father and listens in on mother's phone calls to Baxter. She repeatedly tells the lawyer to buy the cops off once and for all, regardless of the price. Baxter finally calls back and tells mother that it is all set, but to be sure she should destroy everything belonging to father, including everything in his safe deposit boxes. Johnny knows that there is nothing interesting in father's study—only his guns and ammo and his books; but the safe deposit boxes are something he has forgotten to scope out. He steals the keys to the boxes from father's desk and forges a note to the manager of the First Union Bank in Scarsdale Village. The old fart buys it hook, line, and sinker, chuckling over the twelve-year-old boy doing banking errands for his dad. Johnny walks away from the bank with a brown paper bag full of blue chip stocks and a black leather-bound diary that looks like a bible.

Johnny walks to the train station, intending to go to the movies in the city. A very un-Scarsdale-like bum tries to panhandle train fare from him. Johnny gives him the stock certificates. Once on the train heading toward Manhattan, Johnny opens up the diary and reads his father's words. The words prove conclusively that what he saw on June 2, 1957 in Ossining niggertown was for real.

Since 1948, alone and with the aid of a Sing Sing Prison guard named Duane McEvoy, father had tortured and murdered eighteen women, some in Westchester County, some in upstate cities adjoining his favorite duck hunting preserves. The mutilations, sexual abuse, and ultimate dismemberments are described in vivid detail. Johnny forces himself to read every word. Tears are streaming down his face and the ferris wheel memory battles the words for primacy. The benevolent whirling object is winning as the train pulls into Grand Central Station. Then Johnny gets to the passages that prove how much his father loves him and everything goes crazy.

> The boy is so much smarter than me that it's scary.
>
> Brains are everything. I've been able to keep Duane as my lacky for so long because the dumbfuck knows that *I'm* the one who keeps *him* from getting caught. When Johnny killed the rats and shot the dogs I saw him go cold almost overnight, and when I saw him go smart and wary and cautious too, I knew I was scared. I wanted to go to him and love him, but staying away makes him stronger and more fit for life.
>
> Johnny boy is like an iceberg—cold and 7/10's below the surface.
>
> He's probably afraid to kill human prey; too manipulative, too asexual. It's going to be interesting watching him hit adolescence. How will he attempt to prove himself?

Johnny walks through Grand Central, openly weeping. Coming out onto 42nd Street, he throws the death bible into a storm drain and hurls a silent vow to his father: he will show him that he is afraid of nothing.

Fall, 1957. Johnny considers potential victims at Scarsdale Junior High. To fulfill his father's legacy, he knows that they must be female. Beyond that first essential qualification, he sets his own criteria: All his prey must be snooty, giggly, and stay late after school participating in kiss-ass extracurricular activities, then walk home via the Garth Road underpass, where he would be waiting with a razor-sharp Arkansas toad stabber like the one Vic Morrow wielded in *Blackboard Jungle*.

Johnny's selection process narrows as he stakes out the underpass. Finally he settles on Donna Horowitz, Beth Shields, and Sally Burdett, grinds who remain until after dark each day in the Chem Lab, washing test tubes and brown-nosing Mr. Salcido for a good grade. Stab. Stab. Stab. Johnny sharpens his switchblade every night and wonders if father ever bagged three at once. He sets the execution date: November 1, 1957. The three grinds will walk through the underpass at their usual time of 5:35 to 5:40, giving him twelve minutes to bump them off, then hotfoot it over to the station and catch the 5:52 to the city. Stab. Stab. Stab.

November 1, 1957. At 5:30 Johnny is stationed on the left-hand side of the Garth Road underpass, wearing blue jeans and a hunting vest that he has scavenged from his father's left-behinds. The vest has loops to hold shotgun shells and hangs down to his knees. The toad stabber is affixed to his belt in a plastic scabbard.

The three victims approach the underpass right on time. Donna Horowitz notices Johnny and starts to giggle. Sally Burdett hoots, "Is that Johnny Havilland or Chucko the Clown? Dig that crazy vest!" Johnny draws his knife as Beth Shields sidles past him, taunting, "Wimpdick, Wimpdick." He lunges and snags the stiletto on his vest pocket. The blade pokes his ribcage and he screams and falls to his knees. The girls gather around him and shriek with laughter. Johnny sees a kaleidoscope of the Caesarean birth, the ferris wheel and his father joining in the laughter. He screams again to drown it all out. When that doesn't work, he bangs his head on the pavement until everything goes silent and black.

The banging continues. When a woman's voice calls out, "Dr. Havilland, are you there?" the Night Tripper is catapulted back to the present. His office, the projector and a portable movie screen come into focus. The voice must belong to Linda Wilhite, banging on his outer office door. His first conscious thought of his now destroyed childhood void is appreciation for his very own God, who did not give him the courage to break down the void until he had given him the courage to kill, and earn his father's love. His destiny had been dealt with split-second accuracy.

"Dr. Havilland, are you there? It's Linda Wilhite."

The Doctor got to his feet and took a deep breath, then rubbed his eyes. His steps were rubbery from the sodium Pentothal jolt, but that was to be expected—he was, technically speaking, a newborn creature. Trying his new voice, he called, "Hold on, Linda. I'm coming." Hearing his familiar baritone, he walked to the outer office door and opened it.

Linda Wilhite stood there, looking uncharacteristically nervous. "Hello, Linda," Havilland said. "Are you all right? You seem slightly on edge."

Linda walked past the Doctor into his private office and took her usual seat. When Havilland followed her in, she said, "I've been having some very strange, violent fantasies. I've even bought a gun." Pointing to the movie screen and projector, she added, "Are those the visual aids you mentioned?"

Havilland sat down facing Linda. "Yes. Tell me about your new fantasies. You look full of stress. Are you sure you want to quit therapy under such conditions?"

Linda twisted in her chair, clutching her purse in her lap. As the last fuzziness from his Pentothal trip died, Havilland saw that underneath her nervousness she was very angry. "Yes, I still want to quit therapy. *You* look full of stress. Woozy, too. Everyone is full of stress. These are stressful times, don't you know that, goddamn it?"

Havilland raised placating hands. "Easy, Linda. I'm on your side."

Linda sighed. "I'm sorry I barked."

"That's all right. Tell me about the new fantasies."

Linda said, "They're weird, and variations on my sweater man fantasies. Basically I'm just menaced by the same type of man I used to have the hots for. I fantasize being chased by men like that. The fantasies always end with me shooting them." She reached into her purse and pulled out a large blue steel revolver, grasping it by the barrel and cylinder. "See, Doctor? Do you think I'm crazy?"

Havilland reached over and took the revolver from Linda, holding it firmly by the smooth wood grips, sighting it at the movie screen. "I'm proud of you," he said as he handed it back, butt first.

Linda returned the gun to her purse. "Why?"

"Because, as you said, these are stressful times. You're a strong person, and in stressful times strong people go beyond their beyonds. Move your chair over here. I want to run a little home movie for you."

Linda pulled her chair over to where it was facing the screen. Havilland got up and threaded a length of film through the projector's feeder device, then hit the on switch and turned off the wall light. A series of blank frames flashed across the screen, followed by a jerky panning shot of a bedroom, followed by more blank frames.

Then a blond woman in a nurse's uniform began to undress. Close-up shots caught everything fallible about her body: a small abdominal scar, networks of varicose veins, patches of cellulite. When she was naked, she did an awkward vamp dance, then lay down on a mattress covered by a single blue sheet.

A nude man joined her, averting his face from the camera. The couple moved into an embrace, broke it, and moved to opposite sides of the mattress. The woman looked bewildered and the man mashed his face into the sheet. After holding these poses for long moments, the woman rolled underneath the man and they faked intercourse.

Linda clutched her purse and said, "What is this, amateur porno film night? I thought this was going to be a therapy session."

"Shhh," Havilland whispered. "You'll catch the drift in just a few seconds."

The screen went blank, then filled up with a long shot of the blond woman, now dressed in her nurse's uniform, leaning against the bedroom wall. Suddenly a man, also clothed, threw himself on top of her. The screen again went blank, then segued into an extreme close-up of a transparent plastic pillow. The muzzle of a gun was pressed to the pillow. A finger pulled the trigger and the screen was awash in red. The camera caught a close-up of a man's face. When Linda saw the face she screamed "Hopkins!" and fumbled in her purse for the gun. Her finger was inside the trigger guard when the lights went on and the man from the movie jumped out of the closet and smothered her with his body.

23

LLOYD slammed down the phone in response to Dutch's news: the two women and one man that Hollywood Division detectives had leaned on with "behind the green door" and "beyond the beyond" had immediately clammed up, first threatening the officers with lawsuits, then going into repeated recitations of the phrase "*patria infinitum*." No breakdowns, no recantings of past sins, just indignation at police scare tactics and the rapid expulsion of seasoned cops. Dutch would be deploying a new team of detectives for runs at the guru worshippers, but they would probably be in mantra comas by then. There was only himself, Linda and her magnum, and the unknown quantity of William Nagler.

Lloyd checked the clock on the kitchen wall. 7:45. Linda would still be at her "therapy" session. He could wait and call and ease his mind, or he could move. The ticking of the clock became deafening. He locked up the house and walked to his car.

Headlights flashed across the driveway as he slipped behind the wheel, and a panel truck pulled up in front of his unmarked cruiser. Lloyd got out and saw Marty Bergen step in front of the headlights and jam his hands into his pockets. A gun butt extended from his waistband.

"My lawyer glommed me a writ," he said. "Fred Gaffaney almost shit shotgun shells."

Lloyd said, "Amateurs shouldn't pack hardware. Beat it. I've got no stories for you."

Bergen laughed. "When I was on the job I was in love with my piece. Off duty, I always made sure that people could see it. I was in love with it until I had to use it. Then I dropped it and ran. Jack's dead, Hopkins."

"Tell me something I don't know."

"It's on me. It's all on me."

"Wrong, Bergen. It's the Department's and it's mine."

Bergen kicked the grill of the Matador, then stumbled backward into the hood of his truck. "I *owe*, goddamn you! Can't you see that? All I ever had was what Jack gave me, and even that was all twisted. Some piece of shit took him where he shouldn't have fucking gone and made him feel things that he shouldn't have fucking felt, and it was *me* that he felt them about, and I owe! Don't make me say the words, Hopkins. Please don't make me say the fucking words."

Lloyd sent up a prayer for all guilt-driven innocents seeking jeopardy. "What do you want, Bergen?"

Former L.A.P.D. Sergeant Martin D. Bergen wiped tears from his eyes. "I just want to pay off Jack."

"Then get in the car," Lloyd said. "We're going to Laurel Canyon to good guy-bad guy a suspect."

William Nagler was not at home.

Lloyd parked across the street from his two-story redwood A-frame and walked over and knocked on both the front and back doors. No answer, no lights burning and no sounds of habitation. After checking the mailbox and finding two catalogs and a Mastercard bill, he returned to the car and his improbable partner.

"Are you going to open up this thing?" Bergen asked as Lloyd squeezed in behind the wheel.

Lloyd shook his head. "No. I don't trust the fourth estate. Just play the interrogation by ear. You ever work plainclothes?"

"Yeah. Venice Vice. I'm going to be the good guy, right?"

"No. You've got booze breath and you need a shave. You're big, but I'm bigger, so I can play savior. I'll ask the questions, you just be abusive. Just imagine yourself as a typical fascist pig out of the pages of the *Big Orange Insider* and you'll be cool."

Bergen laughed. "You're the kind of joker who hands out compliments one minute, then rags people who hand out compliments the next, which means one of two things—you either love to give people shit, or you don't know where your own head is at. Which one is it?"

With his eyes on Nagler's front door, Lloyd said, "Don't jerk my chain. If I didn't want you here, you wouldn't be here. If I didn't understand what you have to do, I would have busted you for carrying a concealed weapon and kicked your ass back to the slam."

Bergen scratched his razor stubble and poked Lloyd in the arm. "I apologize for saying I didn't like your style. What I should have said was that you *have* style, but you don't know what to do with it."

Lloyd turned on the dashboard light and stared at Bergen. "Don't tell me about style. I read some of your early stuff. It was damn good. You could have been something big, you could have said things worth saying. But *you* didn't know what to do with it, because being really good is really scary. I know fear, Bergen. Two niggers blew away your partner and you ran. I can understand that and not judge you for it. But you had the chance to be great and you settled for being a hack, and that I can't understand."

Bergen toyed with the knobs of the two-way radio. "You Catholic, Hopkins?"

"No."

"Tough shit, you're going to hear my confession anyway. Jack Herzog taught me to write. He ghosted my first published stories, then edited the ones I actually did write. *He* formed my style; *he* was the one who had the chance to be great. It's weird, Hopkins. You're supposed to be the pragmatist, but I think you're really a romantic innocent with an incredible nose for shit. It's funny. Jack gave me everything I have. He made me a derivative fiction stylist and a competent journalist. He'd been writing a novel, and I was serving as *his* editor, helping him hold it together as he got crazier and crazier. I've never had the chance to be great. But if I had *your* brains and drive and guts, I'd be more than a gloryhound flatfoot."

Lloyd turned on the radio and listened to code ones and twos. "It's a stalemate, Marty, and a life sentence for both of us. But we're lucky we can play the game."

Bergen took the pistol from his waistband and rolled down the window and took a bead on the moon. "I believe that," he said.

Two hours passed in silence. Bergen dozed off and Lloyd stared out the window at William Nagler's driveway, wondering if he should make a run to a phone and call Linda; wondering also if Havilland's worshippers were in contact with each other and if the already hassled followers had alerted Nagler to the approaching heat. No, he decided finally. Havilland was too well buffered. The worshippers probably had no way of contacting Havilland or each other besides Havilland's pay phone communiqués, which logic told him were rigidly pre-scheduled. *His* investigatory parries were buffered against discovery. Then the truth hit. He was pumping himself up with logic because Linda was part of the game and part of him, and if she fell the game was over forever.

Shortly after ten o'clock, a silver Porsche convertible pulled up in front of the A-frame. Lloyd nudged Bergen awake and said, "Our buddy is here. Follow my lead and when I touch my necktie interrupt me and buzz him with 'behind the green door' and 'beyond the beyond.' This guy had nothing to do with Jack Herzog, so don't even mention his name. You got it?"

Bergen nodded and squared his shoulders in preparation for his performance. Lloyd grabbed a flashlight and opened the car door just as a man got out of the Porsche and crossed the sidewalk in front of the A-frame. Bergen slammed his door, causing the man to turn around at the foot of the steps. "Police officers," Lloyd called out.

The man froze at the words, then walked forward in the direction of his car. Lloyd flashed the light square in his face, forcing him to throw up his hands to shield his eyes. "It—it's—ma-my car," he stammered. "I've got the pink in the glove compartment."

Lloyd studied the face. Blond, bland, and cultured were his first impressions. He pointed his five cell at the ground and said, "I'm sure it is. Are you William Nagler?"

The man stepped off the curb and stroked the hood of the Porsche. Touching its sleekness gave an edge of propriety to his voice. "Yes, I am. What is this in regard to?"

Lloyd walked up to within inches of Nagler, forcing him back on the sidewalk. He held up his badge and played his light on it, then said, "L.A.P.D. My name is Hopkins, that's Sergeant Bergen. Could we talk to you inside?"

Nagler shuffled his feet. Lloyd held his light on the little dance of fear and saw that the worshipper was pigeon-toed to the point of deformity. "Why? Have you got a warrant? Hey! What are you doing!"

Lloyd turned around and saw Marty Bergen leaning into the Porsche, feeling under the seats. Nagler wrapped his arms around himself and shouted, "Don't! That's my car!"

"Cool it, Partner," Lloyd said. "The man is cooperating, so just maintain your coolness." Lowering his voice, he said to Nagler, "My partner's a black glove cop, but I keep him on a short chain. Can we go inside? It's cold out here."

Nagler brushed a lock of lank blond hair up from his forehead. Lloyd eyed him openly and added competent and smart and very scared to his initial assessment.

"What's a black glove cop?"

As if on cue, Bergen walked over and stood beside Lloyd. "We should toss the vehicle," he said. "This bimbo's a doper, I can tell. What are you flying on, citizen? Ludes? Smack? Dust? Give me thirty seconds inside that glove compartment and I'll get us a righteous dope bust."

Lloyd gave Bergen a disgusted look. "This is a routine questioning of burglary victims, not a narc raid, so be cool. Mr. Nagler, can we go inside?"

Nagler's feet did another fear dance. "I'm not a burglary victim. I've never been burglarized and I don't know anything about any burglaries."

Lloyd put an arm around Nagler's shoulders and moved him out of Bergen's earshot. "All the houses on this block have been crawled," he said. "Sometimes the guy steals, sometimes not. A snitch of mine heard a tip that he's a panty freak, that he checks out all the pads he crawls for lingerie. What I want to do is check for fingerprints on your bedroom drawers. It will only take five minutes."

Nagler jerked himself free. "No. I can't allow it. Not without a warrant."

Pointing at Bergen, Lloyd whispered, "He's the senior officer, I'm just a forensic technician. If I can't print your drawers, he'll go cuckoo and frame you on a drug charge. His daughter O.D.'d on heroin and it flipped him out. He's about one step ahead of the net, so it wouldn't do to rile him. Please cooperate, Mr. Nagler, for both our sakes."

Nagler looked over his shoulder at Marty Bergen, who was now squatting and examining the front wheel covers of his Porsche. "All right, Officer. Just keep that man *away* from me."

Lloyd whistled, drawing Bergen away from his hubcap scrutiny. "Mr. Nagler is going to cooperate, Sergeant. Let's make it quick. He's a busy man."

"Dopers always are," Bergen said, walking over. He gave the Porsche a last glance and added, "I'll bet it's hot. We should check the hot sheet. We could get us a righteous G.T.A. bust." Leaning into Lloyd in a pseudo drunk's weave, he whispered, "What's my job inside?"

Seeing that Nagler was walking ahead to open the door, Lloyd faked a coughing attack, then said sotto voce, "Toss the pad for official papers, especially anything pertaining to property in Malibu. See if you can find something illegal to squeeze him with. Be menacing."

Nagler unlocked the door and turned on a light in the entrance foyer. He pointed inside and shivered, then wrapped his arms around himself and moved his inwardly bent feet together so that the toes were touching. Lloyd thought of a frightened animal trying to protect itself by curling into a ball and blending in with the scenery. The fear in the man's eyes made him want to strangle John Havilland for his complicity in that fear and strangle himself for what he might have to do. He caught Bergen's eyes and saw that his bogus partner was thinking along parallel lines and hoped that his rage would hold for the duration of his performance. When he felt his own rage subside in a wave of pity, he resurrected it by thinking of the guru-shrink slipping through loopholes in the legal process and said, "Let's sit down and talk for a minute first, Mr. Nagler. There's a few questions I have."

Nagler nodded assent. Lloyd walked through the foyer into a living room furnished with plastic high-tech chairs and a long sofa constructed of beanbags and industrial tubing. Bergen sauntered in behind him, going straight for a portable bar on casters. Sitting down in a lavender armchair that creaked under his weight, Lloyd saw western movie posters beam down at him from all four walls. Nagler perched himself on the edge of the sofa and said, "Will you *please* make this fast?"

Lloyd smiled and said, "Of course. This is a charming living room, by the way." He pointed to the posters. "Are you a movie buff?"

"I'm a free-lance art director and an amateur filmmaker," Nagler said, leveling worried eyes at Marty Bergen. "Now please get to your questions."

Bergen chuckled and poured himself a large shot of Scotch. "I think this pad sucks, and I think this bimbo is just holding down this art director gig as a front for his dope racket." He downed the drink and poured another. "What are you dealing, citizen? Weed? Speed? *Dust*? That's it, Hoppy! This is a *dust bust*!"

Nagler fretted his hands and pleaded to Lloyd with his eyes. Bergen guzzled Scotch, then blurted out, "Jesus, I'm gonna be sick. Where's the can?"

Lloyd waved an arm toward the back of the house as Nagler drew his feet together and slammed the edge of the sofa with outwardly cocked wrists. Bergen took off running, making gagging sounds and holding his hands over his mouth. Lloyd shook his head and said, "I apologize for my colleague, Mr. Nagler."

"He's a terrible man," Nagler whispered. "He has a low karma consciousness. Unless he changes his life radically, he'll never go beyond his low efficacy image."

Lloyd noted that the recitation of the mini-spiel had had a calming effect on Nagler. He honed his own spiel to razor sharpness and said, "Yes, I do pity him. He has so many doors to go beyond before he finds out who he really is."

The razor drew blood. Nagler's whole body relaxed. Lloyd threw out a smile calculated to flash "kindred soul." Thinking, *hook him now,* he said, "He needs spiritual guidance. A spiritual master is just the ticket for him. Don't you agree?"

Nagler's face lit up, then clouded over with what looked to Lloyd like an aftertaste of doubt and fear. Finally he breathed out, "Yes. Please get on with your business and leave me in peace. *Please*."

Lloyd was silent, charting interrogation courses while he got out a pen and notepad. Nagler fidgeted on the edge of the sofa, then turned around when footsteps echoed behind him.

"*Achtung,* citizen!"

Lloyd looked up from his notepad to see Marty Bergen hovering next to the sofa, holding a glass freebase pipe out at arm's length. "Thought you were cool, didn't you, citizen? No dope on the premises. However, you overlooked the new possession of drug paraphernalia law recently passed by the state legislature. This pipe and the ether on your bathroom shelf constitute a misdemeanor."

Bergen dropped the pipe into Nagler's lap. Nagler jerked to this feet and threw his hands up to his face; the pipe fell to the floor and shattered. Bergen, florid faced and grinning from ear to ear, looked at Lloyd and said, "This is fucking ironic. I wrote an editorial condemning that law as fascist, which of course it is. Now I'm here enforcing it. Ain't life a bitch?" He reached into his back pocket and pulled out a wad of paper. "Check this out," he said.

Lloyd stood up, grabbed the papers and walked over to the shivering worshipper. Steeling himself against revulsion, he said, "You have the right to remain silent. You have the right to have legal counsel present during questioning. If you cannot afford counsel, an attorney will be provided. Do you have a statement to make regarding that paraphernalia, Mr. Nagler?"

The answer was a series of body shudders. Nagler pressed himself into the wall, trembling. Lloyd put a gentle hand on his shoulder and felt a jolt of almost electric tension. Looking down at the worshipper's feet, he saw that they were twisting across each other, as if trying to gouge the ankles. The brutality of the posture made Lloyd turn away and seek out Marty Bergen for a semblance of sanity.

The image backfired.

Bergen was standing by the bar, guzzling Scotch straight from the bottle. When he saw Lloyd staring at him, he said, "Learning things you don't like about yourself, Hot Dog?"

Lloyd walked to Bergen and grabbed the bottle from his hands. "Guard him. Don't touch him and don't talk to him; just let him be."

This time the answer Lloyd got was Bergen's grin of self-loathing; a smile that looked like a close-up of his own soul. Taking the bottle with him, he walked to a small den off the living room hallway and found the phone. He dialed Linda's number and let it ring ten times. No answer. Checking his watch, he saw that it was 10:40. Linda had probably gotten tired of waiting for his call and had left.

Lloyd put down the phone, knowing that he had wanted the comfort of Linda's voice more than her confirmation of Havilland's prints on the magnum. Remembering Bergen's wad of paper, he reached into his pocket and extracted it, smoothing it out on the desk beside the phone.

It was a real estate brochure listing properties in Malibu and the Malibu Colony. Attached to the top of the front page were "complimentary" Pacific Coast Highway parking stickers for the period 6/1/84 to 6/1/85. A soft "bingo" sounded in Lloyd's mind. Beach area realtors gave away the hundred-dollar-a-year resident stickers to their preferred customers. It was a solid indication that Nagler had property in Malibu—property that he let John Havilland use, but held the deed to for tax purposes and secrecy. Havilland would undoubtedly *not* let his worshippers confer with him at his office or Beverly Hills condo—but a beach house owned by an *especially* trusted worshipper would be the ideal place for individual or group meetings.

He read the name of the realtor on the front of the brochure—Ginjer Buchanan Properties. The phone number was listed below it. Lloyd dialed it on the off-chance that an eager beaver salesperson might still be at the office. When all he got was a recorded message, he called information and got a residential listing for a Ginjer Buchanan in Pacific Palisades. He dialed that number and got another machine, this one featuring reggae music and the realtor's importunings to "leave a message at the tone and I'll call you from the Twilight Zone."

Thinking of the Los Angeles Police Department as both the keepers and inmates of the Twilight Zone, Lloyd rifled the desk drawers looking for official paper pertaining to Malibu property. Finding nothing but stationery and invoices for movie equipment, he walked down the hall looking for other likely rooms to toss. The bathroom and kitchen would probably yield zilch, but at the end of the hallway stood a half-opened door.

Lloyd walked to it and fumbled at the inside wall for a light switch. An overhead light went on, framing a small room filled with haphazardly discarded movie cameras, rolls of film, and developing trays. The floor was a mass of broken equipment, with plaster chips torn loose from the walls. Noticing a Movieola that remained intact atop a metal desk, Lloyd peered in the viewfinder and saw a celluloid strip showing a pair of inert legs clad in white stockings.

He was about to examine the equipment more closely when singing and chanting blasted from the living room. Walking back to investigate, Lloyd saw and heard a hellish two-part harmony.

Marty Bergen was standing over a kneeling William Nagler, strumming an imaginary guitar and singing, "They had an old piano and they played it hot behind the green door! don't know what they're doin', but they laugh a lot behind the green door! Won't someone let me in so I can find out what's behind the green door!"

When Bergen fell silent, fumbling for more verses, Nagler's chanting took precedence. "*Patria infinitum patria infinitum patria infinitum.*" Muttered in a droning monotone punctuated by the worshipper's banging of his prayer-clasped hands against his chest, the words seemed to rise from a volition far older and darker than John Havilland or his murderer-father. "*Patria infinitum patria infinitum patria infinitum patria infinitum patria infinitum.*"

Bergen snapped to Lloyd's presence and shouted above the chanting, "Hi, Hoppy! Think I'll make the top forty with this? Green Door Green Door Green Door!"

Lloyd grabbed Bergen and shoved him to the wall and held him there, hissing, "Shut the fuck up now, and don't drink another drop. Go toss the rest of the pad for Nagler's I.R.S. forms and income tax returns. Don't say another fucking word, just do it."

Bergen tried to smile. It came out a death grin. "Okay, Sarge," he said.

Lloyd released Bergen and watched him ooze off the wall. When he shambled away, the chanting became the dominating aspect of the room. "*Patria infinitum patria infinitum patria infinitum patria infinitum patria infinitum.*"

Lloyd knelt in front of the worshipper, watching his trance grow deeper with each blow to the heart, memorizing every detail of the flagellation in order to justify his next move. When Nagler's glazed eyes and heaving lungs were permanently imprinted in his mind, he swung a full power open hand at his head and saw the trance crumble as the worshipper was knocked off his knees screaming, "Doctor!"

Lloyd, knocked loose of his own equilibrium, pinned Nagler's shoulders to the floor and shouted, "Havilland's dead, William. Before he died he said that you were a chump and a fool and a dupe."

Nagler's glazed eyes zeroed in on Lloyd. "No. No. No. *Patria infinitum. Patria infin—*"

Lloyd dug his fingers into the worshipper's collarbone. "No, William, you can't. You can't go back."

"Doctor!"

"Shhh. Shhh. You can't, Bill. You can't go back."

"Doctor!"

Lloyd dug his fingers deeper, until Nagler started to sob. Withdrawing his hands altogether, he said, "He talked about how he used you, Bill. How he got you to pay his phone bills, how he made you his slave, how he laughed at you, how your movies were shit, how you had all that expensive equipment, but you did—"

Lloyd stopped when Nagler's sobs trailed off into a terrified stutter. "Hor-hor-hor-moo-hor-moo."

"Shhh, shhh," Lloyd whispered. "Take it slow and think the words out."

Nagler stared up at Lloyd. The look on his face wavered between grief and bliss. Finally the bliss prevailed long enough for him to say, "Horror movie. Doctor John made a horror movie. That's how I know you're lying about what he said about me. He appreciates my talent. I edited the movie and Doctor said—he said . . ."

Lloyd stood up, then helped Nagler to his feet and pointed him toward the sofa. When Nagler was seated, he studied his face. He looked like a man about to enter the gas chamber who didn't know whether or not he wanted to die. Knowing that the bliss/death part of the worshipper had the edge and possessed the potential to produce lucid answers, Lloyd quashed his impulse to bludgeon Nagler into grief/life. Sighing, he sat down beside the ravished young man and stabbed in the dark. "Havilland isn't really dead, Bill."

"I know that," Nagler said. "He was here this morning with—" He stopped and flashed a robot smile. "He was here this morning."

Lloyd said, "Finish the thought, Bill."

"I did. Doctor John was here this morning. End of thought."

"No. Beginning of thought. But let's change the subject. You don't really think I'm a policeman, do you?"

Nagler shook his head. "No. Doctor John told me that there was a three percent leak factor in our program. I know exactly what the leak was—it came to me while I was chanting. You're an Internal Revenue agent. I paid Doctor John's phone bills while he went skiing in Idaho last December. You checked the records out, because you're with big brother. You also cross-checked my bank records and the Doctor's, and saw that I sent him a big check last year. He probably forget to report it on his tax return. You want a bribe to keep silent. Very well, name your amount and I'll write a check." Nagler laughed. "How silly of me. That would leave a record. No, name your amount and I'll pay you off in cash."

Lloyd gasped at Nagler's recuperative powers. Five minutes earlier, he had been a groveling mass. Now he held the condescending authority of a plantation owner. A "horror movie" and the wrecked equipment in the back room were the dividing points. Thinking, *Break him,* he said, "Didn't it surprise you that my partner knew enough to sing you that song?"

"No. A song is a song."

"And a movie is a movie," Lloyd said, reaching into his pocket. "Bill, it's time I came clean. Doctor John sent me to test your loyalty." He held out the mug-shot strip of Thomas Goff. "I'm the replacement for the old recruiter. You remember this fellow, don't you? There's a guy on Doctor John's program who looks just like him. I know all about the meetings at the house in Malibu and how you bought the house for the Doctor and how you pay the phone bill. I know about the pay phone contacts and how you don't fraternize outside the meetings. I know because I'm one of you, Bill."

First grief, then bliss, now bewilderment. Lloyd had kept his eyes averted from Nagler, letting him feast on Thomas Goff's image instead of his own. When he finally reestablished eye contact he saw that the man had fingered the mug-shot strip to pieces and that his spiel had turned him into clay. Feeling like a bullfighter going in for the kill, Lloyd said, "I also lied when I said that Doctor John said that your movies were shit. He really loves your movie work. In fact, just today he told me that he wants you to both star in *and* direct the script that he's working on. He tol—"

Lloyd stopped when Nagler's grief took him over. "*Patria infinitum patria infinitum patria infinitum patria infinitum.*"

Lloyd thought of Linda and got up and walked toward the den and the telephone. He had his hand on the reciever when a tap on his shoulder forced him to jump back, turn around, and ball his fists.

It was Bergen, looking eerily sober. "I couldn't find any I.R.S. papers," he said, "but I did find our pal's diary under his bed. Renaissance weird, Hopkins. Fucking gothic."

Lloyd took the morocco bound book from Bergen's hands

and sat down on the desk. Opening it, he saw that the first entry was dated 11/13/83, and that it and all the subsequent entries were written in an exquisitely flourished longhand. While Bergen stood over him, he read through accounts of Havilland's "programming," picking up a cryptically designated cast along the way. There was the "Lieutenant," who had to be Thomas Goff; the "Fox," the "Bull dagger," the "Bookworm," the "Professor," the "Muscleman," and "Billy Boy," who had to be Nagler himself.

The entries themselves detailed how Havilland ordered his charges to fast for thirty-six hours, then stand nude in front of full-length mirrors and chant their "fear mantras" into tape recorders, until "subliminal dream consciousness" took over and led them to babble "transcendental fantasies" that he would later sift through for "key details" to translate into "reality fodder." How he paired them off sexually at the "Beach Womb," interrupting the couplings to take vital signs and "stress readings"; how he forced them to kill dogs and cats as "insurance against moral flaccidity"; how the "Lieutenant" interrupted their REM sleep with late night phone calls and brutal interrogations into their dreams.

Alternately using the first person "I" and the third person "Billy Boy," Nagler described how he and Doctor John's other counselees were pimped out to wealthy people who advertised for "fantasy therapists" in privately published and circulated sex tabloids, the weekend "lovemaking seminars" often netting Havilland several thousand dollars, and how the "beach womb groupings" were taped and transcribed by the "Lieutenant," who sometimes served as the "Chef"—concocting mixtures of pharmaceutical cocaine and other prescription drugs that the Doctor would administer to his counselees under "test-flight conditions."

Lloyd leafed full-speed through the diary, looking for incriminating facts: names, addresses and dates. With Marty Bergen hovering beside him and Nagler's muffled chanting coming in from the living room, he felt like the sole outpost of sanity in a lunatic landscape, the feeling underlined by the fact that the diary contained *no* facts—only narrated disclosures peopled with coded characters.

Until an entry dated the day before jumped out at him:

> Helped set up movie equipment at the Muscleman's house in the Hollywood Hills. Doctor John supervised. I showed him how to operate the camera. I hope Muscleman won't break anything. He scares me—and he looks more and more like the Lieutenant these days.

The entry was followed by a blank page, followed by the diary's concluding entry, dated that morning. Lloyd felt an icepick at his spine as he read,

> *It's not real*. They faked it. You can fake anything with new camera technology. It's a fake. It's not real.

Lloyd shoved Bergen aside and walked back to the movie room and searched among the upended equipment for film scraps, finding three strips of celluloid wedged underneath the editing machine. Running them through the machine's feeder-viewfinder, he saw four close-ups of a woman's white nyloned legs, a long shot of a mattress on a carpeted floor and a blurred extreme close-up of a broad-chested man with what looked like an L.A.P.D. badge pinned to his shirt.

The icepick jabbed his heart. Lloyd thought of the white-stockinged nurse that Richard Oldfield had brought to his house twenty-four hours before. The knife twisted, dug and tore, accompanied by a deafening burst of *patria infinitum*s from the living room.

Lloyd walked toward the sound, finding Nagler still in his mantra pose and Bergen standing beside the fireplace, pouring bottles of liquor over the acrylic "firewood" on the grate. "Long-term interrogation, Sarge," he said. "It won't do to get tempted. What's next?" His ghoul grin had become a feisty smirk, and for one split-second Lloyd found a beacon of sanity.

"I'm leaving, you're staying here," he said. "I have to check on someone. Then, if she got my evidence, I have to take our friend's guru out. You stay here and watchdog him. Hang by the phone. If I need you, I'll ring once, then call back immediately."

"I want in on the bust," Bergen said.

Lloyd shook his head. "No. Just having you *here* could cause me lots of grief, and I'm not risking my job or *you* any further." He watched Bergen's smirk go hangdog. "What are you going to do when all this is over?"

Bergen laughed as he poured out a bottle of Courvoisier V.S.O.P. "I don't know. Jack left me close to twenty grand, maybe I'll just see where that takes me." When Lloyd didn't react to his mention of the money, he said, "You *knew* about the bank draft, right?"

Lloyd said, "Yeah. I didn't report it because I knew I.A.D. would try to seize your account as evidence."

"You're a good shit, Hopkins. You know that?"

"Sometimes."

"What are *you* going to do when this is over?"

Lloyd thought of Linda and Janice and his daughters, then looked over at the devastated William Nagler, still chanting at demons. "I don't know," he said.

24

THE Night Tripper sat at the recording console in the Beach Womb, listening to Richard Oldfield and Linda Wilhite make frightened small talk upstairs in bedroom number three. The split-second accuracy of his fate had taken on ironic overtones. Linda's screaming of "Hopkins" combined with the gun in her purse was a tacit admission that the genius cop had figured it out on the same day that he had broken through his childhood void. Richard had blown his chance to kill Hopkins, and his contingency plan to drive Linda over the edge with the snuff film and have *her* commit the murder had backfired. After twenty-seven years devoted to venting his terror through others, it had all come down to himself. He had claimed his father's heritage, gaining autonomy along with the knowledge that the game was over. God was a malevolent jokester armed with a blunt instrument called irony.

Havilland leaned back in the chair that Thomas Goff used to occupy, feeling a conscious version of his dream disengagement split him in two. His left side imagined whirling corkboards, while his right side heard words issuing from the bedroom where Richard guarded the object of his corkboard fantasies. Soon exhaustion crept up. The spinning of the corkboard dominated, while the words played on, like dim music at the edge of sound.

". . . why are you staring at me?"

"Doctor said to watch you."

"Do you do everything he tells you to do?"

"Yes. Why are you making nasty faces at me? I've been gentle with you."

"Because Doctor said to be gentle? No, don't answer, it'll only make me hate you more. For your information, drugging and kidnapping is not a gentle activity. Are you aware of that?"

"Yes. No. You're very beautiful."

"Jesus. Was that movie for real? I mean, there was the awful part, and then this close-up of you. Listen, are you Thomas Goff?"

"I told you my name was Richard."

"All right, but what about the movie. *Was* it real? My mother was killed like that, with a pillow and a gun. Is the movie part of your crazy guru's plans for me?"

"What movie?"

"Jesus. Are you high? I mean, on something besides insanity? You know, on drugs?"

"Doctor gives me tranquilizers and antidepressants. Prescription stuff. He's a doctor, so it's legal and not bad."

"*Not bad*? Havilland's a Doctor Feelgood to boot? No, don't answer, I know he's capable of anything. I'm not going to let you hurt me, you know. Never. Not ever."

"I don't want to hurt you."

"Jesus, you sound like Peter Lorre. Does it turn you on that I'm not scared?"

"Yes. No. No!"

"First responses are always the most honest, Richard. If you or that psychopath downstairs tried to hurt me, I'd kick and bite and scratch and rub lye in your eyes. I—"

"I don't want to hurt you! I've done my hurting! It wasn't good!"

"Y-you—you mean you hurt other women?"

"Yes! No! I mean they hurt *me*. Me! Me! Me! Me. Me."

"Who hurt you? What are you talking about?"

"No. Doctor said I should talk to you, but not about bad things."

"Bad things, hmm? Okay, we'll change the subject. Let me ask you a question. Do you honestly think that those overdeveloped muscles of yours are a turn-on to women?"

"No. Yes. Yes!"

"First responses, Richard, and you're right. A woman sees a man like you and thinks, 'This guy is so insecure that he spends three hours a day at the gym with all the fags and narcissists, building himself up outside so I won't know how scared he is inside.' I've got a lover who's bigger than you and probably almost as strong, but he's got a trace of flab on his stomach and hips. And I dig it. You know why? Because he lives in reality and does a good job of it, and he hasn't got time to pump iron. So don't think your muscles impress me."

"The . . . they're for protection."

"From the people who hurt you? From the *women* who hurt you?"

"Yes."

"Aha, the truth outs. Let me set you straight on something. Muscles don't rule the world, brains do. Which is how a wimp like Havilland can make a slave out of someone big and strong like you. People protect each other with their love, not their muscles. Someone, probably some woman, hurt you really badly. She didn't do it with her muscles, because she didn't have any. You can't get revenge by hitting back at people the way they hit at you, because then the people who hurt you win—by making you like them. Aren't you hip to that?"

"No. It's different with Doctor John. He took me beyond my beyond."

"What's your beyond?"

"No!"

"Hurting women? You can't hurt me, because I'm smarter than you and stronger than you, and because that wimp downstairs told you not to. Some fucking beyond. Brown-noser to a freaked-out headshrinker who's going to end up in the locked ward at Camarillo for life. Who's going to protect you when he's wearing a straitjacket and sucking baby food out of a straw?"

"No! No! No no no no no. No."

"Yes, Richard. Yes. Besides, how many beyonds have you got? One? Two? Three? You don't seem too fulfilled to me. It's old wimpy's beyonds we're talking about, Richard. I almost wish you'd try to get violent with me, so I'd know you had the guts to disobey your slavemaster."

"What makes you think you're so smart and so tough?"

"I don't know. Do you know that I'm not scared of you?"

"Yes."

"Then that's your answer."

"What would you do if I tried to hurt you?"

"Fight back. Watch you get turned on and watch you lose."

"Doctor said you're a whore. Whores are wrong. Whores are bad."

"You almost got me there, but you missed by a few days. I quit. I walked. *I walked*. You can, too. You can walk out the door and wave good-bye to the Doctor, and he'll be terrified, because without you he's just another L.A. fruitcake with no place to hang his hat. Think on that. I'm going to try to sleep, but you think on that."

The Night Tripper awakened, instantly aware that his corkboard dreams had destroyed the music voices in bedroom number three. He checked the console and saw that he had forgotten to hit the "record" switch, then heard a soft male sobbing come over the speakers and pictured Richard distraught over his dictate not to hurt the whore.

Richard was a day too late. Linda was his. In the morning he would sacrifice her to his father's memory. He would end the game on his own terms.

25

DAWN.

Lloyd sped north on Pacific Coast Highway, running on adrenaline, rage, and terror. His jeopardy gambit had become a sacrificial offering, and if the fires had already been fed, he would have to take out the Beach Womb and everyone in it and throw himself into the flames. He looked at the pump shotgun resting on the seat beside him. Five rounds. Enough for Havilland, Oldfield, two miscellaneous worshippers, and himself.

The thought of self-immolation jerked his mind off of the immediate future and back to the immediate past. After leaving Bergen and Nagler, he had driven to Linda's apartment. She was not there, and her Mercedes was not in the garage. Now frightened, he had run dome light and siren to Havilland's Century City office. The night watchman in the lobby told him that he had admitted a very beautiful young woman at about seven o'clock, and that an hour later the nice Dr. Havilland and another man had brought her downstairs, looking high as a kite. "Emergency tooth extraction," the Doctor had said. "I'm not a dentist, but I gave it a go anyway." The two men had then hustled the near-comatose woman off in the direction of the parking lot.

After frantically driving by Havilland's Beverly Hills condo and finding no one there, Lloyd had run code three to the Pacific Palisades residential address of Ginjer Buchanan of Ginjer Buchanan Properties. The woman was not at home, but her live-in housekeeper succeeded in rousing her by phone at her boyfriend's apartment in Topanga Canyon. After Lloyd explained the urgency of the matter, the realtor agreed to meet him at her office with the information he needed. An hour later, at five A.M., he was staring at a floor plan of the Beach Womb.

Then the terror that he had held at bay by movement took over. If he called the Malibu sheriffs for assistance, they would storm the beachfront house S.W.A.T. style, with all the accoutrements of military/police overkill: Gas, machine guns, bullhorns, and the substation's lackluster hostage negotiation team. Loudspeaker amplified pleas, counterpleas and simplistic psychological manipulation that Havilland would laugh at; itchy-fingered deputies weaned on TV cop shows; automatic weaponry fired in panic. Linda in the crossfire. No. The jeopardy gambit came down to himself.

Again Lloyd looked at his Ithaca pump. When the taste of cordite and charred flesh rose in his throat, he pulled over to the side of the highway and a long row of pay phones. Jungle Jack Herzog redux—with a blackmail demand.

He had the receiver to his ear and a handkerchief over the mouthpiece when a strangely familiar vehicle ground to a halt behind his cruiser. Squinting through the Plexiglas, he saw Marty Bergen get out on the driver's side door and walk over to the booths, holding a quart bottle of beer out at arm's length, as though he were afraid of being contaminated. Lloyd slammed down the receiver, wondering how someone so sad could look so scary.

Bergen smiled. "Maintenance jug. I haven't touched it yet. Emergencies only. You look scared, Hopkins. Really scared."

Lloyd grabbed the bottle and smashed it to pieces on the pavement. Only when the smell of beer hit his nostrils did he realize what he had done. "I told you to stay with Nagler."

"I couldn't. I had to move, so I tied him up and split. Is that a misdemeanor or a felony? When I was on the job I never did learn the penal code."

"How did you find me?"

"That one I do know: 413.5—Impersonating a Police Officer. I called the number on the real estate brochure. The woman told me you'd just walked out the door. She gave me the guru guy's address. I was headed up there when I saw your car."

Lloyd started to see red. "*And*?"

Bergen squared his shoulders. "And this is vigilante shit all the way. Where's the backup units? Where's the sheriff's black-and-whites? It's all about to come down, and you're here by your lonesome looking scared. Why? Personally, I think we should go in full bore, fire team, copters, tear gas, snipers, I—"

Lloyd swung an overhand right at Bergen's jaw. Bergen caught the blow flush and went down on his back, then got up on one knee and began flailing with both arms, his eyes squeezed shut. Lloyd started to bring up an uppercut, then hesitated and moved backward into the phone booth. He fed dimes to the coin slot until he realized he had deposited four times the required amount. Cracking the door for air, he deep breathed and dialed.

"Hello?"

The voice was Havilland's. Lloyd cleared his throat and brought his voice up to tenor register. "Doctor, this is Jack Herzog. I've been away for a while. I need to see you."

The Doctor's response was a startling burst of laughter. "Hello, Sergeant. Congratulations on a job well done."

Lloyd said, "I know all about you and your father. Herzog left a pile of notes. Let Linda go, Havilland. It's over."

"Yes, it is over, but Herzog's green door would prevent him from keeping notes, and if you had any evidence, storm troopers would already have assaulted me. And Linda is here of her own free will."

"Let me talk to her."

"No. Later perhaps."

"Hav—"

Lloyd doubled over as a blunt forced crashed into his

kidneys; he dropped the receiver and slid down the wall as Bergen uncoiled his fists and elbowed his way into the booth. Lloyd tried to get up, but stomach cramps forced him to remain bent over, retching for breath.

Bergen picked up the dangling receiver and spoke into it. "Hey guru man, this is Martin Bergen. I'm a reporter for the *Big Orange Insider*. Maybe Jack Herzog told you about me. Listen, Hopkins and I just broke Billy Boy Nagler. He told us all about your scam. The *Orange* is going to do an exposé on you, talk about how you cheated your way through medical school, how you studied pimp techniques with Western Avenue spades, how chronic impotence led you to become a spiritual master. You like it, guru? You feel like consenting to an interview?"

Lloyd got to his feet and shoved his ear in the direction of the receiver, shouldering Bergen partially aside, so that both men were able to hear the tail end of Havilland's scream, the long silence that came in its wake and the calm words that finally emerged. "Yes. An interview. You obviously know where I am. Come over. We'll barter for the truth."

The line went dead. Lloyd shoved Bergen out of the booth and limped over to his car, his abdominal pain abating with each step he took. Grabbing Ginjer Buchanan's floor plan from the glove compartment, he said, "Have you still got your thirty-eight?"

"Yes," Bergen whispered.

Lloyd spread the floor plan out on the hood of the cruiser. "Good. You knock on the front door, I'll go in upstairs on the beach side. There's a woman in the house. She's innocent. Don't go near her. Keep the Doctor talking for at least two minutes. If he tries to pull anything weird, kill him."

26

THE Night Tripper switched on the living room amplifier and the bedroom number three speaker, then walked into the kitchen and found the 1984 equivalent of his 1957 Arkansas toad stabber, a short-bladed, serrated-edged steak knife. He stuck the weapon in his back pants pocket and called upstairs, "Richard, come here a second."

Oldfield appeared at the head of the stairs. "Yes, Doctor?"

"We're having a visitor," Havilland said. "Maybe more than one. Stay upstairs in number three and stick close to Linda. Listen for strange noises. When you hear 'now' come over the speaker, bring Linda down to me."

Nodding mutely, Oldfield about-faced and walked back down the hall. Havilland stared at the front door and counted seconds, savoring each little increment of time. He was up to six hundred and forty-three when the doorbell rang.

The Doctor opened the door, extending his second count to six hundred and fifty, standing perfectly still as he eyed the burned-out figure who had maneuvered at the center of the Alchemist's life and the unseen periphery of his own. "Please come in," he said.

Bergen entered, hunching forward with his hands jammed in his windbreaker pockets. "Nice décor," he said. "Too bad I didn't bring my notebook. I can never remember details unless I write them down."

Havilland pointed to a pair of arm chairs facing the latticework patio and the beach. Bergen walked over and sat down, stretching his legs and cramming his hands deeper into his pockets. Sitting down beside him, the Doctor said, "Where's Hopkins?"

Bergen licked his lips. "Parked over on P.C.H., scared shitless. He's crazy about this girl you're holding, and he's afraid to move because he thinks you'll kill her. He suspects you of all kinds of felony shit, but his superiors won't let him move—no hard proof. We glommed Billy Boy's diary, but all we could get out of it were possible pandering beefs. You're clean, Doc."

Havilland breathed out slowly, wondering if the burn-out's right hand was holding a gun. "Then you really have no intentions of writing an article on me? You came here to offer me a deal?"

"Right. Hopkins and I both want something personal. I want all your records pertaining to Jack Herzog destroyed. I don't want anyone to know that you counseled him. Hopkins wants the girl released safely. If you comply, Hopkins drops his investigation and lets the L.A.P.D. high brass deal with you, and I never write a word about you and your scam. What do you think?"

Havilland let the deal settle in on him. The selfishness of the men's motives rang true, but they obviously didn't know that he knew the game was *over*. "And if I don't comply?"

Bergen pulled out his left hand and looked at his watch. "Then I attack you in print with a yellow journalistic fervor you wouldn't believe, and Crazy Lloyd goes after you with everything *he's* got. A word to the wise, Doc. They don't call him Crazy Lloyd for nothing."

Lloyd skirted the ocean side of the house, looking for the foundation stanchions mentioned on the floor plan. Holding the Ithaca pump in the crook of his arm, he hugged the edge of the sand, shielded from view from within the house by a wooden screen of crisscrossed trelliswork.

The rear stanchion was an ornately carved wooden pole leading up to a second story balcony that was open at the front and enclosed by a trelliswork arbor immediately before the upstairs windows. Lloyd grabbed the pole with his right arm and inched himself up the narrow footholds provided by the carving indentations, holding the shotgun out at arm's length. When he was just underneath the edge of the balcony, he slid the Ithaca pump up and over, wincing at the clatter and scrape of metal. Leaning his weight into the pole, he released his right arm and grabbed the edge with both hands, then hoisted himself onto the tarpapered surface.

Hearing nothing but silence, Lloyd picked up the shotgun and tiptoed over to the enclosure, looking for an entry point. There were no built-in doors, but dead in the middle a section of wood had cracked and separated, providing a crawl space. Seeing no other way, Lloyd wedged himself through, splintering a large network of boards in the process. The sound exploded in his ears, and he closed his eyes to blot out the overwhelming sense that the whole world could hear it. When he opened them, he again heard nothing but silence, and realized that his finger had the Ithaca's trigger at half-squeeze.

Early morning light played through the gaps in the trelliswork and reflected off the second floor windows. Lloyd threaded his way past piles of lounge chairs and over to the windows, hoping to find at least one unlatched. He was about to begin trying the hasps when he saw that the middle window was wide open.

Holding the shotgun out in front of him, he walked over and pulled back the curtains that blocked his view. Seeing nothing but an empty bedroom, he stepped inside and padded to the door. Opening it inward with trembling hands, he saw a long carpeted hallway and heard Marty Bergen's voice *surrounding* him: "We're reasonable men, aren't we? Compromise is the basis of reason, isn't it? We—"

Lloyd pulled the door shut, wondering how Bergen's voice would be carrying from two places at once. Then it hit him: William Nagler's diary had stated that Thomas Goff taped the Beach Womb groupings. The house was obviously equipped with speakers, amplifiers and bugging apparatus. Bergen and Havilland were downstairs talking, while an upstairs speaker was blasting their conversation.

Lloyd pushed the door open and peered out, cocking his ears in order to get a fix on the speaker. The sound of amplified coughing delivered it: The room across the hallway two doors down. Linda was flashing across his mind until Havilland's voice destroyed the image. "But you want innocence for Jack, and you can't have it. Hopkins wants the woman and he can't have her. *Now*!"

And then Linda was there in reality, propelled out of the speaker bedroom by an unseen force. Lloyd jumped out into the hallway when he saw her, catching a blurred glimpse of a moving object that she seemed to be shielding. When Linda saw him, she screamed, "No!" and tried to duck back into the room, revealing Richard Oldfield behind her.

"Hopkins, no!"

Linda stumbled and fell to the floor as Oldfield froze in the doorway. Lloyd fired twice at eye level, blowing away Oldfield's retreating shadow and half the doorframe. Muzzle smoke and exploding wood filled the hallway. Lloyd ran through it to find Linda on her feet, blocking his entrance into the bedroom. She pummelled him with tightly balled fists until he shoved her aside and saw an empty room and a half-open picture window reflecting a descending object on its opposite side. Screaming "Oldfield!" Lloyd pumped a shell into the chamber and blew the reflection and the window to bits, staring into the rain of glass for geysers of red that would mark first blood. All he saw was glass fallout; all he heard and felt was Linda pushing herself into him, shrieking, "No!"

Until a shot reverberated stereophonically from downstairs and the bedroom speaker, tearing him away from Linda and down the hall to the head of the stairs, from which he saw Bergen and Havilland wrestling on the floor for Bergen's .38, kicking, flailing and gouging at each other, twisted into one entity that made a clean shot at the Doctor impossible.

Lloyd fired blindly at the far downstairs wall. Startled by the explosion, Bergen and Havilland jerked apart from each other, letting the .38 fall between them. Lloyd hurtled down the stairs, pumping in another round and taking a running bead on the Doctor's head. He was within a safe firing perimeter when Havilland got his left hand on the revolver and aimed it at Bergen's midsection. Bergen twisted away and brought his knees up to deflect Havilland's arm, again voiding Lloyd's target.

The Doctor's finger jerked the trigger twice. The first shot ricocheted off the hardwood floor, the second shot tore through Bergen's jugular. Lloyd saw *innocent* first blood cut the air and screamed, hearing his own terrified wail dissolve into the sound of his Ithaca kicking off a wild reflex round and the .38 blasting three times in its echo. When his tear-wasted vision cleared, he saw Havilland stabbing Bergen in the stomach with a short-bladed knife.

Lloyd felt everything move into a thunderous slow motion. Slowly he worked the slide of his weapon; slowly he walked to the death scene and aimed point-blank at Havilland's head. Slowly the Doctor looked up from his second generation fate, dropped the knife and smiled.

Lloyd rested the muzzle on his forehead and pulled the trigger. The empty chamber click resounded like hollow thunder, snapping the slow motion sequence, sending everything topsy-turvy and breakneck fast. Suddenly Lloyd had the shotgun reversed and was slamming the butt into Havilland's face over and over again, until a jagged section of his cheek was sheared off and blood started to seep from his ears. Then the speed diminished into a vertiginous absence of light, and from deep nowhere a beautiful voice called out, "Walk, Richard. *Walk.*"

27

THE legal machinery took over, and for nine straight days, temporarily suspended from duty and held incommunicado at Parker Center, Lloyd watched the state of California and the City and County of Los Angeles bury Dr. John Havilland in an avalanche of felony indictments, a barrage of due process based on his ninety-four page arresting officer's report and Havilland's own written and taped memoirs.

The first indictment was for the murder of Martin Bergen. The Malibu District Attorney expected it to be an open and shut case, because a highly respected veteran police officer had witnessed the killing, and because the defendant appeared to have no known relatives or friends likely to press embarrassing lawsuits against either Sergeant Lloyd Hopkins or the Los Angeles Police Department for their jurisdictional foul-up on the "arrest."

Back-up charges were quick in coming, as federal agents investigating the Howard Christie murder moved in and seized *everything* at Havilland's Century City office, Beverly Hills condominium, and Malibu house. His handwritten notes alone led to three indictments for first degree murder, handwriting experts having examined verified specimens of the Doctor's script along with his diary notations stating that he had ordered Thomas Goff to "kill the proprietor of the liquor store on Sunset and the Hollywood Freeway as proof of your desire to move beyond your beyond." Indentical match ups, three murder one indictments and an indictment for criminal conspiracy resulting.

The agents also found the deed to a storage garage in East Los Angeles, and upon checking it out discovered a yellow Toyota sedan and the decomposed body of Thomas Goff. A right index print belonging to John Havilland was found on the car's dashboard. The District Attorney of the City of Los Angeles ordered yet another murder indictment. The federal officers could find no concrete evidence linking Havilland to the murder of Howard Christie, and gave up.

Four days into his forced sequestering, Captain Fred Gaffaney visited Lloyd at his typewriter storageroom/domicile and told him that *any* report that he submitted explaining Martin Bergen's presence at the Malibu house would be accepted if he agreed to edit cut all mention of former officer Jacob Herzog and all mention of the stolen L.A.P.D. files and the security firms and their files. The various prosecutors thus far involved in the case had read his ninety-four page epic and considered it "overly candid" and "potentially embarrassing to the prosecution." Lloyd agreed. Gaffaney smiled and told him it was a wise move—he would have been summarily shitcanned from the Department had he refused. Before he left, Gaffaney added that he would be appearing before the Grand Jury in two days. Was there any information he had held back? Lloyd lied and said, "No."

The worshippers of John Havilland were taken into custody, questioned and released after signing depositions elaborating their relationships with "Doctor John." A free-lance "deprogrammer" of religious cult captives was there to aid the district attorneys and D.A.'s investigators in their interrogations. The combined coercion worked four out of five times, resulting in detailed accounts of brainwashing, dope experimentation, and sexual debasement. Only William Nagler could not be convinced to talk. He screamed his mantra and ranted about "horror movies" and was ultimately released to the care of his parents, who admitted him to an expensive private sanitarium. The D.A.s were pleased overall with their questionings; the depositions would be juicy fodder for the

Grand Jury, and they would spare the sad brainwashees the grief of a courtroom appearance.

Lloyd was not spared that grief. He spoke for four straight hours, almost verbatim from his new arrest report, omitting all mention of Herzog, the security files and Martin Bergen's outsized role in his investigation. He explained Bergen's presence at the death house as a simple case of a bulldog reporter hot on a story. When Lloyd concluded his own story, he did not mention Richard Oldfield or Linda Wilhite and their presences at the house, or how he happened to be unconscious when the first wave of Sheriff's deputies arrived on the scene. When he walked back to the witness table, Fred Gaffaney was there with a wink and glad tidings: his violations of L.A.P.D. canon were only going to cost him a thirty-day suspension without pay, a slap on the wrist for his vigilante hooliganism.

The final witness to appear before the Grand Jury was a Los Angeles County deputy medical examiner, who stated that in his opinion the flurry of indictments leveled at Havilland was overkill, because the Doctor's fall down a steep flight of stairs immediately before his arrest had resulted in severe and irrevocable brain damage. Havilland was destined to live out his years insensate, not knowing who, what, or where he was. The impact sustained by his fall had opened up lesions from a previous head injury, quadrupling the neurological destruction. The M.E. ended with the statement, "I tried to get the man to understand that I was a doctor, that I was there to examine him. It was like trying to explain relativity to a turnip. He kept looking at me so pathetically. He had no idea that it was over."

But Lloyd knew that it wasn't. There was the unfinished business of the horror movie and the big "why" of Linda's behavior at the Beach Womb. And when that was settled, there was the matter of homage to Marty Bergen.

Nine days after the incident the press had dubbed the "Malibu Massacre," Lloyd was released from his "voluntary incarceration" at Parker Center. His thirty-day suspension had twenty-one days left to go, and he was told to remain in Los Angeles for the next two weeks, in order to be available to the myriad D.A.s working on the Havilland case. He was also ordered not to speak to representatives of the media and to refrain from police work on any level.

Returning to Los Angeles at large, Lloyd found that John Havilland had become a cause for ghoulish celebration. The psychiatrist was still front-page news, and a number of nightclub comedians had made him the focal point of their shticks. The *Big Orange Insider* had dubbed him the "Witch Doctor," and the 1958 novelty song "Witch Doctor" by David Seville and the Chipmunks was re-released and climbing the top forty. Charles Manson was interviewed in his cell at Vacaville Prison and proclaimed Dr. John Havilland "a cool dude."

Medical authorities at the jail ward of the L.A. County Hospital proclaimed the Doctor a vegetable, and Lloyd resisted his own ghoulish impulse to visit his adversary in his padded cell and throw the phrase "snuff film" at what remained of his brain. Instead, before going home or partaking of any post-sequentering amenities, he drove to 4109 Windemere Drive.

No L.A.P.D. or Federal crime scene stickers on the doors or windows; layers of undisturbed dust on the junctures of doors and doorjambs. An ordinary looking tudor cottage in the Hollywood Hills. Lloyd sighed as he circuited the house on foot. Stonewall. He hadn't mentioned Oldfield in any of his official reports or earlier communiqués, and the feds who had seized Havilland's property either hadn't come across Oldfield's name or had decided to ignore it. In their fearful haste to deny Jack Herzog, the L.A.P.D. and the F.B.I. were letting the sleeping dogs that were John Havilland's minions lie.

Lloyd broke into the house through a back window and went straight for the bedroom. A mattress lay on the carpeted floor, an indentical visual match to the film scrap he had seen at Billy Nagler's workshop. Reddish-brown matter stained a swatch of carpet near the window. Recalling the adhesive bandage he had found on the front lawn the day before the Malibu apocalypse, Lloyd bent down and examined it. Blood.

Checking the rest of the house, Lloyd found it cleaned of personal belongings. No male clothing, no toilet articles, no legal or personal documents. Food, appliances and furniture remained. Oldfield had fled. And judging from the dust on the doorjambs, he had a good head start.

Driving back to Parker Center, he put all thoughts regarding Linda Wilhite out of his mind, coming to one solid conclusion. Havilland or Oldfield had destroyed the movie. Had the Department or the feds discovered it, he would have heard. Again he was dealing with theory and circumstantial evidence.

It took Officer Artie Cranfield a scant ten minutes to identify the reddish brown matter on the carpet swatch as type O+ blood. Thus armed with facts, Lloyd called the L.A.P.D. Missing Persons Bureau and requested the stats on all female caucasians age twenty-five to forty with type O+ blood reported missing over the past ten days. Only one woman fit the description—Sherry Lynn Shroeder, age thirty-one, reported missing by her parents six days before. Lloyd wept when the clerk ticked off her last known place of employment—Junior Miss Cosmetics.

He had watched her walk in the door.

Tears streaming down his face, Lloyd ran through the halls and out the door of Parker Center, knowing that he was exonerated and that it wasn't enough; knowing that the woman he wanted to love was innocent of the overall tapestry of evil; she had been psychically violated by a madman. In the parking lot, he slammed the hood of his car and kicked the grill and broke off the radio aerial and molded it into a missile of hate. Hurling it at the twelve story monolith that defined everything he was, he sent up a vow to Sherry Lynn Shroeder and set out to plumb the depths of his whore/lover's violation.

A call to Telecredit revealed that Linda Wilhite had bank

balances totaling $71,843.00 and had made no recent major purchases with any of her credit cards. Richard Oldfield had liquidated his three savings and checking accounts and had sold a large quantity of IBM stock for $91,350.00.

A trip to L.A. International Airport armed with D.M.V. snapshots of the two supplied the information that Oldfield had boarded a flight for New York City four days after the Malibu killing, paying cash for his ticket and using an assumed name. Linda had accompanied him to the gate. An alert baggage handler told Lloyd that the two didn't seem like lovers, they seemed more like "with-it" sister and "out-of-it" brother.

Lloyd drove back to L.A. proper feeling jealous and tired and somehow afraid to go home, afraid that there was something he had forgotten to do. He would have to confront Linda soon, but before he did that he needed to pay tribute to a fallen comrade.

Marty Bergen's landlady opened the door of her former tenant's apartment and told Lloyd that the people from the *Big Orange* had come by and taken his beat-up furniture and typewriter, claiming that he promised them to the tabloid in his common law will. She had let them take the stuff because it was worthless, but she kept the box that had the book he was working on, because he owed two months rent and maybe she could sell it to the real newspapers and make up her loss. Was that a crime?

Lloyd shook his head, then took out his billfold and handed her all the cash it contained. She grabbed it gratefully and ran down the hall to her own apartment, returning with a large cardboard box overflowing with typed pages. Lloyd took it from her hands and pointed to the door. The woman genuflected out of the apartment, leaving him alone to read.

The manuscript ran over five hundred pages, the typing bracketed with red-inked editorial comments that made it seem like a complete co-authorship. It was the story of two medieval warriors, one prodigal, one chaste, who loved the same woman, a princess who could only be claimed by traversing concentrically arrayed walls of fire, each ring filled with progressively more hideous and bloodthirsty monsters. The two warriors started out as rivals, but became friends as they drew closer and closer to the princess, battling demons who entered them as they entered each gauntlet of flame, growing telepathic as the guardians of each other's spirit. When the final wall of fire stood immediately before them, they revolted against the symbiosis and prepared to do battle to the death.

At that point the manuscript ended, replaced by contrapuntal arguments in two different handwritings. The quality of the prose had deteriorated in the last chapters. Lloyd pictured Jack Herzog pushed to the edge of his tether by the Witch Doctor, trying to forge poetry out of the horror of his flickering-out life. When he finally put the book down, Lloyd didn't know if it was good, bad, or indifferent—only that it had to see print as a hymn for the L.A. dead.

The hymn became a dirge as he drove to Linda Wilhite's apartment, hoping that she wouldn't be there, so he could go home and rest and prolong the sense of what might have been.

But she was.

Lloyd walked in the half-opened door. Linda was sitting on the living room sofa, perusing the classified section of the *Times*. When she looked up and smiled, he shuddered. No might-have-beens. She was going to tell him the truth.

"Hello, Hopkins. You're late."

Lloyd nodded at the classifieds. "Looking for a job?"

Linda laughed and pointed to a chair. "No, business opportunities. Fifty grand down and a note from the bank gets me a Burger King franchise. What do you think?"

Lloyd sat down. "It's not your style. Seen any good movies lately?"

Linda shook her head slowly. "I saw a preview of one, and got a vivid synopsis from one of the stars. The one print was destroyed, by me. I'd forgotten how good you were, Hopkins. I didn't think you knew that part of it."

"I'm the best. I even know the victim's name. You want to hear it?"

"No."

Lloyd mashed his hands together and brought them toward his chest, then stopped when he realized he was unconsciously aping Billy Nagler's worship pose. "Why, Linda? What the fuck happened with you and Oldfield?"

Linda formed her hands into a steeple, then saw what she was doing and jammed them into her pockets. "The movie was a crazy reenactment of my parents' deaths. Havilland pushed Richard into it. He ran part of the film for me at his office. I freaked out and screamed. Richard grabbed me, and they doped me and took me out to Malibu. Richard and I talked. I hit the one germ of sanity and decency that he had. I convinced him that he could walk out the door like the movie and Havilland never existed. We were getting ready to walk when Havilland called out 'Now!' Marty Bergen could have walked out with us. But then you showed up with your shotgun."

When Lloyd remained silent, Linda said, "Babe, it was the right thing to do, and I love you for it. Richard and I took off running, and you could have put the cops on to us, but you didn't, because of what you felt for me. There's no rights and wrongs in this one. Don't you know that?"

Lloyd brought his eyes back from deep nowhere. "No, I don't know that. Oldfield killed an innocent woman. He has to pay. And then there's *us*. What about *that*?"

"Richard has paid," Linda said in a whisper. "God, has he paid. For the record, he's long gone. I don't know where he is, and I don't want to know, and if I *did* know, I wouldn't tell you."

"Do you have any idea what you did? *Do you*, goddamn it!"

Linda's whisper was barely audible. "Yes. I figured out that I could walk, and I convinced someone else that he could, too. He deserves the chance. Don't lay your guilt on me, Hopkins. If Richard hadn't gotten hooked up with Havilland he never would have killed a fly. What are the odds of his meeting someone else like the Witch Doctor? It's over, Hopkins. Just let it be."

Lloyd balled his fists and stared up at the ceiling to hold back a flood of tears. "It's not over. And what about us?"

Linda put a tentative hand on his shoulder. "I never saw Richard hurt anybody, but I saw what you did to Havilland. If I hadn't seen it, maybe we could have given it a shot. But now that's over, too."

Lloyd stood up. When Linda's hand dropped from his shoulder, he said, "I'm going after Oldfield. I'll try to keep your name out of it, but if I can't, I won't. One way or the other, I'm going to get him."

Linda got to her feet and took Lloyd's hands. "I don't doubt it for a minute. This is getting funny and sad and weird, Hopkins. Will you hold me for a minute and then split?"

Lloyd shut his eyes and held the most beautiful woman he had ever seen, closing out the L.A. end of the Havilland case. When he felt Linda start to retreat from the embrace, he turned around and walked, thinking that it was over and it would never be over and wondering how he could get the Herzog/Bergen book published.

Outside, the night shone in jetstreams of traffic light and in flames from a distant brush fire. Lloyd drove home and fell asleep on the couch with his clothes on.

ALSO BY JAMES ELLROY

BLOOD ON THE MOON

Detective Sergeant Lloyd Hopkins can't stand music, or any loud sounds. He's got a beautiful wife, but he can't get enough of other women. And instead of bedtime stories, he regales his daughters with bloody crime stories. He's a thinking man's cop with a dark past and a relentless drive to hunt down monsters who prey on the innocent. Now there's something haunting him. He sees a connection in a series of increasingly gruesome murders of women committed over a period of twenty years.

Crime Fiction/1-4000-9528-X

DESTINATION: MORGUE!
L.A. Tales

Dig. The Demon Dog gets down with a new book of scenes from America's capital of kink: Los Angeles. Fourteen pieces, some fiction, some nonfiction, all true enough to be admissible as state's evidence, and half of them in print for the first time. Here are Mexican featherweights and unsolved-murder vics, crooked cops and a very clean D.A. Here is a profile of Hollywood's latest celebrity perp-walker, Robert Blake; three new novellas featuring a demented detective who's obsessed with a Hollywood actress; and, oh yes, just maybe the last appearance of *Hush-Hush* sleazemonger Danny Getchell.

Crime Fiction/Nonfiction/1-4000-3287-3

ALSO AVAILABLE

American Tabloid, 0-375-72737-X
The Cold Six Thousand, 0-375-72740-X
Crime Wave, 0-375-70471-X
My Dark Places, 0-679-76205-1
White Jazz, 0-375-72736-1